THE PATH OF SAINTS AND SINNERS

A JOURNEY OF CORNELIA ROSE NOVEL

J.F. COLLEN

EVOLVED PUBLISHING™

www.EvolvedPub.com
Evolved Publishing LLC
Butler, Wisconsin, USA

Books by J.F. Collen

JOURNEY OF CORNELIA ROSE
Book 1: *Flirtation on the Hudson*
Book 2: *Walk Away West*
Book 3: *Pioneer Passage*
Book 4: *The Path of Saints and Sinners*
Book 5: *Bit o' Heaven Ranch*

What Others Are Saying

FLIRTATION ON THE HUDSON (Book 1):
"I was immediately captivated with this story, particularly given the period it was set in and the area where it takes place... J.F. Collen does a fantastic job of capturing the dialect of the time as much as the etiquette and conduct of what was required to be a lady of those times... Nellie Entwhistle is a richly developed character with personality personified and I look forward to the next book in this delightful series. Well done! I am a fan."
~ Feathered Quill Book Reviews, Diane Lunsford

WALK AWAY WEST (Book 2):
"Collen creates an outstanding synthesis of history and personal experience that bring readers into a world that moves from a comfortable one to one which, by choice, embraces austerity and adventure... Readers looking for a fine stand-alone story of a venture out West and the characters' motivations for both undertaking the unknown and remaining and growing as a couple will find *Walk Away West* an invigorating novel of change and challenge. It works well either as a follow-up to Nellie's previous adventure [*Flirtation on the Hudson*] or as a stand-alone historical novel for newcomers."
~ Midwest Book Review, D. Donovan, Sr. Reviewer

"What I particularly love about this author's style is her ability to convey a wonderment and understanding of the physical environment the pioneers were passing through. Her prose is melodic, almost to the point of musicality and her descriptions vivid and real enough to transport the reader right into the wagon, alongside Nellie and her family, as they negotiate the dangers of the trail. One can truly feel the barrenness and spread of the western prairies, along with the power of the crystal-clear night sky through Collen's melodic prose... A fantastic read that I can highly recommend and one of the best I've had in a long time."
~ Readers' Favorite Book Reviews, Grant Leishman

Dedication

For my loved ones. You help me stay the course.

TABLE OF CONTENTS

THE PATH OF SAINTS and SINNERS

a novel by

J.F. COLLEN

CHAPTER 1
It's a Lovely Day

Emigrant Camp, Great Salt Lake City, August 1857

Their bespoke Conestoga wagon shook as his footsteps pounded up the wagon steps.

Her honey-blonde hair, jumbled upon a pillow, obscured her slumbering face as it bounced with the motion of the six-foot man hurling himself on the makeshift bed.

"Cornelia Rose Entwhistle Wright, wake up and face your destiny," the intimate voice of Obadiah whispered in her ear.

A tingle ran from Nellie's ear all the way to her toes. *Our romance forever sizzles just below the surface,* she thought, and smiled.

"My dearest husband," she said, refusing to open her eyes, ignoring the smell of fresh brewing coffee percolating her senses. "Mere minutes have passed since you and my daughters bade me get an hour of shut eye."

She felt wet kisses slide over her chin as his soft mustache inched toward her lips.

"Not true," Obadiah said, and laughed in her ear.

Nellie relented, but only one eye's opening worth.

Obadiah Weber Wright nibbled his wife's neck as he crooned, "We let you sleep for two- and one-half hours. I need not remind you that throughout our long journey on the California Trail, over mountain, river and prairie, not once did you luxuriate abed in the late morning. Such decadence can only occur in this Great Salt Lake City, destination of our dreams."

He opened his pocket watch with the hand not caressing her shoulders and squinted an eye at it. "'Tis time to rise and face our new city, our new adventure, yea, our new life, before the day is bisected by the high noon sun."

Returning his attention to his wife's soft shoulder, he continued his kisses, sending delicious tickles down her spine. His murmured words added yet another layer of enthralling delight.

"You have twelve minutes before the morning transmogrifies into afternoon."

"Then I shall recline abed that entire twelve minutes." Nellie pulled his chin closer to her mouth and began her own soft kisses.

"Bringing the tenderness of night closer in reach."

She reveled in the tender touch and closed her eyes again, but Obadiah cleared his throat, kissed her on the cheek, and pulled her upright.

She balked at his change in mood, and teased, "Further dallying could serve a dual purpose: extending our tender feeling, and avoiding the morning altogether, thus successfully eluding the menacing grasp of morning sickness for the day."

"My invincible Cornelia Rose, you shall not fall prey to that base plague of lesser women." Obadiah released Nellie's hands so he could scramble out of the bed.

She flopped back down.

Perhaps my husband fails to realize the many months this nausea, the scourge of pregnancy, afflicted me. Through the river crossings, the oppressive heat, and the endless walking, this malaise has plagued me. In all my two-and-twenty years, I do not recall feeling this poorly, this unlike myself, for such a long duration.

Tenderness shone from his eyes as Obadiah gazed at Nellie lying on the bed. "My brave pioneer woman, gather your strength and your winsome ways, for we must indeed now venture forth. Our future awaits. Do you not yearn to at least see our long-sought destination?"

'Tis not my dream to dwell so far from home amongst these strange creatures calling themselves 'Latter-day Saints.' Can the chore not wait until I am better rested from my night of midwifing?

Nellie shook her head without voicing any of these thoughts, and held out her arms.

Obadiah grinned and dropped back into them.

A few kisses later, their two daughters popped their heads into the wagon cover's opening.

"Arise, sleepy head. Embrace the start of my new position as federal judge of Utah Territory and our new life," Obadiah said, with a conspiratorial wink at their daughters.

Nellie sat bolt upright and tried to run her fingers through her hair. She bit back a yawn, not quite stifling it, as she tugged her hand through a snarl.

The girls giggled as they tumbled into the wagon around them.

"We see a fancy house," lisped three-year-old Elizabeth.

"Not as grand as our house in Sing-Sing," said Emma, with the gravitas of someone decades older than her five years.

Nellie, rousing herself both physically and psychologically for the new day ahead, felt her spirit plummet at those words. *Our New York home on the hill overlooking the mighty Hudson River surely looms majestic in my memory as well. Mercy, 'tis over two thousand miles and many months of weary travel away.* Her heart thumped painfully. *When shall my memories hearten rather than grieve me?*

She sought solace in recalling her first glimpse of the Great Salt Lake City from Emigration Canyon. *A small mercy: civilization appears below.* From high atop the mountain trail, she'd seen paths intersecting neat blocks of land composed of houses, strips of gardens, and pastures for livestock grazing. *How organized and cozy, like a carefully crafted patchwork quilt.*

She stretched, trying to release the pinch in her neck. *Yet this city looks unlike any town in the States. The Mormon people's attempt to hew cultivation from an ungodly bit of uninhabitable land has the perverse effect of deepening my estrangement from home.*

She shook her head trying to clear her thoughts, wondering why her heart now lurched into despair, when they had finally triumphed over the hardships of the trail. Buffalo stampedes, raging rivers, sicknesses, contaminated water, to list only a few of the maladies, failed to deter them. *Flirted with disaster, yea we surely had, but we emerged from the journey's adversity unscathed.*

'Tis foolish to feel homesick now, she chided herself. They hovered on the verge of attaining their own home and joining this thriving civilization.

"If I tidy my hair," she said with all the enthusiasm she could muster, "I shall most certainly be pioneer-ready in a jiffy. We shall parade to the finest house in Great Salt Lake City."

The girls beamed in delight as she blinked back tears and re-combed her hair into a tight bun, neatly capturing a vagrant strand and securing it with a hairpin.

Nellie caught the hand of each girl as they escorted her down the steps of their wagon, parked in the area designated for California-bound wagon trains.

Obadiah scooped her into his arms and swung her down the last step. "My love, our future now begins," he said. "No harm can befall us now. We have arrived!"

Nellie smiled and held onto her hat as he kissed her again.

"Thanks be to God for our safe arrival and the joy in our family." Obadiah tugged her hand and propelled her through the camp at a fast pace.

She laughed and hurried along, after making sure her daughters followed. Blinking in the harsh sunlight, Nellie strained to see any holdovers from their own wagon train.

Are our traveling companions still here? Have the Claytons stayed behind? How fares the newborn? Was Beauregard Clayton able to convince his ornery wife to rest and recuperate from the arduous birth?

Though curious, she did not risk inciting criticism by raising the subject with her husband. She rubbed her back, sore from the laborious midwifing task of coaxing that breech baby into the world last night, which also depleted her strength for verbal jousting. She squeezed her eyes shut, dazed by both sleep deprivation and sun glare, and popped them open again to see the wagons camped all about her in Pioneer Square.

Did Captain Hines and their former company delay their departure? Her heart leapt with hope, as the adjournment of travel could mean one less infant and mother likely to succumb to death within forty-eight hours of childbirth.

She scanned the busy pioneers, looking for a familiar face. *Is that the oldest Wilton girl?* Nellie peered at the teenager hurrying by with a sloshing water bucket. *No, not Winifred.*

Seeing not one recognizable soul in this hive of busy bees, her dashed hope felt like a punch to the gut. While she had slept, their wagon company, with all their companions traveling the long distance from Council Bluffs, Iowa, must have pulled up stakes and resumed its trek toward California gold. Yet they wound their way through an encampment just as crowded as yesterday, packed with strangers. The overfilled campground offered no friendly faces, as another company of emigrants had replaced her wagon train's.

She caught herself lingering, scanning the crowd, still clinging to the hope that the Claytons had delayed travel and attended to their newborn. Nellie shook her head and stretched her legs long to keep step with Obadiah's excited stride.

I must expunge all thoughts of Missus Clayton's bizarre words of audacious inference of an untoward relationship between myself and her husband, Beauregard. For surely my agitated sensibilities and exhaustion produced those unsuitable tingles of emotion.

The Wright family hurried along. Oblivious to her quandary, Obadiah waxed poetic as he lectured her in the protocol necessary when meeting the Governor of Utah Territory.

Her daughters alternated between gasps of surprise and delight as they scampered through the city. They ping-ponged between the places of interest and their parents, chattering like magpies.

Nellie grinned, feeling her skirts constantly tugged as she and Obadiah strode past the sights. The girls giggled at the chair perched precariously on a roof, advertising the cabinetry skills of the proprietor of the shop below, and doing so far more effectively than the wooden sign under the chair bearing the word *CARPENTER*.

Tug: "There's the shoemaker," shouted Elizabeth, pointing to the boot on top of a trim white house, displaying a sign *BOOTMAKER*.

Tug, tug—one on either side of her skirt—and both girls cried, "The tin smith!" at the cup and lantern over the door of the tin maker.

Another tug, and a whisper, "What does ZCMI mean, Mama?" Emma, proud of her ability to read the letters, looked up, her adorable little face scrunched in question.

Obadiah advised, "Zion Cooperative Mercantile Institute."

Nellie joined the girls in their blank stare.

"It's the general goods store of the Latter-day Saints," he explained.

Their hurried pace slowed as they approached a large, thatched-roof, open dwelling that hummed with groups of men conferring. Nellie overheard snatches of conversations discussing crops and livestock.

"Welcome to the Bowery, weary pioneers!" shouted a stocky man, touching his moth-eaten hat in a mockingly deferential manner. "Let me point you in the direction of our vast stocks of provisions, at our *special* pioneer prices." The man gave a sly wink.

Cornelia Rose's stomach churned with distaste. He held up two ears of corn, and she caught a glimpse of mold at the bottom of the browning, dried husks.

The group of men around him laughed.

Weary travelers must negotiate with a slimy snake oil salesman?

CHAPTER 2
People Are Strange, When You're a Stranger

The Bowery, Great Salt Lake City, August 1857

Faces in the crowd gawked at them. Laughs and sneers sounded under the Bowery's thatched roof.

Shy daughter Emma shrank away, attaching herself to Nellie's skirt, while little Elizabeth tightened her grip on her mother's hand.

Nellie felt her stomach clench, and wondered if it was fear or her morning sickness migrating to afternoon. She raised her eyebrows at Obadiah.

"Good day to you, sir," countered Obadiah cheerfully. "We do not require comestibles."

"Good," muttered a man in the clutch of men staring at them. "We would not sell our valuable produce to you anyway."

Nellie felt her eyebrows climb even higher on her forehead. *What devil's lair have we stumbled into?*

"Perhaps you seek lodging?" the sleazy man spoke again. "I can point you to a nice spot in the middle of the Public Square in Ward Eight, where we welcome immigrants. Howsoever, it is not waterproofed against the weather like this here Bowery," he said with a disingenuous smile.

"Right obliged for the information," said Obadiah, tightlipped but with a friendly nod.

They picked up the pace of their footsteps.

"Why do we encounter such open hostility?" whispered Nellie to Obadiah. "Would not all immigrants be welcome with open arms? Who would desire huddling in the open square, sleeping like vagrants in town after months of lack of proper accommodations during the trek across the continent?"

"Wife, do not fret," Obadiah said with a frown, looking down at the upturned anxious faces of their daughters. "I am sure Governor Young has seen fit to make suitable arrangements for us."

A tall, sparse man with the swagger of a bureaucrat, leering within earshot, took four swift steps away from his group and detained Obadiah with a firm hand on his arm.

"Look he's head red," whispered little Elizabeth. Nellie pressed her lips together and gave her a stern look, and Elizabeth took her pointing hand and put it behind her back.

"Very few travelers tarry here. You're not welcome to restock the wagon here, so yer kind must move along."

Tarnation! Nellie grimaced. *This surly man's antagonistic greeting does not bode well for our future here. Enmity rears its ugly head in our first encounter with Mormons?*

Obadiah turned and looked the man squarely in the eye. "We travel no farther. As newly appointed United States Federal Circuit Judge, I and my family come to settle amongst you."

The discussion in a nearby group stopped at these words, and scoffs and jeers erupted.

Hardly the respect I anticipated these words would engender. Nellie peered anxiously around them. The men did not appear openly hostile, just disdainful. She glanced at Obadiah and read dismay in his eyes, even though he sought to hide it behind a poker face.

The intimidating man tucked a long wavy shock of red hair back under his big brimmed hat, and tried to hide a smirk under his bushy mustache.

Betsy makes a fair point! Nellie pulled her youngest daughter's hand up to her lips and kissed the index finger. The striking red hair rather dandified this man and lessened his intimidating manner.

"I was told to keep my eagle eye out for one of them Federal circuit judges. Is it Obadiah Weber Wright I have the pleasure of encountering?"

A frown hip-hopped across Obadiah' face. "So it is. And whom do I have the honor of addressing?"

The big man looked slightly confused, as he puzzled whether or not he had been insulted.

The sides of Nellie's lips pulled up in amusement. The dapper dress of this brash man further belied his ominous affect, and his speech hinted of a touch of genteelness.

The tall, sinewy man grasped the lapels of his long, full wool coat with two hands, puffed out his chest and said with a smirk, "Wild Bill Hickok." He stuck out his chin as if asking 'what's it to ya?'

Charming! Nellie hid her own smirk. With such a prominent, protruding proboscis, almost highlighted by that red mustache, it was a wonder his nickname was not 'Duck Bill' Hickok.

"Pleased to make your acquaintance, I'm sure," said Obadiah.

Nellie hoped that only she could detect the generous portion of sarcasm sprinkled on Obadiah's words.

"And your profession?" Obadiah asked.

"Marshal," Hickok drawled as he leaned back on his heels and stroked his sides, where rested the handles of two pistols. "Where is your posse of army, whot was ta escort ya?"

Obadiah's poker face now sported a frown of consternation. Picking his words with care, he said, "I see no necessity for a protective posse. I come lawfully and in peace."

The imposing man scowled at them.

Suddenly, Mr. Hickok slapped his buckskin-clad thighs and threw back his head, and a big belly laugh erupted from his fancy waistcoat area. The crowd relaxed into guffaws.

"That's the spirit!" he said. "Why *would* you need a posse?" he added with a sly slant to his eyes.

A thought niggled at the edge of Nellie's memory, and she scoured her brain to retrieve it. In her vast research of the West and its budding 'civilization,' she'd encountered the name Hickok in numerous reports of clashes between pro-slavers and the Jayhawkers in Bleeding Kansas. Could this man be the same scout and bodyguard for General Lane, the sure shot fighting in the Jayhawker's antislavery army to protect a black boy from being beaten? If so, he must have some conscience, some morality.

But howfor appears he here? Aloud, Nellie said, "Thus, as Marshall, I presume you are charged with protecting lawful citizens?" The notion to challenge this man's braggadocio popped into her head and she verbalized it before she could think better of it.

Tarnation! When shall I learn prudence, not to mention a lady-like reticence?

She felt Obadiah stiffen with disapproval.

In response, the man put his hands on his hips, pulled back his long wool coat, and revealed the two pistols hanging on a bright red sash.

Suddenly, the strange man's hands sprang to his pistols.

Nellie suppressed a gasp, and her little girls leapt behind her skirts.

But the big man frowned and jerked one hand past his gun and extended it toward Obadiah.

Nellie's sigh of relief caught in her throat as she watched Hickok yank Obadiah by the elbow, pulling him away from his family. The burly man pushed her husband forward in the open air a few paces away from the neighboring building.

Obadiah, recovering from the surprise, planted his feet. "Unhand me, sir. I will not be juddered about."

Hickok dropped Obadiah's elbow and dusted his fingers on his waistcoat, his mustache twitching with laughter.

Nellie and her daughters let out their unconsciously held breath.

"I merely wish to propel you farther past this thatched roof toward the Tabernacle." Once again, Hickok pulled Obadiah forward.

Nellie grasped her still trembling daughters' hands and followed, trying to hear what the 'wild' man said.

"My instructions, good sir, are to find you and introduce you to Brother Ellis Smith, our probate judge—elected by the board of Saints. Once you have become properly acquainted, I shall turn you over to his tutelage."

Obadiah stopped and yanked his elbow from Hickok's grasp. "I am obliged to you, sir," he said. "But *my* instructions are to report only to Governor Young." He crossed his arms over his chest.

James Butler Hickok—Nellie suddenly remembered his given name from her reading—pushed his hat back and scratched his head, sending his surprising red curls cascading down his back. "I thought surely someone sent by the United States would know: Brother Brigham's status as governor has been placed in jeopardy of termination."

Obadiah and Nellie exchanged uncertain looks.

"Word from the horse's mouth," said Hickok, "whispering down the trail, says *your* president James Buchanan, opposed as he is to the dominance of our faithful Saints in the political arena here, has taken it upon himself to appoint a new governor, some Alfred Cumming, without even notifying our leader. Our Prophet shall discern the proper response. I would advise a fellow pioneer to keep an open mind and choose his path and his steps wisely." Hickok pointed to Obadiah's feet.

Choose his path? As a Territory of the United States, why would the response be anything other than a welcome to the new Governor?

Nellie whispered in horror, "Must we fear skirmishes brewing?"

Could the small inklings of this trouble taunting us on the trail manifest in conflicts far worse than I imagined? Have we stumbled into a quagmire of political distrust already?

Obadiah stroked his mustache, not responding to Nellie, deep in thought.

An ominous silence hung in the air.

At last, Obadiah said, "Thank you kindly for your advice. It seems, under the circumstances, I shall be much obliged if you would introduce me to Judge Smith. I shall take the rest of your discourse under advisement. And indeed, I will need directions to the capitol, so I might introduce myself to the new governor."

Hickok's lips twisted in an ugly smirk. "It don't make no never mind to me, sir. However, the new governor ain't here yet. I believe his progress has been somewhat impeded." Another loud, big belly laugh emanated from the commanding man.

Nellie jumped and her girls looked terrified. She thought his self-proclaimed moniker 'Wild Bill' might suit him after all.

"But I sure can point you to the capitol building. Right this way." Wild Bill pulled Obadiah around and jerked a big finger in the opposite direction. His face hardened as Nellie and the girls turned their heads in that direction too.

"To where are you pointing?" asked Obadiah.

"*To Fillmore City*—about a hundred miles away," roared Hickok, slapping his buckskins again and howling, and some of the groups looked over and chuckled. "Your precious States officials should have advised ya o' the whereabouts o' our capitol!"

One of the men observing them, eavesdropping on the conversation, piped up. "I am whole hog helpful when it comes to doin' in our enemies, but this fella ain't gonna harm us. C'mon now, Hickok, don't lead a lamb to slaughter. This here capital and the legislature moved back to good ol' Salt Lake City after that big shindig this past Christmas."

Wild Bill's hands jumped to his gun handles, and he growled at the man.

The hapless man didn't flinch, just stood his ground and stared at Hickok. "I don't think it right to mess with the unarmed."

A nebulous statement, about whom? Usually that statement implies a limited mental capacity, but does the man literally mean we carry no firearms?

"Looky here, Brother Spencer," said Hickok. "The capitol *building* still stands in Fillmore, so I am directing the man to it. For all we know, the appointed governor's posse could be escorting him there. This fella didn't ask to speak to the legislature."

Obadiah clapped the friendly Brother Spencer on the back and said good-naturedly to Hickok, "My good man, you've had your fun. Now do me the kindness of indicating the whereabouts of Judge Smith. I shall leave you in peace as soon as you provide me that service."

Marshal Hickok patted his massive cluster of curly locks. "You'll be missin' a glimpse of the grandest capitol ever under construction, thanks to Brother Spencer, but... right ho. I'll learn ye, in fairness, that new man, Alfred Cumming, the pretender to the governorship, will probably seek residence in this fair city, but only the good Lord knows when he shall arrive. I am certain that he too will petition to see our Prophet Young, the true governor, the governor-of-the-people."

Hickok glared at Nellie. "I would counsel against yer bringing yer womenfolk when meeting either governor." He scowled and added, "Womenfolk belong in the home."

"As soon as we have a home, we shall most assuredly consider your advice," Nellie said, taking a firm step, with both girls' hands in hers, to follow her husband.

Hickok led them back to the open-sided dwelling. "This here *Bowery* functions as both an outdoor house of worship and social meeting spot. Within this watertight structure we supervise the settlement process. President Young erected this structure's predecessor the minute we entered this valley. We faithful must have a sacred place to worship the Lord."

"What kind of business has you interruptin' our agricultural committee meeting?" an ornery-looking man said.

A cauldron bubbling with dissent, Nellie thought, her eye appraising a cluster of men again engaged in boisterous and agitated discussion.

This new man separated himself from the group. "Brother Elias, " said Hickok, and jerked his thumb at Obadiah. "This here is the U-nited States' appointee whom our hallowed Prophet told me to look out fer."

"Pleased to make your acquaintance, Judge Smith." Obadiah stepped forward with an outstretched hand.

"I wear too many hats to have this head only belong to judging, although I reckon justice is the overriding unifying factor," said Judge

Smith, in a not unfriendly tone, but with a wary look on his face. He kept his hands attached to his lapel.

Obadiah retracted his hand and stuck it in his waistcoat.

The judge frowned. "Let's see now, young fellow, I don't reckon I remember what your name was supposed to be."

With determined politeness, Obadiah nodded and said, "I am Obadiah Weber Wright, my wife Cornelia Rose, and my daughters Emma and Elizabeth."

"Yes, yes, time for them niceties later," said the judge, waving away Nellie's greeting and dismissing her with a curt nod. He turned the full glare of his gaze on Obadiah. "I don' rightly know why that dammed President Buchanan is firing up people and sending 'em out here on false pretexts. Why, our Governor Young has this territory in tip-top shape. Marshal Hickok will testify to it. He has the Governor's ear."

"Did he cut it off with his sword?" whispered Emma, terrified eyes meeting Nellie's smiling ones.

Nellie scooped her frightened older daughter into her arms while Elizabeth clung to her skirts. Nellie whispered through smiling lips, "No, no, my sweet pumpkin. It is an expression grownups use to indicate that someone listens to them with great attention."

Smith pointed to Hickok, who nodded and touched his broad brimmed hat.

Smith continued, "Prophet Young devised a brilliant system, organizing every facet of a Godly society, working so well, we don't hardly need any judging. Mind you, the Church is a higher authority anyway than them fools that run the old United States. We adjudicate our own folks. Don't see why Buchanan is sending that coward Cumming, and don't see *why* we would need the likes of you."

The judge scowled down at Obadiah, who sucked in an audible gulp of breath.

Nellie felt her two girls again trembling against her.

Hickok chuckled.

The crowd of men swarmed around them.

They do not appear a motley crew. Let us hope they remain civil. Yet there appears nary a woman in sight.

This observation did little to relieve her anxiety.

Mercy, women may well not be permitted here, in a place where the men transact business and discuss politics. Do they willingly keep to their place in the home?

Obadiah drew himself up to his full six-foot height and cleared his throat. Suddenly, he turned to a man listening to the exchange almost at his elbow. "Where are we?" he asked.

"Beg pardon?" the man answered.

"He don't even know his whereabouts?" snickered a fellow at the man's elbow.

"I asked you a question, sir," Obadiah boomed. "What is this place called?"

"Why, this is the Great Salt Lake City," he replied. "Are ye lost?"

"Have ye got cotton between the ears, man?" asked Hickok.

The crowd roared with laughter.

Obadiah looked grave and nodded his head no in answer. In a slow, deliberate tone, he asked, "And where is this Great Salt Lake City located?"

"In Utah Territory," the man replied.

Obadiah nodded, hands still jauntily clasping his waistcoat. "That's right. Utah Territory. Created by the Compromise of 1850, President Millard Fillmore himself appointing Brother Brigham Young as *first* Governor of Utah Territory."

The crowd nodded and muttered agreement.

"So, my good man, of what is Utah a territory?"

The man answered promptly, "Of the United States, ye fool."

"By jingo," said Obadiah, pointing a finger in the air. "Aye! Of the United States." He looked around at the curious, unfriendly crowd. "Of the United States of America. Good sirs, are we not all citizens of the United States of America?"

There ensued some general grunts of assent.

"We ain't in Utah Territory. President Young named our promised land Deseret," shouted one man.

"Land of the honeybee."

"Like our Book of Mormon promises. Our honeybee symbolizes our industry and cooperation."

"We are building the Kingdom of God on earth!" shouted another. "We don't need no scalawag's aid."

"Yeah. Leave us our 'popular sovereignty.' We don't want the blessing of the United States of America."

"There ain't no place for infidels here," shouted an uncouth-looking man lurking in the background.

"That may be so," conceded Obadiah. "But we have Treaties and Agreements that tell us we are all here in Utah. That's right, Utah Territory, and under whose jurisdiction does the Territory of Utah belong? To the United States. Moreover, each one of us has a voice in overseeing our government in the States by means of a vote. That's right, we are part of the United States, and Utah Territory has a vested interest in those United States, and a vested interest in keeping the States around to protect Deseret and allow it to flourish."

"We got our own armies for that," a man in the crowd declared.

"Now see here," Obadiah continued. "I have been deputized to act on behalf of those United States to administer justice. You, good sir, have just confirmed this is the United States Territory of Utah. As we have just established, the Territory of Utah, notwithstanding your learned Judge Smith's opinion, *still belongs to the United States.*

"Therefore, good sirs, you must respect the nation that gives this territory the protection against foreign invasion, the freedom to form itself, and the freedom to practice your faith. I trust your faith has the largesse to respect the nation of which you are *still citizens,* and allow me to perform my duties to protect those United States-granted freedoms, as I have been deputized by your nation."

Nellie beamed, and before she could stop them, her two little girls clapped. She glanced around assessing the faces, and saw some men looked less hostile, and a few even appeared persuaded.

Judge Smith broke into a grin. "With liberty and justice for all!" he shouted, and clapped Obadiah on the back.

The group broke out in a cheer.

Nellie almost snorted. *Is that sincerity or sarcasm emanating from the shyster, pettifogging lawyer?*

Hickok sniffed and said, "I guess this fella don't let his guns do his talking."

Judge Smith pulled Obadiah's arm and leaned in to stare at the younger man. "All right, you young whippersnapper, I suppose you are entitled to your opinion. Howsoever, we as a people have been scorned, insulted, betrayed and, if the truth be told, persecuted by agents of the United States of America."

Obadiah surreptitiously freed his elbow, but kept his eyes locked on Smith's.

Smith continued, "Therefore, you must concede we have a right to believe in our principle of blood atonement. After all, we merely hope to save the infidels and federal agents from the fires of hell."

Obadiah stepped back and pulled his waistcoat straight as he and Nellie exchanged glances.

Good Lord. This miscreant's incendiary words shall incite the crowd's animosity again.

Obadiah cleared his throat, "Now, let us adopt reasonable thinking—"

The judge cut him off with what Nellie thought was a sinister laugh.

Before either she or Obadiah could think of appropriate words to stem the tide of hostility, the judge changed his tone. "A point of order: since I am preaching freedom for us to follow our faith, I reckon I can allow you to follow yours."

Nellie let out an audible breath and clasped her shaking hands together.

Judge Smith again clapped Obadiah on the shoulder.

This man distorts a friendly gesture into one of domination and aggression.

The judge continued, "Ye might want to investigate an alternative means of income for supporting your family, though. As wot I told you originally, Prophet Young has this here territory running like a well-oiled machine, and there ain't much *federal* judging to be done. Why, currently, I am managing the finances of our fine newspaper." He jerked his thumb towards the west. "The Lord encourages industry with the promise of prosperity."

Nellie turned her head in the direction Smith pointed, peered over the heads of the men, and saw an imposing two-story brick building bearing the sign *DESERET NEWS.*

"I daily increase my wealth and stature between adjudicating disputes," the judge said. "But ye go and set yerself up, and keep me abreast of your goings on." Judge Smith dismissed him with a wave of his hand.

The assembled men, realizing the show was over, turned back to their business.

Obadiah turned to Nellie, took her arm, grasped Elizabeth's hand, and escorted them out into the open air.

"More's the pity, that was a bit unexpected," he said, a mild expression sitting easily on his face.

"Yes," Nellie agreed, still frowning and clutching Emma. "It is not every day one meets both a cockalorum and a snollygogger in one visit."

"Papa, your words learned those men good," offered Emma, suspended in an awkward spot in Nellie's arms as she scuttled, her daughter slipping, to get as far from the Bowery as quickly as possible.

"Yes, Papa, splendid," echoed Elizabeth, as she looked up at him while trying to match his big stride.

"I must agree with our daughters," huffed Nellie, as they scurried along.

Obadiah gave a grin, and slowed his step a bit, mid-stride. "Then, by the hornspoon, it is unanimous! I was splendid!"

Nellie caught his hand and smiled. "Mayhap we should end our day upon this high note of triumph."

A thundercloud crossed Obadiah's face, but Nellie rushed on. "I fear darkness shall overtake us soon."

"Darkness?" Obadiah sputtered. "'Tis August! Darkness shall not approach until nigh eight o'clock in the evening."

Nellie swallowed. *My husband despises exaggeration. I must choose more persuasive words.*

"I suppose," she said, "but certainly, calling hours are passed by this time of day. I know you are anxious to begin our future, but I fear 'tis the better course of valor to return to camp now." She looked expectantly at Obadiah.

Obadiah hesitated, and Nellie knew he would not leave without a fight.

She felt herself shrink in the face of her husband's ire, but she stuck to her guns, terribly rattled by the ugly incident. "We must feed our little charges. We must re-group. We cannot settle such an important matter as our entire future on an empty stomach and no rest."

Elizabeth said, "Papa, I'm ex-scared. Weren't you scared?"

Emma said, "I still shake with fright."

No longer waiting for Obadiah's permission, Nellie scooped her younger daughter into her other arm. "Our Guardian Angels surrounded us and protected us. Moreover, your father has matters well in hand. So, we shall return to camp and rustle us up some supper."

CHAPTER 3
I Made It Through the Rain

Great Salt Lake City, August 1857

Determined to shake the pall cast by the intimidating encounter with the men in the Bowery yesterday, Nellie searched for a new topic of conversation as she cooked yet another breakfast in a trench. "Surely, our friendly pioneer friend, Hannah Tapfield King, has arrived by now."

Emma piped up from her seat on a log. "Mama, 'twould be wonderful to find Missus King."

"She makes good biscuits," seconded Elizabeth.

"That's the cherry on top, Betsy," said Emma. "I would be happy to just see a friendly face."

Nellie caught Emma's hand and gave it a reassuring squeeze. *Mercy! This hostile environment takes quite the toll on my constitution. I cannot even fathom the damage it does to my precious daughters.*

"Did she not take Parley Pratt's Road?" Obadiah shook his head. "I doubt she shall arrive for many days. Did I not foresee delay and difficulty? As you will recall, I advised the Golden Pass Road impassable due to its dire condition."

"How much longer could a short-cut take?" Nellie asked.

The question had its desired effect. Her daughters giggled and their collective mood eased.

Obadiah's grin widened. "Do you not wish to thank your mastermind husband for staying the course and finding the most efficient route to this fair city? Or did you wish to spend several more weeks camping along the trail, sleeping atop all our earthly possessions?"

"I like camping in our wagon," said Emma. "It's fun to snuggle all together at night."

"Bugs like it too," said Elizabeth.

The family looked at her.

"Just like Mama 'splained. Squished together, bugs don't have to go far to feast on every one of us."

They all laughed.

Obadiah announced, "Today we continue our foray into the future. Everyone spend a minute on your toilet. We must look sharp for the Governor." Still jolly, he grabbed his cup and razor and began to mix his shaving soap into a lather.

The girls ran into the wagon for ribbons.

Nellie finished the breakfast cleanup, noticing the increasing swell of her abdomen every time she bent over the dish tub.

Chores completed, she hastily re-combed her hair and rinsed her face. She longed for the luxury of a bath. Partial cleaning with cold water could not hold a candle to a long soak in a tub in a warmed room.

Even in her nightmares, she never would have thought she would still be homeless the day after arriving at her destination.

"Here we go on our magical adventure," said Emma with a smile.

"I didn't bring my magic wand," said Elizabeth, pulling as if to turn around to retrieve it.

Nellie picked a stick up off the boardwalk. "Today I shall cast a magic spell over this stick and its magic will flow." She waved her hand over the stick and mumbled, "Abracadabra."

As she handed it to Elizabeth, Emma said, "I need one too!"

Obadiah snapped a branch off a tree overhanging on the path. "Stolen magic," he proclaimed and handed it to Emma. "On information and belief, I report this wand was the property of a fey garden gnome."

Elizabeth turned her gaze, eyes round as saucers, on her father. "He won't cast a bad spell on us for stealing his wand, will he?"

Nellie rolled her eyes and swished her skirt over Elizabeth and then Emma. "I have cast a protective spell over you so the gnome can cause no harm."

"Will that protect us from that mofit too?" asked Elizabeth.

Nellie and Obadiah looked at each other. *Mofit?*

"She means *Prophet*. Prophet Young," explained Emma.

Would that it could! Nellie thought. "We don't need...."

"I shall protect us," Obadiah interrupted. "We have no need of magical protection. We have our wits and our earnest desire to fulfill our responsibilities to protect us."

No doubt I would have responded differently, but Obadiah makes a fair point.

The intensity of their discussion led the family to cross an intersection without checking for oncoming traffic. A horse and buggy charged up the street. Startled, they dashed to the edge of the road.

Shaking from the all-too-near miss, Nellie wondered if they might in fact need a magic incantation to keep them from harm.

Surprise at the horses reigned to a neighing stop right in front of them cut her new worry short.

In the middle of the road?

The carriage's driver jumped down and opened the compartment door, and a stout middle-aged woman sprang out.

"Missus Cornelia Rose Entwhistle Wright," she said. "Like a magical mirage you appear on the street the very moment I speak your name to my confidant, Samuel Francis!"

Nellie rubbed the carriage dust from her eyes. "Missus Hannah Tapfield King. Merciful heavens, 'tis fortuitous in the extreme to again encounter you unexpectedly."

The stout British woman said, "Daily I look for you in the waves and trains of emigrants arriving in the Public Square. I thought, surely, I should see you at one of the welcome feasts the Saints serve to the new arrivals, or at one of the tables where Sister Sluce provides clean clothes to trail-maltreated children. I even checked the faces of the stricken children at the infirmary receiving medical treatment from Doctor Hovey, for fear one of your precious daughters suffered from a disorder your own expertise could not combat."

Nellie frowned and glanced at Obadiah, who looked equally bemused, even as she moved forward to embrace her friend from the Overland Trail.

The Saints serve welcoming feasts? Supply immigrant children with clean clothes?

"Surely, you, yourself have only just arrived?" asked Obadiah.

Nellie suppressed a grin. *Hannah already here after Obadiah just congratulated himself on avoiding the shortcut? Mayhap Golden Pass proved most expeditious after all.*

Hannah steamrollered right past the question. "I told myself I shall never find you in the hundreds of wagons parked in the Public Square in Ward Eight, whilst their occupants found jobs and arranged for lodging, but nevertheless I still searched. And now I found you, in the nick of time."

"Do you leave again, after only just arriving?" Nellie asked.

"Praise God our Lord and Savior, no! We only just arrived yesterday."

Nellie and Obadiah exchanged a glance and suppressed smiles.

Her friend loved to add a bit of drama and exaggeration for their entertainment.

"Mister King and I, and our entire entourage, shall move to a fine house in the eleventh ward under Bishop William A. McMaster tomorrow. My son-in-law has it all arranged."

Nellie tried to say something, despite feeling flabbergasted at the contrast between her family's reception and that of Mrs. King's family, but Hannah talked over her feeble attempt.

"Now our reunion joins the multitude of grand reunions I witness in the square!" Hannah clasped Nellie's hand to her heart. "The unmitigated *joy* pouring into my soul upon arriving to the sound of our holy Prophet Brigham Young preaching! The wonderful welcoming words of the gospel lifted my spirit to ecstasy, and love for all mankind filled my bosom."

Would that a little of that love spilled out to your fellow Saints *so they might spill some drops on the parched tongues of the non-Mormon immigrants. Tarnation, 't would be ecstasy to receive any treatment better than thinly veiled hostility.*

"The feting of our corporeal bodies with soup nourished me. Supplying beef, potatoes, pies, sugar and coffee — all the wants of those who had just come in from their long and tedious journey across the plains replenished us. The generosity of the Saints astonished me." Hannah continued to list the largess of the 'Saints' in the welcome she received.

Nellie felt as if her entire family stood there with their mouths open in amazement.

Hannah beamed at them. "But the wonder and awe I felt as they alleviated the suffering and supplied the needs of our poorer brethren pales in comparison with my awe in discovering you! Bless the Lord, oh my soul, and give thanks for all his benefits, for he indeed has been gracious to me to allow me to see for my very own eyes you and your little brood safely within the walls of Zion, enfolded by the Promised Land."

Now breathless, Hannah leaned over and gathered Emma and Elizabeth into her arms. "Just as soon as you locate lodgings, come to Bishop McMaster's guest house and we shall rekindle our friendship." She smiled up at Nellie.

Without waiting for any reply, Hannah turned on her heel and rushed back to her carriage. "Ta ta, for now," called Mrs. King over her shoulder as her driver and her young male companion assisted her in mounting her carriage step.

Dust swirled over the Wright family as they stood watching Hannah's retreat.

"Fiddlesticks," exclaimed Obadiah. "That woman's words bowled us all over more effectively than her horse ever could."

Nellie stared after the carriage, shaking in a trepidation not provoked by the near collision of Elizabeth and the horse, or even the force of Hannah's whirlwind of words. A wave of despair deluged her spirit, triggered by Hannah's inadvertent confirmation that the Wrights were not welcome there. Her heart plummeted to the ground and a deep foreboding for their future swamped her.

Establishing a home in this hostile territory when we have a perfectly good one back in New York? Mercy, the idiocy of this decision plagues me. I fervently wish I had never agreed to this journey. How I wish on all the stars in heaven we had turned our wagon around at any one of the many adversities we faced and retreated homeward.

"After weathering all sorts of storms whilst traveling, we find ourselves stranded in quite the turbulent climate," Nellie ventured, but bit back further words when she looked at her daughters. Mercifully, their spirits seemed revived by the unexpected encounter with their acquaintance from the trail.

"Missus King *always* pops in when we don't expect her," said Emma.

"Yes." Elizabeth shook her head up and down with such vigor, Emma burst out laughing. "Therefore," Elizabeth continued, "we should always just 'spect her."

"I see the logic," said Emma.

Both girls giggled.

Nellie smiled. "I see your logic as well."

"Magic can happen any time," Elizabeth said earnestly.

"Of course," said Emma, hugging her little sister.

Cheered despite her nagging misgivings about their predicament, Nellie said, "Yes, magic makes its own opportunity."

"That is why we should always expect it," Emma confirmed.

"Even when we don't 'spect it," Elizabeth chimed in.

"We travel around in delightful circles," Nellie said.

Her daughters joined hands and spun around in a circle.

Nellie tugged at a lock of hair already sprung from her bun. "But what course shall we pursue now?" she asked, the purpose of their journey evading her.

"Why, we find Governor Young, or even the new governor, 'Coward Cumming,' of course," replied Obadiah, his daughter's cheer warming his disposition as well.

Nellie balked, not interested in encountering more Mormon hostility. She stalled for time. "We must feed our little charges, and we must re-group. We cannot settle such an important matter as our entire future on an empty stomach."

"Did we not just feast on breakfast?" asked Obadiah. He grabbed her hand and gave it a reassuring squeeze.

True. Nellie shook her head. Her trepidation at this meeting quite overwhelmed her. She searched for other ways to delay another potential altercation.

"Can we explore this perfectly appointed town before we have a meeting?" asked Emma.

Elizabeth jumped up and down. "Yes! Let's look at all the gardens and buy some fruit!"

Offering a silent prayer for her girls' timely suggestions, and without waiting for Obadiah's opinion, Nellie took her daughters by their hands and said, "To market we shall go, and the finest fruit find! Then, we shall rustle some dinner for lunch and strike again in the afternoon."

"Eat *again*?" Obadiah said. "Did we not get this far last night and stop for that same activity?"

Nellie frowned and glared at him.

Obadiah laughed and scooped both his daughters into his arms. "Must I *always* feed you? Just like little birds who consume their whole weight in food daily?"

They strolled down the street.

I must curb my runaway fears and restrain myself from longing for my well-constructed house in Sing Sing, nestled in the bosom of my family. Oh, Papa, Ach! Mutter, I miss you. And all my brothers, and all my sisters, even Agnes! Not to mention the friends, aunts, uncles, and cousins I left behind.

"Z... C... M... I..." read Elizabeth. "What does that spell, Papa?"

"ZCMI," repeated Emma. "Papa already explained—"

"I remember," said Elizabeth with a defensive scowl. "But here 'lion' starts with a 'Z'?"

"Whatever do you mean?" asked Nellie.

"The Lion Cooperates Business," replied Elizabeth. "Why do the Saints spell *lion* with a Z?"

The group giggled.

"It may well be a lion, determined to get the lion's share, that we are dealing with," agreed Nellie. "But Elizabeth, the company's name is Zzzzzion Cooperative Mercantile Institute."

Elizabeth looked back at her silently, with her trademarked rounded eyes.

Obadiah frowned but made no comment.

The group came upon a gentleman emerging from a shop that emitted enticing aromas.

"Yum, the sweetest smell we smelt since we left home," announced Elizabeth.

"Cinnamon," said Nellie, and she and Emma sighed simultaneously.

"If it is a bakery," declared Emma, "it should have a big piece of cake nailed to the roof, in the fashion of the cobbler and the tinsmith!"

Elizabeth nodded, her little face taking on a grave, determined expression. "Then I would climb up and nibble it just like Gretel did in that fairytale!"

"And risk the wicked witch, or maybe the business lion, wanting to eat you?" breathed Emma. Her eyes widened, aghast at her sister's foolishness.

"Girls, don't let this heavenly scent cause your imaginations to wander too far." Nellie laughed.

"Mama, do they have cake here, just like at home?" asked Elizabeth.

My fears must be contagious.

"My darlings, the cake may not be precisely the same as we make at home, but nevertheless, let us celebrate our arrival here. Come, we shall reconnoiter to see if there is anything inside that strikes our fancy." Nellie took the girls by the hands and brought them into the shop.

Several minutes later, with a giddy whirl of skirts, Nellie ushered her children back out onto the street, each girl clutching a little box tied with string.

Obadiah stood looking at the sky and twirling his mustache. "'Tis rather a conundrum, taunting me since that encounter with the swaggering Hickok and his crafty accomplice, Judge Smith."

Nellie's smile vanished as all her worries rushed back.

"A series of fits and starts confronts us," said Obadiah. "A new capital established in Fillmore City, a huge building to house the legislature planned. They sat one season, only the first section of the legislature, after completing only one wing of the capitol. Yet last year the government returned to the Great Salt Lake City, and a new governor appointed, yet the old governor still firmly ensconced."

"From whence have these facts suddenly appeared?" Nellie was now puzzled as well as frightened.

"Whilst you drooled over confectionary treats...."

"Hardly!" Nellie snorted and Obadiah raised his eyebrow. "One powdered sugar cruller and one berry tart hardly a bakery make. Why, at home in Sing Sing, my *Mutter's* fine Viennese *sachertorte* and *apfelstrudel* obviated any need for a bakery, but when the weather conspired to deplete the joy of standing by a hot oven, Spindler's fine bake shop tempted all with fresh bread, divine biscuits, and berry pie — in almost every season."

"By the hornspoon, Cornelia, capture thy runaway tongue! 'Tis of little use to compare everything here to the life we left in New York. We must approach our adventure in this place with an open mind, allowing ourselves to appreciate the joys contained in this new life."

Stung by the rebuttal, Nellie hung her head. Then contriteness washed over her. "Yes, I see your wisdom. 'Comparison is the theft of joy.' I must take this maxim to heart and endeavor to approach the riches this new life may contain with an open heart. Now, wherever did you obtain a newspaper?"

"I found a more comprehensive and interactive, but less reliable, source. A passerby heard my mutterings and gave me a brief history of the location of the capital and the capitol. Then he waxed poetic about the machinations of politics.

"As nearly as I can figure, based on what the chap said, and the little news which reached us on the trail, President Buchannan appointed an Alfred E. Cumming new governor of Utah Territory in July. Fearing Young's resistance, he then assigned a military escort to accompany Cumming to Great Salt Lake City to take up his position. Yet, Brigham Young received no official notification and still governs here." Obadiah shook his head and stroked his mustache, deep in thought.

"The question is, quite literally, where to go from here? Mayhap to find the new federally appointed Cumming? I'll wager then, to Fillmore?"

"'Tis quite the 'Irish huddle'." Nellie mused. "Who then truly *is* the governor of Utah Territory at this exact moment?"

Obadiah tugged his mustache and, looking confused, shook his head. "As near as I can figure, gubernatorial power remains in the hands of Brigham Young. That big fellow Bill Hickok alluded to this strange turn of events, and now we have some clarification. Sometime in the near future, I believe, leadership shall pass to the new man. I shall verify my orders. But I do believe I was instructed to report to Brigham Young, and by gum, that is what I intend to do." Obadiah brushed his hands together as if he were disposing of the whole mess. "Done and dusted."

"There's a storm brewing. Strange machinations abound. Find you this not alarming?" Nellie said, her voice getting a bit shriller.

"This is a city. I am sure we are safe from Indian attack here. Further, this discussion must be tabled until we tuck our little pitchers with big ears into bed,'" Obadiah said sternly.

Has he deliberately misunderstood my misgivings and suspicions?

Nellie would not be put off so easily. "Methinks the order said to present yourself to *Governor* Brigham Young. If President Buchanan appointed a new governor, how can you report to Young?"

The girls looked up at Obadiah with wide eyes.

"Let us not fret, and let us not make haste," Obadiah said at last. "We have only just arrived at our new home. We must take some time to assess the situation, and get oriented, both geographically and politically. What say you fine ladies to a sip of sarsaparilla, and a nibble of whatever heavenly concoction is hiding in those parcels, and then a mosey through this fine town to see what she has?"

Nellie began to say 'is this not what I have just counseled' but kept her mouth closed, and found satisfaction in the ratification of her strategy, even if her husband believed he devised the plan himself.

"Sarsaparilla!" exclaimed Emma.

Elizabeth just clapped with happiness.

"But what if they don't have sarsaparilla in this town?" asked Emma, looking worried again. "We had trouble enough finding sweets we recognized."

"Or what if they do, but they don't want us to have any?" said Elizabeth.

Amen, my prescient little three-year-old.

Nellie met Obadiah's eyes over their heads as they took the girls' hands.

Nellie squeezed Elizabeth's hand, warm in her own, and was surprised when Elizabeth screamed.

Nellie and Obadiah looked at her in surprise.

Elizabeth yowled again and pulled her hand away.

Nellie dropped to one knee and examined her daughter's hands. "Mercy, here is our culprit. My sweet pumpkin, you have a splinter."

Elizabeth burst into tears.

Surprised, Nellie said, "But it is just a little thing, easily fixed." She tried to yank it out with just her fingernails, but a small part broke off and remained under the skin.

Elizabeth howled.

"I have some soothing witch hazel, and we shall apply it the moment we return to our wagon. But for now, hold your father's hand with your other hand."

While Elizabeth looked at her father, Nellie pulled her broach off her shirtwaist.

Is it better to wait until I can sterilize this, or relieve the pressure now from that angry infection already starting to pus?

Tarry a moment, Nellie told herself. *Did I not enclose a sterile needle pinned to a scrap cloth in this carpet bag of necessities I always lug along?*

Emma saw Nellie pull her bag off her shoulder, and realized they must continue to distract Elizabeth. "Betsy, look at the roses in full bloom tucked along that beautiful white fence!"

Taking no chances, Obadiah turned his daughter's head away from Nellie's movements, in the direction of a truly picturesque late summer garden. "The Last Rose of Summer," he sang.

In a flash, Nellie extracted her needle from its linen case in her bag. In one quick motion she swooped over Elizabeth's finger, darted the needle under the splinter and gently pushed it out the way it went in. Elizabeth tried to snatch her hand away, but Nellie held on tight, and Emma turned Elizabeth's head away and pointed as Obadiah continued his verbal guided tour of the garden in front of them. Nellie rooted in her bag with her other hand searching for her packet of witch hazel.

Tarnation!

She had applied the last of her witch hazel salve to Obadiah's sunburn, back on the Overland Trail.

Mercy, now I shall have to send all the way back to Mister Hart's apothecary in Sing Sing, New York for more. These Hamamelis shrubs only grow in the East.

Her right hand kept searching her bag as her left still held little Elizabeth's.

Eureka! I shall use the aloe vera gathered in the big Sandy desert. It shall function as both an astringent and unguent, thus sealing the little cut.

Elizabeth looked at her mother with her big, round eyes filled with fear at the coolness of the gooey aloe. "Tell me when to be ready," she said, lower lip trembling.

Nellie, Emma, and Obadiah chuckled.

"Your mother's superior surgery skills strike again! You felt nothing when she removed the splinter," Obadiah said, with a big smile and a hug.

"It hurted anyway, but I am brave," said Elizabeth, nodding for emphasis.

"Betsy, your courage is an example to us all," said Emma, and gave her sister a squeeze.

Nellie and Obadiah exchanged another smile over the tops of their daughters' heads.

I could not be prouder of both of my girls.

The walking tour continued, and as the girls marveled anew at the city's wondrous signs of civilization, they again began to chatter.

Taking advantage of that cover, Obadiah said in a low voice, "I feel I must disclose I have not been quite forthcoming reporting additional information I have gleaned. We have arrived at a very difficult time in the relationship between Mister Young and his Kingdom, and our United States. Since our arrival, I have discerned from various sources that a mere month ago, all the federal employees were ridden out of town on a rail."

"Literally?" gasped Nellie.

Obadiah *shhhhhed* her.

"Quite likely," he replied grimly.

"What about judges, such as yourself?" Nellie whispered, her voice constricted with fright.

"Judges, justices, constables... in general, any critics of Young's faith, the whole kit and caboodle. Must be how that Hickok earned his position of marshal. Howsoever, it seems that Governor Young has had his troops stand down, and he shall withdraw his Proclamation of Martial Law."

"His troops? Martial law?" A note of hysteria crept into Nellie's voice.

This is a fine time to tell me, now that we have arrived. Mercy. Must we flee home? Surely! And I can retrieve my own new supply of witch hazel blossoms. She felt a hysterical laugh escape her lips as wild thoughts tumbled, one on top of the other.

Obadiah glared at her, and she calmed herself for the sake of her children.

"We shall discuss this further tonight," he said, "as our custom, when we need not censor our words. Howsoever, I felt I must alert you that not only shall I have a more severe test of my fortitude in carrying out this assignment than I anticipated, but this situation likely brooks no opportunity for *Saints* or neighbors welcoming *us*."

Nellie's worried eyes did not leave his face. She barely noticed the establishments they passed.

Obadiah shook his head. "One further worry: *still-acting* Governor Young issued an edict that no person shall be allowed to pass through this territory without registering with Mormon tribunals and receiving his permission."

Clayton! Nellie's heart leapt to her throat. *This decree further jeopardizes his safety. As if resuming travel to California with a day-old infant and his unpleasant wife did not provoke enough threat to life.*

She gritted her teeth. "Has our old wagon company *registered* and been granted permission to proceed through southern Utah Territory along the California Trail?"

Obadiah shrugged his shoulders. "I assume, as they camped in the designated area visible to all the *authorities*, Captain Hines made all the necessary disclosures."

An irrepressible note of hysteria crept into Nellie's voice. "Merciful Lord, we pray, protect our comrades in our former wagon train!"

Obadiah nodded. "It is with great sadness that I contemplate the fate of our dear wagon company. Let us bow our heads in prayer for their safe passage through Utah Territory."

Nellie and Obadiah bowed their heads as they walked.

Silently, she prayed, *Dear Lord, keep my former traveling companions safe. Especially... Lord, my heart wrenches with fear at the thought of noble*

Beauregard Cornelius Clayton, intent on shepherding his days-old son and his ornery wife away from the perils of the Great Salt Lake City instead silently trudging into danger.

"Yea, perils designed by fellow men may well prove more trying than nature's fury," Nellie said. In her worry about her friends and companions from the journey, she forgot her own predicament.

The girls prattled away, blessedly oblivious, crafting the rules for some elaborate game.

Obadiah cleared his throat and said, "Further, and just as importantly, let us maintain our habitual breadth of view, and keep our faith that our good deeds shall shape our future in a positive mode."

"Nellie!" someone shouted.

Nellie looked at Obadiah in surprise. "Another Nellie resides in the Great Salt Lake City? Whosoever shouts must seek another person. Who would know me?"

The Wrights all turned around and looked as a woman ran up the boardwalk toward them.

"Lucena Parsons!" Nellie grabbed the young bride in an ecstatic hug, relief at seeing a friendly familiar face causing her to cling a little desperately to the young woman.

"Mercy," said Lucena. "How long this day has been, and me not seeing anybody but strangers! My heart busts with joy at the sight of you, Cornelia Rose. This town sprouts a cornucopia of fresh vegetables, the likes of which we have not seen since leaving Wisconsin, yet no meeting house within miles that *we* could attend."

"Everybody's cup runneth over at the sight of us," Elizabeth said, and ran to Lucena and hugged her legs.

The adults burst into laughter.

"Halleluiah, little cherub," Lucena cried. "I cannot fault your reckoning, Precious!" She resumed her train of thought as if there had been no interruption. "Yes, the enterprising Mormons already harvest many crops, even this early in August. We shall make up for lost time and dine like kings! All things considered, the abundant food and water confirms my decision to persuade Mister Parsons to rest over here and continue our journey to Californie next summer."

Rejoice, for my dear sweet Lucena shall not fall victim to the fate of other unwary wagon trains at the hands of the Mormons. Mercy droppeth like dew from the heavens! But what of Clayton?

Lucena gave Nellie a radiant smile, which cheered her a bit. "I did get tiresome sick of only finding chokeberry and black currants on the trail."

Tears sprang to her eyes as Nellie said, "My gratitude to the bountiful harvest that lured you into wintering in this city overflows. I shall cherish your companionship. Relief in having a friend and confidante in this cold location washes over me like a warm rain."

Her pretty young face twisted in consternation, Lucena asked, "Do you mean the Great Salt Lake City hosts temperatures below zero, or that it's residents are unwelcoming?"

Nellie gave a short laugh as a few tears splashed on her cheeks, despite her best efforts. "I meant the city hosts hostile hosts!"

"Saints alive!" said Lucena.

"Yes, the *Saints* are alive and dominant. That is the problem." Downright merry now that she had a friend, Nellie pressed her puns a little further onto Lucena's good nature.

Lucena threw up her hands in mock despair. "Oft I embrace the challenge of deciphering your witticisms, but these two utterances more aptly resemble riddles. I gots to stand in front of the school Marm and diagram those pesky sentences." She grinned at Nellie, who opened her mouth to explain.

"No, do not speak!" Laughing, Lucena held up her hand. "If I am to winter in a place with you as my sole trusted female companion, I must sharpen my wits. I gots ta do this by myself. I'll untangle this snarl of yarn alone. I used *host* to mean *offer*, and you used it to mean both that and someone receivin' guests... and the *Saints* are—"

"Splendid deductions!" Nellie interrupted her. "Fit for a host of saints!"

"Another meaning—a big ol' group of Mormons!" Lucena gave Nellie an enthusiastic hug.

"You have perforated my puzzle, and I shan't stump you any longer." Nellie returned the hug, grateful for the appearance of this happy angel in the midst of hell. "Perhaps I am the one who should move...."

Lucena's face pulled into an astonished expression.

"...Migrate to a different form of parlor games."

Lucena's astonishment turned into a mock stern expression. "You'd better stay right here the *entire* duration of my inhabitation of this foreign land. I could not, nay *shall not*, bear it without you." A smile once again accentuated the pretty features of her face. "Furthermore, the head-achin' words you thrust upon me shall make me all the brighter for it, for I do so love being merry."

Nellie laughed. "Brilliant!" Then she realized Lucena did not detect her own inadvertent pun. Rather than pointing it out, she said, "'Tis your bright, sunny personality that warms my heart and eases my burdens. I shall cherish our additional moments together."

Emma and Elizabeth could wait no longer for the attention of their 'aunt' and crowded around her. They each grabbed one of her hands and showered them with kisses. "Aunt Lucena, will you live next door to us?" asked Emma.

"Missus Parsons shall at least live nearby for this coming winter," said Nellie.

The little girls jumped up and down, and Elizabeth threw her arms around Lucena's skirt.

"Do you know where there's some sarsaparilla?" asked Elizabeth.

"Betsy, Aunt Lucena just moved into town, same as us," said Emma. "Of course she does not."

"Emma is right, Betsy. I do not know, but just as soon as Mister Parsons concludes his conversation with your father, I shall make it my mission to find out." Lucena leaned down and hugged both girls.

Nellie noticed Lucena clinging to them in relief. She then looked at her husband, deep in conversation with their fellow waggoneer. Both men wore grim expressions on their faces.

Whatever trouble brews now, Lord, thank you kindly for arming me with a friend to face the difficulty surrounding us.

Relief written all over her face, Lucena now turned a blind eye to the heated conversation of the men and struck a merry tune with Nellie's daughters.

Nellie reached over and hugged Lucena again, who squeezed Nellie's hand and winked while continuing to sing.

Nellie caught a few snatches of distressing words from her husband's conversation through the stanzas of *Oh! Susanna*.

"...breastworks...."

"...elaborate stone formation."

"...like shootin' fish in a barrel, attacking anyone walking through those passages."

Unable to control her curiosity any longer, Nellie burst into the tête-à-tête between her husband and Mr. Parsons. "Who is being shot at like fish in a barrel?" she demanded.

Obadiah put a restraining hand on her arm as if to prevent her speech. "Hold your horses now, Cornelia. Mister Parsons communicates a bit of enlightenment as to some strange developments, which we must carefully consider, deduce the intent, and check for accuracy before—"

"Now *you* hol' on just a cotton-pickin' minute there, Captain Wright!" interrupted George Washington Parsons. "This here is accurate intelligence, which I have on the best authority."

"Personal observation?" asked Obadiah, his eyebrow raised in a mild, curious expression.

Mr. Parsons practically spluttered his reply. "No! Not personal observation, mind you. I arrived in the same wagon company as you. None of us noted anything out of the ordinary."

I did!

Nellie's mind raced as she recalled the strange stone foundations that lined the high mountain walls crowding the narrow trail through Echo Canyon.

I noticed the stone arranged like a man-made fortification! I remember distinctly. But I shan't blurt my observation. I must exercise restraint and discern all the information Mister Parsons knows.

"I got my word directly from a Mormon scout by the name of Abraham Owen Smoot," Mr. Parsons continued. "He told me them Mormons was arming for a resistance to the new governor. A fellow by the name of Cumming, newly appointed Utah Territory Governor by Mister President John Buchannan himself, travels here now. An Army platoon of 1,500 soldiers escort him! 'A course, old Mister Smoot says, our President didn't tell Governor Young—not any of this. Them Mormons discovered this via news reports and gossip, jest like us pioneers. But Smoot saw Colonel Alexander and the United States troops begin their journey here hisself." Parsons shook his head and looked a bit sympathetic to the Mormon plight. "This has ol' Brigham Young in such a dander, he's raising an army and mounting a protection of his kingdom."

Nellie listened with her mouth hanging open in surprise and dismay.

Tarnation! Gossip confirmed, making our situation more precarious than even the terrible scenarios unfolding in my worst nightmares. The United States Army on the march? Tarry a moment, shall that harm us or protect us?

"Mayhap an ambush awaits the arrival of the new governor," said Parsons.

"Political ambush, surely," replied Obadiah, unruffled.

"Is Young's strategy to shoot the new governor from the newly erected breastworks along the ridge top of Big Mountain as the envoy of our United States Army escorts him through Mormon Flats?" Nellie asked, hysteria rising in her voice.

Lucena broke off her singing, even though the little girls continued, and looked at Nellie.

Once again Obadiah grabbed her elbow and squeezed it to restrain her speech.

Lucena said, with a large smile, "I heard a fellow talk in the Public Square where all them Mormon pioneers get welcomed. He says Governor Young called for martial law in the Great Salt Lake City, so that should protect us."

Nellie and Obadiah exchanged looks but Nellie dared not correct her optimistic friend in front of her baby girls.

Lucena frowned. "I am sure I don't rightly cotton what kind of law 'marshal' is, but it sounds like it involves a peace-keeping sheriff. Besides, this unrest brews far away in the Great Salt Lake City, so we need not be concerned."

Mr. Parsons, Obadiah, and Nellie stared at Lucena, mouths agape.

"Whatever put a bee in you all's bonnet?" she asked.

Merciful heavens, does Lucena's excess of good humor leave no room for common sense?

Nellie took her gently by the arm. "Did you forget, *we* have arrived in the Great Salt Lake City?"

"Mercy, I clean forgot! Yes, we're jest stopping here temporary, on account of all them ripe vegetables."

I shall wait for the penny to drop....

"Heavens! *We* stand in the Great Salt Lake City!" Lucena exclaimed.

Obadiah's firm voice calmed and focused them. "Now regard this town carefully."

Everyone glanced up and down the street.

"It appears business as usual. No one rushes around as if preparing to flee. No one storms the shops gathering provisions as if *Armageddon approacheth*. These pieces of information remain unconfirmed. We must adopt a reasonable approach and assess the situation once we have garnered more facts."

"That's all well and good, but what are we to do in the meantime?" asked Parsons.

"I shall secure us all some temporary lodging and hasten to obtain an audience with Young, to get the accurate information right from the horse's mouth," Obadiah replied.

Parsons nodded. "That's a fair approach. I am far too road-weary to rush back to the Californie Trail. Further, learnin' the devil *here* might serve us better than heading into the wilderness just as winter approaches. We don't want to end up in the arms of the devil mother nature we can never learn."

Nellie swallowed hard.

I must restore equanimity, especially for myself!

She shook Obadiah's hand off her elbow and pulled her arm through Lucena's. "My *Farmer's Almanac* advises an October blizzard is no stranger to these parts."

Obadiah clapped the younger man on his back and said, "We shall rendezvous back at the emigrant camp after I have sussed the information necessary to form a plan."

Lucena and George Washington Parsons hurried away, with a nod of farewell.

"Papa!" Elizabeth impatiently tugged on her father's coattails.

"Mama!"

Nellie realized both daughters vied for their attention.

"We have walked through many wonderful streets, but we still have not found sarsaparilla!" Emma protested. She looked at her little sister. "We enjoyed sarsaparilla in Sing Sing."

That was all Elizabeth needed. "When can we go home? I want to go home!"

Nellie's heart lurched. *My lament exactly!* She forced a brave, determined smile.

Obadiah bent and gave both girls a hug. "If this town does not contain a proper establishment where a fine family like us can imbibe in a thirst-quenching sarsaparilla, then we shall at once shake the dust of this town from our feet and head on to Fillmore!"

Nellie reached over and squeezed Obadiah's hand.

Neither was at all sure what they would find as they continued through town. They only hoped that lack of sarsaparilla would be their worst problem.

CHAPTER 4
If You're Going Through Hell, Keep on Going

Great Salt Lake City, August 1857

The search for sarsaparilla proved fruitless.

While the Wrights *oooed* and *ahhhed* as they meandered through the streets, they failed to find an establishment that served beverages.

Nary a saloon in town. How strange.

Obadiah leaned over and whispered in her ear, "I do recall reading that one part of the Latter-day Saint's sacred scripture, the Doctrine and Covenants, prohibits church members from consuming wine and strong drink. Thus, no public drinking establishments, which significantly lessens our chances of finding a nicely brewed sarsaparilla."

Discouragement wrapped over Nellie like a heavy woolen cloak, dropping her shoulders and hanging her head.

"Beer does not seem to be mentioned, so rouse your cheer, as we may yet find a brewery," Obadiah said with determined optimism.

I must refrain from allowing these setbacks to obscure my gratitude for a safe arrival, family intact, in the Great Salt Lake City. But tarnation! Our safety seems threatened anew at every turn. Moreover, the peculiar ways espoused by these people deepen my dread. How shall I ever learn these mores, or learn to avoid offending anyone whilst skirting them?

She tugged a stray lock of hair. Shaking her head to stem the new downward spiral of worry, she tucked that lock firmly into place with renewed resolve and turned her thoughts to a litany of gratitude, reciting like a mantra.

Thank you, merciful Lord for your continued care and protection. Thank you for the gift of my family. Thank you for the preservation of their health. Into your hands I command my spirit and my anxiety for our future.

Nellie glanced down the street, once again admiring its crisp intersection, at right angles, with the street running parallel. The entire downtown area consisted of a grid of streets, bordered at each edge by streams funneling fresh water directly from the mountains.

"Why is there so many rivers, right in the city?" asked Emma.

"We find ourselves in an arid climate, so we shall experience very few rainy days. These cleverly engineered streams bring us water from the mountain springs for irrigation."

"Mayhap that is why the pretty little buildings look sunburned, Mama," said Emma.

"Adobe buildings often mature into this color, from their days standing staunchly in the sun."

"Why don't they paint them pink?" asked Elizabeth. "That would be a pretty color."

Nellie smiled at her daughters' wondrous prattle as they ambled through the bucolic but bustling streets.

Her smile froze on her face as she discerned unusual movement. A large building came into focus with armed guards pacing in front.

Tranquility of mind arrested, yet again.

She paused and looked at Obadiah for reassurances, but he strode forward as if he found nothing untoward in the sight of guns brandished by hostile men.

Mercy me, every man in this place wears his pistol upon him. Is it a sign of the wildness of the West or of a heightened alarm in the Mormon community?

Nellie grasped her daughters' hands more firmly and scurried along behind her husband. Quaking with a fear that nauseated her susceptible stomach, Nellie stopped her family in front of a square enclosed by a high wall.

"Mama, look." Emma pointed. "These building *are* painted a lovely creamy white. Someone important must live here."

"*Very* important," seconded Elizabeth. "Look at all his soldiers."

"These are the dwellings of Governor Brigham Young," said Obadiah.

"Not important enough to paint his house pink," Nellie observed with a hint of panic in her voice.

Obadiah glared a 'get ahold of yourself' look.

After clearing her throat to rid the lump of dread lodged there, Nellie said, "Just attempting a bit of levity for the sake of our daughters."

Our still sarsaparilla-less daughters.

A statue of an eagle spread its wings over the main gate to the compound. Another set of armed guards stood on either side of the arch.

The gatekeeper looks familiar.

She gasped. "Why if it isn't Wild Bill Hickok!"

Obadiah approached him.

Nellie and the girls hung back, not wanting to interfere.

The men spoke in low voices and Nellie could not catch their words. One of the guards blocked her view of Obadiah, but she could still see Hickok, almost continually shaking his head in the negative. At last, she heard the man speak and caught '...half four this afternoon.'

Obadiah tipped his hat and returned to his family.

"I have been granted an audience at a half after the hour of four," he said, with a smile.

The little girls giggled.

She failed to see the humor in the denial of their entry into the almighty Brigham's fortress. Why did Young surround himself with such security? Did 'Wild Bill' function less as Marshall and more as a bodyguard for Brigham Young?

Suddenly, out of nowhere, Lucena breezed in front of her, interrupting her dark thoughts.

Lucena's voice sang with her usual optimistic, if not misguided, vivacity. "We found a place for us to stay! I mean all of us, including your little girls." She grabbed Nellie's hand and squeezed it with happy enthusiasm.

As if I would have stayed somewhere without my babies? raced through her mind.

Lucena skipped off with a wave of her hand. "I promised Mister Parsons I would immediately return to his side once I located you. We rest at a farm stand, conversing with the locals and ogling the bushels of strawberries."

Watching Lucena's high fashion skirt swirl down the boardwalk boosted Nellie's spirits as much as her friend's merriness. She smiled.

Obadiah held out his arm as if he were inviting Nellie to a pleasant, afternoon stroll. With a cheery smile and a crisp bow, he said, "My dearest Cornelia, our scheduled appointment provides us with just enough time to continue our search for some sarsaparilla, or perhaps that dinner you proposed, but not cooked over a trench, instead at a fine establishment. There must at least be an inn somewhere in this town."

***

Three hours later, they returned to de facto-governor Brigham Young's compound, which seemed to consist of several dwellings, barely visible behind a ten-foot-high stone wall.

"All they have is tops of houses. Why do they have a too-high fence?" asked Elizabeth.

"At least we can see the beehive," said Emma, craning her neck to scour the architecture of the edifices, pointing to the model beehive perched atop a large observatory dome.

"Can the bees see it way up there? Do they fly that high?" Elizabeth asked, squinting at the sky.

Suppressing a smile, Nellie answered, "It is a stone model of a beehive, not one with actual bees."

Elizabeth looked doubtful, as if that answer did not satisfy her.

"Goodness," said Emma, as they once again approached the eagle-topped gate. "'Tis a grand adobe edifice, handsomest in town!"

"The white hurts my eyes," agreed Elizabeth, with such a silly shake of her head, her sunhat flew off.

"Saints in heaven, a two-storied tenement, festooned with balconies? 'Tis by far the finest house in the city," Nellie said, shading her own eyes against the glare of the dazzling white adobe finish. "Must have cost a pretty penny," she whispered to Obadiah. "How does a man fund a private observatory in the middle of the wilderness?"

Nellie bent to a tug on her skirt, but caught a quick glimpse of uncertainty in Obadiah's eyes.

"Is that house haunted?" Emma whispered, big gray eyes round with fright. "It looks so lonesome."

Nellie's head swiveled to the far right and saw a rather dilapidated big house, with green shutters askew around a few small windows, blinds drawn to irregular lengths. Now she looked uncertainly at Obadiah.

Obadiah smoothed his mustache and said, "On information and belief, Mrs. Young is sole commander of the house on the right."

Brigham Young's mother?

This statement only raised more questions in Nellie's mind, but before she could formulate a question, Mr. Hickok walked toward them and escorted them under the eagle arch towards the two-story balconied house. Nellie smiled when she saw both Emma and Elizabeth duck under as they stared up at the angry-looking eagle with the prominent talons.

Perhaps in an attempt to be polite, Hickok pointed to the grand building and in an officious tone said, "I present the Beehive House, newly constructed in 1854 as the home of our Prophet and his family. I shall escort you to the entrance to his office, attached to this building."

Their small procession made its way past the recently completed mansion.

Nellie admired the variety of trees lining the path. Apple, pear, peach, apricot, all heavy with ripening fruit, tickled her nose with their enticing scent as they proceeded.

Glancing at Nellie, Hickok said, "The Prophet dotes on fruit. We have orchards of each of these types laid out in the back, producing abundant crops every year."

Nellie raised her eyebrows.

"Hells bells," Hickok continued. "We don't neglect grape cultivation either."

Nellie nodded her admiration of the garden, trying to count how many long months had elapsed since her tongue tasted the sweet nectar of apricot.

She glanced at Obadiah, who surreptitiously adjusted his cravat and tugged at his vest as they walked.

Nervous ticks betray his unease. She reached for his hand to squeeze it.

As they wended their way along the path, Hickok pointed down the main street. "Tithing store and *Deseret News* printing office reside beyond the Lion House," he said, and steered them toward the entry of the building.

The girls exchanged frightened glances.

"Where is the lion?" whispered Emma.

Elizabeth silently pointed to a building on the right directly adjacent to the one they approached. "Do lions live everywhere here?" she asked.

"'Tis a *statue* of a lion, peaceful and lying in repose," Nellie whispered back with what she hoped was a reassuring voice, despite feeling apprehensive about the whole encounter herself.

"That is the house with lots of chimneys," Emma advised Elizabeth.

"But when we looked over the wall it looked like a garden of chimneys not attached to anything," Elizabeth said.

"Why would anyone make that?" asked Emma reasonably.

"True," said Nellie in a low voice, hoping Hickok would continue talking to Obadiah and not hear her. "Everything we have seen thus far bears the mark of utility. Notice there are no flower gardens, only trees and bushes bearing fruit. Even the fancy features of this grand building are practical, with windows open to let in air and light, and balconies to enjoy fair weather."

"Prophet Young's office entrance," Hickok boomed, waving them toward a big wood door.

The raw scent of the new pine of the doorframe overwhelmed Nellie as she stepped through its opening into a large two-story room.

A tall silent man stepped aside to allow their entrance.

A butler? Mercy, we have regained civilization.

Rows of desks loomed before them, like sentries guarding a tomb. Three clerks bent, scribbling industriously, over desks on each side of a center aisle. Six men hunched over tall yellow pine desks along the wall, dipping pens in ink, inscribing large ledgers, and blotting their entries with a quiet, efficient purpose. No head rose from this work to look at the cluster of visitors surreptitiously scrutinizing the room. The commotion of the Wright's entrance did not seem to register.

Nellie puzzled at their lack of curiosity and the room's purpose as she tried to evaluate its details through her peripheral vision. Bookcases of honey-colored box elder-wood drew her gaze to the walls, as the gleam of their high polish mirrored the sunlight streaming through the big windows. It's magnified sunny glow poured over the industrious stooped heads.

I have entered the beehive and now view the drones!

Side-stepping the scribes, the tall grave man opened inside doors to reveal a larger, more expansive room. More light streamed from large windows on the street-facing side of the house, creating a warm ambiance and illuminating every detail of the architecture. A narrow balcony circumscribing its entire perimeter capped the room's upper story.

The girls tilted their heads and stared at the balcony and high ceiling until Nellie gave them a throat-clearing warning.

The balcony resembled a viewing gallery. She observed numerous chairs grouped in untidy rows in both the balcony and the first floor of the room, as if ready for an assembly. On the opposite wall, a large platform, encircled by a railing, faced the gallery running round the upper story.

The tall man maintained stony silence, his forbidding stare inhibiting questions.

The girls angled fearful eyes upward, darting glances between the formidable man and their parents.

Suddenly, as if cued, the butler's voiced boomed and the girls jumped. "This chamber hosts both territory government business as well as Sunday worship."

Elizabeth ran behind Nellie's skirts at the sound of the man's voice. Nellie gently pulled her forward while giving her a reassuring squeeze of her hand, never taking her eyes off the man, out of politeness.

He glared down at Elizabeth and continued, "The clerks to our right work for the Brigham Young, Trustee for our Church. Those on our left are employed for the benefit of Brigham Young and Company. On the Sabbath, our prophet stands right here, gracing us with his preaching." He pointed to the pulpit.

"I presume you wish to present yourselves to our prophet, our president of the Saints, our Territory's Indian Affairs Agent, and our Governor, Brigham Young. After which I can assign you a seat for services in the Tabernacle or the Bowery."

"I am afraid you misunderstand, sir. While I *have* come to pay my respects to Mister Young, it is solely in his capacity as Governor. I am Obadiah Weber Wright, the newly appointed United States judge for the Utah Territory."

"My mistake, sir." The butler bowed and ushered them forward. He opened a door to a slightly smaller room.

A grand desk presided in front of a few chairs and sofas, filled with men, clustering at the door. A large safe sat with an expansive solid air before a sidewall, almost obscuring a small door.

Mayhap the door leads to the 'sanctum sanctorum,' the private quarters of the Saint.

Seated at the desk was the Latter-day Saints' President Young himself, reviewing papers and mumbling under his breath.

Nellie evaluated the plain, neat room, noting it exhibited a store-bought rug and a rich mahogany desk, most likely imported all the way from New York. She stood on her tiptoes to see the 'prophet' held court from an expensive embroidered mahogany chair.

The doorman formally presented them to Mr. Young. "My most excellent Prophet and President, may I present Obadiah Weber Wright, newly appointed circuit judge to Utah Territory."

The men clustered around the table all stared.

Nellie opened her mouth to introduce herself to the infamous man, but a glare from Obadiah silenced her.

Although his posture and his bearing exude authority, I cannot fathom why such a sanguine, portly man with such bland features commands such deference, respect, and yea, even reverence.

A pleased expression graced Brigham Young's face, but he did not stand to greet them. He merely gestured for them to come closer and stretched a limp hand across his desk to shake Obadiah's.

"I had faith you would come to introduce yourself to me. At last! We have been waiting for you," he said warmly.

Someone must have reported the commotion at the Bowery, thought Nellie.

He turned to Nellie, "Is this your only wife?" he asked.

Somewhat taken aback, Nellie looked at Obadiah.

"Why, yes sir," said Obadiah. "May I present Cornelia Rose Entwhistle Wright, Your Honorable."

Honorable? That entreats debate.

Nellie curtsied, but did not drop her eyes, as was the custom. She stared directly and boldly into his eyes.

His mouth kept smiling, but his eyes did not. He said, "As you say."

Nellie turned to her children and introduced them, to avoid having to say anything to Young, or puzzle out what he meant by his greeting.

"Fine, fine," he said, with barely a glance at the girls. "Wright, are you any relation to New York Governor, Silas Wright, junior?"

"Most definitely, sir. He was my father," offered Obadiah.

Young frowned.

Does this man bear a grudge against Obadiah's father which will further sour an effective relationship with my husband?

"Of course," Obadiah added, pride stealing into his voice, "he was also a United States Senator."

Ignoring Obadiah's added information, Young replied, "Son of a governor, eh? I have examined your *curriculum vitae* extensively. Sir, you and I have some business to discuss."

He rang a bell, and the obscured door instantly popped open.

A young lady around twenty-years-old sprang into the room.

"Clarissa," said Young, "take Missus Wright and her daughters into the kitchen and introduce her to the women."

"Your wife?" Nellie inquired.

"Yes, yes, of course," he replied absentmindedly, having mentally dismissed her, his attention already focused on the business of getting Obadiah oriented.

CHAPTER 5
Harmony

Brigham Young's Compound, August 1857

Nellie, still holding her daughters' hands, followed the girl through the door and discovered that it opened directly into the heart of the main house. She and her daughters paused to survey the hubbub of activity. Women and children of all ages, shapes and sizes scurried to and from a large door carrying all types of bundles.

It must have been baking day.

A large warm kitchen enveloped the Wrights.

Thwap!

They jumped and looked left.

A deliveryman dumped sack after sack of flour, stacking them in a pile right next to the door.

A middle-aged woman opened one of the potbellied ovens and extracted a steaming loaf of bread. The scent wrapped around the Wright women and welcomed them into the heart of the house.

Emma stood still, enthralled by the bustle, nose wrinkling in delight at the wonderful aroma emanating from the fresh bread.

Filled with the cheerful din of many voices, the sunlit room accommodated many women, working, talking, and laughing. Countless trays of ingredients lay on a long pine table. Smaller tables hosted an assortment of females stirring big bowls, measuring spices, kneading dough, shaping cookies, forming piecrusts, slicing meat, and arranging fruit.

"Mama, so many pies!" Elizabeth cried, pointing to a table along the wall laden with dozens of pies.

Nellie pulled her mouth together in a straight line and furrowed her eyebrows at her. Elizabeth put her hand under her pinafore.

"It's not polite to point," said Emma in a hoarse whisper, and some of the older women nearby smiled.

A rather robust woman entered from a room beyond the passage, dusted the flour from her hand onto her apron, and introduced herself to Nellie. "Welcome, I am Lucy Decker. Welcome to Deseret and The Beehive House."

After all the time on the trail and the many months without a kitchen, the bustle and commotion of the many women in the well-appointed room flustered Nellie.

Mercy, this kitchen is larger and busier than Grand Central Station!

"Why, thank you for your hospitality," she said timidly. "Verily, you are as industrious as a bike of bees."

And I thought the drones outside worked in a beehive! Quite the hubbub of activity buzzes before my eyes. Yet, who is the mistress of the house? Are all these women boarders?

As if reading her mind, a younger woman approached Nellie, took her hand, and led her to a small table at a far corner of the big room. Nellie perched on a wood chair drenched in a direct beam of sun.

"I am Ellen Young," said the pretty young woman. "We don't all live here. Some of us still live in Harmony."

A most nebulous illumination, Nellie thought. She said in a cordial tone, "I contrive this appears quite harmonious."

Most of the women giggled.

Why is that funny?

"Harmony House is the moniker for the series of log houses that Brigham built for all of us when we first settled here."

Maintaining her erect posture, Nellie balanced on her chair, confused and silent at this information. She stared at the lacy curtains framing a large window conducting golden sunshine into the room.

A pleasant-looking middle-aged woman spoke up, pointing to two of the women. "Mary Ann and Lucy moved here with Brigham just this past year, upon the completion of the house and the government office."

Elizabeth whispered, "Mama, *she* pointed."

Nellie just shook her head, pressing her lips together to prevent a smile as she scrambled to process and interpret this information.

What criteria forms the group 'all of us' to qualify them as recipients of newly built houses?

She twisted in the chair to embrace her daughters on either side of her, as some of the women moved closer to sit near her.

"I am Harriet. Most of us have now moved to the Lion House right next door," offered a dark-haired beauty.

The women's expectant faces all seemed to wait for her reply.

Nellie licked her lips and tugged a stray strand of hair.

"Didn't Papa say that Missus Young lives in that scary house next door?" said Elizabeth in a stage whisper.

The women tittered.

"I apologize," said Nellie. "We just arrived yesterday, and I fear my daughters and I struggle to ascertain our bearings."

The women all stared, all the while continuing their busy endeavors.

"I do believe we were given some misinformation," Nellie tried to explain. "A guide advised that Missus Young lives in the house with... uh... the green shutters."

"That may well be where I am headed," said the dour-looking Mary Ann through pinched lips.

"Don't mind Mary Ann Angell." A laughing girl speckled with white flour waved at the Wrights from across the room.

"Enough of our confidences!" declared Lucy Decker with her hands on her hips. "Enlighten us as to your circumstances!"

All the ladies began asking questions at once.

"Was your journey tolerable?

"How many wagons in the train?"

"How did you endure the tempestuous weather?"

"What of the savages? Were there skirmishes?"

"Brigham always counsels 'tis far less costly to feed an Indian than to fight him'," Ellen said as if quoting from scripture.

"Anybody die on the trail?" asked Mary Ann Angell.

Nellie drew in her breath in dismay.

"Hush, Mary Ann!" they all cried in unison.

"Pardon Mary Ann Angell!" Lucy Decker smiled. "She is often out of humor."

Nell gratefully accepted the proffered cup of tea as two of the younger girls brought cups for her daughters, who were still standing stiffly and shyly on either side of her.

"'Tis difficult to find a commencement point," she said. Yet immediately her mind jumped to Clayton and his wife and their new baby. *Have they left? Did they catch up with the wagon train? Is the baby all right?* Then, blushing, she remembered Clayton's hug. She stroked her own undelivered child, still invisible beneath her voluminous petticoats. *It was just the heat of the moment, the trauma of the nearly tragic birth,* she told herself sternly.

Shaking her head to clear it, she tried to organize her thoughts into a report.

"Tell us something," one girl implored.

"Anything, it doesn't matter," Harriet cried.

"Just give us some news," said a cheerful pump matron standing next to an oven.

"Yes, we tire of the same old story here," explained an earnest-looking girl. "Spare us *one* day of having to discuss Prophet Young's favorite, Emmeline Free." She giggled, and all eyes looked at a pretty young girl sitting at a sunny window sipping tea.

"Favorite child?" inquired Nell.

"No silly, wife," growled one woman.

"So naive," sputtered another.

"I am not our Prophet's favorite, so much as his first," said Lucy Ann Decker.

"What does that make Mary Ann Angell?" retorted a saucy-looking younger woman.

"I keep the Beehive House in good order," continued Lucy Ann Decker, as if the interrupter had not spoken.

"*I* keep the Beehive House in good order," argued Mary Ann Angell.

Nell tried not to gasp.

Of course.

Tarnation.

My unparalleled stupidity and naiveté leave my conversation skills stymied. Missus Hannah King and Rosalinda Wells and even Missus Clayton surely gave me enough hints and warnings, yet I stumble into this lion's den as defenseless as Daniel.

She stared at all the women in the large kitchen.

Where do the wives end and the daughters begin? she wondered.

She had read horrible tales of harem-esque polygamy and mistreatment of women in Utah Territory, but had dismissed them as only rumors. After all, conflicting reports abounded. Yet now she sat in the midst of a large gathering of what could only be polygamous wives.

Flustered and still speechless, Nellie hoped the bustle and chatter of the women around her shrouded her consternation.

Bewildered at the multitude of women and the horde of children in the room, she could not even imagine sharing a husband. *'Tis onerous enough to observe Mister Wright attain important decisions with only a nod to my opinion. 'Twould be insufferable to share that trace amount of attention with another wife. Or, far more trying still, the horror of my husband heeding the counsel of some other wife. Or several other wives, and not me!*

She tried to guess how many of the present company of women fell in the category of wives. She estimated Brigham Young's age at fifty-five. Some of the women appeared long past that half-century marker, yet some were mere girls.

She scanned the room. Were the young girls children or wives?

I shall coax whatever virtue I can from this situation and ignore the babes-in-arms.

She could not help but fret, *will I be the only woman in Great Salt Lake City whose husband has but one wife? How difficult and lonely a life shall I lead as a non-believer? At least I have Lucena, if only for this winter. Thank you, Lord God Almighty!*

She abandoned the useless speculation, determined to engage in polite conversation. "Where should we begin?" she asked her daughters, who still stood, nervous, as if attached at either of her elbows.

I blame them not for their hesitation to mingle with the other children.

"At the beginning, with our boat ride from Grandmama's house?" responded Emma.

"When you were captured by the Indians," said Elizabeth, simultaneously.

Exclamations of delight mixed with a chorus of questions.

As a cordial conversation evolved, gradually Nellie's tension eased. Her daughters, too, loosened their hold on her arms.

A girl about Emma's age, bearing a small plate of cookies, enticed her girls to a corner of the room. From time to time, she glanced over and saw them chatting with offspring of Brigham Young who stitched samplers.

"Were there any fellow Saints in your company?" asked Lucy Ann Decker.

"Not within my train," replied Nellie. "However, I did meet a lovely woman, Missus Hannah Tapfield King, who also just recently arrived."

"I thought Elder Haight's new wife was on your train," said Clarissa, the woman who had brought her into the kitchen. "Didn't you tell me that, Margaret?"

Margaret, another stern-faced woman nodded.

"Why, yes," replied Nellie, "she was."

"Then why say you there were no fellow Saints?" questioned Margaret.

"I am not of the Mormon faith," said Nellie, tension and caution causing her voice to be barely audible.

"Neither are we," said Emmeline Free, emphasizing her words with a curt nod. "We are members of the Church of the Latter-day Saints."

"Infidel," mumbled Ellen.

As the other ladies buzzed with conversation, Nellie caught whispered words: 'heretic,' 'poor soul,' and 'dammed.'

Clarissa sniffed, "We were advised that our new federal judge accepted salvation as a Latter-day Saint."

"That is an inaccurate evaluation of our current situation." Nellie tried to be diplomatic. "I apologize for the misunderstanding," she felt compelled to add.

She thought she heard a woman in the corner murmur, "You'll not tarry here long then." And her companion answer, "It was nice to know you." They giggled.

"Hush," said Lucy Ann Decker. "We must welcome our guest and make her feel comfortable."

Margaret sniffed, "President Young exhorts us, 'If our neighbor wishes salvation, and it is necessary to spill his blood upon the ground in order that he be saved, spill it.'"

Nellie gasped.

Ellen chastised Margaret, "Hush. This blood atonement merely hastens all our reformation and safeguards better adherence to the divine Word."

"We daily demonstrate salvation by our good example," said Harriet brightly.

"Mayhap the Lord will aide us in her conversion," a young woman declared.

Not on your life! Nellie cleared her throat with determination and tried to think of a polite way to continue conversation with this.... *Wife? Daughter?*

Suddenly, Elizabeth gasped and ran to Nellie, burying her face in Nellie's lap.

Nellie's face turned beet red and dead silence fell over the room.

"I apologize for this unbecoming outburst," she said, and bent her head to the quaking Elizabeth.

"Ugh, ugh, a-scusting," the little girl sobbed.

Although overcome with embarrassment, Nellie's daughter's mispronunciation of 'disgusting' softened her heart.

What care I for the judgment of these ostracizing women?

She whispered, "Whatever troubles you, Betsy?"

Elizabeth cried, "It's his hair! She makes flowers out of real hair."

Nellie looked across the room where a girl about seven-years-old dangled some pretty handiwork of a cloth with several flowers appliquéd in black thread.

Why would anyone pick black thread for flowers? Nellie wondered.

The girl shrugged and said, "To honor my father, I have woven his hair into a fine work of art, in the form of these beautiful flowers, thus preserving it forever."

With this announcement, Emma blanched and crept away from the other little girls toward Nellie.

Once again Nellie was at a loss for words.

"Bravo, Zina," a large woman said, a small smile lighting her rather melancholy face. "A lovely keepsake."

Certainly, the child's mother, Nellie thought as she hugged her own daughters tighter.

"Hair cushions are the common way to keep our needles sharp and free from rust, as I am quite certain you ken," said Lucy Decker.

A silver-haired woman, laboring with pen over paper, not participating in the baking, interjected, "Why not honor her father, and our president of the Saints, with the fine arts? Poetry, in my case. From little Zina, illustrations fashioned from his hair."

"Thank you, Eliza Snow. Yes, our father, so just, so gentle, so noble." Skinny little Zina beamed.

The sharp-tongued Eliza Snow continued, "I shall read aloud the verses I have just penned to pay homage to him."

> "But to the Saints, God will all things restore,
> As pure — as perfect as they were before;
> And more endearing thro' the contrast giv'n,
> In our estrangement from the laws of heav'n.
> Truth to his neighbor, every man shall speak,
> And heav'n bred confidence will bless the meek.
> In princely grandeur — Godlike majesty...."

Mercifully, at this moment, the door opened and the butler announced, "I advise our guest, Missus Wright: President Young requests your presence in his office. Time for departure."

Does Eliza Snow warn me with her dire poetry?

Nellie thanked many of the ladies individually, struggling to remember as many names as she could. The crabby woman, not merry but Margaret, silver-haired, frosty-penned woman named Eliza Snow, Lighthearted Lucy Ann Decker, favorite, Emmeline Free, Caustic Clarissa.

"I shall surely come calling again, as soon as I am settled," she promised.

Horrified at what she had just said, Nellie knew she would fulfill that grim promise only if no other women resided in the entire town.

The butler showed them through the pantry, fragrant with many loaves of warm bread and cooling tarts, and then through a bedroom.

"Mama, why are we walking through a bedroom?" said Elizabeth loudly.

Dear Betsy, the thought crossed my mind as well.

"Whose bedroom is this?" asked Emma.

Nellie frowned her daughter's lips back into a clamped-shut position, but all three Wrights tilted their questioning eyes expectantly at the butler.

He sniffed. "This room functions as Our Prophet's private office. However, it is commonly known as his Excellency's bedroom."

His bedroom! Connected to the public meeting room and his main office? If this isn't the height of impropriety. How untoward!

With that thought, Nellie and her daughters were ushered back into the President's more public office.

Brigham stood next to a wall with a large map of the continent of North America, all the new United States Territories colorfully prominent in the middle.

Alas, the many wearily trudged miles which separate us from home, Nellie thought.

"I anticipate a satisfactory working relationship with you, Judge Wright. I ascertain and assert the utmost confidence you possess the requisite skills for this job. I perceive a keen, insightful mind, an ability to comprehend the subtleties of this position, a flexibility as to methodology, excellent oratorical skills, and the diplomacy to juggle a myriad of sensitive matters."

Nellie raised her eyebrows. *What motivates his excessive praise? Truly, his accurate assessment of Mister Wright's attributes denotes a keen power of assessment, but the man's word choice provokes great anxiety in me. Why the need for 'flexibility in methodology'? I fear a sinister motive behind these charming commendations.*

Brigham extended his hand to shake Obadiah's.

"A man's accomplishments are but a reflection of his beliefs," replied Obadiah.

Mr. Young's face twisted in thought at the enigma of that reply.

CHAPTER 6
'Cause I'm a One-Man Woman

Temporary Lodgings Block 61, Great Salt Lake City, September 1857

As the Wrights settled into their temporary quarters, a small cottage rented next to Lucena and George Washington Parsons on the outskirts of town, across Third Street South from Pioneer Square, Nellie watched yet another wagon train depart.

'Tis rather unusual to see that space empty, Nellie ruminated, glancing through her window as she inventoried the meager supplies remaining from their grueling trip.

Ever since they had arrived, a continuous influx of emigrants had flowed through Pioneer Square. The bareness of the space added to Nellie's unease. She determined to ferret out the explanation for the pause in arrivals.

The thought, *The Lord worketh in mysterious ways*, crossed Nellie's mind later that morning when she turned the corner of West Temple Street and chanced to encounter the mistress of the Beehive House, Brigham's wife, Mary Ann Angell Young on the way to market.

I do believe this woman bears the dubious title of first wife to that infernal man. Surely, she will be privy to kingdom politics.

Nellie paused to introduce herself, but Mary Ann Angell Young said, "I know who you are."

Taken aback by her rudeness, Nellie blinked in surprise.

Mary Ann said, "Do you take me for a fool? I met you that day they dragged you into the lair of the Beehive House."

As Nellie stood there tugging her hair and trying to think of a polite response, she was surprised to see a look of great embarrassment darken Mary Ann's already overburdened countenance.

Mary Ann bought her nose very close to Nellie's and through clenched teeth blurted, "Brigham Young was a widower when he courted me." Mrs. Young sniffed. "I entered not into a plural relationship, at least not of my own volition." She stepped back and adjusted her shawl.

Nellie tugged her stray hair again. Uncertain how to respond to Mary Ann's pent-up aggression, she settled for patting the strange woman on the hand and offering a reassuring smile.

Without any further prompting, Nellie learned this Mrs. Young vociferously objected to the duties and responsibilities inherent in being the Prophet's wife.

"Women and children tramp through my house at all hours of the day. The crowds never cease! Then we must entertain fellow Saints and Gentiles alike, with dinners and teas, music, or dancing. I far prefer a more solitary life." The unhappy woman rearranged the vegetables in her basket, and her grim mouth turned further down at the edges.

Nellie observed Mary Ann's agitated state and deduced her deep discontent originated with the arrival of the first 'plural' wife at her doorstep. She wondered how Mary Ann must have felt watching her husband court multiple women, and then perfect them into wives, long after vowing love and fidelity to her.

"Mercy," said Mary Ann, "my trials shall never cease as long as I abide in that citadel of sinners. Why, I would even prefer that old house with the green shutters right there. Its air of abandonment rather suits me very nicely, I'll have you know."

From Mary Ann's very informative chatter, Nellie learned most of the women she met at the Beehive lived in the Milk House, the name 'about town' for the row house next door. Mary Ann wanted nothing to do with the harem rooms in the house that only the Prophet Brigham called 'new Harmony.'

Nellie suppressed a smile. Plural wives all living together under one roof seemed the antithesis of 'harmony.'

Perhaps the dwelling received its name ironically?

Mary Ann insisted she wanted a house of her own. "If I have my druthers, one day Brigham shall, still grudgingly, I am sure, install me and my eight children into that rather neglected old house. I shall gladly allow Lucy Ann Decker to play hostess at the Beehive House."

Mary Ann sniffed. "The other wives must settle for a few rooms for themselves and their children in the Lion House."

Yet another name for the Harmonious Milk House? Would that I had quill and paper to take notes of this woman's speech!

"Those lesser *wives* rooms' décor corresponds with the amount of esteem with which Brigham Young accords them."

Nellie envisioned a poor wife, only skin and bones, sitting on a broken chair huddled by a puny fire, eating stale bread with six children, noses running, squabbling over who's turn it was to have the small assigned portion of gruel for their supper.

She drew in her breath in horror. *Surely, Mary Ann only means some apartments have finer rugs and wall hangings than others?*

Mary Ann confided to Nellie, "Whilst I decry the trappings of hosting all manner of people for the various forms of social gatherings, I certainly concede the importance of good relations with the United States. Some people in this community simply do not understand the challenges presented to our way of life."

Nellie frowned. *Quite the inscrutable, ambiguous statement. Does Mary Ann object to the internal politics of her espoused way of life, or does she chastise the United States for its interference?*

Mary Ann sniffed, "One good thing about Mister Young I *will* say. While he closed the border to outsiders and now requires permits to traverse our cherished Deseret, he does see your husband as an opportunity rather than a threat."

Finally, some interesting intelligence gleaned from this conversation.

The confirmation that the borders were closed made Nellie question how wagon trains now obtained permission to travel through Utah Territory. She pondered if she could press Mary Ann for information about United States mail delivery.

I must seek clarification. This status severs my ties to home, but how completely? Will I receive letters from my loved ones back in the States? Newspapers? Or do these tense relations threaten my very survival?

Heart racing, Nellie collected her runaway fears and considered her words carefully, to ensure she did not alienate this source of information. She only asked, "An opportunity?"

"Yes, your Mister Wright offers a chance to set the record straight about the goodness and righteousness of our faith community here," said Mary Ann.

Nellie narrowed her eyes, trying to glean Mary Ann's meaning. *First words dripping with bitterness, now words of praise? Further enigmatic answers, not entirely enlightening.*

Later, as she gently pressed some pears to ascertain ripeness at the market, a sudden thought struck her. Maybe Mary Ann was hinting that Young would try to manipulate her husband into pleading the Mormon's cause in communications with the United States.

She flushed with instant anger. *That base fellow Young! Tarnation! I shall endeavor to thwart his efforts to groom Obadiah as a mere mouthpiece for Young's views any way I can.*

At dinner that night, Nellie tried to engage Obadiah in talk of his work, to allow him to broach the subject of the state of affairs in this territory, but he turned every attempt into silly banter with the children.

"What number do you deduce when you multiply six times three?" he asked Emma with a merry wink.

Emma cocked her head. "Eighteen!" she replied with a triumphant smile.

Obadiah beamed. "My brilliant daughter."

"Give one to me," shouted Elizabeth.

"Certainly." Obadiah twirled his mustache. "If you go to market with Mama and she buys two pears and one apple, how much fruit does she have?"

Elizabeth giggled and looked at her fingers. She held up two fingers on one hand and one on the other. "This much."

"Very good," said Obadiah. "Now let's count them together."

Nellie said, "Did you know that both apples and pears are fruit? So you can count them on one hand, because they go together."

"Like our family," said Emma. "We are all different people, boys and girls, but we go together."

Beaming, Obadiah and Nellie exchanged glances of wonder and pride. Nellie hugged both of their daughters.

Love glowing from his eyes, Obadiah said, "Let us fill our lives with this joy and mirth every night."

Her daughters laughed with delight, clamoring for their father to tell them a story after supper.

"The reading and telling of bedtime stories," Obadiah said, "is your mother's dominion. You may come kiss me goodnight in my study when you are scrubbed and suitably attired for bed."

The faces of the little cherubs fell.

With a change of heart, Obadiah tousled their hair and sang them a silly song.

After Nellie finished tucking her daughters into their cozy comforter and singing them to sleep, she joined him in his study. She threw more kindling on the fire and settled herself in her newly acquired rocking chair. It was not quite as elegant as the one she was forced to abandon in Sing Sing, but she deemed it quite serviceable.

"Exhaustion quite overwhelms me. I wish nothing other than to sit and enjoy quintessence of the day." Nellie smiled and allowed herself a moment to stare into the fire, enjoying its crackle. "No matter that my weariness lulls me into inactivity. Housework never ceases, and idle hands are the devil's tools." She sighed and picked up the first sock in the mending basket.

"Darn this sock!" She giggled at her pun, and glanced nervously at Obadiah, lest he think she was cussing.

Absorbed in his work scribbling in his ledger, he hadn't even noticed her presence.

Nellie rocked, darned, and marshaled the information she had uncovered during her first week in the Great Salt Lake City.

"I had an interesting discussion with Mary Ann Angell Young, the first Missus Young who is actually the second Missus Young," Nellie said, leaning close to Obadiah, dangling her darning, as well as a puzzle in front of her husband.

"The first Missus Young is really the second Missus Young?" Obadiah absentmindedly repeated as he scratched his mustache, barely tearing his eyes from his documents.

Nellie leapt from her chair so fast she almost launched her new rocker into the fire. She perched on the arm of her husband's chair, waving her darning needle and suspending a sock dangerously close to Obadiah's candelabra. "Originally, Young was married to Miriam Angeline Works, but she died of consumption after two children and eight years of marriage."

Obadiah mumbled a barely audible, "You don't say."

Undeterred, Nellie continued, "Thus, when Young married Mary Ann Angell, she was not a plural wife, because he was a widower. They were married for eight years, and Mary Ann had six children, before Young decided to take his first plural wife. He married Lucy Ann Decker in 1843."

She sat back down in the rocking chair and leaned toward the fire to examine the sock for more holes. "No wonder Mary Ann takes umbrage at life in the big house. Furthermore, every year since 1843, Young has added two or more wives to his harem. It is difficult to determine the exact number of wives he currently feeds, as some have died and two or three have even divorced him."

Nellie knew she was mostly talking to herself, but she wanted to parse the whole Young household so she had a clear sense of how this society worked. "No wonder some of the wives appear young enough to be Brigham's children! Many *are* younger than Young's children."

She giggled. "Mercy, that sentence twists upon the tongue."

She scrutinized the next sock and continued. "And the Clarissa that I met was not Young's daughter, but his wife. Yea, she was not the daughter of Lucy Ann Decker, but rather the sister!"

Obadiah flicked an annoyed look at his wife. "How ever does this prattling, this untangling of wives, aid me in *my* endeavors and position?"

Wounded, Nellie blinked. Warmth crept up the back of her neck, but she merely shook her head and observed, "I would surmise this information shall be of far more importance to you than to me. I only wish to acquire clarity so that I do not embarrass the family with a *faux pas* when addressing a member of Brigham's household, at an important social gathering like a dinner or a concert. You, however, must understand this structure to better adjudicate the Mormons' civil lawsuits and other judicial matters. Did you not take notice of the legal divorces of a few of his wives?"

Suddenly, Obadiah was interested. "It is not possible."

"I have it on good authority." Nellie cocked her head considering whether a muttered statement from an anonymous woman baking bread in the Beehive truly represented 'good authority.'

Mercy, now I am cross-examining myself without my attorney husband even opining.

"With all those wives, 'tis logical 'twould breed a few malcontents," Nellie reasoned.

Obadiah shook his head. "Impossible. The divorces could not be legal. Do you not see the conundrum? The United States cannot grant a divorce. Since polygamy is illegal in the United States, the plural marriage would never be legal in the first place, thus it cannot be legally put asunder."

Nellie smiled at her husband's fine reasoning, but decided to play devil's advocate. "Howsoever, the United States has not yet made polygamy illegal in its territories."

Obadiah sat with a nonplused expression on his face that Nellie found most satisfying.

She took a deep breath and plunged into a full discussion of this most distasteful subject. "And what say you to address the rampant polygamy we have found surrounding us? This practice goes against all I believe, and just as importantly, compromises your position. How can you adjudicate here, with Mormon ways violating many fundamental laws, not to mention values, of the United States? Further, how in heaven's name would you even *entertain* a hearing of a marital dispute among Mormons? *The conundrum* prevents any State's rubric for adjudication of marital disputes. The entire practice of multiple wives flouts the law you were sworn to uphold."

Obadiah rose to the bait. "Nay, to the letter of the law this is untrue. As you so correctly underscored, polygamy is prohibited in the United States, but there is nary a mention of it in the laws governing its territories. Thus, I must adapt our divorce law to accommodate this dilemma, for I am afraid there is little I, one solitary judge, can do to curb this practice," he said with an impatient shake of his head and a small grin.

I note nary a sign of remorse.

Nellie rolled her eyes and kept stitching the hole in the sock. "Polygamy embodies the quintessence of the fundamental differences between the Mormon mindset and philosophy and the principles of the United States. 'Tis a momentous task you undertake if you try to meld these two distinct convictions, or even merely try to exist simultaneously in these two different worlds. The issue of multiple wives—"

"Imagine the multiple issues of the multiple wives," interrupted Obadiah with a sudden grin. "It is small wonder that their church courts have any time to hear any other disputes besides marital ones. Multiple wives could keep a man, and the land's courts, busy around the clock."

Nellie refused to see the humor in the situation. "In our short time here, I have witnessed deplorable subjugation of women sufficient to plunge our entire civilization back into the Dark Ages." She wrenched her hair out of her eyes and tucked it away, but it popped right back out of its bun. "Invisible, women function as mere factotums, running the family enterprise behind the scenes. 'Tis little wonder no Mormon man ever *mentions* his wives, much less than cite his wife's, or any other woman's, opinion on a subject. The next step shall be to revert to veiling them in public, or forbidding them to leave their dwellings." Nellie tugged her stray hair with a vengeance, twisting it in knots like those in her stomach.

She glared at Obadiah, waiting for his retort.

He merely smiled, put down his quill, hopped around his desk, and pulled her from her chair. He drew her towards him, and in a flash, she was in his warm embrace.

Merciful heavens, the pressure of his hand on my back effects a magic elixir to the nagging pain I tried to ignore all day.

"My beautiful factotum," he whispered in her hair.

Does this at all acknowledge my opinion, or recognize any of the tasks I undertake and juggle daily?

Nellie pulled back and leveled a long look at her husband, her eyes flashing. Seeing only acceptance and love in his, she focused on their large reservoir of love.

"My apotheosis of a wife," he whispered.

The floodgates of love opened with that high praise, and she melted into Obadiah's arms, all bitterness and rancor driven from her heart.

"We shall find a way forward, my darling Cornelia Rose," he whispered into her neck as he caressed her shoulders.

CHAPTER 7
(S)He Blinded Me with Science

Great Salt Lake City, September 1857

"I thought I might find you here!"

Nellie raised her nose from sniffing honeydew melon for ripeness to see Lucena Parsons hugging her daughters. They responded with enthusiastic squeals.

Nellie smiled as once again, the spirited Lucena appeared with an impish grin filling her with good feeling and kinship. "How goes your settling?"

Lucena's face fell. "Miserable. It seems we dwell amongst the glummest, most ornery bunch of folks. Moreover, I overheard scuttlebutt concerning an evacuation of the town before the United States troops come here to burn them out."

Nellie scrambled to find soothing words for her young friend while her mind worked furiously to assess this rumor and determine its danger. Her head spun. *I barely have sufficient time to accustom myself to the outrageous deviation in lifestyle presented by the many multiple wives in the Great Salt Lake City. Now I must also contemplate the new treachery afoot in Young's bellicose threats to preserve his fiefdom?*

Unexpectedly, Lucena broke out in a broad grin and tossed Elizabeth up into the air.

"Wheeeeee," chuckled Elizabeth while her older sister looked on and extended her hands in a nervous preparation to catch her.

Nellie blinked in surprise.

"If our Mormon landlady evacuates, we shall not only dwell rent free, but I shall enjoy free run of the picturesque house and reap the benefits of the well planted garden your house and mine share," said Lucena. "Mayhap then I can eat as many apples as my heart desires."

Merciful heavens! This woman thinks like an optimistic half-wit!

Nellie put her hand on Lucena's arm as if to warn her of the true urgency of the situation, but then thought the better of it. *First, I must ascertain the veracity of this rumor.*

Nellie and her daughters joined in Lucena's bubble of laughter with relief.

Even if it be a short, deceptive interlude, Nellie fretted.

***

The girls skipped as they made their way through the market, passing a cornucopia of fruits and vegetables, toward the butcher stands.

Their carts laden with good food, the party joked and walked along State Street toward their houses.

Suddenly, Obadiah appeared, striding toward them deep in conversation with a tall uniformed man.

Nellie's gaiety evaporated.

So engrossed in his discussion with an officer of the United States Army, Obadiah walked right by Nellie without noticing her.

She turned around after him and clutched his arm to detain him. "Mister Wright, do me the honor of introducing me to your companion," Nellie said, latching on to him as if she had been trotting besides him the whole time.

Startled, Obadiah looked as if he would refuse.

His companion halted, smoothed his mustache, and extended his hand. "Please introduce me to this lovely young lady," said the army officer.

Nellie smiled. *How I have missed courtly civility. The Mormon men are courteous, true, but calculating. They appraise women as if they evaluate chattel.*

Obadiah shook his head with reluctance and pulled his own mustache in frustration. "We have little time to dally...."

The officer only planted his feet more firmly and swept off his hat. "I shall do the honors myself, if you can afford no time to be civil. Finest lady —"

"No, she is my wife," Obadiah interrupted.

The officer blinked, but then regained his composure. "From hobnobbing with the Mormons in Iowa, I know, around these parts, the definition of the term 'wife' expands and contorts with quite interesting fluidity."

Realizing her mouth gaped in surprise, Nellie shut it, thinking, *A rather flummoxing observation.*

Lucena shook her finger at Obadiah. "Mister Wright, your words implied that Nellie can't be a lady because she is your wife."

Dumbfounded, Obadiah and Nellie exchanged suppressed smiles.

You master the obvious, my fair friend. Nellie shook her head. *Nevertheless, Lucena's perception surprises me. I must not underestimate her intelligence. Yes, one way or another, Lucena lends levity to any situation.*

"Captain Steward Van Vliet, meet my fair wife, Cornelia Rose Entwhistle Wright," Obadiah said hastily.

As Nellie curtsied and the captain bowed, Lucena asked, "What about me?"

Obadiah coughed. "Never to be overlooked, might I have the pleasure of introducing Lucena Parsons."

The captain made a move to kiss Lucena's hand.

"Lucena *Pfuffer* Parsons, if'n' we're all gonna be formal." She giggled.

The captain plays quite the courtier.

Obadiah cut the amorous gesture short. "Truly, you take liberties with the hand of *Missus George Washington* Parsons, who honeymooned on the Overland Trail."

Obadiah's words seemed not to register, as Van Vliet continued to smile at Lucena and the young bride giggled.

"Enough with this frivolity." Obadiah ran a finger along his mustache, as if dismissing the matter. He turned toward Nellie. "My dear, the captain and I have important matters of state to discuss. He just concluded a difficult negotiation with Governor Brigham Young, and he must brief me on the particulars."

Obadiah turned to depart, but Nellie said quickly, "Then may we resume our conversation over dinner? I can offer you some of the bounty you see here." She held up her grocery basket and added, "I usually do not sing my own praises, but I have honed my cooking skills quite enticingly over the years."

Frowning, Obadiah gave an impatient tug to his mustache. "We cannot fritter our precious time away, lounging at table."

"*Au contraire,*" said the captain. "I raced over a thousand miles from Leavenworth City, the last one hundred or so virtually alone, accompanied only by Bill Cody, a mere boy of a scout, to nip this disaster in the bud. I thought better of jeopardizing the lives of thirty good, loyal men when the death threat only involved myself."

Nellie visualized the captain patting himself on the back.

"I seek no finer reward than a hearty meal, right from the home's hearth. This delicate negotiation shall consume several days. It surely affords time to dine in such pleasant company. What say you to tomorrow night?"

Obadiah did not reply.

Nellie glanced at him.

He wore a neutral expression.

Does anger hide behind my husband's poker face? Certainly, no hint of welcome, yet not inhospitable. He, too, seeks more information on this volatile situation from this man.

She said, "Saturday night would be the perfect evening to host guests for the first time in our new Great Salt Lake City abode. We abide in the former home of Henry Heath, Block 61, across from Pioneer Square. I look forward to welcoming you at half six."

Both Obadiah and the Captain took out their pocket watches, as if to synchronize them. Both thought the better of it and sheepishly tucked them back in their respective pockets.

Nellie swallowed a smile.

With one hand on the hilt of his sword, the captain smoothed his mustache in a dashing gesture with the other, and replied, "An evening with citizens loyal to the United States shall be a comfort, the perfect antidote for the next day's activities."

At Nellie's raised eyebrows, the captain explained, "The following morning, on the Sabbath, I shall attend the Saints' meeting at the behest of the Prophet himself."

Lucena looked up from tickling Elizabeth. Over the child's giggles, she asked, "Can me and Geo come too?"

The captain stepped forward. "Yes, I insist you attend. Afterall, there is always time for the finer things in life." He extracted Lucena's hand from Elizabeth's clutches and kissed it.

"Of course," barked Obadiah. "I happily extend my wife's invitation to you, and your *husband* George Washington Parsons."

Unfazed, the captain confirmed, "And your husband as well." He retained Lucena's hand for too long while she blushed and batted her eyes.

Nellie pulled her young friend's arm away from the captain. "Then it shall truly be a lovely dinner party."

Later that evening, she sat in her rocker and let down the hem of Emma's dress.

My eldest child grows like a weed despite the heavy toll exacted by the trek on the Overland Trail. She gazed into the fire and counted her blessings. *Firstly, a fireplace! 'Tis a joy and a blessing to bask in its effortless glow, quite the luxury after digging a trench night after night for cooking and warmth.*

She shook her head and sighed, trying to exhale the former grueling burden. She knew that, in spite of the arduous demands of the trail, blessings showered down upon them.

Our gracious God wrapped us in a cocoon of love, protecting us from not only the ordinary travails of the trail but, more importantly, from overwhelming tragedy.

With the children now tucked in bed and sound asleep, Nellie took a mental break from organizing the housework, but her hands remained busy. She let her mind wander over the unexpected and astounding differences already encountered in Salt Lake City civilization, as she pulled out some wool and cast on stitches, knitting needles flying over the beginnings of new winter stockings.

Lascivious promiscuity permeates this city. True, I view this situation from the vantage point of my Catholic upbringing, but bigamy transgresses not only my values but the mores of even the rather agnostic society of the United States.

It was little wonder Mary Ann took umbrage at the role of hostess. How wounded and betrayed must she have felt when Young took a third wife. Nellie speculated on the actual number of women married to Prophet Brigham. Thirty? Forty? A few more days of sleuthing revealed some of Young's wives had their own houses, and pairs of wives shared separate dwellings scattered all over town. Further investigations and introductions to other town folk had led her to the conclusion that the older wives of Brigham Young looked worn and rejected, and some of the younger wives seemed brazen.

What makes a woman want to marry someone else's husband? As she listened to the fire's merry crackle, she abandoned her stocking project and reached for smaller needles to make a layette for the new baby.

In this day and age, unmarried women had no rights and few ways to sustain themselves. Young claimed he married mostly poor widows. He wed all of Joseph Smith, the faith's founder's, wives to rescue them from the pitiful condition called 'widowhood.' He boasted that their status, elevated back to 'wife,' provided them shelter and rejuvenated their financial situation.

But still... taking them as wives conjures many unsavory images.

Nellie's first impression had been that all the wives got along remarkably well.

Were they not all cooking together, social as a quilting bee, when I was first introduced?

But now she realized the women gathered at the Beehive House that day, baking and kibitzing, comprised only a few of Brigham's wives and only some of his daughters. Young's entire harem consisted of many different personality types. He seemed to have a broad range in his taste for women. The personality conflicts alone engendered many disagreements. The 'sharing of a husband' kept the cooking pot of conflict simmering with jealousy and bickering even amongst the wives close enough to live and share their daily meals together.

Nellie cut some cloth and basted the seams of a baby bunting, dreaming of her expected child. *A new baby cooing and playing with his older sisters! Is it a boy?*

She glanced at Obadiah and a loving smile sprang to her lips. *'Tis true I already included Mister Wright in my list of blessings. Howsoever, it bears repeating. Through all the trials of life and the ordeals of our journey, our love grows stronger. May we continue to be of like mind and purpose, facing all adversity together.*

Obidiah tore his gaze from his papers and said, "My reconnoitering so far leads me to a preliminary conclusion: we need not fear the Saints. They aspire only to continue to live in harmony and build their Kingdom of God."

"Harmony? Will they *all* join the wives of Brigham in the Milk House?"

Obadiah looked quizzical.

Rather than explaining, Nellie's smile turned into a frown as she asked, "Is that why the Mormons prepare for Armageddon?"

Obadiah shook his head. "We have no confirmation of that rumor. My discussions with Van Vliet this afternoon revealed a tense situation, but not yet one beyond redemption. 'Tis my philosophy, and yours as well, to walk a mile in another man's moccasins before decreeing judgment. The Mormons suffered persecution. Time after time, they were forced to flee the communities they had just built. They fled homes in New York. They founded a new community in Ohio, and then in Iowa, only to be persecuted and finally expelled from each location. All Brigham Young asked of the United States was ten years' peace here to regroup and rebuild."

Nellie shook her head. "They have had their ten years. They arrived in this territory in 1847, yet they remain insular and unwelcoming."

"True. Howsoever, the States only left them in peace because this land was thought useless. Now that the industrious Saints built a brilliantly engineered civilization from a desert by irrigating the runoff from the mountains, the States have renewed interest in their thriving community. 'Tis rotten luck for these Saints that gold has again been discovered, for they find themselves sitting in the middle of a thruway to California, their land overrun with emigrants."

"Much like the Paiute and other tribes that lived in this area," Nellie observed.

"True." Obadiah tugged his mustache. "That's a whole different kettle of fish, smelling no better. Since the tribes have already been unseated from this land, let's leave that problem for another discussion.

"As I was saying, the Mormons built a community in the middle of a wasteland, in Mexican Territory, a thousand miles from anywhere, where they hoped to be autonomous and free from persecution forever. The influx of immigrants and the creation of Utah as the United States' Territory after victory in the Mexican War shattered their plan."

"Did I read a falsehood?" Nellie asked. "Does not Brigham Young himself seek statehood, and the protections that status affords? Do not the Church of the Latter-day Saint celebrations include the reading of the Declaration of Independence, and the reverencing of the Constitution?"

"Far more complex and nuanced particulars constitute this matter," Obadiah began.

Nellie interrupted, "Young must have understood, as a Territory, federal officials and our way of life must make inroads into this insular community, in order to assimilate into, and make congruous, their civilization with the rest of the United States. Moreover, as he himself is Governor, he swore to uphold the United States Constitution and support the federal judges and sheriffs assigned to this territory."

Obadiah did not argue, which gave Nellie the small satisfaction of inferring that he agreed with her line of reasoning.

Nellie lifted her feet toward the fire, and despite their contentious conversation, a cozy contentment slid over her like a warm blanket.

Obadiah cleared his throat. "In truth, the briefing I received, just before our departure, warned that circumstances here conspired to increase the difficulty of excelling at this job."

Nellie sat bolt upright, needle suspended, good feeling evaporated.

"Over the last seven years, a succession of federal officers, judges, Indian agents, and surveyors came to this territory only to find the Governor would circumvent or reverse their decisions. I learned many federally appointed officials complained to Washington that Governor Brigham Young thwarted all their efforts to fulfill their responsibilities."

Nellie shook her head. *Thwarted* all *their efforts?* "Do you mean...?"

Obadiah held up his hand for silence, and sighed. "I was advised that federal surveyors were told 'you shall not be suffered to trespass on Saints' lands.' An Indian Agent wrote to his superior in Washington, 'Young has been so much in the habit of exercising his will, which is supreme here, that no one will dare oppose anything he may say or do'."

Nellie sat dumbfounded.

Winking, Obadiah said, "But never you fear. I shall not endeavor to break Young's will. I shall *bend* it. Besides, Young had himself designated Indian Agent, so he shan't have to parry the decisions of yet another federal officer."

Nellie barely heard Obadiah's consoling words. *Before we left? These issues were within Mister Wright's purview, and he did not enlighten me?*

"I see your reaction, and I must advise, these several incidents do not a precedent make. I believe in my capacity to rectify this situation." Obadiah playfully admonished Nellie with his wagging finger. "Do not underestimate the ability of your humble servant to open the lines of communication and forge a cooperation between the authority of our States and that of the Saints."

Nellie's mouth formed a grim line, and she tugged viciously at her stray hair. "You concluded I lacked the intelligence required to receive this information and engage in dialogue evaluating the merits of our journey and the new life we hope to establish?"

"I never said anything about your lack of intelligence," Obadiah replied.

Blinking back tears, Nellie said, "You never considered I should be privy to pertinent information regarding our prospects?"

"I am the head of this household. I had the situation well in hand," Obadiah said, abruptly rising from his chair.

Nellie opened her mouth to meet his challenge, but Obadiah's face suddenly softened. Smiling, he leaned closer, planted a kiss on her lips, and whispered, "Hush. Have you no faith in my abilities? Do you feel my skills and charms unequal to this challenge? Do you not trust my superior intellect? I shall not allow Young to circumvent or reverse my decisions.

"Will you thwart me in my efforts to establish my name as not only an expert judge, but a skilled negotiator and cunning diplomat?"

Frowning, Nellie closed her mouth and gazed at him.

He turned his back to her and poked the fire. "We shall put this behind us and remain committed to our choices and our partnership." With a pleasant nod he reoccupied his seat, retrieved another stack of papers from the corner of his desk, moved his candelabra a bit closer, and adjusted his glasses.

Nellie watched her husband retreat into his work.

Must I follow his decisions blindly like some imbecilic wench, unschooled and uneducable?

Obadiah lifted his head and looked her in the eye. As if he read her thoughts, he said, "I hoped to spare you from the potential adversities concomitant with my new position. I shall not place my manly burdens on your lovely shoulders."

She stared at him through wet lashes.

Have I no voice in our future?

She could not find words to express her despair.

"Of course, I still welcome your thoughts on our joint enterprise. However, you must recognize I, not you, toil in my position. By myself. Thus, I alone must make the necessary and relevant decisions concerning my employment."

I've been hornswoggled!

Still furious and feeling duped, she shook her head.

Obadiah jumped around his desk and swept her into his arms. "I love you with all my heart," he whispered into her neck. He re-deposited her into her chair, sitting her down on her knitting needles.

Nellie pulled them out from under her, and the thought to brandish them in his face flashed through her mind.

Oblivious, her husband rounded the corner of his desk and buried himself back in his documents.

I must... I must....

She stared into the fire and forced her breathing to slow.

Lord, please endow me with understanding and forgiveness, I beseech you. I must....

I must finish this layette, as there is less than a half hour left in the life of these candles.

CHAPTER 8
Garden Party

Home, Great Salt Lake City, September 1857

Nellie avoided looking at the flour sprinkled on the floor, from the 'help' of her daughters, as she rolled her dough once more. "I shall cross the city and pay a visit to Hannah whilst I travel to the butchers and select a fine cut of mutton for our festive dinner tonight. If I locate her before I shop, I shall purchase enough to invite her and her husband as well."

"No, do not invite the Kings." Obadiah dismissed the idea without even raising his head from the newspaper.

"Whyever not?"

"Dreadful idea. A woman of questionable alliances."

"Husband...." Nellie began advocating for her position.

He looked at Nellie and pulled at his mustache, frowning. "Did you not hear the captain say he shall relish a night amongst solid United States citizens? Missus King hails from England, thus not a citizen. Moreover, as a recent convert, Missus King may well assert with zealous enthusiasm that this be the Kingdom of God and not subject to any other sovereignty."

He shook his head and delivered his verdict. "Ghastly table conversation. No invitation."

Her face fell, but she acknowledged the wisdom of his rationale.

"Your lack of intuition surprises me. Do you not usually counsel *me* to be more sensitive to the wants and needs of others? Or in your zeal to reunite with your companion, did you overlook the propriety, nay, incongruity, of assembling such personalities?"

Nellie shrugged her shoulders. "Mayhap I merely surmised that with the Parsons in the mix, Hannah could only contribute a welcome voice of conventional conversation."

"Ignorance is bliss." Obadiah laughed, jumped up, caught her in his arms, rolling pin and all, and spun her across the kitchen.

My clever husband and his amazing double entendres.

He covered her with kisses, his mustache tickling its way down her neck.

His signature move — this oft-felt embrace continued to thrill her to her core. Breathless, she pulled away and he set her down, but her head kept spinning and a wave of darkness threatened to overwhelm her. She grabbed the edge of the table to steady herself.

"I see you still find my charms disarming." He chuckled.

"Surely I do," she gasped, laboring to catch her breath. "But in my condition, any trifle disturbs my equilibrium." She used her free hand to rub her now noticeably round stomach, and a little flutter from within rewarded her.

Could that be a kick?

"Nonsense. You share the constitution of thoroughbred mares." He smiled and kissed her again, then strode out of the kitchen, and the door swung shut behind him.

Gallant, charming man.

Nellie smiled, still gripping the table with one hand and feeling her child within flutter.

I must subjugate my distempered feelings. Most likely he does not realize his frivolous spin felt unpleasant in the extreme, and might have done me harm, had I not immediately stopped him.

I must not succumb to grumpiness, rather rejoice in his joy.

***

"Zounds!" Captain Van Vliet pounded on the table.

The two little girls jumped, and tears sprang to their eyes.

Oblivious, the captain continued, "I left my escort behind upon a scouting report that Mormon raiders lurked ahead on our direct trail from Kansas City. Dang nab it! I would not be derailed from delivering my top-secret letter from General Harney directly to Governor Brigham Young himself."

"I beg your pardon," said Nellie, and catching the captain's eye tilted her head toward her daughters.

"Apologies, little ladies," roared the captain.

Startled again, Emma burst into tears.

"Confound it," he continued, as Nellie gathered Emma into her arms for a hug. "Little girl, are you not aware, these Mormons have been lied about worse than any other people?"

Elizabeth buried her head into Nellie's shoulder.

Goodness, the irony of Obadiah thinking Captain Van Vliet would object to Hannah's sentiments on this subject.

She smiled at the captain and he continued his rant. "I promised old Brigham that I shall stop this 'Expedition' at all costs, personally cease the movement of the United States Army if necessary! Even if I must track down my West Point classmate, William Tecumseh Sherman to help me hold 'em back. Hell, I'll get the ear of my old Mexican War chum Zach Taylor. He must still be able to throw some weight around in Washington, even if he no longer is top dog."

"Former *President* Taylor?" asked Obadiah, clearly impressed.

'Tis quite the name to drop into our conversation.

"Young merely seeks to prevent harm to his people. Plain and simple, that's the bottom fact."

Nellie gave voice to her disagreement. "The rumours abounding in the marketplace belie such sentiment." She shivered, and her daughters looked at her with petrified eyes. She pulled Emma into her lap. "Snatches of conversation overheard whilst marketing left me in dread of blood-thirsty *Saints*! They threaten belligerent and violent responses to the United States Army Expedition."

Before the captain could reply, Obadiah, ignoring Nellie's comment, asked, "Can you offer us a more precise definition of *Expedition*?"

Visibly relieved that he need not respond to Nellie, the captain replied, "The Expedition functions as a precautionary action. Our Army's mission is simply to escort new federal appointees to their designated positions and ensure their assumption of duties. Afterward, the deployment of troops shall act as a *posse comitatus*. They shall maintain the peace and establish at least two, perhaps three, new United States Army camps in Utah."

"Utah shall feel like an occupied territory." Nellie trembled, glancing at her daughters' stricken faces.

Captain Van Vliet drew in his eyebrows and looked as if he would take her to task for her cowardice.

Loathe to miss the serious discussion, but wanting to protect her daughters from fear, Nellie excused herself from the table. "I shall clear our dinner plates, and my daughters and I shall attend to some domestic duties."

Lucena sprang up, upsetting a dirty plate and flinging a fork at the captain.

With quick reflexes, the captain caught it and placed it in Lucena's hands.

Did I just witness a surreptitious squeeze?

Looking at her hand, Lucena confirmed the squeeze with a blush.

'Tis impossible to surmise if the blush originated from the pleasure of the flirtatious gesture, or the embarrassment of fork flinging.

Collecting herself, Lucena said, "Please, allow me to clear the table and scrub some dishes with your daughters. All this talk of politics bowls me over. I do believe I need to let that scrumptious feast set awhile in my tummy before I even *think* about consuming that fine dessert I smelled when I entered your home."

Without waiting for an answer, Lucena picked Emma up from Nellie's lap and looked at Elizabeth. The three-year-old did not need any further prompting to take a dirty plate from the table and skip into the kitchen.

The other dinner guests sat in complete silence as the girls traipsed back and forth ferrying dishes to the kitchen. Through the open window, Nellie heard the happy sound of the little girls begging for a turn at the water pump handle, and then the gush of water.

Van Vliet broke the companionable silence by clearing his throat and resuming right where he left off. "I do concede a very real threat of violence from both sides of this conflict. Thundering Thor, the fanatical Mormons threatened my very own life. I took it seriously, mind you, and made a rapid, thousand-mile journey from Leavenworth with a hardy band of thirty men in light wagons."

Nellie tried not to roll her eyes at hearing, yet again, Van Vliet's self-aggrandizing story of his trip to this city.

Oblivious to any reactions from the group, Van Vliet's rhetoric rolled on. "Speed, *speed* comprises the key factor to avoiding crisis, I tell you. We sent the bulk of the troops toward Fort Laramie. This situation called for a direct, yet diplomatic approach. After my death threat, yea, for that very reason, I left my hardy regimen 150 miles from here at Camp Scott and my scout, fifteen-year-old Bill Cody, a deuce of a cowboy by-the-bye, and I snuck into the Great Salt Lake City on my own."

This tale confirms the worst rumors, the substance of my nightmares.

Van Vliet looked around the table as the rest of the party digested this news, and continued. "Now, I've gotten a good reception from the Prophet himself, based upon my years in Iowa Territory, where I, as erector of military posts along the Oregon Trail, established a rapport with the Saints' community there. Why I *believe* we obtained and *retained* a mutual respect and feeling of trust. Thus, Young parleyed with me.

"I confronted him directly, at one point, asking him about the incident with Judge Stiles."

Incident? Nellie looked at Obadiah, nodding along with the conversation, and made a mental note to ask her husband about that conflict.

"Governor Young looked me directly in the eye, he did. Not hesitating for a moment, Young expressly denied personal complicity in the destruction of the law offices of United States Federal Judge Stiles."

Nellie blanched.

Merciful heavens, does this incident presage a direct threat to our family's wellbeing? Is not my own Federal Judge worried about suffering the same fate?

She studied Obadiah, but his face remained unperturbed.

Van Vliet shook his head. "Yea, I believe the man. Young confided his fearfulness to me. Yessir, he is afraid he shall perish by the same fate that befell his predecessor, Prophet Joseph Smith.

"I told him right then and there, I says, 'I do not think it is the intention of the Government to arrest you. They merely wish to install a new governor of this territory'."

Van Vliet sat back gazing at those assembled.

The kitchen door opened, and Emma walked in carrying a pie. Elizabeth followed, gingerly holding Nellie's good pitcher, sloshing cream everywhere. Lucena rushed in right behind them, a stack of plates wobbling in her hands.

Nellie leapt to help Lucena steady the plates, judging Elizabeth the less likely of the pair to drop her burden.

As the girls served the dessert, the captain said, "I've made it my personal responsibility to avoid bloodshed here. The Mormons arm their men as we speak. Yessir, on my return to Washington, I shall travel directly through Big Mountain Pass, where, on information and belief, I shall find breastworks, fully constructed and undoubtedly manned.

"Then I shall inform every man in the United States Army's chain of command, starting with appointed-governor Cumming's posse and working my way up to the Commander-in-Chief himself, that that the route through Echo Canyon would be a death trap for a large body of troops. I hope to stave off any bloodshed by advising the Army of the delay tactics of the Mormons, and request that the Commander-in-Chief, in return, assure the Mormons they shall not be persecuted for their religious beliefs."

Abruptly, he smiled his charming smile.

Mercy, the West Point cadet smile! 'Tis ill-conceived and irrational that this charming officer's West Point smile immediately assuages my qualms. I fear some behaviors learned in my formative years are hard to unlearn.

Nellie, head reeling from the dump of information from Van Vliet and the memories evoked by his practiced smile, asked, "Who would like to try my sweet potato pie?"

CHAPTER 9
Whiskey for My Men, Beer for My Horses

Home, Great Salt Lake City, September 1857

"May I offer you some spirits to whet your whistle as we converse?"

Obadiah gallantly poured some whiskey from a bottle that mysteriously appeared at their back door this morning.

Payment of some kind for Obadiah?

Nellie closed her eyes and visualized the Irish blended whiskey that always filled their finest crystal decanter on their étagère in New York. Real whiskey constituted a nicety from home for which even Obadiah pined.

"Amen and Alleluia," the captain answered, rubbing his hands together. "All I get out of Brigham in the way of refreshment is a damnation of whiskey. That does not fill my glass! Hell, he even damns the whiskey makers."

"This comes straight from the still but should do the trick." Nellie smiled.

"Zounds! I sat in that service and heard with my own ears every one of those Latter-day Saints swear with their lives they would not allow any 'invaders' to penetrate their kingdom."

"*Kingdom?* 'Tis strange to hear a Territory of the United States called a kingdom." Nellie shook her head and tugged at a strand of hair straying across her face.

"Aye, there's the rub," said Obadiah. "Whilst I already have grown fond of the charismatic Young, the scoundrel is nurturing a theocracy under our very eyes."

"By the sword!" Van Vliet made a noisy swallow of his gulp of whiskey. "A ropy, more turgid swill of suds, I never did see." He scrunched his face.

Does the captain refer to Young or to his drink?

Thinking it must be the latter, she said, "Each pint of that vile whiskey contains enough poison to turn a corn cob white. 'Twas a pity, every worker along the way of the trail seemed to imbibe the stuff.

Often it seems workers willingly allow themselves to be swindled out of a weeks' worth of wages to maintain this deadly habit. Except the Mormons, of course, who are forbidden to partake."

"As I have gleaned from my time in Illinois, and lest I forget, reminded every one of my few nights in this city." Van Viet hung his head. "As I said, my friend the Prophet reviles the whiskey maker as the devil incarnate in our midst, but, heaven help me, I crave a real drink!"

With doleful puppy dog eyes imploring Nellie, he said, "Have pity on a soldier, ma'am, trying to avert a war. Do your bit for peace and pour me a dram of your fine scotch imported from New York."

Nellie looked surprised. How did Van Vliet guess they had carefully carried just one bottle of authentically aged Scotch over the entire length of the Overland Trail?

Van Vliet winked at her and tapped his head, as if to say, 'It only makes sense.'

Obadiah retrieved the bottle from its hiding place in the back of the cupboard, and poured a stingy dram.

Van Vliet took a gulp and closed his eyes, relishing the flavor. He followed this with a tiny sip. "I will savor the rest, I promise. You have not wasted this precious liquid on a boorish oaf, but rather lavished it on a sophisticated fellow who knows its worth and cherishes each drop."

Nellie smiled. "'Tis truly a pleasure to share it with a friend who appreciates its golden nature."

The captain settled himself into the straight-backed chair on one side of the fireplace, and Obadiah took Nellie's rocking chair.

Nellie stood next to her husband.

I must purchase another guest chair. 'Tis a dilemma. If I run to the kitchen to get a stool, I shall miss all the conversation.

Van Vliet said, "I did attend Sunday service as promised. The emotional speeches I witnessed! The fear and anxiety of the community! Young announced the approach of the Army, and the appointment of the new governor. He confirmed to his followers his belief that his religious authority was more important than any secular position."

Spellbound, Nellie and Obadiah waited while Van Vliet took a sip and shook his head.

"Young reminded the community of prior conflicts when they lived among the gentiles. His community gasped in horror reliving the persecution. Men rose and spoke of their obligation to protect their many wives and defend their religious beliefs. I saw the Saints raise their hands in a unanimous resolution to guard against any *invader*."

Nellie gasped.

Any time I dare to hope for tranquility, I hear of more incendiary speeches. "What can be done?"

"Persuasion. Negotiation. Diplomacy," the captain replied, a grim determination settling on his features. "I rose and tried to persuade these resentful Mormon people that the Army had peaceful intentions. Young replied that he sought to avoid conflict too, saying, 'If we can keep the peace this winter, I do think something can avoid the shedding of blood'."

Nellie let out a breath she hadn't known she was holding.

Van Vliet looked at them steadily and said, "It shall be my noblest endeavor: I swear to find that something."

Nellie felt a tiny bit of renewed hope at that oath. *In my few days acquaintance with Van Vliet, I surmise if someone could help this situation, surely, it is he. Can he and my husband recruit other men to help maintain the peace and prevent death?*

"I shall continue to interview leaders and townspeople, encouraging them individually to avoid conflict and seek peace. But, as I said previously, speed is the key. Thus, on the fourteenth I shall return East through the Mormon's fortifications in Echo Canyon, so that I might fully inform the Army of the actual threat to concord."

A terrible thought struck Nellie. *My word, the confirmed fortifications imprison us here as fully as they exclude States citizens from entering.*

Van Vliet stood and, without waiting for any further reactions, threw back the last dram of whiskey and put on his hat. He faced Nellie, grasped her hand, and looked into her eyes. "Now you must seal our friendship by promising to remain neutral in this unfortunate situation, trying to see good and right in both sides of the skirmish."

Nellie smiled, bringing her warm, kindhearted eyes to meet the charming man's eyes. "'Tis only our Christian duty, to look with love and compassion upon our neighbor and to seek commonality rather than division."

Holding her gaze, Van Vliet reiterated, "I truly believe these people have been unfairly persecuted, and diplomacy, not arms, constitutes the salve to right the wrong."

He flashed his West Point smile again and said, "Now, one more dram of the good whiskey for the road? Please don't give me the swill. It isn't even good enough for my horse!"

CHAPTER 10
If We Stick Together, We're Safe and Sound

Home, Great Salt Lake City, October 1857

In the early morning light, while their little girls slept, Nellie and Obadiah again took advantage of having a proper bed and bedroom, now that their wagon days had ended.

"'Tis a true gift from God to awaken in the arms of my most beloved husband, with the night's passion still simmering between us," she whispered.

She smiled at the sun, planted a soft kiss on the slumbering Obadiah, and rolled over, but he stirred to life and began caressing her.

She felt his lips slide deliciously from her mouth to her ear and then all the way down the side of her neck. She arched her back as his hands came into motion, stroking her shoulder and blazing a path for his lips across her back. The wet kisses sent her squirming as his hot breath on her neck lit her whole body on fire.

Once again, our passion heats to a boil, transporting us to ecstasy.

"Would that I had the morning to explore every inch of this sensuous skin," he whispered into her back.

She flipped over and began her own exploration.

'Tis strange to share relations with my husband without rocking the whole room.

Nellie almost giggled aloud, but a deep desire to melt into his strong body quickly replaced the fleeting thought.

"We may not have the leisure of time," she whispered back, "but we shall make the time we have well spent."

Ecstasy surrounded her.

All too quickly, they lay again in each other's arms, blissful and content.

"Mama, we are awake," Nellie heard as she drowsed.

"Our cherished little girls awake to further brighten our day," Obadiah whispered into her neck as Nellie stretched.

***

Nellie hummed as she pulled oats from the larder and poured batter onto the griddle, smiling at her girls' chatter, and her spirits soared on top of the world.

With my loving husband at my side, with my beautiful girls clustered around me, how can we fail at any undertaking if we, ourselves, dwell in peace and harmony?

Obadiah came into the kitchen dressed in his best clothes, his hair groomed and mustache trimmed.

"Why are you sporting your Sunday-go-to-meeting attire?" Nellie asked, noticing the pancake batter splatter that missed her apron and landed on her sleeve.

"Did you forget, we go to the Bowery to hear the prophet speak?" said Obadiah, kissing each of his daughters before picking up his fork and attacking his pancakes.

"Tarnation, I did!" Nellie flew into action, scouting out her daughters' best dresses as she frantically wiped batter from her sleeve.

Obadiah laughed. "Do not fret, we still have over an hour before we must be there."

***

Dressed in their best, my little angels assemble among the Saints, Nellie thought as she led the family to their seats.

As they sat in the shaded Bowery listening to Brigham Young perform his public discourse, Nellie gazed at the congregation. Her attention lapsed, and she turned a critical eye on her daughters' attire.

Blessed Saint Bridget, how did the deplorable state of their best frocks escape me? Merciful heavens, my little angels look more like ragamuffins!

The wear and tear of travel had exacted a high toll on both girls' clothing.

"These people are free," Brigham shouted from the pulpit. "They are not in bondage to any government on God's footstool. We have transgressed no law, neither do we intend or have occasion to do so, but as for any nation's coming to destroy these people, God Almighty being my helper, they *can not* come here."

Quite the dramatic pauses between the words 'they can not come here,' Nellie thought, frightened shivers running down her spine.

The congregation rumbled a loud, "Amen."

Wide-eyed, Emma and Elizabeth jumped at the passionate roar of voices responding to their prophet. They squirmed in their seats, anxiously looking at the angry congregation.

Pleased with the effect, Brigham Young continued, "We have borne enough of their oppression and hellish abuse, and we will not do so anymore, for there is no just law requiring further forbearance on our part. I will not have troops here to harass the priests and make hellish rabble in efforts to drive us from the land we possess, for the Lord does not want us to be driven, and has said, 'If you will assert your rights, and keep my commandments, you shall never again be brought into bondage by your enemies.'"

Now even Nellie stirred in her seat.

More accurately, I join my daughters' squirming with apprehension. Surely, the majority of this rhetoric sounds defensive, and the overall import could well be the Saints *fear more persecution. But mercy! A bellicose threat seems to underlie every well-chosen word. The man breathes fire and brimstone! Does their Lord truly exhort them to assert their rights against the United States and repel its armies?*

Nellie studied the composed countenance of Obadiah, who remained serene.

Does he not fear for his family, if not his own person? Tarnation, if I had my druthers, we never would have settled in this Godforsaken place.

She shifted again in her seat to put her arms around her daughters and pull them close.

Looking at the pulpit, she saw Young gather his breath and continue to stoke the fire of his followers' fears.

"We are invaded by a hostile force, who are evidently assailing us to accomplish our overthrow and destruction." He paused for effect and gave the congregation a meaningful look, finessing his mesmerizing oratory skills. "Our opponents have availed themselves of prejudice existing against us, because of our religious faith."

"Amen," shouted the congregation, some rising with fists in the air.

Nellie clutched her daughters more tightly to her.

Young held up his hand. When the commotion subsided, he proclaimed, "We shall not sit idly by. We shall institute martial law. We shall repel the United States Army. Moreover, no person shall be allowed to pass into, through, or from this Territory without a permit from the proper officer."

People stood and shouted. Some flocked to the pulpit to swear personal allegiance to Young and The Church of the Latter-day Saints.

In the hubbub, Nellie whispered to Obadiah, "Utah Territory spans more than 600 miles. More importantly, the principal emigration trails to both Oregon and California cross it. This proclamation prohibits all transcontinental travel."

"Other routes exist," Obadiah replied.

Nellie marshaled her arguments.

But she had no need to voice them, for Obadiah shook his head and revealed his acknowledgment of her fears. "Or, far worse, unsuspecting pioneers shall continue to travel this route and pay for their lack of political knowledge with their lives."

The Wrights slipped out of the open-air meeting, undetected in the uproar.

His face still set in a grim expression, Obadiah stroked his mustache with one hand and pulled Emma along with the other.

Nellie, panting and half running to keep up behind him, jostled Elizabeth in her arms as her thoughts scrambled through her brains. "We must gather other federal appointees and other Christians and pray," she said, swiping her hair to keep her vision clear.

Cocking his eyebrow as if amused, Obadiah said, "Did not one service suffice today to provide a healthy dose of religion?"

Nellie panted, "Listening to Young proclaim his murderous, vengeful words, *does not* denote worship of our Lord. I see little correlation."

Obadiah stopped so suddenly, Emma, Nellie, and Elizabeth bumped into him. "We must retain our acumen. You heard Captain Van Vliet. Diplomatic channels remain open and good men hope to employ reason and negotiation to salvage this situation. It is not yet time to panic. Even warring philosophies can align for a common purpose—to prevent bloodshed. We must band together and keep our wits about us. This shall deliver us safely to the other side of this enmity."

Nellie said, "But the numerous supply trains and the posse for the governor traveled right behind us. Not to mention the many waggoneers we encountered from time to time on the trail. What of these innocent people? Where are they? Have we no duty to warn them before they find themselves caught between these two *philosophies*?"

"We shall assess the situation after Sunday dinner. In the meantime, my taste buds are primed in anticipation of your savory rabbit stew, followed by the treat, untasted since last Christmas, of plum pudding."

The girls squealed with delight at the mention of the pudding.

Thank you, Lord, for granting my girls some small pleasure to mask the fear of martial law or invasion, Nellie prayed.

Mercy! Which one is worse?

Equanimity fully regained, the girls laughed and skipped as they made their way home.

Back to our temporary dwelling place in Block 61, Nellie mentally corrected.

"Look at those huge stones!" said Elizabeth.

"They must be building a grand palace," Emma marveled.

The group breezed past a large square with massive foundation stones laid out for construction.

"Erecting their temple," explained Obadiah.

"Building a grand house of worship?" asked Emma.

'Then why do they cover those stones with sand?' Elizabeth asked.

How curious! Nellie thought, and aloud said, "Mercy, they *do* appear to be throwing cartloads of dirt over that formation of stones. How very observant of you, my pumpkins. I shall enquire as to the extent of this project."

***

The next day Hannah sent a note inviting Nellie for tea.

Reading it, Nellie said, "The social niceties continue in the Great Salt Lake City. All must be well." But doubt permeated her words.

Obadiah gathered Nellie into his arms and hugged her so hard he squashed her hat, and said, "Did I not tell you diplomatic channels shall assure tranquility?"

At tea, Nellie shook her head and confided to Hannah, "Tis the strangest thing. Martial law has been declared, yet only in the Saints' meeting house. There appears no visible effect on the town."

Hannah placed her hand over Nellie's and replied, "'Tis all posturing and puffery. I trust in the Lord. You observe that the Lion of the Lord, Prophet Young, remains comfortably situated in his mansion, petted by his harem, leisurely walking to his counting house to oversee his vast commercial enterprises."

Nellie smiled. *These reassurances, coming from one of the* Saints *truly comfort my excited sensibilities.* "True. None of his wives in the Lion House exhibit any signs of agitation. No one prepares for travel or burns their garden in anticipation of relocation."

Hannah's face suddenly darkened. "Yet the rhetoric disturbs me to my soul. Lord, sustain my faith! It brought me to the depths of despair to see my neighbor burn his harvest, at the direction of President Young, pack up all his belongs and his kin and head South. Dear God, comfort my wounded heart for these sights quite stir terror in it."

Nellie's fears reared large again and her mood fell into despair.

Lucena laughed.

Nellie gaped at her in surprise.

"As Hannah observed," Lucena said, "you don't see Brigham following his own directive. His pear trees bear such an abundance of fruit, me or any other passersby can pluck their goodness right from a tree, any time. I've made pear sauce from ones lying unclaimed on the boardwalk."

Nellie's small smile acknowledged the logic in this.

"Furthermore," Lucena continued. "Our neighbor Edwin Bird flew the coop, *not* burning his garden which lies between our houses. God in his infinite mercy hid all evidence of the abundant harvest before the man left. Now Mister Parsons and I enjoy the bounty, reaping where we did not sow."

"Mercy," said Nellie. "That shall sour the *prophet's* milk."

"I hope so." Lucena giggled.

But Hannah glowered. "Foolish girl. The Lord, our Savior and protector from the Destroyer, shares His abundance with us all. Moreover, the Prophet's only sin is an excess of caution in protecting his flock."

Lucena looked crushed, and Nellie could think of no rejoinder.

CHAPTER 11
You've Got a Friend

From her position at the cutting board, Nellie stared out the window into her garden. Anxiety and melancholy gripped her.

I wonder how my family fares? I realized it might be many a year before I laid eyes upon them again, but I never anticipated the ultimate injustice of not receiving any news from home.

Suddenly, she rubbed her eyes as if to confirm she was not dreaming.

Clayton? Could it truly be Mister Clayton who appears out of the wilderness like a welcome phantasm from home?

The apparition opened the back door and breezed in, pausing to seize Nellie's hand and squeeze it hard. "Nellie Entwhistle," he murmured.

Blushing, and trying not to shake her hand from the force of his squeeze, Nellie thought, *That certainly felt real.*

Beauregard Cornelius Clayton rubbed his own eyes with a weary gesture. He laid a misshapen brown paper package and his Winchester on the kitchen table and sat his massive frame down with a sigh. "Cornelia Rose Entwhistle *Wright*, the sight a' ye blesses me sore eyes. I feared I would never lay these eyes upon you again."

"Welcome Mister Beauregard Clayton. 'Tis quite a surprise to find you at my kitchen table." Nellie tried to still her racing heart.

Mercy, what in tarnation? How comes this man here? I feel I conjured him with my despondent thoughts.

She stood silent for a moment, knife arrested in mid-chop. *I cannot enquire as to the whereabouts of his wife and baby, for what if they are dead? When last I saw them, his baby was less than a day old, and the hazards of the trail claim many a newborn.*

Or have they been killed in some sort of horrible accident?

Nellie shook her head, offered her family friend a smile, and chose neutral words. "Where have you come from?"

He just sat there, his tight lips set in a straight line.

Yet he looks happy.

A frown wrinkled her brow as she glanced at him, but suddenly his eyes sparkled with his trademarked twinkle.

Nellie's smile returned.

Those magic eyes!

Ever the enigma, Clayton's silent presence somehow warmed Nellie's heart. She shook her head and poured some water from a pitcher into her kettle, then set it on the potbellied stove for tea.

Here sits silent Mister Clayton, appearing out of nowhere, offering no immediate explanation for his presence. Shall I be forced to wheedle it from him one word at a time?

"My current occupation: scout, for the United States Army," Clayton offered, and then his lips returned to their straight line.

Nellie opened the breadbox and retrieved the last quarter of her nut bread loaf. After slicing it, she smeared a piece with a generous helping of butter and topped that with a glop of strawberry preserve.

Biding her time while he gobbled it down, almost in one bite, she crushed some lavender and mint leaves and threw them in the bottom of her teapot to let them steep. Clayton remained silent while she pulled out a chair and sat across from him.

When he extended his arm for another piece of brown bread, she saw pus oozing from a gash running up his arm from his wrist.

"Mister Clayton, we must attend to this at once!"

"Shoot! It's tolerable. I chunk biled water and a lavish amount o' lye soap upon it."

"Jumping juniper!" Nellie drew in her breath, wincing in empathy. "That must have stung worse than a swarm of wasps. Whilst I applaud your thought to clean the wound thoroughly, I do fear your cut is infected."

"Dinna fash yersel'. I dinna come here to have you attend to my wounds. I am as tough as whitleather. 'Twill sort eventually, I am sure."

Why did you come? How traveled you here?

"First things first," she said. "Mayhap you shall indulge me and allow me to ply my midwifery skills. Whilst usually you are correct, if a wound has been cleaned with boiled water, other than a salve to expedite healing, little else is needed to mend. In this case, infection afflicts your wound. Simple ministrations, before gangrene sets in and you lose a limb—"

Clayton snatched his hand away. "Now see here, Miss Nellie!"

"—are required." Nellie grabbed it back. "I shall brook no arguments. Certainly you cleaned it quite thoroughly, thus I suspect contaminated water caused this malady."

Somewhat mollified by Nellie's blame of the dirty water rather than his own care, Clayton did not further resist Nellie's probing examination of his arm.

She restrained the gasp that threatened to escape her lips. "Mister Clayton, I am afraid you must remove your sleeve to allow me to see the full extent of the swelling.

As his shirt came off, her gasp escaped, not because the wound was worse than she expected, but because of the muscular chest revealed.

Mercy, I puff like an ingénue, overcome with sentiment. I am an experienced professional, yea, a married woman. The romantic lure of his unclothed chest should not distract me.

She tried to hide her emotional response to his naked flesh as she examined the wound with brusque efficiency. Angry red streaks emanated from a well-sewn gash, engorged with pus, climbing Clayton's forearm towards his shoulder.

"Mister Beauregard Cornelius Clayton," she said, using his full name to further emotionally distance herself. "How fortuitous you should arrive at my kitchen table before your whole arm became just a memory. I must apply my most potent salve forthwith and give you instructions for the care of this wound, which must be followed meticulously if we are to prevent further harm and facilitate healing."

She busied herself pouring hot water from the kettle into a trough-like bowl she usually used for baking loaves of bread. After adding Epsom Salt and stirring, she placed Clayton's forearm in the solution, turning it so the wound would soak.

"I thought you said I cleaned it proper," said Clayton.

"Yes, and you did. This solution shall educe the toxins and help us combat this nasty infection. Next, I shall prepare a poultice for daily use and a salve to help resolve the infection and promote healing. You must apply this salve directly to the wound *daily*, with a fresh bandage, in order to reverse the course of this ailment."

She tried to get the conversation back on track as Clayton's forearm soaked and she prepared the medicines from her stock of herbs. "Mister Clayton, what project has occupied your time since we last met?"

Silence.

The soft fizz of a new teaspoon of Epsom salts dissolving in the water supplied the only sound in the room.

Just when she thought she could wait no longer, Clayton said, "I set Becky up real pretty in the little town of Ogden, but that was after... after the scare." He took a bite of a third piece of bread.

"I worried you took the southern route. Vicious rumors circulate here of Indian hostility and attacks on innocent emigrants."

Clayton shook his head. "Why go through the desert? I thought to meself. Moreover, why stay with this train at all? With the right reasoning gone—"

Did Clayton intend 'Wright reasoning' as a pun, or do I only overlay it for him?

A man of few words would certainly acknowledge the loss of Obadiah Wright as co-captain of the wagon train, and sometimes the sole voice of rational thinking for the whole company, with a clever conundrum.

"—I doubted Hines, in sole command, had the intellect to see the company through safely. But after only traveling a short distance, my poor forfochen Becky had a powerful sore head, and then me bairn took the colic."

Nellie almost interrupted to diagnose the exact health issues of the pair, but then thought the better of it.

Shaking his head, Clayton continued, "I took it as a sign confirming your advice: me little family were not fit to face crossing those Promontory Mountains. I let the tow gang wi' the bucket and got her set up bonny. We bide awee when some regular army guy, a Captain Van Vliet, comes waltzing through town on his way back to Fort Bridger. I'll tell ye, he took a bit of a detour if you don't mind my saying. I shook my head and thought 'the man needs a better map.' But he told me he was after finding a few good scouts."

Clayton paused to gulp the last of his bread.

"Mighty obliged, Nellie," he said through his loud chomping. "A man can only get so far on chipped beef and hard tack." He swallowed and looked at her.

Wordlessly, Nellie poured him some tea. "Cream? Sugar?"

"I don't usually imbibe such fancy fixins, but it's been so long since I tasted cream, much less than *sugar*, I dare say I shall have the works." He paused to recover his train of thought. "Now, Becky was settling in real nice with a lovely lady who reminded her of her mum. Soon I realized there was no employment for me in Ogden. I was not of the right persuasion."

Discriminated against because of his religion, Nellie guessed. She took a sip of her own tea while waiting for the rest of the story.

"'Twould be a hard knock winter whilst we waited for spring and the chance to either move on or find a bit o' land. I told Van Vliet one of his scouts would be me."

Nellie listened in astonishment.

Clayton's mouth returned to its natural closed straight line.

"Scouting! So, you returned to Fort Bridger with Van Vliet?"

Clayton seemed to have exhausted his words, and he simply nodded his head yes.

"I heard rumors that Wild Bill Hickok took a posse of men and burnt the fort to the ground. Does it still stand? Did you find the federally appointed Governor Cumming? Were you stuck in the storms? Did Van Vliet get back to Washington? Did you go with him?"

Clayton stirred his tea. "Ay, Hickok... a nasty piece of a man, truly. A Dark Angel, the Mormons call him. I meself wouldna disparage the term 'angel' to be associated with the likes of him."

Clayton passed his large hand over his forehead and winced at the pull of pain at his stitches. He smiled, but his eyes remained sad. "As to ta rest o' your other well considered inquiries, I must reply I've little more information for ye. We both sort through speculation and conjecture. When Van Vliet returned to Washington to make his report, I accompanied him only so far as the end o' the canyons."

Clayton's lips resumed their straight line, and Nellie felt more than a twinge of empathy for this weary man.

How might I elicit at least his speculations as to the truth of our situation here?

But she only said, "As soon as you finish that concoction, you shall drink this clove, Echinacea, and honey ginger tea."

"Clove? I ha'n't seen neither hide nor hair o' that heavenly spice since I left New York. Where did you procure clove?"

"I traveled with a healthy portion, though my supply diminishes more rapidly than I would like."

Clayton sniffed the air. "Aye, just ta smell it warms the cockles o' me heart. I should don my best duds with the honor you confer, using it on the likes of me."

She turned back to business to hide her blush. "Did inclement winter weather deter your progress?"

"Sure," said he. "But the real worry hit me like a mad granny cuffing a bairn caught red-handed stealing her warm pie. Remember that spot at the eastern foot of Big Mountain at Mormon Flat, where ta trail turns sharply to the northwest and passes along the foot of a ridge as it heads up the mountain?"

Nellie did recall it, and clasped her hands together. "Yes, it was a beautiful but narrow path, rimmed by steep mountain walls dotted with barberries."

"That warn't all that topped it."

She looked into Clayton's eyes and, for an instant, saw them twinkle. When his grim hard look returned a second later, she thought she had imagined the fleeting sparkle.

He cleared his throat. "On the ridge atop those beautiful sheer cliffs crowding the trail, Mormon militiamen built a defensive breastworks—a low wall of stacked rocks—from which they await, ready to fire down upon any United States troops which may happen to pass along this well-trod route."

Nellie shook her head. She felt the small hope she'd held to, that the breastworks did not exist, extinguish. She had reasoned that her confirmation came from Van Vliet, a man prone to exaggeration, but Clayton never spoke unless he spoke the truth. And now he confirmed the ugly speculation that armed men populated the stone foundations fortified along the Overland Trail.

"Ay, along the pass through the canyons, the only way into Salt Lake from the East, hides over one *thousand* militiamen, shivering and waiting. My scouting reveals the savage and fiendish way the Mormons prepare to mutilate and mow down the Army of their own nation."

He shook his head, grabbed her hand, and looked into her eyes. "I knew I must warn ye. They've fortified every entrance to this city, and have their men stationed along the trails by the tens of thousands."

Terror clutched Nellie's throat. She could not speak.

Will Young corral all non-Mormons, and imprison us as enemies? If they prepare to do battle with the United States Army, will they expel us from the city?

Surely not!

Just this morning, several of the Missus Youngs stopped to chat with Nellie on her way to market. Lucy Ann Decker Young, the wife who seemed to run the whole female enterprise, could not have been more cordial. Nellie stared at the man at her kitchen table, trying to corral her runaway thoughts and assess the risks to her family with objectivity.

Did Clayton abandon his scouting position merely to warn me?

At this disconcerting thought, Nellie looked down at the table. The package thrown there by Clayton stared back up at her. One side looked collapsed, as if someone had deliberately smashed it with a hammer.

Merciful heavens, protect us from maltreatment such as this parcel received.

"Around the fifth of October, myself and a boy by the name of William Cody keek Lot Smith and his band of hooligans attacking the United States Army provisions wagon." Clayton shook his head and stared into his teacup, then returned it to its saucer.

"You 'keek'?" Nellie asked.

"There goes meself again, Scottish words sneaking into me speech. We observed them from a hidden position. We snuck up on them."

Nellie grimaced.

You don't have to translate the English for me! She recalled Van Vliet's mention of a scout by that name.

Any shred of the mirage twinkle annihilated, Clayton banged his injured fist on the table and winced. "Dang fool, Colonel Alexander. We had 'em. We had that Lot Smith, that Wild Bill Hickok, and them Mormons, and we could'a prevented the shenanigans. Why the hell did he not give the order to attack, but rather let them lickspittles destroy United States property and necessary provisions?"

Nellie replied, "The troops accompanying the newly appointed governor have strict orders not to fire upon citizens of the United States. My husband advised, they must function as a *posse comitatus*."

Clayton raised his eyebrows in disbelief. "I well ken the orders. But how will the posse get them here in one piece when them devils stampede our animals and burn our supply wagons? No sir. Cumming and his band won't have an easy time of it getting to Fort Bridger. Mormons have burned every blade of grass along the whole trail. The train's remaining animals will die of starvation. And now there's naught left of the razed supply train, increasing the already good chance they will *all* starve to death before the snows let up enough for them to enter the Great Salt Lake City."

She jumped up and exclaimed, "It seems Young's incendiary preaching has transformed into deeds. They 'no longer sit idly by.' He incited his people to repel the United States Army." She pulled Clayton's arm from the solution, applied the salve, and began bandaging it.

Clayton resumed his story. "Nevertheless, seeing as whot his orders were, Van Vliet went on his merry way to convince diplomacy to work her magic. Armed with the knowledge of what it would take to reign in King Brigham Young, Van Vliet shall attempt to persuade Washington to avert the catastrophe brewing here.

"Me and the kid scout, Cody, we trekked back here. However, Van Vliet was my ticket on the way out. Without him, on the way back, had to sneak past them Mormons lying in wait to mow down anyone passing through the narrow emigration trail."

"Mercy, that must have been quite the feat."

"I proved the family rumors true. I have some Indian blood mixed in me Scottish constitution, for Cody and I passed stealthily and unnoticed during the wee hours just before dawn."

Clayton shook his head and looked down at his hands. "Yessir, 'twill be a long hard winter for them lads wait'n up in them mountains. Jest sitting there, with little shelter, let alone any comforts, while a dang mad man here uses them as pawns in his lust for power.

"There's no sense to it on either side of the coin. Them poor Mormon foot soldiers perch, frozen in place."

"Quite literally?" Nellie asked.

"November snowstorms raged through those mountains," Clayton replied. "The cold and ice afflict punishment on both sides alike.

"Snowbound and lacking supplies, the United States troops' new commander, Colonel Albert Sidney Johnston, decided to spend the winter at what is left of Fort Bridger. The men may be rough enough, and have enough pounds on them to endure starvation conditions, but what of the poor womenfolk traveling with the new governor?"

"Does Missus Cumming in fact accompany her husband?"

"That brave Lady Cumming trudges through snow, along with the rest of them, as we speak. We anticipate their arrival at the burnt-out fort any day now."

Clayton passed his hand over his face and took another swig of tea. "We have received one improvement in circumstances: that old Granny of a General replaced by a savvier Colonel. Yep, our new leader, Colonel Johnston, decreed, 'The Mormons have... placed themselves in rebellion against the Union and entertain the insane design of establishing a form of government thoroughly despotic, and utterly repugnant, to our institutions.'

"This new Colonel aims to take action." Clayton smiled. "That gives us a bit o' hope."

Nellie sat and digested all this information. *Mercy, when has this mysterious here-to-for silent man ever uttered so many words at one time? He must have used a year's worth of words in this one conversation!*

Grabbing her hands, Clayton used his sparse words urgently. "You must escape. Flee this place festering with strange heathens calling themselves Christians."

Nellie looked down at her swollen belly, and raised her eyes to this mysterious man who suddenly popped back into her life. "But where can we find safety? These are troubled times both here and in the States. Discord reigns."

"I heard folks in the mountains of Ken-tuck is pretty well off and sheltered from all the politics. Mebbe we could get some land there."

Who is 'we'? Surely not he and I?

"Becky's powerful mad at me."

I see the hurt in his eyes.

Clayton sighed. "I am trusting the Lord she'll come to her senses, leave her adopted kinsfolk and return to me. Mebbe jis 'til this sit-i-ation resolves."

Until the world is free of problems?

Nellie suppressed a smile and tamped down the tiny flame that ignited at the thought that Beauregard Cornelius Clayton could be asking her to escape with him.

Feeling as unwilling to talk as Clayton, she stared at the wood of the table. When she raised her eyes, still at a loss for words, she glanced at the misshapen box, grabbed it, and latched on to it as a topic of conversation. "What have you carried through thicket and thin wood here, Mister Clayton?"

The twinkle sparkled again in Clayton's eyes. "Aye, a parcel truly rescued from hell, or at least a burning inferno. As I watched the supplies burn, the Mormons ran away. My young scout Cody and I pulled as many containers from the flames as we could. I ensured Missus Governor Cumming, and any other female traveling with the governor's posse, a source of two types of food, at least for a few weeks, when we wrested a couple sacks of cornmeal and flour from the mess, as well as a packet of desiccated vegetables."

"And this package?"

"What to my wonderin' eyes did appear but two boxes, banged and bashed, yet unburned. One sent all the way from England to a Missus King residing here in the Great Salt Lake City. And lo and behold, one addressed to you. I had no choice then but to come and find you. The Lord himself gave me a sign."

Nellie peered at the label. "Saints be praised! *Meine Mutter's* unmistakable handwriting decorates the parcel."

She picked up her kitchen knife and cut the string holding the parcel together, and sliced open the brown paper. A stack of letters, written in many different hands, surrounded a small box.

"Clever. The stationery provides some cushioning to the treasure contained within," Clayton observed.

Nellie blinked rapidly to hold back her tears as she opened the box.

Bespoke ornaments, familiar from childhood and handcrafted in Germany, sparkled and swam in her tear-filled eyes.

"Treasure indeed," she finally whispered. She removed them one by one, savoring their beauty, until only broken glass remained in the package. "Regrettably, two are smashed."

"Yea, but since you were sent a baker's dozen, ye still have eleven ornaments to grace yer tree," Clayton said, with an optimism Nellie willed herself to adopt.

"'Twill be a bit of heaven and home all dancing among the candles on the tree." Nellie smiled as the tears streamed down her face. "Treasures protected by a trove of letters. I can see already I have one from each member of the family." Ignoring those tears, she cleared her throat to make her voice more cheerful. "Even at this distance, I sense the love from my home wrapped around each ornament and coursing through each letter."

She smiled at her friend and said, "Mister Clayton, I rejoice that you traveled to find me. Against all odds!"

She'd first encountered this peculiar man as a colleague of her father's during the construction of the Croton Aqueduct. She had many memories of acts of kindness by this friend of her family, in spite of his silent, foreboding manner.

"A fitting tribute to an astonishing family woman," said Clayton.

Blushing, Nellie covered her embarrassment with directions for Clayton. "I assume, based on your scouting report, that you do not have the required pass for traveling within Utah Territory."

"I shan't grace that man, illegally retaining power in open rebellion with the United States, with a *request*, that I, a loyal citizen of the United States, be allowed to travel unmolested through this free country."

Nellie clasped his hands and gave one final check to the bandaged one.

Clayton softened and the twinkle returned to his eye. "Howsoever, for piece o' mind, I can furnish written orders from Van Vliet, friend to both the United States and the Mormons, upon necessity."

Relief flooded Nellie.

Clayton noticed and grinned.

Blushing furiously now, Nellie corralled her thoughts and returned to business. "Don't forget to apply that salve and take your tea."

"Aye."

"It grieves me to see you return to the wilderness. Correction. I have confidence in your ability to survive any tricks of Mother Nature. I simply loathe the thought of the wilderness teaming with Mormons gunning for bear. Mister Clayton, please be careful."

"I'll exercise me customary caution. What's for ye will no go by ye," said Clayton.

Nellie blinked. *Scottish idioms provide quite oblique statements to unravel.*

"I'd best be getting back on the trail. No time to tarry about, having tea! You've provisioned me well. Now I'll be finding my cohort scout and resuming me duties."

Suddenly, Nellie realized she had continued to hold Clayton's outstretched hands, and now she tried to jerk hers back, but Clayton tightened his grip and hung on.

He looked into her eyes and said with a twinkle, "Lang may yer lum reek."

Nellie burst out laughing. "You leave me with yet another Scottish riddle?"

Clayton smiled and the twinkle shone brightly from his eyes. "Na. 'Tis just a wish for yer continued health and prosperity. Now keep yer head ta ensure our paths shall cross again."

Nellie squeezed his hands and said, "Thank you, Mister Clayton, for safe delivery of my gifts from home. Thank you too, especially, for your scouting report. Forewarned is forearmed! May God shine his protective light upon you, my friend."

She pulled her kindling bag from the pantry and stuffed it with a jar of her newly made jam, another loaf of fresh bread, some cheese, tea, and the bandages and salves for Clayton's injury, and thrust it all into his hands.

He smiled and his eyes beamed their twinkle one last time before he disappeared out the back door.

Nellie stood stock still for a moment, appreciating all that Clayton had brought her. She clutched the precious ornaments from her mother, grateful for the newly arrived piece of home and her mother's thoughtfulness. But for this package, Clayton might not have found her, and she might never have received his scouting report. She felt less defenseless now, armed with this important information clarifying the true nature of her situation.

Thank you, Lord, for the gift of a friend.

CHAPTER 12
I'm Dreaming of a White Christmas

Beehive House, Great Salt Lake City, December 1857

Nellie danced through the steps of preparing a light lunch. "Tonight we shall feast on an Advent supper."

"Huzzah, Mama. 'Tis only four days until Christmas," confirmed Emma.

"Right. In addition, we received an invitation to dinner and dancing as Brigham Young's guests at The Beehive House."

"Inside the palace?" asked Elizabeth.

"Will other girls be there?" asked Emma. "Can we wear our finest dresses?"

"Yes, yes, and yes!" Nellie sang. "'Twill be a fine party. Missus King advises that almost the whole town was invited."

The girls clapped their hands and Nellie smiled. "Now run and feed the chickens. We must attend to our chores."

Nellie looked out the window as she tidied the kitchen.

Her daughters danced with glee as big puffy snowflakes, the size of quarters, magically dropped from the sky and surrounded them.

Wonder and awe filled Nellie's heart. She dashed out into the fairy-like swirl, grabbed her daughters' hands and twirled them around.

Joy shone on all their faces.

"Thank you, Lord, for the bounty of your numerous gifts," Nellie shouted.

Her girls giggled and shouted, "Thank you, God. Thank you for snowflakes."

"The snow comes down in different directions at the same time," observed Elizabeth.

"Is it crossing winds, Mama, or cross purposes?" asked Emma.

My grave scientist, endeavoring to decode the riddles of nature. Aloud, she answered, "I would wager cross winds and air currents. Cross purposes might only be found among God's creatures that can reason."

"As when Elizabeth and I rush into the parlor from opposite sides and crash in the middle like these flakes here?" shouted Emma, as she raced toward her sister.

It does my heart good to see the snow entice even Emma to caper about like a pixie.

"Mama, the flakes are so big we can see the magic pattern of each one that lands on my arm," Elizabeth squealed with delight. "We do not even need Papa's looking glass."

Nellie giggled. "You mean his magnifying glass."

Faces wet with melted flakes, they ran back inside. Nellie stripped the boots off her daughters' feet and rubbed their cold toes. She wrung their wet socks into her laundry basin, water trickling happily down its sides. Soon the smell of wet wool drying before the fire mingled with the aroma of brewing coffee.

Nellie drew in a deep breath, letting the pleasure and comfort of the moment envelope her. The pungent aroma of fresh coffee evoked images of the Overland trail. She pictured grinding beans in the open prairie, sometimes by using the heel of her shoe. She remembered the coffee pot percolating over the fires she laboriously built each night in a trench. Even as she visualized the faraway grand scenery the whiff evoked, she realized that smell, mingled with damp wool and burning wood, now signified home.

She poured a fresh cup of coffee and took a big gulp.

Tarnation!

She gagged and raced to the washbasin. She vomited the coffee and a little bit of something else.

Lord, have mercy! I must serve my husband his brew before the thought of its contact with my stomach causes a repeat performance.

I had hoped the taste of coffee would not trouble my innards this trimester. I must content myself with merely savoring its aroma. Or prepare it like it is served to children: one cup of warm milk with a spoonful of coffee.

The evening sparkled with starlight, and moonlight-lit frosted trees glowed, as the Wrights skipped down the boardwalk to the Beehive House.

"We count ourselves lucky, among the privileged *gentile* visitors entertained at the Beehive House," Nellie said, a happy lilt lifting her voice. "I've heard tell of wonderful dancing parties filled with laughter and sweets at *Saints* Christmas celebrations."

"This event shall prove the rule," confirmed Obadiah. "All afternoon during my meetings, I heard the musicians practicing."

Inside the foyer, the Wright females stood bathed in soft twinkling candlelight, eyes shining as they viewed the opulent setting of the party. Wreaths and bows hung everywhere and tables groaned with cornucopias of food. A trio of musicians played dreamy waltzes from a corner on the far side of the ballroom. The festive atmosphere enveloped them as a servant took their wraps. Fashionably clad ladies dotted the large music room with splashes of color. Their dresses shimmied and swished as they circulated, the whisper of silk wrapping around the soft hubbub of happy conversation.

"The dark finery of the men provides the perfect accentuation of the colorful rainbow of the ladies' Christmas gowns," whispered Nellie.

"Splendiferous," agreed Elizabeth.

"Just like our grand balls at home, Mama," said Emma.

Perspiration dampened her hands as butterflies fluttered in her stomach.

Goodness, suddenly mingling with the Saints' *highest society feels quite daunting.*

She swiped at her forehead and adjusted her hands in her gloves.

I hope to heavens my gloves hide and absorb my sweat.

Nellie gave a nervous giggle. *Goodness no, not sweat! Have I become a common deckhand aboard a ship? Horses sweat, men perspire, women merely glow,* she heard her mother's voice chide her.

Mercy, after all this time and these many miles how I still miss meine Mutter. Nellie's face flushed further with a wave of homesickness. *I yearn for my entire family, even the oft-antagonistic sister Agnes!*

She looked at the lovely house, aglow with candlelight, alive with music, all so familiar, yet tinged with a strange Mormon overlay, skewing the picture to twist it just slightly into something unfamiliar. She sighed and remembered the Christmas soirees at her parents' large estate, and even the glorious Christmas parties she held in her modest home back in Sing Sing.

Merciful heavens, frontier standards elevate my house to a palace! Only a mere two years have passed? An eon's worth of changes, surely, since I dwelt in my homeland amongst the civilized.

Lucena Parsons arrived and shrieked, "My word, ain't this purdy!"

Before Nellie could reply, Lucena had both Nellie's daughters by their hands, escorting them to the buffet table for cakes and punch.

Obadiah reappeared at Nellie's side, bowed low, and took her hand.

Nellie experienced a flashback to the first time she met Obadiah.

My handsome man distinguished himself at young sister Anastasia's debutante ball. Mercy, he cut a fine figure in his military Academy jacket. I can still picture his gloved hand clutching the hilt of his sword. Mayhap he too felt butterflies! I remember to this day our witty exchange of bon mots. 'Twas a challenge to hold up my end of the conversation. Yet exhilarating. My one disappointment: he failed to ask me to dance.

Nellie laughed, for Obadiah smiled into her eyes and immediately led her into a Virginia reel.

My happiness with my husband grows in leaps and bounds evermore.

Breathless after two reels and a several waltzes, Nellie and Obadiah stopped for a drink. With her first sip, three men joined them and ensnared Obadiah in deep conversation. Just as Nellie worried some new political mischief commenced, the men burst out laughing.

Relieved, she sipped her punch and tapped her foot to the music.

Lucena joined her. "Them purdy cakes is the best thing about this party. These poor Mormon women. Their men are as far from saints as ye can get. None of these *spiritual wives* seem the least bit happy. They are a poor and deluded lot, even at a holiday party."

"'Tis quite a pleasant gathering, with everyone on their best behavior," said Nellie with a grin. "See, even Mary Ann Angell Young is smiling."

"You call that a smile? I call that a grimace. Or maybe something is stuck in her teeth. Can the lot of them, made slaves to the will of these hellish beings they are calling men, be neighborly all night long, or will the façade drop at the chime of midnight?" asked Lucena.

"Remember your Christian charity, have a little faith," chided Nellie. "Each woman here has displayed most admirable characteristics in direct conversation."

"I 'spose I shall do my Christian duty and try and help each one individual. That's the ticket." Lucena darted suspicious glances over her shoulder.

"You have no reason to suspect trickery afoot," Nellie reassured her friend.

Looking over her glass of punch, Lucena whispered, "I jest don't trust that man as far as I could throw him. I jest learnt underground passages run from Brigham's houses to Kimball's on the north, and Woodruff's on the southwest."

"Whatever could be the reason the *Lion of the Lord* needs underground passages?" Nellie asked, lowering her punch glass.

"Fiddle-faddle, you're the one with the imagination. You tell me," retorted Lucena, with a pretty toss of her head. She lowered her voice again. "Also, he's got some apartments under the Lion House, where he secretes his wealth and punishes his refractory wives."

Nellie looked skeptical and began to speak.

Lucena's eyes widened. "Wait, is *that* why they call it the Lion House? Because Brigham is the *Lion of the Lord*?"

Nellie stifled a giggle.

Lucena held up her hand. "I know, I know. You solved that riddle a long time ago. But I have a new riddle to solve. Why does the Lion have apartments *below* the house if not for some dark and despicable reason?"

Nellie began to object. "Have you verified —"

"All right, I cannot vouch for the truth of this assertion. I offer it merely as rumor. I am credibly informed, however, that all the carpenters and masons who worked on the lower story of this building have disappeared."

Lucena frowned and rubbed her head. "All I know is not a meaner group exists on this Earth than this very set of men that calls themselves Latter-day Saints. I know'd many instances where they cheated men out of a whole winter's worth of work, simply because the worker men did not belong to their Church. 'Tis not too much of a stretch of imagination to know that some of them that was cheated just disappeared, on account a to prevent the word from getting out."

Nellie shook her head in disbelief.

"I take some consolation in the thought that you don't believe it could be true. Mebbe I can breathe a sigh of relief." Lucena shrugged. "I thank the Lord I don't have to join them. I can just watch their antics and shake my head. Any who, this is only a temporary stop 'til the weather gets better for travel, so I 'spose if I just mind my Ps and Qs we'll be just fine."

Nellie could not dismiss the rumors of malfeasance as easily. She searched for Obadiah in the crowd and sped to his side.

"Rumors run rampant that the *prophet* has underground tunnels to facilitate many kinds of nefarious activities conducted behind the scenes."

Obadiah shook his head and looked at her. "We must not fall prey to every allegation coming down the pike."

"Come, let us dance," Nellie said, postponing the discussion for another time.

Obadiah laid a restraining hand on Nellie's arm. "Our previous dancing must suffice. I must continue my conversations with my colleagues. Diplomacy, a strict taskmaster, demands vigilant application. This social gathering affords an excellent opportunity to strengthen my personal rapport with key figures in the community."

Nellie stared at him. "But it's a Christmas party."

"Precisely," said Obadiah. "And you, my savvy wife, must join the cause."

He turned away and Nellie looked around. *Now I must locate someone with whom to open diplomatic channels?*

Mary Ann Angell stood at the cucumber sandwich tray.

Is she guarding it against infidels?

Nellie checked her posture and glided to that Mrs. Young sporting a merry smile. "Just the person I seek! The hostess of quite the lovely party, herself, stands before me. My most sincere wishes for the happiest of Christmases in your beautiful home."

"'Tis a relief to be at home. Two years ago, Prophet Young foisted the state house in Fillmore City upon us as the site for our Christmas celebrations. The shock to my system has not yet abated. I thank our Lord Jesus Christ we are here in the Great Salt Lake City, surrounded by our domestic comforts."

"Were you not able to celebrate here last year either?" asked Nellie, trying to ooze empathy for Mary Ann Angell Young.

"Why no. We celebrated here. We held our gatherings here, I distinctly remember, for we all rode sleighs to the ice dam and celebrated outdoors on the second day of Christmas. It would have been far too warm in Fillmore last year to find snow and ice."

Nellie shook her head, confused. Did Mary Ann not have a whole two years to recuperate from her trauma?

As if in answer to her unspoken question, Mary Ann said, "Rest assured after the misery and deprivation of travel to Fillmore, and then the last-minute jury-rigging of the necessities for a festive gathering, it takes quite fully two years to recover."

"I would imagine," Nellie said, leveling what she hoped was a sympathetic gaze on her hostess. *Deprivations? This woman knows nothing of true deprivation. I cannot even imagine her on the Overland Trail.*

Mary Ann fiddled with her fan. "I fear my cantankerous humor grows with each advancing year. Alas, in truth, those deprivations did not hold a candle to the trials we withstood, with God-given fortitude, thank you, Lord, on the trail from Nauvoo, Illinois. Still, I oft shake my head at the tortures I have had to suffer from the decisions of my husband."

Merciful heavens, she has suffered deprivations. I should not have judged her so harshly. How many times must I learn the lesson: one never knows the trials one's neighbors have endured.

A woman, resplendent in green taffeta, joined their conversation.

"Sister Sousa, a good evening to you," said Mary Ann, almost pleasantly.

Oh, yes, Sousa! I have met this woman before. Thank you, Mary Ann, for reminding me of her name.

"'Tis quite a lovely party, Missus Sousa," said Nellie.

"Quite!" agreed Sister Sousa. "We are dozens of Saints gathered here, freely and sociably partaking of all the good things of earth!"

"Yes, we thank the Lord for His bounty," said Mary Ann.

"Such a splendid dinner," agreed Nellie.

"I hope you did not eat your fill," said Sister Sousa, shaking her finger at Nellie.

Nellie drew in her breath, about to voice her affront.

Sister Sousa laughed and leaned in. "Caroline Wooley advises additional suppers shall be served at one and three o'clock in the morning! We are encouraged to promenade all through the night."

"Jumping Juniper," squeaked Nellie, summing up her relief at not being chastised for overeating, and astonishment at the length of the party.

The ladies looked askance at her rude exclamation.

Nellie apologized. "Please forgive my outburst. This gathering boasts such a lovely extravagance."

Mary Ann sniffed. "We Saints have earned the right to rejoice in the bounty with which the Lord rewards our arduous toil. We have created a cultured civilization in a wilderness that still erupts in barbarism by hand of the natives of this land."

Nellie raised her eyebrows but did not comment. Quite the statement to puzzle later. *Does Missus Young refer to a particular incident?*

In the ensuing awkward silence, Nellie said, "In my youth, I would have relished dancing the night away, but now with my little charges in tow, 'twould be unconscionable to deprive them of sleep into the wee hours of the morning."

Both women's mouths puckered as if in disapproval.

"'Tis lovely to have occasion to celebrate as a family in our new community," Nellie hastened, using a broad platitude to restore amity to the conversation.

"Yes," said Mary Ann. "Quite. Did you realize that locally grown foodstuffs comprise the majority of the feast?"

Emmeline Young skipped into the conversation. "Missus Wright, did your daughters enjoy Clara Decker Young's social for little girls?"

Nellie frowned. *I am sure they would have, had they been invited.*

Realizing her error from the expression on Nellie's face, Emmeline hurried on. "No matter, a simple oversight in extending invitations. There are so many new immigrants this Christmas."

"Never you fear, Cornelia Rose, my darling." Hannah Tapfield King chose that moment to join their conversation. "We set aside a sufficient store of molasses to ensure a plenteous supply of candy canes, so *all* the children enjoy one on Christmas day. All are welcome at the table of the Lord. We shan't overlook your delightful daughters."

Nellie chose the high road. "How lovely! I know my children have not tasted a sweet that scrumptious since we left New York."

"Yes, sweets constitute a Yuletide luxury," confirmed Sister Sousa.

But Sister Sousa's voice barely penetrated Nellie's senses.

Suddenly the sound and vision of her mother's Twelfth Day of Christmas party surrounded Nellie. She felt transported through time and space into her parents' great mansion at Sing Sing-on-the-Hudson. She again witnessed her girls sharing a candy cane, in their fanciest Christmas dresses on that Little Christmas. She perceived their happy laughter.

She saw it and heard it as clearly as if she still stood in the midst of that party. The joyful bursts of the red of the poinsettia plants tucked in every corner of the great house contrasted with the green of the holly draped on every wall, over every door. Mistletoe hung in every grand archway, with couples lingering underneath. Dazzling light radiated from the many chandeliers and sconces populating the ballroom, accompanied by the melody of music and the murmur of conversation. The whole scene swam in her visualization, threatening tears.

Mercy, it still leaves stardust in my eyes, even now in my memory.

Eliza Snow Young approached, her dour expression visible as she barreled down on Nellie. The three other women melted away; only Hannah remained. A stalwart friend, Hannah grasped Nellie's elbow and stayed at her side.

"Missus Wright." Eliza faced Nellie with a frown, pulling her from her flight of fancy. "Have you suspended your pagan beliefs long enough to join us Saints in a proper celebration in anticipation of our Savior's birth?"

Nellie opened and closed her mouth.

I appear like a damn fool loblolly!

No. Nellie tugged her recalcitrant hair with determination.

Eliza Snow wins the moniker 'harpy'!

Eliza sniffed. "If we wish to be superfine flour, we must be willing to be ground."

Emma and Elizbeth ran up to the group of women, and Elizabeth chattered, "Mama, all the children are drinking the grownup punch."

Nellie blushed. *They remember their prohibition from drinking the punch last Christmas and think this concoction contains alcohol.* "Mercy, my sweets, no need for alarm. The punch recipe differs greatly from the wassail Aunt Agnes served in Chicago last year. Children may drink this."

Relieved, they ran off to sample some.

"A nice, wholesome punch," scolded Eliza Snow Young.

I made no comment on the nature of the beverage, Nellie groused to herself.

Brigham Young suddenly appeared in front of them. "There is no call for divisive sentiment in this Yuletide season. After all, Christmas day and the birth of our Savior rapidly approach."

So, you do enjoin malicious statements but only in the Christmas season?

Nellie blushed as the brazen man's eyes boldly swept over her figure, lingering on her breasts and at last coming to rest on her eyes. He locked her in his stare.

Reprehensible. How ever do all these women tolerate the attention and advances of this portly, pompous man?

Nellie tried not to shudder.

Eliza Snow raised her eyebrows in disbelief. "I would surely think you, of all people, Prophet Young, would champion my efforts to set this infidel upon the right path."

Young stepped closer to his wife Eliza and drew her away from Nellie, whispering something in her ear. As Young released Eliza, Nellie heard "...keep your enemies closer."

Hannah squeezed Nellie's arm and murmured, "I pray to Almighty God to open my sisters' hearts a bit wider to embrace all who struggle on the road to paradise."

Before Nellie could respond, one of the younger Young women— *I'm not sure if she holds the honor of being a wife or a daughter* — struck a chord on the piano and a crowd gathered around to sing. The band took a well-deserved break, sitting down and wiping their faces, gratefully guzzling liquid refreshment.

"Let the caroling begin," said Nellie.

"It came upon a midnight clear," sang Lucena, a bit off key.

What my dear friend lacks in pitch she more than compensates for with volume!

Nellie giggled and hurried over to stand by her side, grateful for the reprieve from forced socialization.

In between songs, Lucena leaned closer to Nellie and made amusing observations about their fellow party guests. "Like I said, I must keep my sense of humor. I must endure this charade until spring."

Suddenly, Lucena bent down and pointed to the floorboards. She whispered fiercely, "I think I see the hidden trapdoor! It can only be the entrance to the labyrinth of hidden rooms."

Nellie pulled her friend upright and said firmly, "This is not the time to test idle gossip for its veracity. Perhaps the source of your information merely made sport at your expense."

"You must believe me," said Lucena, her eyes full of accusation.

Nellie sighed and rubbed her eyes. "I doubt the truth of any statement regarding our scalawag host. Part of me thinks the rumor not *un*true. We shall ferret out the truth, together, but not during a Christmas time celebration."

Just then the band struck a lively dance tune. When the sound of a trumpet hit Nellie's ears, she looked over at the musicians in surprise. While they were caroling, the refreshed string musicians exited and brass instrumentalists replaced them.

"Quite ambrosial," gushed Hannah. "This music fills my spirit with such joy I fear it bursting! I shall find Mister King for a dance, forthwith." She gazed around the room. "On second thought, I will ask Samuel Francis. He has younger feet and fresher limbs."

Nellie tapped her feet and looked for Obadiah, longing for another dance.

Emma and Elizabeth rushed over. "Look, Mama," said Elizabeth. "They gave us honey taffy to enjoy on Christmas Day."

"And cookies in animal shapes made from sweet dough," said Emma. "Can we set these aside with our cloaks so we can take them home?"

"Fiddlesticks," said Elizabeth, looking down to hide the telltale chocolate cookie crumbs suspended on her upper lip.

Nellie laughed. "I am sure you may each enjoy one cookie now and ask for another to take home with us for Christmas."

She could almost smell the wonderful Viennese pastries her Grandmama Pffernuss concocted. She recalled in vivid detail the first Christmas her mother permitted her to bake with her grandmother. Her gladness at this remembered triumph plunged into melancholy.

My heart longs for the Christmases spent cooking at the hearth in Sing Sing, New York. What grand company I kept, preparing feasts with my kinswomen. Not to mention the joy of Christmas caroling and our gatherings around the Tannenbaum. I can picture Mutter proudly hanging each of her precious ornaments handcrafted in Deutschland. *Decorations festooned every nook and cranny of the grand house, even in the kitchen. I pine for the scent of fresh pine! Tarnation! I would even settle for the Christmas spent last year in that mud hole called Chicago with Agnes.*

She sniffed.

At least we gathered with faithful family and sang carols.

She grinned.

Not to mention our many toasts with wassail, on many more nights than just the traditional Twelfth Day of Christmas!

As her daughters chattered and tucked their treats away in their cloaks, Nellie gave a final tug to her stray curl.

I must introduce some of my home customs to our celebration here in this wilderness. I must incorporate my faith into these festivities.

"I shall re-create a Midnight Mass!" she blurted.

Of course! We must observe our own faith. I know the mass rites so well, I can repeat them for the children. I am sure Lucena and George, for a start, would join us. I am sure they shall welcome the reprieve from Brigham Young and the tirades he calls sermons. Perhaps I can even find other Catholics here to join us.

Her daughters ran back into the ballroom, and in the excitement of her scheme, Nellie almost ran alongside them.

"Lucena," she called, when she spotted her friend. "A most brilliant idea just struck my fancy. On Christmas Eve, we shall gather at my house and re-create a Catholic Midnight Mass to properly celebrate Christmas."

Lucena grabbed Nellie's hands and swung her around in a joyful circle, the long train of Lucena's dress swinging wildly in her exuberance. "My Cornelia Rose! Always using that wonderful brain of hers to dazzle me with her magic ideas."

Executing a full 180-degree twirl, her beautiful dress swirling around her, Lucena stopped her pirouette with a curtsey and said, "On behalf of myself and my husband, I accept your invitation and promise to bring my most somber Nativity self, complete with a joyful singing voice. Every day I taught school, I sang with my pupils. I know all the verses to all the mass songs!"

Lucena skipped over to tell her husband the news. She moved so swiftly, startled dancers stepped out of her path and gave her wide berth. George's look of concern exploded into a hearty laugh when he learned the cause of her excitement.

Obadiah was at Nellie's elbow in a flash. "What rattles Lucena all out of kilter?" he asked, in a *sotto voce* tone.

With a saucy tilt to her head, Nellie replied, "I just invited her to a re-creation of a Midnight Mass at our house on Christmas Eve."

Obadiah's mouth tightened. He smoothed his mustache.

Nellie felt all her joy burst like a hot air balloon popping. Her stomach clenched with pain. Even the baby inside her seemed to shrink. "Whatever can be the matter?"

"Do you never think of the import of your actions before you leap headlong into some foolish enterprise?"

It inures to your benefit that I don't, for had I premeditated our journey, I never would have joined you on our trek westward to this horrible destination.

Nellie grimaced. "Whatever could be the issue with having friends join us on Christmas Eve?" she mumbled, knowing Obadiah would lose no time in detailing deleterious effects she had never considered.

"Did you not stop to think the practicing of a different religion in the Mecca of the Mormons might cause difficulty for me in fulfilling my duties here, prime of which is to continually maneuver around the current Governor and President of the Mormons?"

Nellie hung her head.

"This clandestine practice of what Prophet Young considers heretical rites shall undo months of my arduous endeavors to establish a working rapport with this man."

Nellie's heart and her head sank lower.

"Did you never wonder why we, almost *alone* of all the federally appointed professionals in this town, have not been tarred and feathered or run out of town, much less than permitted, rather than thwarted, to fulfill my duties? My hard work, my months of diplomatic negotiations, accruing into a working relationship with the Prophet." He shook his head in disgust. "Now I shall be forced to watch all that good work undone as that loose-lipped Lucena broadcasts your intention to engage in what Prophet Young perceives as pagan rituals. Zounds! 'Tis simply outrageous and difficult to bear."

"Does the man not espouse religious freedom?" Nellie lifted her head incredulously.

"Only for his own faith," Obadiah replied through tight lips.

"That hypocritical humbug," Nellie exclaimed softly.

Obadiah glowered at her. "Be that as it may, enumerating the faults of the man shall not facilitate execution of my job."

"Is not your duty to uphold the law?" Nellie frowned, amazed at her own courage to contradict her husband.

Obadiah glowered.

Nellie pursued. "Does not the law of our land here include the Bill of Rights? Should *we* not be able to enjoy religious freedom?"

"Speaking theoretically, of course, yes," said Obadiah with an impatient shake of his head.

Heartened by Obadiah's concession, Nellie said, "Thus it is not against the law of the Great Salt Lake City to pursue the religious practices of our choice?"

Obadiah grabbed her arm and practically growled at her, "Of course it is not illegal, *per se,* but woman, do not ignore our reality. I subsist here whilst performing a job in a homogeneous community that seeks freedom from the persecution it suffered in the States. I understand their reactive intolerance toward the religions of their former persecutors. Moreover, I grasped this concept instantly, that I might remove at least one obstacle blocking establishment of an effective relationship with the head of this faith, this community, yea, this entire Territory."

Nellie looked at him with love in her eyes. "I well know your struggles to inaugurate yourself in your appointed position. I strive daily to facilitate your endeavor. Howsoever, you must recognize, I face the same struggles creating a home for our family, amidst this truly foreign land with different climate and culture. Furthermore, I gave up home and hearth to join you on this journey. 'Tis not to follow *my* dreams that we undertook this charade."

Obadiah's face softened, just a miniscule bit.

"Please," Nellie said. "I long to repatriate with my family. I long to immerse myself in the familiar landscape of my youth, engaging in all the traditional activities I always enjoyed as a child. Especially at this time of year, I want to be home. Indulge me in this one request."

"*One* request? What about the goliath Christmas tree?" Obadiah glowered at her again.

Nellie sighed. "I shall forgo my *Tannenbaum* and settle for that puny branch you call a Christmas tree *if* you will permit me to re-create, as best we can without priest or Blessed Sacrament, a Nativity mass. After all, and I cannot emphasize the importance of this enough, we must inculcate our daughters in the spiritual practice of Christmas. The trappings and traditions we can always modify later.

"Please. I'll give up the *Tannenbaum*. Afterall, I only possess eleven Christmas ornaments from *Mutter*," Nellie confessed, her eyes resuming their merriment. "Even a *Tannen* branch can hold eleven ornaments."

Obadiah nodded, his mustache in a straight line, his eyes only a tiny bit more compassionate at the mention of Nellie's severe homesickness. "I concede that 'twould be a proper and fitting tribute to both Christmases past and Christmas present."

Elizabeth skipped into the room. "Where's the Christmas present?" she asked.

Obadiah winked at his daughter, then glowered at Nellie. "But our event must retain the utmost secrecy. And if Lucena is party to—"

Emma arrived in the conversation and asked, "Our Christmas celebration must be secret?"

Obadiah's face took on a darker shade of grim. He gave Nellie a meaningful look.

"Yes, we shall host a secret Christmas celebration this year," said Nellie, assuming an air of gaiety. "We shall stage many surprises and secret aspects of our multiple day worships for the birth of our Lord and Savoir."

"Goody-good." Elizabeth clapped her hands.

"Yes." Emma nodded.

Nellie and Obadiah breathed a sigh of relief. "Good."

Our one big secret shall hide under the guise of many little secrets. Now to convince Lucena!

"Just like the early followers of Christ," said Emma, not missing a trick. "Too bad we don't have a cave. We could mark it with a picture of a fish so everyone would know where to gather for Mass."

"What about the big scary cave along the trail where we tried to find the treasure?" Elizabeth turned to Nellie.

Which one?

But Emma knew. "Cache Cave! Where all the Mormons signed their names. And we only found one lady's."

"But we found Missus King there." Elizabeth turned puzzled eyes to her sister.

Nellie's heart lurched at their fractured remembrances of the walls, extending into the darkness of Cache Cave, covered with emigrating Mormon's signatures.

And that rascal young drover, that jackanapes, Virgil Ralston frightened us all half to death!

She chuckled. *Mercy, now I wax nostalgic, and feel homesick for even the events and people encountered on the Overland Trail.*

We shall have our own proper Catholic Christmas Eve celebration, or as near to it as I can muster. We can gather and break bread.

Emma broke into Nellie's thoughts. "'Wherever two or three are gathered in my name, there am I in their midst,'" she quoted, and the two girls skipped back onto the dance floor.

Nellie stared after them in amazement.

She turned toward Obadiah to share this wonder with him. "My precious daughter, quoting scripture!"

He smiled and embraced her. "'Tis little wonder they quote scripture. 'Tis merely a reflection of your daily lessons."

Nellie looked down to hide the tears in her eyes.

He put his hand under her chin and drew her up until her eyes looked into his. "I meant to compliment you. No need for tears. My precious Cornelia Rose, I share your joy in our precious offspring. The wonder of our daughters is a testament to your excellent child-rearing skills, as well as your shining example as a teacher. I am proud of your efforts on their behalf. You are all a credit to me."

She sniffed.

Dare I trust my husband holds no rancor for making a Christmas celebration without consulting him?

She said, "All the more reason to reinforce our mores with a celebration of our faith in as close to a traditional observance as I can imitate."

"I agree."

Nellie could hardly believe her ears.

These words sound almost apologetic. Mayhap he regrets his harsh tone?

The floodgates holding back her love, while her inner anger festered, released, and she was inundated by her passionate respect for her husband. She threw her arms around his neck and whispered, "My dearest heart, I truly love thee."

Obadiah brought his lips to hers in a quick kiss. "I promise more admiration of your attributes later." He winked.

She blushed and they parted ways. The world stood righted again. She straightened her posture and headed toward the buffet table.

However, she determined not to let her renewed feeling of love for her husband deter her from imparting her faith, world views, and culture to her children. She vowed to make Midnight Mass a yearly tradition in her home, until she could help establish a proper Catholic Church.

Or I surrender and return home to New York.

CHAPTER 13
A Whiter Shade of Pale

Home, Great Salt Lake City, January 1858

With the first pangs of labor came an intense pang of homesickness.

Sadness swept over Nellie and plunged her mood into darkness. Her sense of loneliness sharpened her dread of the ordeal to come, until her heart hurt with a pain as acute as a contraction.

Merciful Heavens, how shall I endure the trials of this birth without the skilled midwifery of Missus Rafferty?

Nellie longed for the company of her midwife and teacher as much as she missed her mother's practical wisdom. She tried to fortify herself with the knowledge she'd gained, not only from her training as a midwife but also her own experience of childbirth.

But the waves of contractions brought waves of memoires.

Thank you, Lord, for delivering my mother to my kitchen door before I recognized the signs heralding Emma's arrival. And Mutter diagnosed the imminence of Elizabeth's arrival during the raging blizzard of '55. How accurate her judgment! I believed I still faced a day's worth of anguish, and Elizabeth arrived less than three hours later!

The love and warmth of her memories of Emma's and Elizabeth's births wrapped around her and surprised her with comfort.

Until another swell of pain crashed her back on the shores of misery.

Jumping juniper! Bereft of meine Mutter, how shall I fare?

Tears once again blindsided Nellie and she could no longer blink them back.

'Tis onerous enough to proceed sans *midwife, but impossible to soldier through without the experience or comfort of my mother.*

This wave of homesickness combined with an actual contraction to form a perfect one-two punch to the heart and gut.

Lucena glanced up from their group writing exercises. "Mercy, you're as white as a ghost. What ails you?"

Nellie grabbed her abdomen and said aloud, "Nothing."

Lucena stared at Nellie's rounded figure. Suddenly, she stood up so fast she knocked her chair over and the slate flew out of Elizabeth's hand. "No, no, no! I cannot be privy to such events."

Nellie burst out laughing and crying as her friend backed away, toward their front door.

Nellie's two little girls stared from their mother to Lucena in astonishment.

"Aunt Lucena, what events?" asked Emma.

"Lucena Pfuffer Parsons, tarry a moment," Nellie sputtered, in between hiccups.

"There's not a moment to spare," said Lucena, reaching behind her, feeling the wall for the hook where she'd hung her hat.

Nellie swiped the tears from her face, put her hands on her hips, and gasped for breath between spasms of laughter.

Or is that already another contraction?

"Lucena Ellen Pfuffer Parsons, I have attended hundreds of births in my capacity of midwife, and as you can see, I have birthed two children of my own. I assure you: 'tis a very rare occurrence when this process truncates to as little as a few hours. My own two labors have lasted 15 hours and then 8 hours respectively."

Nellie pointed first to Emma, then to Elizabeth.

Lucena opened her mouth to argue while, hat in hand, she inched toward the door.

"Therefore," Nellie said, a stern warning ringing in her voice that stopped Lucena in her tracks. "I must impose upon you to please bring word to Missus Hannah Tapfield King that I am in need of midwifery services. I urge you to fetch her back here yourself."

Lucena shook her head and said, "Mercy, no. No! First of all, you know I scarce abide that woman. She puts on high and mighty airs. 'Heighho-ho, the Mormons are *God-like* creatures.'" Lucena mimicked.

Nellie, in spite of her compromised position, stifled a smile at the accuracy of the impersonation.

"And second of all—" Now Lucena shook her head so hard Nellie got a headache. "—you won't catch me steppin' back through your door for love nor money."

"Have I offended you?"

"Cornelia Rose, pretty please. If I get any closer, I'll be so scared I won't never have any children of my own."

Nellie suppressed another smile. "I remember you uttered those exact words when you stumbled upon me employing my midwifery services for Missus Clayton."

Lucena's face wore a sheepish expression, and she poked at Nellie's rug with her toe. "Well, I won't never have a baby."

"I merely request you come back so you might collect my daughters and entertain them with an appropriate distraction." Nellie giggled, and then gulped, as an identifiable contraction shot across her abdomen.

Lucena considered for a bit. "All right, I can do that. You know'd I used to be a school Marm back in Janesville, Wisconsin before I married my young George Washington." She flew out the door still clutching her hat.

"Or else we could go picking chokeberries. The kind that's juicy and sweet." The words floated back to them from the closed front door.

Nellie giggled. *A school Marm? With that grammar?* She couldn't even summon a picture in her head.

"Mama," Emma began.

Nellie held up her hand. "It's time your little brother or sister made an entrance into our world. When Aunt Lucena comes back, you shall have a lovely day of fun with her, and by the time *you* come back, you can meet your sibling."

The girls squealed in delight.

"I have the perfect thing to do whilst we wait," said Emma. "We can write a welcome on our slates."

Elizabeth agreed, shaking her head yes, but then shaking it side to side to watch her braids flap in her face until one of her ribbons popped off.

Nellie rose and walked to the kitchen. "While I wait, I shall prepare a stew in anticipation of dinner with a new family member."

Please, God, let the ordeal be over before our supper, she prayed. Feeling guilty, she added, *I accept whatever length labor you grant me. Please only hear my prayer for a healthy baby.*

A short time later, enticing smells emanated from the broth percolating in the pot. The girls' happy chatter filled the kitchen with loving sounds as Nellie hummed, *Way Down Upon the Suwanee River,* and her daughters joined in singing.

Nellie suspended her knife over the chopping block.

Merciful heavens! The contractions seemed to have abated. Goodness, I hope I did not seek aide prematurely.

Just as Nellie finished chopping the dried bay leaves and thyme, her kitchen door burst open and two women blew in on a gust of air and snow.

Without a hello, Hannah said, "I assured her you shall feel blessed by her presence."

Nellie eyed the heavyset woman behind Hannah, who shook off her cloak and raised her unsmiling face to Nellie.

Hannah pulled Nellie by the hand and brought her to sit at the kitchen table. "I brought Missus Mary Ann Angell Young, proud mother of five, to assist you. As you may surmise, she possesses *endless* experience in birthing, far more qualified than I. I fear my back will not strengthen to bear this load."

Nellie jumped back up from the table, ready to send them packing. *I shan't allow grim-faced Missus Young, the second, to assist in the birth.* She felt like crying and shouting, 'I want *meine Mutter!*'

Hannah gave a wink and a little chuckle. "I imagine we all know circumstances demand midwifing here, oft on a weekly basis!"

"I fear the contractions stopped," Nellie blurted. "My humble apologies for dragging you fine gentlewomen away from the comfort of your hearths in such inclement weather."

"Nonsense," said Mary Ann. "If a momentary lull occurs, as I am sure you are fully aware, you must ambulate and engage in other movement of the limbs to keep the labor progressing."

Nellie raised her eyebrows. Perhaps this woman would prove less dire and more beneficial than she first thought. At least Mary Ann seemed to understand this part of labor.

"Moreover," Mary Ann continued, "as I recall, you, yourself are trained in midwifery, so I shall merely humbly assist performing the ministrations you cannot perform on yourself."

Nellie nodded.

Quite satisfactory. Now if she could smile occasionally, she might not resemble the grim reaper.

Nellie obediently trotted around the room and then ran toward the pantry in search of another clove of garlic. As she reached for the right clay pot, another contraction rewarded her. She hurried back into the kitchen, clutching her side.

Mary Ann gave a smug look, and the corners of her mouth turned from frowning to almost a straight line.

My prayers answered! Almost a smile and mercifully not 'I told you so.'

Nellie said, "We may make progress after all, if only Lucena—"

The kitchen door flew open and Obadiah appeared, saying, "Why does Lucena hover about our hen house shrouded in snow like a ghoulish specter, entreating me to fetch our daughters for her? Does she fear some type of contagion in our house?" He stopped short when he saw Hannah and Mary Ann.

"Please forgive my lack of manners, ladies." He swept them an exaggerated bow and attempted a joke. "Have I interrupted a tea party to which Lucena was not invited, thus feeling the need to haunt us in protest?"

"It does the heart good to hear your jest," Hannah proclaimed, "for surely you know your wife shares all the Lord's good and bountiful gifts with her neighbors!"

After the ladies explained the situation, Mary Ann said, "Missus Wright, please take this opportunity to rest and build energy for the ordeal to come."

Nellie obliged and lay down for a nap.

***

To her surprise, she'd fallen asleep immediately. She awoke in total darkness, quiet permeating the house. Disoriented, she tried to remember why she lay in bed.

It must be well after four if the sun already set. How could I have slept for over two hours?

"Tarnation! The contractions stopped," she said.

Hannah poked her head into the Nellie's bedroom. "Heighho! Our Mary Ann predicted the cessation. She surmised you could not have fallen asleep if labor pangs still shot through your body. Your guardian angels surround you with love and protection, thus I shall retrieve your babies from that Parsons woman and follow Missus Young home. Just send word as soon as your pain resumes."

***

As Nellie and her daughters walked through the market stalls the next day, it seemed everyone in town wanted to know the state of Nellie's labor.

"We thought our town would be favored with an increase in population yesterday," said Lucy Ann Decker Young with a kind smile.

They both examined the newly arrived beautiful fabric rolls as they waited for the dry goods store owner to measure out coffee beans.

Nellie shook her head. "I am afraid this baby maintains his own schedule."

"Then you believe it is a boy," asserted Lucy Ann. "Certainly, you can't take stock in another girl."

"I welcome whomever the Lord has in store for me," said Nellie, taken aback at the callousness of the remark.

***

Mary Ann Young appeared at the back door the next morning. "No progress yet?" she scolded, untying her hat and sniffing at the bread and honey sitting half-eaten on the kitchen table. At Nellie's negative head shake, Mrs. Young's face puckered in deeper disapproval.

As if it were something I could control!

"Tell me, Missus Wright. You felt no labor pains at all yesterday or this morning?"

Nellie looked at her kitchen floor in embarrassment. "Only periodic mild contractions, which cease as soon as I sit down."

"Good Lord have mercy! Do not sit down!"

Nellie repressed an angry retort. "Of course, I increased my activity all day yesterday, but to no avail. When I lay down to sleep last night, all contractions ceased."

"I shan't tarry here today too. I cannot sit around waiting to be a godmother." As she spoke, Mrs. Young, the second, retied her bonnet and bustled toward the door. "I shall check in on you periodically, but by all means, send that flighty woman, your next-door neighbor, to fetch me as soon as you feel the requisite progression of affairs."

Nellie crossed her arms.

I'll be a lily-livered hedge-pig if I elect you godmother to my issue, she thought at Mrs. Young's back hurrying out of the door. *Furthermore, I take umbrage at your insult of my dear friend.*

Nellie shut the door firmly behind the cross woman. *And stay out!*

The day wound its way from start to finish in a series of dreary tasks with sporadic episodes of mild, hope-inspiring pain that disappeared as soon as Nellie sat down. Nellie's interaction with her daughters brought the only solace from her state of suspended dread.

Their chatter and antics fill my soul with sustaining love and joy. I can bear this trial of prolonged trepidation too.

The next morning, Nellie jumped out of bed as if she were shot out of a cannon at the first crow of their rooster.

I mustn't tarry, even though every bone in my body demands further rest. Surely, today my child shall enter this world.

She stumbled to the kitchen, lit the potbellied stove, and placed her hands near the fire's glow for an instant before shutting the 'belly's door.'

Glory and praise to God for the quick warmth emanating from this sumptuous stove.

Renewed relief surged around her, protecting her like her house's solid four walls shielding her from the stormy weather. She prayed for the safety of all those without this precious shelter, whilst she luxuriated in front of a glowing stove.

Nellie remembered Beauregard Clayton's scouting report.

I envy not Missus Alfred Cumming, forced to camp at a site stripped of its fortress characteristics and reduced to mere rubble. "Please, Lord, keep this remarkable woman warm and fed until circumstances allow her to rejoin civilization."

She clutched her dressing gown around her throat with one hand, grabbed the kettle with the other, and ran out to the pump in the back yard in her slippers. The inch of snow, deposited overnight, encased her yard in a fairyland of frost.

If I run so fast my feet barely touch the ground, I shan't regret not stopping for my boots.

Madly, she primed the pump and then held her kettle under the spout.

Mercifully, our temperature hovers somewhere between light frost and freezing our pump.

She ran back inside, threw the kettle on the stove, and looked down at her feet.

Wryly she reflected her conservation of the three minutes required to bother with boots might just have cost her a pair of slippers. *Once again, penny wise and pound foolish.* She shook her head while chastising herself.

But I cannot surmount the difficulty of bending down.

She jumped!

Hannah King suddenly stood right in front of her, stooping to remove her beautiful leather boots.

"Merciful heavens, you gave me quite the start," Nellie said, clutching her heart.

"Enough to send you into labor?" Hannah chuckled. "For, Lord bless us, that was my very intention. Ordinarily, decorum dictates I wait to be invited inside, but with the snow still swirling and that recalcitrant baby stubbornly refusing to join us, I thought I just might try a different entrance." She gazed out the window. "Why were you *outside*?"

"Fetching water for tea."

Is the reason not obvious?

"Have you no one to fetch water? In your condition? At very least, Mister Wright?" At Nellie's negative headshake, Hannah continued. "Heighho! How trying such things are. This lack of Godly empathy saddens my soul. My Mister King hops about at my slightest intimation of need. I cannot fathom the rationale of a man who neglects his wife, especially at this time. Where in heaven's name is he at this hour?"

Nellie blushed in fury.

In bed, sleeping, but that is none of your concern. She said, "Mister Wright busies himself with important legal matters, thus providing for our family."

"Do not emulate the strange behavior of that Missus Cumming, content to struggle out there in the wilderness rather than put some sense into her lame pretender-to-the-governorship of a husband. I wager a complaining and disobedient spirit composes her nature, and 'tis the Lord's plan to punish her. Why would she choose to spend a winter in the frozen mountains when the temperate climate of our fair city, the height of civility and civilization, awaits a few days easy walk from their hideout?"

Nellie's head spun. "Surely, you lend no credence to the rumours that duly-appointed Governor Cumming and his faithful wife *choose* their exile from a warm bed, a roof over their heads, the Great Salt Lake City and civilization?"

Hannah wagged her finger. "There are two sides to every story. I simply advise, examine the source of your information and do not believe every tongue-wagging gossiper you encounter."

"I do not wish to be argumentative, but I hardly base my information on the prattle of tattle baskets and quidnuncs. Thus, I might offer you the same advice." Nellie felt her temper rise and angry words spring to her lips.

But Hannah interrupted her train of thought. "Now does pain overwhelm you? I hoped a verbal nettling might induce labor."

"But...." Nellie closed her mouth.

Did Hannah truly believe the Cummings camped near the demolished fort out of preference?

"Your midwifery skills include quite the interesting assortment of techniques." Nellie could not resist asking, "You do know, as a bottom fact, that Wild Bill Hickok, the notorious *angel of death,* led a group of the faithful to raze the fort and destroy the United States Army's supply wagons simply to—"

"Cornelia Rose," a new voice interrupted. "I'll thank you not to repeat unsubstantiated rumours to one of the faithful, especially as she is our guest." Obadiah appeared in the doorway, tousled head and sleepy eyes metamorphosing into a stern, polished look with one swipe of his hand over his hair.

Startled eyes no doubt betrayed her hurt at her husband's reprimand as Nellie explained, "Missus King and I merely exchange outrageous rumours in order to induce the end of my confinement."

Hannah covered Nellie's hand with her soft gentle one. "Surely, our discussion prompted some movement from our long awaited one."

Nellie closed her eyes, tried to will a contraction, and rubbed her hand across her distended abdomen. "Maybe...."

Emma and Elizabeth burst into the room. "Where is our sister?" they demanded in unison.

Nellie felt as if her brain were swaddled in cotton. "Your...?"

"The baby," Emma answered.

"How could you forget, Mama?" asked Elizabeth.

Nellie burst out laughing.

Soaking wet feet, ruined slippers, no warming tea, surprise visitors.... I am quite at my wits end.

She could not stop laughing.

The harder Nellie tried to justify her mirth to the astonished faces surrounding her, the more she could not stop laughing. She laughed so hard tears streamed down her face.

Now the faces looked worried.

As if I have taken leave of my senses.

Nellie laughed. "Hic! Hic. Everything," she gasped, before a fresh spasm of hiccups silenced her.

"Everything," she tried again. Suddenly a pain shot across her abdomen, and she clutched at her side.

"It worked!" exclaimed Hannah. "Your laughter acted as the catalyst. The Lord endows your baby with a quick wit and an enhanced sense of humor."

Obadiah's frown increased and he reached for his daughter's hands to pull them out of the kitchen.

"What worked?" asked Emma.

"Hush now, we must go visit Aunt Lucena," said Obadiah.

"Not without my breakfast," announced Elizabeth. "Mama promised we could have buckwheat griddle cakes today and I, for one, shall not go visiting without a proper breakfast."

Nellie laughed.

Now where has my little pumpkin ever heard those words?

Once again, hysteria threatened, but another contraction curbed her desire to laugh. Suddenly somber, she said, "Yes, I did promise griddle cakes. Moreover, you are correct. None of you shall depart without your breakfast. Now sit at the table, all of you, and I shall heat the griddle."

"Bless the Lord!" said Hannah. "Do not tax your strength. You must rest, right this very instant, to conserve your energy for what surely now begins in earnest."

Nellie shook her head no. "First of all, I had this same amount of activity yesterday, but all forward progress stopped in the evening the second I lay down. Thus, I anticipate the same heartbreaking sequence shall transpire again tonight."

She whisked around the kitchen as she spoke, measuring milk, and cracking eggs into a bowl.

Obadiah said, "I see the logic in that." He looked at the glum faces of his daughters and tried to lighten the mood. "Besides, I am *hungry!*"

Nellie laughed, her usual genteel, sane laugh, and her daughters broke out in relieved giggles. Buckwheat flour and a pinch of salt joined the wet ingredients, then she walked, whisking the mixture, into the pantry in search of a pinch of sugar. Changing her mind, she wheeled around and folded in the remaining dollop of applesauce from the batch pureed last week.

"I delight in sharing this blessing of the Lord and handiwork bestowed upon me by my kind and loving friend," said Hannah, and sat down at the table.

The girls scurried to and fro bringing plates, forks, and napkins to the table.

Soon the tempting aroma of griddlecakes permeated the kitchen, along with freshly boiled coffee and sizzling sausages.

Even Obadiah lingered at the feast, so full of love, laughter, and delicious food that he delayed his usual dash to his office.

Nellie cherished every second of the warm love of the gathering, as she timed her twinges.

Here stands the home I had hoped to create, filled with love that will never end. Here laughs the family we can only enhance with each small addition. Tarnation! Here may or may not erupt a contraction signaling the imminent increase in the number of Wrights at this table.

Finally, Obadiah rose, still wiping his lips with his napkin. He smoothed his mustache and smiled at the assembled diners. "I loathe ending this delicious feast almost as much as I hate leaving your merry company, but my responsibilities summon me. Further, I must increase my labor for the impending increase in mouths to feed."

"*Your* labor?" Nellie quipped.

Obadiah smiled.

Keeping her cheery smile, Nellie clamped her mouth closed as a painful contraction rose. "All good things must come to an end. Girls, grab your shawls. I shall tidy our kitchen. Loving husband, please bring our daughters, plus this currant jelly, to our neighbors and deposit them with Lucena for a day spent in play."

Chairs tipped in the excitement of the girls' freedom at release from their cleaning responsibilities and plan for a day spent in frivolity.

The door had barely closed before Nellie vomited her breakfast all over the floor.

Hannah scrutinized Nellie's face and said, "Excellent work, my dear. I shall recall your charming husband and dispatch him to fetch Missus Mary Ann Young."

Nellie giggled.

As if my proper gentleman of a husband would stoop so low as to fetch someone!

But her giggle threatened to provoke hysterical tears again as an even stronger contraction gripped her. She felt the blood drain from her face as she swayed and grabbed the kitchen table, gasping. The intake of air, putrid with vomit, made her gag, and the last remnants of her breakfast threatened to rise.

She looked at the table as she swiped at her mouth.

Merciful heavens, I can see whole chunks of the wizened apple I mixed into the batter.

And she threw up again.

"Perhaps your baby shall arrive sooner than we dared dream," said Hannah, and led Nellie to the bedroom.

CHAPTER 14
The Beat Goes On

Great Salt Lake City, February 1858

Glory be to God on this splendid day.

Nellie nursed the baby to the jubilant sound of the girls pretending to be ladies in the finery of Nellie's old gowns. With her one-month-old baby contented and again asleep, she began dinner preparations, soaking some day-old bread in milk for a bread pudding. Humming cheerfully, she tore the rest of the old bread into little pieces and poured vegetable broth on top, to soak them for a savory stuffing for tonight's dinner of quail.

A disagreement rose over who should carry Nellie's fine beaded bag and who would be stuck with the worn needlepoint purse. The girls' voices grew shriller.

"Hush, you shall wake the baby," said Nellie, looking up from her chopping at the big table.

"It is always Emma's turn for the fancy pocketbook," shouted Elizabeth.

"I am older, and hence, it is simply common sense that I would have the finer bag," said Emma, reaching for the purse.

"No," shrieked Elizabeth, pulling the bag away from her.

Emma tugged back, and beads erupted from the bag, spewing all over the floor.

The baby woke and his outraged crying joined the girls'.

"Mama, I am sorry," cried Emma.

"We broke the beautiful bag," sobbed Elizabeth.

No apology from James. His cries just grow louder. Nellie shook her head. *Such fanciful thinking.*

"*We* didn't break it," Emma said. "*You* did!" She reached two hands to her sister and pinched both Elizabeth's cheeks.

Elizabeth slapped Emma.

Nellie scooped up the baby, trying to comfort him before starting peace negotiations.

Horrors, my sweet daughters exhibiting monstrous behavior!

As she opened her mouth to scold, the two girls looked at each other and burst into fresh tears. Crying, they both said, "I am sorry!" at the same moment. Hugging each other, crying, they repeated, "I'm sorry, I'm sorry."

"You can have the pretty purse next time," said Emma.

"No, you can," sobbed Elizabeth.

Nellie softened. "My dearest little ladies, I think you now see the consequences of fostering discord instead of loving solicitude. You must bear this lesson in mind, for selfish disregard for your sister's feelings profits you not."

Looking at the ruined purse on the floor, Nellie could not help feeling angry still, despite her daughters' immediate penitence. She shook her head. "It makes no matter now. Neither of you need to be selfless, for there is no longer a pretty purse for either of you."

"Mama, we are both sorry," said Emma.

"Yes, I see that, but—"

"We shall pick up all the beads and help you sew them back on," said Elizabeth.

I must change my own heart and accept their apology.

"That's a fine bunch o' colleens, as your grandpapa would say." Nellie smiled, still hugging James to keep him from resuming his protest over the argument of his sisters.

The girls worked hard at picking up the beads while Nellie again attempted making dinner, but every time she settled James in his bassinet, he started to cry. She tried to cook one-handed, but it was nearly impossible. At last, she tied James papoose-style to her chest so she could finish stuffing the fowl.

'Tis long past time to insert it in my beehive oven. Tarnation, the clock shall chime midnight before it cooks to an edible temperature.

Task finally completed, she glanced out the window and noticed the position of the sun on the mountains.

Too late!

Her shoulders slumped in dismay. *Dinner shall not be ready when Mister Wright returns from his daily labor at his office. He shall be most displeased.*

Panic threatening, she scanned vegetables in the root cellar to see what she could prepare to accompany the poultry. Then she changed tack when she realized she could not afford to further retard the cooking process by opening the oven door to insert the vegetables.

She slumped into a kitchen chair.

Of course. Now *my daughters play in complete accord, and sweet little James sighs deeply in his sleep.*

She kissed her slumbering baby on the top of his head, too weary to stand up and get back to work.

The front door banged open and her daughters squealed, "Papa!"

"Hello, my little kumquats," teased Obadiah.

Tarnation! she almost cried out loud when she heard Obadiah's voice

"What's a kumquat?" the girls shouted.

"A fruit that grows far, far away," Obadiah replied.

Mercy, no! He could not possibly have returned early! What could have abbreviated his labor?

She grabbed at some ingredients and redoubled her efforts to finish cooking. Engrossed in her work, she tuned out the happy chatter in the parlor.

Obadiah snuck into the kitchen and grabbed her from behind.

Nellie jumped and dropped the saucepan, splattering hot brown sticky gravy everywhere.

James awoke with a start and burst into a wail at her sudden movement.

"Mercy! Now I wish my only concern remained that I did not have enough arrowroot in the pantry to thicken the gravy," she shouted, tossing the pan on the stove and throwing up her hands.

"Cornelia, how very uncivilized of you, greeting your high-spirited husband with a surly manner," Obadiah's smile turned into a scowl. "Your humorless attitude repulses me. Your ill temper quells my excellent spirits."

"And you have ruined our gravy," Nellie retorted, face twisted in anger.

"'Tis but a trifling occurrence. You can make more. I, on the other hand, have had my good nature trespassed upon."

Nellie choked with anger. "I can make more? Why must you advance your good humor at *my* expense?"

"You must not realize how very homely you look when you allow anger to twist your face like an old witch," Obadiah said.

Nellie wanted to strangle him. She wanted to smite him with her stare. She stood stock still, her one-month-old baby tied to her chest screaming, too angry to move.

"Tsk, tsk. Now your mouth hangs open like a codfish from the Atlantic." Obadiah shook his head.

Biting her tongue, Nellie gathered her wits to blast him with both barrels.

Emma suddenly tugged on her skirt. "Mama, whatever is the matter?" she asked. "Are you and Papa having discord where loving solicitude should reside?"

Hearing her daughter repeat Nellie's own words snapped her anger in half. She sighed, a long and shaky sigh, while Obadiah watched with one eyebrow raised.

"How uplifting, Emma, that you embraced my words to your heart." Nellie bit back her fury but her words still sounded sharp.

She scooped Emma up with one hand and kissed her soft cheek as she bounced up and down to calm James.

She reached her other hand out to Obadiah and said, "Let us begin again. Welcome home, dear husband. My heart leaps with joy when we reunite at the end of a long day."

Obadiah scowled at her but took her hand and gave it a squeeze.

At least this altercation prevented the inevitable question, 'How long will I have to wait until our repast?'

Nellie swirled and kissed the heads of James and Emma.

"How long will I have to wait until my evening repast?" asked Obadiah, still holding her hand.

Nellie allowed Emma to slide to the floor and blinked back tears.

"I merely inquire for I must depart within the hour for an evening meeting with Governor Young and Thomas L. Kane."

"Thomas Kane?" Nellie put her hurt behind her and focused on this new development.

"You must recall the esteemed lawyer, Kane, President Buchanan's crony and fellow Pennsylvanian. I am certain he shall play a crucial role in removing the contention between our newly-appointed governor and Mister Young."

"Is this the same attorney Kane, the Mormon sympathizer, who brokered Brigham Young's original appointment as Governor as part of the Compromise of 1850, permitting Utah to join the United States as a Territory?"

Obadiah nodded. "Yes. The man arrived just a week ago. He still recuperates from an unknown illness. Brother Amasa Lyman found

Kane and his servant sick in the desert. Kane must have taken the southern route and avoided Big Mountain."

"You place trust, and hopes of amicable settlement, in the man who, with John Hyde, lobbied President Fillmore to allow Young's assumption of the power of the governorship in the first place?" she asked.

"Emphatically yes, for I do take this as a good sign. Young knows he has an ally in Kane, therefore, he in turn shall trust Kane's proposals for an end to hostilities."

"So, you have confirmation of actual hostilities?" The panic that seized her heart at this thought caused Nellie's voice to shake as she spoke.

"Only in the sense that President Buchanan's failure to notify Young personally of his termination as governor has renewed Young's fear of religious persecution for himself and his followers. Thus Young strategizes to maintain his mission and the integrity of his kingdom of Deseret."

"Integrity? It seems integrity is a virtue Young clearly lacks. His strategy to date smacks of treason! A seditious refusal to accede to our government's wishes."

Obadiah looked at her with a quizzical expression on his face. "I thought you too rational to make a simpleton's dangerous oversimplification of our current political situation."

Further infuriated by the insult Obadiah heaped on top of his lack of concern for her feelings, Nellie pressed her point. "Brigham Young's term as territorial governor expired in 1854. This being the 1,858th year of our Lord, even Young must acknowledge his tenuous hold upon the governorship. Surely, he concedes that he presides only on an interim basis, and thus must accede to his replacement."

"Your sweeping generalizations distort the complexity and nuance of this situation," said Obadiah. "We must acknowledge that all matters, both religious and secular, revolve around Prophet Young's adjudication."

"Adjudication? Hah! 'Whim' applies more aptly. All matters evolve according to that arrogant self-aggrandizer's whim and fancy. Young has been so much in the habit of exercising his will that no one dares oppose anything he may say or do," Nellie retorted.

Obadiah stroked his mustache. "I'll concede some element of arbitrariness, and a bit of a swelled head, but in diplomatic matters, in order to obtain accord, one must examine the facts from the adversary's point of view."

At least he sees that Young is an adversary, Nellie observed.

"My dear, you shall see, a large part of diplomacy relies on the formation of trustworthy relationships. I shall help build a strong foundation of understanding that accommodates, as best one can, the plight of the other. What conclusions *should* Young draw when rumor, not official notification, advises him of the sudden termination of the mail contract with the United States, and the appointment and dispatch of his replacement, not peacefully or routinely, but in the company of the Army?"

Nellie gasped. "Merciful heavens, all rumors ring true? We surge toward armed conflict? I suspect, although you defend Young, your own frustrations with his foibles simmer beneath your cool analysis."

"Do not jump to conclusions. I can only confirm the facts: the mail contract with the States is canceled, and a new governor has been appointed."

Disappointed at the paucity of information she gleaned, and despondent at the news that she would receive no mail from home, Nellie jiggled the baby up and down as she tried to finish cooking. She saw the futility of making another gravy, too dejected to care if the partridge slices tasted dry.

At last, they all sat at the table, James still hanging papoose-style on Nellie's chest.

She ate rapidly, almost giving herself indigestion, anticipating James's angry, hungry cries resuming any second. She shoveled an herb-encrusted piece of partridge onto her fork and crammed it into her mouth as the expected baby cry rose over the happy table conversation.

The rest of the night was a jumble of nursing while undressing and dressing the girls for bed, reading them a story, and singing them to sleep.

Nellie carefully placed her new son in his bassinet.

James finally sleeps! I shall start with the mess in the kitchen and work my way along to tidying the parlor. Disorder must be rectified.

She looked longingly at a chair at the kitchen table.

No! I shan't sit, for I will never resume my duties.

She cleared the table and looked at the pile of dirty dishes in the washtub.

Perhaps just a short nap shall energize me.

Nellie climbed the stairs to her bedchamber and, fully clothed, dropped on the bed.

She didn't stir until she heard baby James crying.

***

"Do not be deceived by Brigham Young's belligerent public posture," said Obadiah.

All eyes swiveled in his direction.

Nellie flushed with anger. She had hoped to keep the discussion of politics out of just one social gathering.

After I expended all manner of exertion to titivate the house, prepare a feast, lay a beautiful table, and seat our guests for optimum harmony in conversation, the first words out of Mister Wright's mouth plunge us right into the very subject I hoped to avoid. Could he not at least have waited until dessert?

"The Prophet never intends to force a showdown with the United States," declared Obadiah.

Visible relief broke over Thomas L. Kane's face. "Good man," he said, and heartily slapped Obadiah on the back. "My sentiments entirely. We attorneys must maintain reason in this matter. Surely, the rest of the world has lost their respective heads! But we lawyers alone, skilled in debate and persuasion, shall broker a peace. We *must* use our skills to turn the heads of the warring factions to peaceable solutions."

"My mantra exactly, good sir," said Obadiah. To emphasize his enthusiastic support, Obadiah followed suit and clamped his hand on Kane's shoulder.

There was a brief awkward moment where both men stood connected like a broken chain, and then Obadiah slid his hand down Kane's arm and shook hands firmly.

Nellie raised her eyebrows.

Perhaps this line of thinking shall cultivate civility.

Kane cleared his throat. "The Saints hold themselves not as foe to the United States, but rather as allies. Nay, we are countrymen. I formed a lasting bond with many of the brethren during our time in Nauvoo, and I feel only sympathy for the suffering they have endured in the name of righteousness."

Which is the side of righteousness?

Looking around the table as he spoke, Kane leaned forward as if to emphasize his earnestness. "I am called to smooth away the wrinkles of this misunderstanding. We must each follow our own path, true, but there is naught preventing us from allowing those paths to run parallel and unmolested. Good sir, Justice Wright, you speak truth. The Saints fled Nauvoo, Illinois for a space of land outside the ownership and jurisdiction of the United States. Brigham Young asked only for a decade to establish a peaceful kingdom for his people. Yea, that has passed, but now the United States knocks at the kingdom's door."

Nellie could contain herself no longer. "The Mormons emigrated more than a decade ago, when Mexico controlled this land. The end of the Mexican War and the ceding of this territory to the United States now fill the pages of history books. True, Young organized a 'free and independent' government in 1847, but the 'kingdom' has been part of the United States since the very next year, when Congress organized the Territory of Utah."

"I well remember," agreed Kane. "And in deference to their suffering, I thought recognizing the Prophet Brigham Young as the Governor of the Territory the best course to ensure the Saints' survival."

I well ken. 'Tis you we must thank for the perpetuation of the rule of King Brigham.

Nellie sighed.

Methinks the man doth argue too much. No one in this room openly challenges our First Amendment right to separate church from state. Perhaps Attorney Kane merely marshals his thoughts verbally to arm himself with solid reasoning for battles to come.

Obadiah cleared his throat. "I hold hope in the pundits' summations of 'Buchanan's Blunder.' Our President Buchanan embarrassed himself mightily by overreacting and sending the United States Army here before even advising Governor Young of his replacement. Just at a time when the States roil from an economic downturn spurred by a financial panic." Obadiah twirled his mustache, then continued. "Not an ideal time to increase expenditure on our military. The press criticizes him soundly for the costs involved in the dispatch of a squadron of fifteen hundred men. Let's hope this censure results in Buchanan's explicit reconciliation overtures, with olive branch in hand."

Will this discourse slow our menu such that I shall be forced to nurse James as my guests finish the main course?

Taking matters into her own hand, Nellie said, "These discussions offer hope to the ladies that this conflict simmering beneath our daily lives shall be peacefully resolved. But now let us turn our attention to this delicious soup and the abundance of vegetables from our harvest gardens, which keeps us so well fed even in the dead of winter."

Lucena made a loud slurping sound and then covered her mouth, spoon still inside it, with her hand. A short laugh of embarrassment, almost sounding like a bark, caused a splutter of soup to fly and land on the table. "If'n' you want us to talk happy, don't bring up death."

At Nellie's frown, Lucena whispered, "You know, *dead* of winter...."

Nellie laughed and broke the tension. "My dear friend, you are quite right. I must choose my words more judiciously. Let me only speak of winter in terms of skating parties and nights spent cozy in front of a fire."

The other ladies smiled, and happy chatter resumed.

CHAPTER 15
California Dreamin'

Home, Great Salt Lake City, March 1858

Emma and Elizabeth rushed to the baby crib while dressing themselves and got James gurgling with pleasure and excitement too.

Nellie faced the day with her usual happy energy, ignoring her fatigue from her sleepless night.

It goes with the territory, she thought, happily using a new slang.

An easy delivery and a plump happy baby now two months strong proffer the best reward for the nine months of grueling sickness and the long day of labor. What care I that I spend my nights nursing instead of sleeping?

Nellie opened her front door and drew in a deep breath, savoring the freshness of the air swirling downward from the mountains and wafting through the valley. The early spring sun caressed her face and she closed her eyes, thanking God for the blessings surrounding her. She stepped one foot out the front door and bent to collect her bucket on her way to the morning milking of her cow, Hildegard.

People hurried past her garden gate, flying in all directions.

"Whatever could be the trouble?" Nellie wondered.

She spied George Parsons charging up the street and taking the steps into his house two at a time.

Alarmed, Nellie dropped her bucket and ran to the Parsons'. Not even bothering to knock, she charged in.

Lucena stood in her nightdress and dressing gown, lovely with sleepy eyes and tousled hair.

Mercy, she is with child!

George Washington Parsons blurted the punch line. "Brigham just issued a scorched earth policy for the Great Salt Lake City!"

Nellie gasped, but Lucena stood immobile, confusion replacing the sleepy look on her face.

Nellie shouted, "He gave an order to burn the town and scatter elsewhere?" She caught Lucena's now terror-stricken eyes.

George commanded, "Lucena, start packing. We must distance ourselves from this lawless, senseless place and its people."

Nellie said, "No. We must ascertain more information. What provokes this command to flee?"

George turned to Nellie, opened his mouth, then closed it, and said at last, "I'll be hog tied and horse whipped if I know."

"I myself heard Heber C. Kimball speaking yesterday, but I didn't pay no never mind," said Lucena. "I mean the man has fifty wives. If none of those poor miserable women listen to him, why should I?"

Nellie frowned as she waited for Lucena to continue. Finally, she said, "Can you recall any words he spoke which may shed light on this subject?"

"That Apostle Kimball, he holds some tittle like high mucky muck." Lucena shook her head as Nellie silently agreed. "Whot I did heard, that demon Kimball declare, 'I will fight until there is not a drop of blood in my veins. Good God! I have wives enough to whip the entire United States.'"

Lucena took a deep breath and stared at Nellie. "All the preaching and teaching heard in this valley and them poor women's rights is trampled underfoot. Are they gonna keep being obedient to the rulers when not a one of them has as much liberty as common slaves in the South?"

"I wait for the penny to drop," said Nellie.

Lucena started. "Good Lord, have mercy! He's getting his *wives* to fight us? That there Kimball's sentence is just *wrong* for so many reasons. I am leaving. I am."

Nellie whirled to the door. "I shall find Obadiah. He sits at table, waiting for cream for his coffee. He shall have the bottom facts."

As she rushed across the Parsons' front garden and leapt over their little picket fence Nellie thought, *I shall demand an explanation as to why, since my husband is privy to the machinations of that evil Brigham Young, he forewarned me not of this latest disaster.*

She charged into the kitchen.

Obadiah sat reading the morning *Deseret News*. Without extracting his nose from the paper, he held up his coffee cup for cream.

Nellie lifted the back of the kitchen chair and dropped it heavily onto the wood floor.

Obadiah blinked and glanced at her.

"Young issued an order to the *Saints* to evacuate the city and burn it to the ground?" she asked in a low, murderous voice. "We must flee into the wilderness?"

Obadiah's mustache quirked upward with his eyebrows. "Are we *Saints*?"

Nellie shook her head in annoyance. "We must flee?" she repeated.

"We *are* Saints?" Obadiah teased, further irritating Nellie with his calm, condescending question.

Obadiah must have sensed he now played with dynamite. "My sweet Cornelia Rose, *we* are not ordered to scorch the earth and make for greener pastures, only the Mormons who fear the approach of the United States Army.

"I take my cue from Governor Young. I do not see him, or any of his wives, packing. Thus I feel, as a faithful implementer of the Constitution and a loyal citizen of the United States, there is no cause for alarm, and even less reason to pull up stakes and leave our happy home."

Nellie caught her tongue in her teeth and tried to take a breath, but she could not control her panic and anger. "So when the United States Army opens fire on the town, none of the bullets shall find their mark in our family because our Army shall magically know we are loyal citizens and not rebellious Mormons?"

Obadiah fixed a steely look on Nellie, which usually sufficed to silence her.

Not this time.

Heedless of his mounting ire, she plunged on. "Thus, we shall continue to traipse about our daily business, never fearing battle, for *we* are not the object of the Army's mission. That fact alone shall suffice to protect us from any harm. There is no likelihood of any confusion, or any chance we may be caught in the crossfire."

Nellie's chest heaved in and out with anger and fear. She almost snorted in contempt of her husband's blasé attitude.

Obadiah rose and shoved the table. His coffee splashed everywhere. The grating of the table on the wood floor startled the baby, and he woke up with a loud cry.

"Cornelia Rose, you heard it from the very man who accomplished his purpose: Kane's mission succeeded resoundingly. Scouts confirm he arrived at Governor-elect Cumming's camp and convinced Cumming to come to the Great Salt Lake City *without* the United States Army escort."

Nellie picked up the baby and stood, mouth closed, thinking. "The same camp of extreme deprivation at burned-out Fort Bridger?" She shook her head. "Is Brigham not privy to this intelligence? Why would he issue a new scorch and burn order if Kane accomplished his purpose?"

Unfazed, Obadiah replied, "Brigham issued the decree two days ago, before we received the intelligence. This very morning, Kane's scout arrived and confirmed that Cumming, his wife, and the other officials in their entourage agreed to finish the journey to Salt Lake City without the Army, or even a platoon of dragoons."

Nellie stood there soothing the baby, feeling uncertain.

George burst through the kitchen door with Lucena, still in her dressing gown, in tow.

Emma and Elizabeth ran in from the sitting room, dragging their dolls, looks of alarm on their little faces.

"We's leaving today," George panted.

"Not when Lucena is with child," Nellie blurted.

All movement ceased as everyone stared at her.

"How do *you* know *that*?" asked Lucena. "I mean are you sure?"

George growled, "You'd tell your confidante that before you would tell yer own husband?"

The two little girls exclaimed and ran to hug Lucena.

"A real little baby to play with our brother?" asked Elizabeth.

Nellie patted the now-screaming brother, placed him under her chin, and applied a skilled, soothing hand to his warm little back. With only one more complaining cry, the baby nestled in and resumed his snooze.

Nellie caught Lucena's hand with her free one and pulled the younger woman to her. In her ear she whispered, "I have suspected nigh this fortnight. However, my suspicions were not confirmed until I saw you in your dressing gown."

Lucena pulled back and looked at Nellie in horror. "Am I already fat?"

Nellie grinned and pulled her in closer. "No, my silly friend, your breasts have swelled quite noticeably, and your skin has taken on an altogether different, healthy cast."

To the group, Nellie announced, "As a midwife, of course I observe telltale signs long before others. I have studied long and hard and practiced my skill. Mercy, it's my *business* to notice. I do apologize, however. I broke my own code of ethics when I blurted the news aloud. I know fully well this information *always* demands delicate dissipation.

Howsoever, in the heat of the moment, in the alarm of the decree....
Mercy, I do hope you both can forgive me."

Nellie put her arm around Lucena and looked questioningly into
her eyes.

"Of course," Lucena said, and tweaked Nellie's stray strand of
hair.

Still panting and looking overwrought, George flared his nostrils
and asked, "When will George Washington Parsons Junior arrive?"

Nellie suppressed a smile. "We need a bit more information to
predict accurately —"

"Don't start pretending ye don't have the eddy-cation to tell me
now," George ordered. "Will he be borned within the next few weeks
before we can clear the borders of this Territory?"

Nellie's lips widened into a smile. "That much I can predict. I
assure you, your wife shall not birth a baby within the next few weeks.
I do believe you can expect your baby near the end of summer or
beginning of fall."

"Plenty of time to be settled into our own place in California." He
grabbed Lucena around the waist and pulled her toward the door.
"Why we might even be millionaires before my little heir arrives. This
gives us plenty of time to get things established."

"But tarry a moment! Obadiah confides some information only he
seems to be privy to, as to what shall transpire."

Lucena shook her head. "Fiddlesticks, it don't matter. I take this as
a sign I should not spend one more minute with this petty,
complaining, miserable people. I should just die of humiliation if I am
shot by a soldier in our United States Army when it storms this crazy
city, trying to quell them bellicose Mormons and teach them civility.
What will become of those men, the Lord only knows. All I know is I
don't want our Army thinkin' *I'm* one of *them.*"

Obadiah openly smirked at this statement, and Nellie tamped
hysterical laughter down into her stomach.

"Lucena, you should not travel in that condition!" said Nellie.

Lucena raised her eyebrows. "Why ever not, Cornelia Rose?
There's as much comfort on the road as living among these thieving set
of pirates. Besides, everyone travels in this condition. Of the women, I
mean. No man never did. *You* did. At this stage, who would know what
condition I'm in? Exceptin' you, of course."

Laughter fled as an overwhelming sadness deluged Nellie, threatening to generate tears. *Another friend sacrificed to this God-awful place.* But she saw the resolve in both Lucena's and George's faces and knew the futility of further arguments. Blinking back the tears, she asked, "Can you at least wait long enough for me to prepare some herbs and ointments for you in anticipation of the events to come?"

"Of course," replied Lucena with a merry shake of her head. "I shall not leave without those. Moreover, fret not. I heard tell there's springs along the way with water so hot you can boil an egg in five minutes. And enough ducks to keep us better fed than here."

Now Lucena addressed the sobbing Emma and Elizabeth. "I say, do not fear. Your Auntie Lucena shall return, and I shall bring your cousins back to meet you. Or, you can come to Californie to visit, just as soon as we's settled."

George Washington Parsons stood up straight. "It being March, we will take the southern route, advantaging ourselves of the warm but not yet too hot desert trail. We'll cut across Death Valley lickety-split and then skedaddle up them Sierras in May, when they've had good and proper time to warm up."

"But what about your vegetable garden, Aunt Lucena?" asked Emma.

"You won't ever see what you planted," said Elizabeth.

"Well, I ain't planted anything yet. Its only March." Lucena crossed her arms.

Sensing there was no changing their minds now, Obadiah clamped George on the back. "You have a plan then. Let me see if I can't help you arrange some traveling companions and a guidebook to get you to your new destination."

"Maybe we'll ride out with some of the faithful fleeing this city at the direction of their almighty god-king," said George, tight-lipped and humorless.

Lucena hugged Nellie again. "I'm sorry we're a-goin', only because I don't want to leave you here. Getting to Californie was our original dream. We just derailed it a bit on account of the winter coming and—"

"The delicious vegetables?" chimed in Elizabeth.

Everyone laughed, breaking the tension.

"Fiddle-diddle! I was agona say 'the chance to stay with our new-found family,'" Lucena said. "But I didn't want to start myself bawling, jest like I am now."

When Lucena gave a big hiccupping sob, Nellie gathered Lucena in her arms, and Emma and Elizabeth grabbed her skirts.

"Unfortunately, the humors excited by the child you shall bear might cause you extremes in emotions," Nellie said, trying to soothe Lucena.

Lucena pulled out of the embrace, a look of horror on her face.

"With the help of the Lord, the journey should not prove overly taxing," Nellie rushed to assure her.

"Mister Parsons speaks with wisdom. Fortuitously, early spring, from this starting point, offers the perfect conditions to travel to your California destination," agreed Obadiah.

Lucena waved a dismissive hand. "I ain't speakn' to the journey. I jest am skeered because my mother and George tell me I exhibit far too much emotion in the first place. What am I going to be like in *this* condition?"

Everyone laughed again.

George said, "Should I not be the one deathly afraid? Do not fret, sweetkins. I shall be right beside you steering you through the storm of emotions, just as I always do."

After two more rounds of goodbye hugs, the door slammed shut behind the retreating couple.

"Does Aunt Lucena lack some sense," asked Emma, "thinking we shall visit? After all, notwithstanding the reassurances you gave them, Papa, isn't California a whole dangerous mountain journey away?"

My sweet, practical girl, wise beyond her years. Would that she was less knowing and her 'Auntie Lucena' a little bit more.

"Truly," said Nellie, "right now the difficulty of the journey makes visiting improbable, but the day may come when a locomotive line reaches all the way to California, and when it does, we shall jump on board and find Aunt Lucena."

She gave her daughters a hug and said, "You have fifteen minutes to play until breakfast is ready."

Reassured, they scampered down the hall.

Nellie turned to Obadiah. "If the Mormons do burn the city before they go, there will be nowhere to stay. Even if they just don't plant their gardens, there will be nothing left to eat."

"Cornelia Rose, whilst you make a fair point, I do believe Young will retract this order post haste."

She still fretted, "The United States must have conceded more than just assurances Governor Cumming would not bring the Army posse along with him. What further incentives were unjustly bestowed upon Young to sweeten the pot?"

Obadiah raised his eyebrow and tugged at his mustache, as if he would deny her reasoning. "Kane spoke optimistically about the rest of the accord he will broker. Buchanan has offered restoration of full citizen's rights in exchange for a declaration of intent to abide by the constitution and swear allegiance to the flag. Thus, just like the martial law order allegedly in place since October, this simmering situation shall not bubble into a boil. I am privy to additional diplomatic channels very vibrantly engaged in preventing a showdown. I have reassurances not only from Attorney and Diplomat Thomas L. Kane in the makeshift camp outside burnt-out Fort Bridger, but also from our friend Captain Van Vliet in Washington—there shall be no violence."

"Not counting, of course," said Nellie, "the Mormons' continued raiding and looting of our States' Army wagons or the burning of the houses here in Salt Lake City." *Two can play that smug game.*

Obadiah crossed his arms, the ends of his mustache pulling into a deeper frown. "Other concessions shall be required of Young."

"Would that this accord is struck and our worries may cease," Nellie conceded. "In the meantime, we shall remain in the crossfire of any conflagration if all does not go according to plan. Moreover, Kane has only obtained Cumming's assent to the terms, not Brigham's. So they could walk into town and Brigham could refuse to relinquish power."

"True," said Obadiah.

Perhaps it was because he could think of no rebuttal, or perhaps it was a tacit acknowledgement of the intelligence of her reasoning, or perhaps it was simply to reassure her, but he unexpectedly burst out laughing.

Startled, Nellie did not resist when Obadiah swept her into his arms and covered her with kisses.

CHAPTER 16
I Heard It Through the Grapevine

Home, Great Salt Lake City, March 1858

Nellie smiled into the soft, brown-speckled, leather side of her cow Hildegard as she completed the morning milking.

Market day! Going to market energizes my humors almost as much as a full night of sleep. I shan't weep because I have not seen such a night in... oh, so many months. No.

Despite the early morning chill, her fingers flew through their tasks in the barn.

Back inside her house, she heard the hum of activity. Accentuating the positive, Nellie's thoughts of strolling through town, greeting neighbors on the way to market, warmed her more than the crackling stove with her kettle whistling atop.

She caught snatches of happy chatter as her little girls, awake early on market day, looked for ribbons to make their clothes 'fancy.'

A headache threatened to cloud her spirits, due to an impending cold coupled with her chronic lack of sleep. While James slept soundly, Nellie nipped into the pantry and crushed a bit of lavender, added some lemon balm, and inhaled the mixture deeply. She straightened her shoulders and stretched her neck.

That should stem the tide.

"Praise the Lord, all is well but a little congestion. I shan't let this miniscule malady prevent me from enjoying our blessings of the day. Thank you, Savior, for our good fortune," she prayed.

She scrambled around pumping water, scrubbing out the porridge pot, and washing the dishes.

The girls' sense of duty escalated on marketing day, and they eagerly wiped the table and swept the floor.

Nellie changed a dirty diaper, disposing of the waste and tossing the cloth in the soaking bin. As she dressed the baby, she kept one eye on the sweepers.

"Hurrah," shouted the girls when they saw her put on her bonnet. "We are finally ready to go!"

"Yes, retrieve the perambulator." She gathered her purse of coins, her shopping bag, and her gloves.

She inspected her girl's attire with her usual critical eye. Now, in addition to their signs of wear, their dresses hung too high above the knee. Emma's looked washed out. Elizabeth's dress fared far worse—the hem sagged down in the back, material frayed around a patch, and a new rip gaped on one shoulder.

Did I not just mend the other shoulder? Mercy, Elizabeth's bonnet bends at an unnatural rakish angle, and she only wears one glove.

Elizabeth hung her head when she saw her mother looking at her one bare hand, and tried to explain.

Drat.

"No matter, Elizabeth, just wear your one glove and you can search for the other upon our return. Otherwise, we shall never get to market."

She loaded James into the pram and off they went.

It was a beautiful day in Great Salt Lake City. Nellie took a deep breath of the fresh air wafting from the majestic Oquirrh Mountains. She turned her head and looked up to the tips of the Wasatch Range to her right, still capped with snow.

God's glorious handiwork simply surrounds our dwelling with grandeur!

Gazing at the towering mountains filled her with wonder and awe, whether on a daily stroll through the streets of Great Salt Lake City, or peeking out of her window as she cleaned the bedchambers.

As she listened to the girls' excited chatter, she drank in the blue of the cloudless sky and felt the cool breeze of the late winter day ruffle that stray lock of hair that never stayed in place. The smell of spring permeated the air.

They took a short stroll up the neatly organized Second West Street, each dwelling separated by a garden, and turned right on South Temple, which brought them to the center of town. The haze of good feeling so completely engulfed Nellie that the charred remains of fruit-bearing trees in several gardens barely penetrated her consciousness. She lifted the baby buggy over the rivulet of mountain runoff water streaming down the street's water ditches, and her daughters hopped over it, safely crossing them away from the partially abandoned neighborhood to the sole business street. As they passed the post office, the girls squealed with delight upon realizing their destination: the dry goods store for some material for new dresses.

Nellie pushed the pram into the store and her daughters squeezed in around it. The bell tinkled over the door, announcing their presence, and the little group gawked at the abundance of materials and goods ready for the purchasing.

"Felicitations and glad tidings of the day," a cheerful voice called from the back room. A short man emerged, black garters pulling up his sleeves, wiping his hands on a rag. "Well I'll be a cocked hat! If it isn't Missus Wright." The gentleman smiled and scurried behind the big counter.

"Wilburforce Wainright Wells, as I live and breathe, what a delightful surprise to see you in the Great Salt Lake City. Why the last time I laid eyes on you, you and my dearest Rosalinda trudged away on a cutoff path to the Oregon Trail. How ever did you contrive to return here?"

"Well, now, Missus Wright, that is a long and sad tale, perhaps best left for another time, when your little scouts occupy themselves elsewhere." He gave a sad smile.

Correct. Yet if my recollection of his character proves accurate, Mister Wells shall inform me of the particulars in great detail, and promptly, in spite of this need for restraint.

Nellie smiled and waited.

Mr. Wells did not disappoint her.

He brightened, and in his loquacious, optimistic way launched his long story... backwards. "Howsoever, all misfortunes lead the way to fortuitous turns of events. As it happens, just five days ago, when we entered town, I chanced to make the acquaintance of the proprietor of this fine establishment. I immediately sought employment here, and upon being advised only a lowly stock boy position would welcome the likes of me, I turned away, heavy-hearted. But the Missus scolded and told me we must reconstitute our finances. Thus, at Rosalinda's behest, I swallowed my pride, ate crow, and returned."

Nellie stood staring at him, momentarily at a loss for words, still stunned to see the husband of her dear friend standing before her, much less than telling one of his long, drawn-out tales.

"By the Saints!" Wilburforce winked. "Pun intended. I humbly accepted the lowest position, befitting a twelve-year-old boy with only modest intelligence. But by Jingo! I must have performed with stellar alacrity, for after just one day of stocking and unloading like no other stock boy in history, Mister Kearns, the proprietor of this here Kearns Dry Goods Establishment...."

I hope he does not sprain his arm from patting himself on the back.

"...tendered the whole management of his *entire* mercantile operation to me," he concluded, tucking his thumbs into his waistcoat.

"Astonishing!" Nellie said. "Whatever could be the cause of such hasty action?"

"I assure you, 'tis no thumper. My stellar performance, just as I have related, no exaggeration, won me the whole kit and boodle." Wilburforce drew himself to his full 5'4" height and looked offended.

As if he had never had to defend himself against a charge of hyperbole.

She said, "Absolutely. I am sure your work evidenced an eager obedience, a quick mind and outstanding work ethic, altogether an exemplary performance. Howsoever, you must grant, on its face, the gesture of entrusting a store full of inventory and a shopkeeper's whole livelihood to a stranger does seem rather unusual."

"'Tis only temporary," Mr. Wells admitted with a chuckle. "Mister Kearns mumbled something about emergency business out of town, urgent travel required. Upon swearing upon my good honor, a promise to extract only my wages from the cashbox, be fully accountable and keep the store in good stead for him, I was handed an apron and a set of keys. Mister Kearns should be returning bimonthly."

In two weeks or two months?

Fear raced through Nellie's heart as frantic thoughts tumbled through her brain. *Yet another prosperous Mormon family pulling up stakes, fleeing town, at Young's incitement to war? Brigham's 'scorched earth' policy continues? Did I not notice the vacant houses on our path to the market? Have negotiations ceased? Have diplomatic channels closed? Why does Obadiah not immediately apprise me of all developments?*

She renounced these thoughts and forced herself to listen to Wilburforce Wells.

"After one additional day of intense training on the whole operation... *voila*... here I stand, sole proprietor myself. Better than any Oregon land claim could offer, even if it were free of displaced tribes scalping pioneers right and left."

"Merciful heavens! You encountered...?" Nellie interrupted herself to locate her daughters.

Wide-eyed and open-eared, they stood on either side of her, absorbing Mr. Wells's entire tale.

Wilburforce cleared his throat. "Suffice it to say, me and Missus Wells settled ourselves just down the street in Block 79. We rent a house left unburned and partially furnished by a man named Elijah Fordham, and we hope to make ourselves a right proper living with me as the trusted employee of Mister Kearns in his fine Dry Goods establishment."

He motioned around the establishment. "I thank the good Lord for the frugality and parsimony of the Mormons. Even at the request of their revered Prophet, they balk at burning their thriving enterprises. It seems enough sacrifice, even to them, to pull up stakes and resettle. I am one lucky Gentile that I reside a step above destruction of good material."

"Goodness!" exclaimed Nellie. She looked down at her girls who still hung on every word. "And when did you begin this next exciting chapter of your life in the Great Salt Lake City?"

"Today is my first day at the helm of this good ship enterprise." Mr. Wells beamed at her.

Nellie shook her head. "My mind whirls like a spinning Jenny at this unexpected turn of events. I trust all in the family are well? And whatever became of Lemuel? I am quite curious to hear further details."

Uncharacteristically, Mr. Wells said no more.

Mercy, horrific events surely transpired, for Mister Wilburforce Wainright Wells, known for his rambling tongue even when he has naught to say, to exercise this much discretion in speech.

She said, "Prithee, 'tis a welcome, pleasant surprise. It is a right pleasure to see you. I shall call upon Rosalinda forthwith! 'Twill surely act as an elixir for my ills to reacquaint with my intimate companion."

Emma and Elizabeth stood stock still, on either side of the pram, as if mesmerized by Mr. Wells's saga.

"Shall we get down to business then? I seek material for new dresses for my two girls."

The magic words 'new dresses' broke the spell. The girls squealed again and jumped up and down, clapping.

Nellie gave a smile at the respite.

Thank heavens the prospect of a new frock buys me some time before the barrage of their questions. Such startling information to process and absorb. Why did Rosalinda not seek me the second her feet touched the city limits?

She caught the girls' hands and they faced the counter.

Wilburforce Wells smiled and reached for the black velvet. "Only the finest for the Wright family, I assume. This is imported from—"

"Ahem," she coughed, her smile frozen on her face. "I believe...." Her mind searched frantically for words with enough diplomacy to avoid offending Wilburforce by rejecting his overpriced and overreaching suggestion, while at the same time not embarrassing herself or Obadiah by her frugality.

"Summer awaits, just around the corner. Thus, I believe calico more suits my fancy," she said in a rush.

The girls jumped up and down again and she swung their hands in relief.

"My little ladies, what color would we like?"

Their eyes grew round as they leaned their heads back and looked at the multiple rows of bolts of material.

"Pink," shouted Elizabeth.

"Lilac," shouted Emma at the same time.

Nellie frowned, regretting Mr. Wells giving them a choice.

Can I afford two separate cloths? Won't Obadiah already disapprove of my unilateral decision to spend money for dresses for both girls?

She cringed, already hearing him chastise her: *'I see nary a fault with Emma's dress. If it be too faded for Sunday wear, certainly Elizabeth requires no further addition to her wardrobe than a perfectly adequate play dress.'*

But I've already promised Elizabeth a new dress of her own — new, unworn.

It would be her first. Hand-me-downs, albeit beautiful ones, from not only Emma but all the older cousins, had filled her clothing needs. Now Elizabeth reached the age of realization of the slight.

After all, Obadiah commands a respected position in town now. Even if this town rapidly transforms into a ghost town as I stand here....

Moreover, what could be the cause of Rosalinda's reticence to call upon me? I am her dearest friend. At least this side of the Continental Divide!

Halting her runaway thoughts, Nellie considered the purchase at hand.

I must present well-turned-out girls when we appear at services on Sunday. If I sew another ruffle on the bottom of Emma's dress, I can stretch its use as an everyday dress for several more months.

She reached a decision. She would buy Elizabeth a new Sunday dress, Emma's old one being too old for Elizabeth to wear to Sunday services, even if it be only for the Mormon congregation. No, *especially* for the prosperous Mormon's worship. The Wright family must exude prosperity, despite the obstacles placed in their path.

Would that one day we have a choice of a church of a different denomination. But for now, we must embrace our enemy and keep our ear low to the ground, which is only possible if one attends the service, to hear, right from the horse's mouth, the latest conniving of Brigham.

Nellie tugged her hair until she reached another decision. She had promised both daughters new dresses; now she must honor her own word.

After all, calico possesses the honor of least expensive fabric. I shall trim the frocks with some lace and 'twill seem luxurious to my daughters. All sorts of ribbons and trimmings festoon my old cambric gown. It shall be none the poorer for the purloining of a few. Besides, I no longer foresee any occasion to wear such fancy garb and, in any case, a total reworking can only improve my dress. My resolve increases with the certainty that my daughters shall rejoice in their new finery.

"Mister Wells, show us both your lavenders and your pinks," Nellie said with a decisive nod of her head, and she pressed forward to the counter.

"Ma'am, 'twould be my pleasure. As a matter of fact, you arrived at a precisely perfect moment. We seem to have a temporary lull in demand and thus a cornucopia of lavender calicos to make your heart sing, and pink to make your toes dance, and some fabric with both lavender *and* pink!"

His verbosity lends itself handily to the task of shopkeeper, obviating any disadvantage his inexperience might cause.

The girls tried to jump up on the counter, pulling up and shimmying their toes up the front. That failing, with one accord they took a step back to watch Mr. Wells unroll the bolts of fabric. Nellie stifled a smile as her daughters raised themselves on tiptoes, swaying as they tried to balance.

After filling the long counter with as many choices as he could, Wilburforce paused, a shrewd glint in his eye, observing which materials Nellie fingered.

He noticed the two girls step back agin, craning their necks for a better view.

"This is certainly not acceptable!" he said and stomped over to them.

The girls panicked. Emma shied away and Elizabeth hid behind Nellie's skirts.

But Wilburforce charged right past them. He rolled a pickle barrel over to the counter, stood it next to Nellie, then turned and swept both girls in his arms and put them on top of the barrel.

They giggled with delight and began to run their hands over the material, exclaiming over the pretty colors.

"Mama, how can I ever decide?" asked Elizabeth.

"Yes," agreed Emma, "every fabric that I see, that is my favorite fabric!"

Nellie laughed. "Mister Wells, mayhap we should leave my darling daughters a bit of time to ogle their choices, whilst you assist me with the rest of my purchases."

She took out her list and kept Wilburforce hopping for ten minutes, finding thread, measuring out flour and sugar, and parceling the spices and herbs she required until her own garden flourished.

"I'll be a paunchy plume-plucked pignut! Why would one merchandise hammers and nails in this location?" Nellie heard Wilburforce mutter to himself as he rounded a corner on his way back to the counter.

"Perhaps your supply of lard is running low?" he asked, when Nellie ticked the last item off her list.

"Thank you kindly, but no. That pig I fattened all fall and killed last month shall keep us stocked clean till next spring. A right plump one was that dear old thing." She smiled and extended her basket, waiting for Wilburforce to start tallying her order.

But his excessive loquaciousness turned into overzealous salesmanship, topped with rumormongering. Wilburforce presented item after item, pressing her to increase her purchases while he told of certain Elders' new brides.

"Look-y here," he said. "You will most definitely require a new needle for the hours of sewing required to stitch your daughters' fashionable new dresses." He led her to the case where different size needles were displayed. "My first sale this morning was to Elder Morill's new bride. She bought four new needles to sew her wedding dress. Might I add, 'twas a beautiful black gabardine, imported from France. You mustn't work this fine new material using your old rusty needles. 'Twould sabotage the endeavor from the pistol start."

"Wilburforce Wainright Wells, my needles lay await in fine form, thanks to the handsome pincushion my daughters helped me make with some love and their baby hair. Just the precise combination of elements to prevent any form of rust, thank you very much," said Nellie, getting impatient to tally her order.

Wilburforce leaned over the counter and said in a low tone, "Have you heard that the States don't abide by Mister Young's story that the Mountain Meadows Massacre was just a bunch of ornery savages?"

Nellie drew in her breath sharply.

Massacre?

Who was murdered?

When did this occur?

Seeing that he had her attention, Mr. Wells continued, "Yessir, I have it on good authority, just this week Congress ordered an official investigation of the Massacre to determine jist what went on what how."

This startling news left Nellie speechless. How could a man so recently arrived in the City already hold an overabundance of knowledge, when she had not heard even a rumor of a massacre?

Wells never noticed her silence. Perhaps from many years of long monologues, Wilburforce never anticipated dialogue.

Does Wells speak of the tribal attack last September on an Arkansans' wagon train bound to California gold? Had that resulted in a massacre? No report of deaths appeared in the Deseret News.

Nellie tugged her stray strand of hair, trying to recall hearing any whisper of bloodshed, much less a massacre.

Is this related to an incident my husband noted in passing, when travelers inadvertently trespassed upon tribal land? Surely an incident such as this needs no further scrutiny.

"I'll be a logger-headed lout," Wells continued, "if the investigation into the Mountain Meadows Massacre does not reveal some malfeasance."

Ordinarily, she held no stock in rumors, as counseled by Obadiah.

But why has Obadiah made no mention of a Mountain Meadows Massacre? *The States launched an official investigation? Surely, as an officer of the court, my husband is privy to federal government official inquiries, especially ones that occur in his own backyard. Certainly his participation in such an undertaking should be part of his professional responsibilities.*

Not even noticing Nellie's silence, having exhausted his knowledge on the subject of the massacre, Wells launched into a long and convoluted tale about the Elders' counsel. She listened with only one ear as she puzzled over Wells's information about the massacre. When she refocused on the drone of Wells's voice citing the instances of collusion among the Elders to proliferate only Latter-day Saint commerce and prevent 'gentile' competition, thus precluding him from capitalizing on his sutler's experience, Nellie tried to interrupt, but to no avail.

She tried another tack. "Girls, have you chosen your fabric?"

The girls both began speaking to her at once, but Nellie felt relief rather than her usual annoyance.

"Mister Wells, whilst I sort out our final purchases of the cloth, and perhaps some trimmings, can I impose on you to make the rest of my goods travel-ready, and tally our bill? I fear my baby James's good humor shall not last much longer. We dare not risk his unhappiness, for the rest of us shall suffer too!"

"I have neglected to properly welcome the new Wright member of the family," said Wilburforce. He reached into the baby carriage and wiggled the baby's foot. "With a new son, might I interest you in the finest wood cradle just crafted—"

James opened his eyes and let out a squawk of protest.

Wilberforce, spurred into action by the threat of a screaming baby, stopped his sales pitches and ramblings immediately. He covered his ears and trotted behind the counter. Without a word, he began computing her purchases and packing the goods into the pram.

Nellie picked up her son and soothed him. "He certainly displays the attributes of a *logger-headed lout*," she whispered to James.

The happy group left the dry goods store with not only lavender and pink cloth, but also a bit of pink material with lilac flowers, and lavender material with pink and blue flowers. At the last minute, Nellie's resolve against Wilberforce's hard sell weakened, and she impulsively purchased some pretty buttons, and both lavender and pink ribbon for trim.

Mr. Wells tipped his cap to her as he followed her out the door. "I sure do thank you for gracing my first day of employment with your presence. Rosalinda shall be delighted to hear...."

James's loud squeals of protest drowned out the rest of Wilburforce's speech.

They hurried back to the house, the girls skipping with excitement and chattering about their new dresses. Her daughters imagined an endless stream of fine occasions for which the dresses would be suitable.

Nellie let them prattle on, the new worry of a massacre consuming all her attention.

***

Nellie wished to dash out the second they finished their delicious supper.

"I must pop in to welcome Rosalinda to the neighborhood. Apparently, she arrived just a few days ago. Mister Wells decried her frenzy of frustration trying to find lodging and establish a proper homestead."

"Our daughters need to cozy into bed," protested Obadiah. "Our son needs nourishment and a settling of his own. How can you think of visiting at this late hour?"

Nellie frowned. "I hold Rosalinda as my dearest companion." She laughed. "This side of the Rocky Mountains, at any rate. Imagine my joy at discovering her presence in this tumultuous, treacherous place. I must see her at once."

"Why has she not called upon *you*?" Obadiah asked, and frowned. "If 'twere a priority, surely by today she could have arranged her affairs sufficiently to call."

"But she did! Wilburforce exclaimed that she sought to meet me today. Ironically, I believe she arrived at our house at the exact moment I stood in the dry goods store, speaking to her husband. I can wait no longer. I must go now."

"You must wait until the morning. After a long day of work and negotiations, I require rest and reflection, not the added duties of childcare," said Obadiah.

Nellie sputtered, "Added duties?"

Obadiah held up his hand. "In anticipation of your proposal that we all go, I balk at the upheaval of the domestic tranquility I hold sacred. Furthermore, there are dishes to be washed and nightgowns to find."

"You have demoted my entire merit to mere domestic servant? Convenient to keep, useful to employ for attending to the house, yet not worthy of updates on the status of the precarious balance of power in this territory?"

Obadiah folded his paper with a sigh. "I see we have broadened our discussion from the inappropriateness of your late night visiting to our very existence in this city in the first place. May I remind you that I am under no obligation to advise you of my decisions for this family, much less than consult with you before making any such decisions."

This statement belies and demoralizes the entire basis for our marriage.

Stung by that rebuke, Nellie stood in stunned silence, like a wounded animal arrested by a shot to the heart.

Oblivious, Obadiah continued. "I have determined we shall not leave until Young himself departs. I know he still exhorts his fellow Saints to burn their farms and re-settle South. I well ken his strategy: he employs extreme measures to prevent the United States Army from profiting from the thriving community established here by the industrious Mormons. But he himself shows no sign of leaving his well-appointed house, his overflowing coffers, or his many wives."

Nellie's stricken face now filled with fear.

Merciful Lord, I have not time to dwell upon Obadiah's shattering of my illusion of a cooperative union. I must ponder the ramifications of the events he has withheld from me, yet now confirms!

"Yea, I know he has sent scouts to determine possible alternative locations for this thriving city, but he shall not leave until he receives their report and finds somewhere viable."

Nellie remained standing, stock-still, while Obadiah continued his tirade. "Moreover, I also know for a fact that diplomatic channels still thrum with activity. Both the United States Federal Government and the Church of the Latter-day Saints toil to find a mutually acceptable resolution to this state of affairs without coming to blows."

Nellie could keep quiet no longer. "In spite of the rampant rumors the Mormons burned Fort Bridger to the ground last fall and sabotaged every supply train, leaving our Army stranded and starving in the early snowstorm in October, you believe they seek peace?"

Obadiah did not reply, just frowned at Nellie while tugging his mustache.

She burst into tears.

Obadiah held out his arms. "Cornelia Rose, my faithful wife."

She buried her tear-streaked face into his waistcoat.

He stroked her hair and whispered into it, "Truth be told, I wish you to remain here only because I am loath to delay for one more moment the quintessence of the day—you and I side by side in front of the fireplace, engaging in convivial conversation."

Nellie lifted her wet eyelashes to gaze at him.

He winked. "Or, far better, engaging in that cherished silent communication—that language only we two share."

He kissed her, and all thoughts of visiting vanished as the familiar pull of desire tingled through her.

CHAPTER 17
Before You Came

Home, Great Salt Lake City, March 1858

Nellie bounced out of bed the next morning before the roosters even stirred.

Today I shall reunite with Rosalinda!

That excited thought propelled her through the morning chores. She provided James with her usual loving chatter during their morning feeding routine, but she made several trips to her pantry to assemble breakfast supplies while nursing, and breakfast landed on the table in record time.

Less than an hour after breakfast, Nellie and her children burst through Rosalinda's front door in an explosion of happiness.

Lemuel jumped on the backs of her daughters as they both hugged Adelaidia. Baby Priscilla crawled to them and tugged at their skirts.

Nellie and Rosalinda watched this chaos from their own embrace.

"I searched for you yesterday," said Rosalinda. "I longed to fly to your side upon arrival in the city, but they veritably trapped us at the Bowery. Just as soon as we moved out of the square and into a rented house, I departed for your newly obtained address. Our good fortune astounds me! Not only have we found a fully furnished house, but it comes with a job for Wilburforce and a full cellar of last fall's harvest."

Nellie grimaced.

First some pleasantries. Then I shall explain her good fortune.

"You just missed Lucena," said Nellie. "She and Mister Parsons fled from town with the first bunch of Mormons brainwashed enough to listen to the prophet."

"'Tis a true tragedy." Rosalinda smiled. "I did enjoy her inadvertent interjections of comedy."

Nellie giggled. "Truly. Howsoever, in these turbulent times, Lucena the jester became a dear and cherished friend. Her companionship at times was the only thing preventing me from snatching up my babies and crawling back to Sing Sing, New York."

Rosalinda raised an eyebrow.

"I concede the point," Nellie cried and clasped her hands together. "I do confess her naiveté provided quite the comic relief to many a tense day. I felt gifted with a new little sister, utterly dependent upon me for guidance and right reasoning."

Rosalinda indicated the bundle in Nellie's arms. "A son! I knew you carried a boy!"

Nellie showed James's little pink face to Rosalinda, who stretched out her arms to hold him.

Baby safely in her arms, Rosalinda smiled and took a deep breath. "I know it has not been that long since I held little Priscilla like this, but I do miss this precious infant phase. Moreover, nothing smells quite so wonderful as a new baby."

Elizabeth ran over holding her nose. "Not all the time!" she said, and ran back over to the other children.

Smiling, Nellie said, "Now delay no further. Regale me with tales of your voyage and the miracle that brought you back to the Great Salt Lake City."

Rosalinda shuddered. "A harrowing experience. No. A series of unending harrowing experiences, too horrible to dismiss as one event."

"The frigid temperatures and the deprivation of food and water?" Nellie asked with sympathy. "Yes, winter roosts early in the mountains."

"Frigid temperatures were the least of our worries. Deprivation? No. I saved many provisions in preparation for extreme deprivation. Cornelia, I am loath to confide even in you. I never want to recall the events that changed our course again." Grinding her jaw, Rosalinda shook her head. "Heaven save me, one incident shall haunt me forevermore."

"Now you simply must purge your thoughts, for any terror might be lessened through examination of the nightmare within the safety of our new home."

"With all due respect, you know not of what you speaketh." Rosalinda wore a rueful expression as she considered Nellie.

"Mercy! It sounds quite the atrocity. Mayhap I do not want to hear your tale."

Rosalinda looked down at her hands. "Perhaps it may alleviate some of the nightmare if I satisfy your curiosity without furnishing the worst of the macabre details."

Nellie nodded. "That sounds mighty considerate of you, for whilst I do want to help you bear the burden of this memory, it gives me no *schadenfreude* to hear of your misfortunes, nor do I have an inkling of desire to hear of blood and gore."

"I shall start at the beginning, at our parting of ways. We trekked for days and finally reunited with the other members of our wagon company heading for Oregon Territory."

At Nellie's blank look, Rosalinda said, "Do you not recall our friendly companion, Sarah Davies? The woman who gave her son's castoffs to clothe poor Lemuel when he crawled out of the river naked and orphaned?"

"Why certainly. I am sure my puzzled look merely reflected my inability to recall the point at which you might have intersected the others from our company, as you left our train after the point dubbed 'Parting of the Ways.' I made extensive study of Mister Wells's prize possession—the trail map drawn by the presidential candidate John C. Fremont. As I recall, Mister Wells planned your change of destination from his constant examination of the routes, hell-bent on using his Fremont-drawn map."

Rosalinda rolled her eyes. "True, you rightly recap the condensed version of the drama."

"But for the elevated status of the man who drew that map, you mayhap would have traveled directly here!" Nellie smiled, lovingly poking fun at her quirky friend.

"Truly, my Mister Wells fixated upon that document." Rosalinda giggled. Then she shook her head. "It proved its worth when circumstances forced us again to change destinations. After our belated decision to strike out to Oregon instead of California, the Fremont map-inspired route led us to intercept our old company train a few miles before Smith's Trading Post. In fact, I do believe 'twas at the foot of Big Hill." Rosalinda pressed her fingertips to her eyes and drew a deep shuddering sigh. "Suffice it to say the few womenfolk left in the train, all except Sarah, had their wits scattered for fear of the Shoshone. Traders at Thomas Fork Crossing had frightened the bejeebers out of them with tales of the restless and vengeful nature of that tribe.

Angered by pioneer trespass across their hunting ground, and failure of the United States to pay its promised annuities, the Shoshone exacted their own price for our crossing. Fear of further attack deprived the company of campfires, singing, and any joy previously felt in travel. All activity required stealth and watchfulness whilst making camp. And whilst Mister Wells and I looked sympathetically upon their apprehension, we did scoff at their stealth."

Nellie raised quizzical eyebrows.

"'Tis well known that amongst all the great stalkers and hunters of the tribes who inhabit this land, the Shoshone top the list. Any *stealth* we employed 'twas folly. Of course, these great warriors knew our exact whereabouts at all times. Thus, it came to pass...." Rosalinda broke off in a sob.

Nellie scooted over on the couch and put a comforting arm around her friend.

Rosalinda buried her face into Nellie's shoulder. Silent sobs wracked her body.

After a moment, Rosalinda spoke into Nellie's shoulder. "Shoshone attacked the wagon train ahead of us. Merciful Lord, Cornelia, there but for the grace of God go I."

Nellie held her and kissed the top of her friends' head.

"The atrocities. Mercy. The agony we witnessed when we assisted the nearly dead and half dead people who survived." She shuddered. "We made our best attempts to help the injured. We buried the dead. We could do nothing for the emotional distress of the few remaining living! Bloody hell. *Bloody hell!* 'Twas neigh impossible to calm the distraught."

Nellie had never heard her friend curse, despite suffering no end of trying situations together on the trail.

"I stumbled upon a woman, great with child, left for dead, lying behind an upturned wagon, bleeding. I had the gruesome task of bandaging her head."

Nellie shook her head, confused.

Rosalinda hung hers. "She was scalped."

Nellie gasped, and reflexively both she and Rosalinda put their hands over their hair.

"Did she survive?"

"Yes, but several other members of her family expired. Somehow, after this woman was left for dead, she managed to crawl to a stream and soak her bleeding head, staying alive until we found her."

Barely whispering now, she said, "We found an infant, brains dashed against a tree and prepared him for Christian burial."

Tears streamed down both women's faces. Sorrow and fear spread through Nellie like a paralyzing poison.

Rosalinda sobbed. "I could not soldier on after this. Mayhap all these free plots granted by the government are in fact on tribal land? We had never inquired, for our destination was always California gold. When we reached Smith's Trading Post, all the news contained reports of attacks on settlers. Even those already settled on homesteads in Oregon.

"Free land? No sir. It seems the land at our new destination rightfully belonged to the Cayuse Tribe. At least that is what a friendly squaw at the post told me. She claimed her tribe of Walla Walla fled from near that land when the settlers began occupying the valley."

Rosalinda examined her hands, shaking in her lap. "I know not what to believe, but that people suffer on both sides of this thorny issue. The squaw, tears streaming down her face, burdened me with her confidences. I could not fathom it—a tribeswoman displaying emotion? I do believe no pioneer had ever been civil to her, much less than sympathetic. She told me, 'All that is left of our tribe in our home village are the remains of my bean and maize plants'."

Nellie could barely process all her friend said. "Such mistrust and ill will on both sides."

Rosalinda shuddered, then sighed. "I cannot fathom a solution. Native peoples deprived of their lands. White settlers duped into occupying it. I just could not imagine living in constant fear and dread of attack. I could not witness any further devastation. The heartbreak I barely survived and the sorrow I witnessed in others far exceeds my wildest nightmares."

Rosalinda wiped a tear and rubbed her heart, as if to wipe away the pain. "What can be done to accommodate the needs of both civilizations now? Except maybe our United States Government should confess—*free land* does not exist. Free *always* exacts a price. Hard work and my own deprivations I am willing to suffer, but not at the expense of a pre-existing tribal nation."

Tears still flowing, Nellie squeezed her friend's hand. "Your golden heart shines with compassion."

Rosalinda sighed. "My anxiety and uncertainty overwhelm me. Perhaps only selfishness motivated my decision, with winter bearing down upon us just as we *settle* into the wilderness. It's not as if already grown vegetables thrived on the promised *free land*."

"Unless you found that squaw's abandoned garden," Nellie interrupted. "You could have been full of beans."

Rosalinda burst into tears.

Nellie wrapped her arms around her friend. "My humble apologies! I merely sought to interject some humor. My heartless and insensitive comment reeks of callousness, when such tragic loss and agony occur on both sides of this issue."

"'Twould be impossible to state such an unbiased opinion if you had seen what I saw," sobbed Rosalinda.

They both shuddered.

"Therefore, Wilburforce and I resolved at Soda Springs to turn around. Fortunately, a trader there told us of the Bidwell-Bartleson route following Bear River, intersecting with the Oregon Trail just after Sheep Rock. Wilburforce again poured over his Freemont maps."

Nellie gave a weak smile and again attempted levity. "How well I remember Mister Wells's statement, spoken so often it became his mantra: 'Drawn by none other than presidential candidate John C. Fremont in exquisite detail so as to guarantee a pioneer cannot lose the Overland Trail'."

Rosalinda's lips twisted but grief prevented them from obtaining a smile. "Yes, surely. It proved its worth, for that map allowed us to realize that since we'd already bypassed Bear River Range, we did not have to retrace our steps, but rather could travel south via the Bidwell-Bartleson route to join you in the Great Salt Lake City. Might as well step into the *Beehive* as travel around it," said Rosalinda, grim line to her jaw.

"A noble pun, my cherished friend," Nellie said.

Rosalinda nodded. She still could not smile. "As I confirmed with my very first sights of the town, we have arrived back in civilization with no fear of Indian attack. Thanks be to God."

Nellie stared at her friend.

Rosalinda shook her finger at Nellie. "I risk life and limb to not only reunite with you, but to join you in your chosen place of settlement, and you, of all people, my wordsmith, have no welcoming, kind words for me?"

Nellie tugged at her stray hair. "Firstly, you risked life and limb *before* you made your decision to retreat and rejoin a civilization which contained me."

Rosalinda made a face.

Nellie winked. "Although I should be insulted, I welcome you with open arms and with humble gratitude, thanking the Lord for your safe return to me."

Rosalinda, using the jesting discussion as a way to let off steam, said, "The Bidwell trail presented many treacheries. Recall—not all the Bidwell party survived!"

Nellie shook her head, almost with an abstracted gesture. "'True, true, but rumor has it, not far from here, this past September 11th, a normally peaceable Paiute Tribe attacked a wagon train of pioneers. Allegedly, more than 100 settlers were killed, many women and children."

"Obadiah's legal terms and phrases creep into your lexicon."

A small smile flitted across Nellie's lips, but it had no strength to lift the frown from her forehead. "Your husband alluded to the rumours and the federal inquest to ascertain the true facts of the tragic incident."

Rosalinda said, "But Indians do not dare to sneak into this huge, civilized city and attack these well-established homes."

"Assuming the culprits of this atrocious act *are* in fact Paiute." Nellie sighed. "Upon reflection, it makes no sense. What riled the nonbelligerent tribe out of kilter?" She paused as fresh fears of nefarious treacheries raced through her heart. *'Tis useless to speculate until I can ferret more information.* She tried to clear her head by shaking it. "Perhaps you are correct. Still acting governor Young also holds the position of this territory's Indian Agent. Thus, whilst there is no fear of *tribal* attack here, our potential from ambush comes from within."

"Have you truly switched camp from a defender of the Saints to an antagonist to their cause?"

Nellie dropped her hair-fiddling hand. "I admit that whilst still journeying here, I maintained an optimistic viewpoint from which I excused any rumors of malfeasance as a confirmation of the sect's persecution. I still cherish the company of individual Mormons. Howsoever, the overarching scenario does give me pause. Did you not wonder at your extreme fortune at finding a fully furnished house, complete with a fully stocked larder and cellar?"

Rosalinda cocked her head and gazed at her friend.

Nellie's hand crept back up to her hair. "Your heart-wrenching story mingles with my oft dire thoughts on the political turmoil here. It percolates just below the surface of my otherwise happy life and leaves me with the burning question: 'Out of the frying pan, into the fire?'"

Rosalinda stirred her tea while looking at her friend, waiting patiently.

Nellie tried to pick her words carefully. "Since our arrival, the stream of wagons through this territory has dried to droplets."

Rosalinda rubbed her forehead. "Speaketh we in riddles now?"

Nellie smiled. "Riddles seem the perfect medium for communicating the fear, rumours, ill-ease and unrest that predominates this town. In fact, the whole town is a riddle, or maybe a puzzle with unturned pieces."

Rosalinda threw up her hands. "Out with it," she commanded.

"Did you not notice any unrest, anything unusual as you approached this city?"

Rosalinda shook her head and tapped her foot.

Nellie slapped her own forehead. "Of course. Now I recall the trail on Wilburforce's map. You did not pass through Emigration Canyon, you journeyed past Sheep Rock, along the west side of the Wasatch Range, through Brigham City."

Rosalinda nodded her head and said, "Correct. Once we crossed Hampton Ford, the journey progressed with little effort. Although winter chased us down the mountain, we trekked through fledgling towns, bunking down for the night in cabins, watching civilization and cultivation increase incrementally as we inched closer."

Nellie gave her hair one final tug and poured out her fears. "But you must have passed the burnt Fort Bridger? The hastily erected Fort Scott where a legion of our United States Army ekes out its survival while a tempest of turmoil percolates in the Great Salt Lake City?" Nellie shook her head and rejected her own theory. "Mercy, no! I've twisted around again. Your path went the opposite way. No matter. Everyone here is on edge. Young has his faithful filled with a steady diet of rumor and incendiary words."

"Whatever plagues this city?"

"The United States Army approaches, accompanying a new governor."

"Replacing Saint Brigham?" Rosalinda rolled her eyes. "Is that not a wonderful development?"

"The *Saint* vows to fight for his job, using his armed forces if necessary!"

Rosalinda gasped. "He marshaled his own army?"

"Obadiah assures me naught shall happen until spring. The new governor, surrounded and protected by a posse of the United States Army, encamps near Fort Bridger for the winter. This stalemate began in November, yet in the meantime, nasty rumours of skirmishes circulate the City. Do you remember Mister Beauregard Clayton from our wagon company?"

Rosalinda stirred more cream into her tea as she thought. "The man that never spoke? I cannot picture him, but I do remember his abrasive wife. The woman's dour expression never changed and she never met a complaint she didn't utter."

Nellie smiled at the accurate summation of the couple. "Dead spot on! The Claytons' destination changed as well. Mister Clayton obtained employment as a scout for a captain in the United States Army trying to broker peace. Thus, Mister Clayton confirmed the hearsay of dark deeds. Clayton informed me that a group of Mormons, led by a notorious henchman of Young, a black angel, Mister 'Wild Bill' Hickok, burnt Fort Bridger to the ground."

Eyes wide and staring, Rosalinda whispered, "Mercy, we *have* jumped *into the fire!*"

"Rumours run rampant." Nellie, pleased to see Rosalinda put down her knitting and pay complete attention, continued, "Loyal States citizens speculate Brigham Young and Wild Bill Hickok conspire to commit treason."

"Have you befriended many loyal citizens?" Rosalinda asked.

Nellie looked sheepish. "To tell the truth, Lucena constituted the entire community of loyal citizens."

"So *she* provided the intelligence that Young engages in treasonous acts?"

Nellie laughed. "When phrased that way, I see your skepticism. But no, I have been privy to the information divulged by various dinner guests, most notably diplomats who have endeavored to broker peace. They and my husband supply snippets of nefarious events involving Hickok and Young."

Rosalinda looked thoughtful. "Might I have stumbled upon this dark angel hanging around the Bowery when we entered town?"

Nellie nodded, a grim expression on her face. "The very same way I made the blackheart's acquaintance. Although I'll wager Obadiah stumbles upon him daily, for I understand the man is attached to Young at the hip."

Rosalinda nodded, processing every word.

"Except when burning forts and destroying our States' Army supplies," Nellie continued.

Rosalinda said, "The man must constantly endeavor to earn his nomenclature of 'wild bill.' Although, with a face like that it isn't any wonder his nickname isn't—"

"Duckbill!" they both said at the same time.

The women enjoyed a brief laugh.

I must cease lest this laugh turn hysterical.

Nellie sighed and said, "In the meantime, spring approaches. Yes, diplomats *may* be able to avert war...."

"*War?*" shouted Rosalinda, astonished.

"Precisely," said Nellie. "Obadiah adamantly holds the Mormons wage no war, nor will there be any armed conflict. But the information Mister Clayton provided indicates that the Mormons devised a detailed plan of deliberate vandalism to prevent the United States Army delegation from traveling to Salt Lake City and installing the new governor. Furthermore, Echo Canyon pass is lined with the *Saints'* Nauvoo Legion, ready to gun down any hapless traveler at a moment's notice."

The children bound in at that moment asking what they could have for their tea.

Nellie gave Rosalinda a warning look over their heads, and their grim conversation remained at its abrupt halt.

CHAPTER 18
Smooth Operator

Nellie's Parlor, Great Salt Lake City, April 1858

"Nellie, I do believe protocol demands: entertaining gentlemen callers must wait until your baby is at least four months old!"

Sputtering with indignation as well as mirth, Nellie jumped up from her couch and whirled as her friend entered the parlor. "Truly, Rosalinda, at times your tongue does quite run askew."

Rosalinda ignored her and rushed to the gentleman, attired in a United States Army captain's uniform, rising from Nellie's settee.

The man took Rosalinda's hand and bowed over it. "Allow me to introduce myself, my fair lady," he said.

"No need," said Rosalinda airily as she watched the man kiss her hand.

He looked taken aback. "Why, madam...."

Rosalinda laughed. "I have already made your acquaintance. You are Captain Laurence Simmons Baker, a former suitor of our dear Cornelia Rose, stationed at Fort Kearney, Nebraska Territory."

"I pride myself on having a memory better than a possum 'membering a sweet tater, but I have no recollection of our previous meeting."

"I dare say it is because you, like many of her multitude of suitors, could not tear your eyes away from our lovely lady," said Rosalinda with a twinkle in her eye.

"Truly. I declare, Cornelia Rose, your beauty of face and figure simply *in*-crease with the number of years you have graced me with your loveliness," Captain Baker drawled, twirling his mustache and beaming at Nellie.

Suddenly, his face twisted in confusion. "Beg pardon? Your words strike me as most irregular!"

"That my friend, Rosalinda Wells, not re-introduce herself?" Nellie asked.

"No," said Baker. "That you still have many admirers."

Rosalinda laughed. "Surely, you do not believe you alone appreciate my dear friend's many attributes?"

I must stop this dangerous conversation before it strays even further afield.

"Rosalinda, do join us for tea. The scent of warm shortbread, at any moment, shall permeate the room and unleash a swarm of now happily playing children, begging for a piece, so please sit and relax *right now* before this fleeting opportunity passes." Nellie put her hand on Rosalinda's shoulder and pushed her into an armchair, and ran to the kitchen for another teacup.

"Now, where were we?" asked Nellie, slipping back into her chair while pouring some hot tea for Rosalinda.

As she handed the cup to Rosalinda, her friend whispered, "Did you get the tempest into the teacup without spilling, as well as the tea?"

Nellie grimaced.

"Old Granny did nothing. Just sat down after throwing together a makeshift, replacement fort," said Captain Baker.

"Old Granny?" asked Rosalinda.

Baker grinned. "There I go slippin' up and givin' you con-fid-ential *information* again, my dearest Cornelia Rose. 'Old Granny' is just my platoon's term of endearment for Colonel Alexander. Yep, his wisdom beams like a possum's grin in the moonlight. Opted to detour around the canyon after Van Vliet's scouting report of the shenanigans of them thousands of Mormons just a-laying await. Bless his pea-pickin' little heart. But then, reason fled, for 'old Granny' retreated, just 'cause of a little October snow. He's so dumb he brought a duck to a chicken fight. He marched us all the way down Bear River, where he could have just taken the city."

"But storming the city would have started a war," blurted Nellie.

"Would have? What do *you* call burning our grass, destroying our food, reducing our forts to rubble, attacking supply trains, 'liberating' our livestock, and giving our horses to the Indians? What would you Northerners call that?"

Nellie and Rosalinda exchanged glances.

My first candid report of the non-war since wounded scout Clayton appeared at my kitchen table.

Scowling, Baker continued. "At least 'old Granny's' replacement, Colonel Johnston, sports some gumption. We now possess too few supplies and no horses, so we dare not attack. We've spent our days constructin' a fort out of the remnants of burnt-out Bridger and the near decimated Fort Scott.

"Completed just in time for Cooke's Second Dragoons to arrive towing the appointed governor Cumming, his wife, and several other Federal officials."

Tarry a moment. Why was Obadiah not offered a protective posse? Or was he? Who decided we should travel here on our own whilst our Army accompanied these judges and town officials?

"Yessir," the captain said, "left us with nothing but donkeys. Turned us into a bunch of jackasses."

Nellie and Rosalinda suppressed giggles.

Captain Lawrence Simmons Baker didn't even notice, he was so engrossed in his own dissertation. "We formed a 'jackass cavalry,' and we would have stopped that damn fool Mormon Lot Smith from further pillaging had we not been loath to directly fire upon that Nauvoo Legion. Hell's bells! Devil feathers! Ah' course, we cannot act against orders and kill our fellow countrymen. But some shots in the air and capturing a few of them? What did that accomplish?"

"I heard a rumor that those protected officials tried your prisoners and found them guilty of treason," said Nellie.

"That dog won't hunt." Baker dismissed this with a wave of his hand. "Killin' a few of them varmints... that might have stopped them cold. Forget diplomacy. You can't make a silk purse out o' a sow's ear. That assuredly won't stop ol' king Brigham from warring against us. Nor will it facilitate his repudiation of his monarchy.

"I say Colonel Albert Sydney Johnston called it right. 'The Mormons,' he declared, 'have placed themselves in rebellion against the Union, and entertain the insane design of establishing a form of government thoroughly despotic, and utterly repugnant to our institutions.'"

The exact words Clayton quoted!

"You mark my words: many a life shall be forfeited to the 'Mormon Conflict'." Captain Baker took a bite of the warm cornbread Nellie just sliced, entirely pleased to have a captive audience for his dissertation.

At that moment, as Nellie promised, the children swarmed their tête-á-tête and ate every last crumb of the cornbread.

"Like the proverbial swarm of locusts," Nellie said, lifting her feet so Lemuel would not trample them in his haste to grab a big slice.

The three adults exchanged more pleasantries as the inundation subsided.

After a convivial chat, Baker said, "I am afeared I must resume my duties. But rest assured, as the spring thaw begins, Johnston prepares to receive reinforcements that will bring our force to almost 5,000 — a third of the entire United States Army. Thus, my fair maidens, we shall keep you safe.

"I beg your leave to depart, my gentle women."

They stood and walked to the entryway.

"Mama, help," cried Priscilla.

Rosalinda waved goodbye and dashed to her baby.

Baker took Nellie's hand and held it for too long. When she pulled it away, his hand caught her chin and forced her to look into his eyes. "My beautiful lady. My dearest, sweetest Rose. How I yearn for you still."

Nellie shook her head. "Merciful heavens, Captain Baker. That ship sailed long ago. We must abandon it at sea."

Baker hung his head.

Dead silence pervaded.

How to make this man leave? He has already overstayed his welcome.

"Then I 'spose it shall not trouble you to learn I am betrothed to be married to a certain filly whots come trotting into my fort and prancing into my heart?"

"Tarnation. You sly devil! What if I had said I longed for your return and hope you make me yours?"

Baker looked confused. "Your heart desires mine?"

"Merciful heavens, no," she said, harsh tone chastising him.

The man had the grace to blush and stammer, "Slap my head and call me silly!"

Nellie said softly, "Your romantic heart quite dominates your faculties. You conjure a certain image of the girl I once was, and you want that which no longer exists. Such a debonair gentleman as you surely should have given up on this hobby of affecting affection for me long ago. Do you merely resurrect it when boredom seeps through your blithe marauding bachelor lifestyle? Shall we agree, again, now, to part as friends, and only friends?"

Baker seized her hand and smothered it with kisses.

"I shall interpret this as ascent. Now fare thee well until our next encounter." Nellie pulled her hand to guide him to the door.

Let us pray that encounter comes without 5,000 of your closest army friends accompanying you whilst you clash with Brigham Young and his forces at my front door.

"I s'pose it's time to piss on the fire and call the dogs then," said Baker. He gave one final kiss to her hand and walked out the door.

Just as she was about to heave a sigh of relief, he turned around on her front walk and swept her a low bow. "I don't know what got a hold a me. Grief, I guess. I do apologize for my ungentlemanly language."

Nellie waved from the front door. At last, she saw the back of his head as he rode his donkey down the street, and released a sigh of relief that spread through her body.

'Tis a mercy to see him retreat from whence he came. Jackass cavalry indeed! Howsoever, I did enjoy this emissary from the past, allowing me to recall, with a trifle too much melancholy, I'm afraid, the joys of my youthful courtships. And the wondrous mansion I was fortunate enough to call home. Mansion! Truly, it did not seem so at the time, for there were far grander homes in Sing Sing. But verily, the Entwhistle home compares like a palace to this humble abode.

After Rosalinda and her brood left, Nellie looked around her sparsely furnished parlor. Only her chest of drawers and her book collection served as tangible ties to her childhood. She sighed again. Many of the comforts of her home were left in New York. She tugged at the strand of hair that always escaped her coiffure and teased her forehead.

But I shan't abandon my connections to my loved ones. I shall stay in touch via post, whenever King Brigham reopens our border, and persist in my hope that one day I will be reunited with my family, whether they journey here, or I return home.

***

Nellie helped Obadiah off with his topcoat when he returned that evening.

"I wonder what jackass hitched at my hitching post?" Obadiah winked.

"Merciful heavens, witty husband. Surely your eyesight does not stretch from Young's office to our house!"

"This is a small, gossiping town, Cornelia. You know full well our movements are observed and broadcast freely." He took Nellie into his arms. "What troubles you?"

"More reports from the States' camp concerning the conflict. Yes, more disturbing reports," she replied.

"I have said from the get-go the Sebastopol strategy of burning the farms north of the City ceased. The tactic has run its course. While I grant you, at first, Young envisioned another permanent emigration for his persecuted people, now that Kane has reported good results from détente, the maneuver functions as a ploy to brush the United States Army back and keep them from storming this great city."

"Sebastopol? After the great Russian retreat in the Crimean War?"

"Yes. I'll grant you, approximately 30,000 people have moved south of our great city into central Utah."

"Why the burning need for this exodus if you have assurances that peace negotiations proceed?" asked Nellie.

"Cornelia, I do admire your ability to inject the levity of a plausible pun even during a difficult conversation." He smiled, then continued with a sterner tone. "However, I have already divulged enough confidential information." Then his arms relaxed around her and he kissed the top of her head. "Confidential information lovingly imparted to make you more confident of the security of our situation."

Only moderately placated, Nellie put her arm around his waist.

Thank heavens for Rosalinda, a true ally behind enemy lines, whilst my husband's allegiances wobble.

I used to think my own thoughts and enjoy my sisters and friends as confidants. Mayhap I should not sustain my dependence upon Mister Wright in any other roles besides husband.

***

With last night's thoughts still uppermost in her mind, it gladdened Nellie when Hannah Tapfield King dropped in for a cup of tea and to check on baby James the next morning.

Rosalinda and her brood arrived soon after. "I come calling early, before the domestic demands of the day completely overwhelm any thoughts of socializing."

As Nellie put on the kettle and set the table for tea, Hannah jumped right into weighty conversation. "My daughter Louisa tells me you had a personal visit from a member of the jackass cavalry. Did you receive any intelligence?"

Nellie laughed. "I depend upon your wit, my lovely friend. My intelligence remains high and in frequent demand, thank you kindly. I did receive a detailed summary of the activities around the old Fort Bridger, which Mister Wright advises may be slightly skewed."

"We must scorn tongues that wag with petty disagreeables rather than proclaim the Good News of the Lord." Hannah dismissed them with a wave of her hand. "Most of the Saints merely exist for the glory of God, continually striving to live lives worthy of a position in His Heavenly Host of Angels. Fear of religious persecution alone incites their defensive activities. The Elders' cry and brouhaha simply ensures our freedom to practice our faith."

Nellie and Rosalinda exchanged skeptical glances behind her back.

What of the cry to extract blood from the gentiles? How much horror and destruction is permissible in the quest to 'preserve their faith'?

Hannah sighed. "Our Prophet and Governor encourages me to abandon my snug little house and move south with the faithful to form new settlements. With all the trials I have suffered, which few women could have borne, I choose to remain here, and dare not face the dearth and wild of a journey again."

Rosalinda and Nellie exchanged glances again.

Rosalinda knows all this information, even if she is not privy to the secret code name 'Sebastopol.' Mercy!

They both had observed the flood of Mormons streaming down from the Northern settlements, all their possessions heaped in wagons, driving past their doors.

Hannah added, "Mister King and my cherished son, Thomas Owen King Junior, joined the ranks of men charged with burying the foundation walls of the new temple and sowing a wheat crop on top."

Nellie said, "I thought the new temple was to be the crowning jewel of our city?"

"Whyever for?" asked Rosalinda.

Hannah replied as she poured herself some tea. "We must protect the Temple from destruction by the Army of the States. Our dear Prophet wisely surmises that the United States Army will not just simply vanish. Nor is it likely they shall knock on our door bearing a peace pipe."

"But we know diplomats work, as we speak, to secure accord between the parties," said Nellie.

"With the assistance of our Blessed Lord, that may well be true," Hannah replied in her dulcet British cadence. "But we faithful heed the warning: there shall be no peace whilst the States Army threatens to invade. Moreover, we obey the call to arms to prevent the hostile appropriation of our fine city."

Interrupting this upsetting conversation, Emma skipped in swirling her new dress. "Auntie Rosalinda, Auntie Hannah, am I not blessed to sport such a beautiful new dress?"

Not to be outdone, Elizabeth popped up behind her. "Mama says that the winter weather shall soon warm mild enough to wear calico starting this month!"

"Yes, spring is here," confirmed Nellie.

Does it bring resolution or further trouble?

CHAPTER 19
It's a Miracle

Nellie's Kitchen Table, Great Salt Lake City, April 1858

The kitchen door burst open and a towering figure panted, "Do not flee!"

"Mister Beauregard Clayton!" Nellie exclaimed. She brushed the crumbs from her apron and tucked a stray strand of hair back into her bun.

Would that I had donned my cleaned and pressed apron this morning.

Obadiah lifted his head from the morning newspaper.

Clayton put his hands on his knees, still struggling to regain his breath. "There's a veritable flood of wagons heading south at the direction of the 'Lion of the Lord.'"

Another wave of Saints forced to abandon all they have built here?

Clayton mastered his breathing. "But I jest arrived in town with Kane. We reconnoitered up to the makeshift camp erected by the governor-elect's posse. My man Kane ostensibly works for the United States government, but I have my confirmed suspicions his true loyalties lie with Brigham Young and his kingdom."

Nellie tried to untangle his words and make some sense out of them. "Kane?" she asked. "Do you mean Thomas L. Kane, the attorney on the diplomatic mission to avert bloodshed during this 'conflict'?

Clayton confirmed with a nod of his head.

"He successfully returned to the hastily constructed Fort Scott after his visit to Washington?" asked Nellie.

Clayton affirmed with another nod of his head.

"While I understand Buchannan did not give Kane direct orders," Obadiah muttered, almost to himself, "he did give his blessing to Kane's efforts to negotiate a peaceful settlement to this political unrest." He clapped his hands together and attempted levity. "If only to distance himself from the outcry against 'Buchanan's Blunder.' Please give us the full report, Mister Clayton."

Nellie, glancing at Obadiah, caught the joviality fading from her husband's face as he rearranged his features into a mask of inscrutability.

Clayton caught his breath and dropped into a chair.

I shan't let Clayton's casual mien offend me since he imparts potentially radical news. She shook her head. *This is no time to let worry over social conventions cloud my mind.*

Clayton had just provided confirmation of Captain Baker's report. The newly appointed governor and his posse had huddled in the makeshift shelter at the decimated fort throughout this whole winter.

"Ol' silver-tongued Tom sure as shootin' did convince the United States Army to stand down," said Clayton.

In the midst of this jaw-dropping news, the strangest observation flitted across Nellie's mind.

Hillbilly talk seems to encroach upon Clayton's Scottish burr.

"I can't rightly figure how," Clayton continued. "But he convinced the new governor to travel west into the Great Salt Lake City without the remains of his bedraggled legion, formerly numbering 2,500 men. Kane and I advance to bring word to Young that if he lets the appointed Governor's small party pass unmolested through his Legion-lined, fortified breastworks, peaceful relations with the United States and full resumption of all territorial rights shall continue. Furthermore, no *Saints* shall be disturbed as long as a peaceful transfer of gubernatorial power passes from Young himself to the newly appointed governor, Alfred Cumming. All will be pardoned."

"Are you speaking of a legal pardon, expunging the treason charges?" Obadiah asked.

Clayton nodded in confirmation.

Obadiah extended his hand to Clayton's and shook it, dropped into the next chair and exclaimed, "Hoppin' Horsefeathers, 'tis the best scouting report I have heard in all my born days! I knew diplomatic channels worked to avoid hostilities, and I knew Young had no real wish to engage in battle with the States. But I am not yet privy to Brigham's inner circle, and information filters through many channels. 'Tis a mercy indeed that placed the proper men here to communicate and assuage the real fears of both sides."

Clayton gave an audible release of air. Suddenly a smile lit his face as bright as if he had switched on an internal flashlight. "The best result of a proper par-ley."

Nellie shook her head. "I hate to spoil the celebration, but we have no confirmation that Young will peacefully cede power to the new governor. Yea, the United States government may offer this extremely reasonable compromise, but will Young, given his history of imperialism, truly relinquish his power?"

Obadiah shifted in his seat.

Clayton stared Nellie directly in the eye. "Cornelia Rose Entwhistle, as I live and breathe, you have a way to dissect the animal and find the heart of the matter."

Nellie's head jerked toward her husband.

Did my husband just scoff at this compliment paid to me?

"As I see it," Clayton continued, "with men like silver-tongued Kane and yer very own husband here on ta side of a righteous peace, they'll soon persuade Brigham Young to see and tout ta many advantages of avoiding the conflict ta king, himself, does not wish to have."

"Without taking up arms," said Obadiah.

Nellie pulled some fresh wizened apple compote from her oven, and Clayton attacked it, barely leaving a quarter for the Wright family.

He gulped down the rest of his tea and shoved back from the table. "A red-letter day surely follows. Judge Wright, I'll see ye at ta negotiations briefly and then I depart, carrying the resolution to appointed Governor Cumming."

He strode out the door, leaving behind a burst of cold air.

Nellie caught Obadiah's eye.

He jumped up from the table, ran for his topcoat, and hugged her goodbye, eyes smiling. "Let us hope our good man Clayton's unusual optimism portends a peaceful outcome to this controversy. I do know that Kane will have to provide the *missing* documentation allegedly stolen from a federal judge, the catalyst for the decision to replace Young in the first place. Yes, to gain credibility, Young must furnish these papers as a show of good faith, but I might yet be of assistance in arranging that matter."

Missing documentation? Stolen papers?

"In any case, your decision to stay in this mostly abandoned town is affirmed yet again," said Nellie.

***

About two weeks later, Clayton again appeared at their back door at breakfast time. "I wouldna believed it, if I hadn't seen it with me own eyes," he said, and he took a huge, hungry bite of Nellie's fresh pumpkin bread.

Does the man eat nothing in between visits to my kitchen?

"Mister Clayton, your dramatic pause leaves me speculating wildly," Nellie said, fear leaping into her heart.

Obadiah raised his eyebrows but didn't reply, he just lifted the *Deseret News* from the kitchen table and began reading the front page.

"Good." Clayton took another huge bite.

A thunderbolt crossed Nellie's face.

"No, mercy no," he sputtered through his full mouth, spewing crumbs. He held up one finger while he swallowed. "No, me words only meant something good transpired." He pointed to the story that caught his eye on the front page. "I dinna want ta appear boorish, talking with me mouth full."

Relieved, Nellie forced herself to be patient while the man took a swig of tea.

Clayton made a face.

"What is wrong?" Nellie fretted again.

He shook his head. "Canna be helped. I'd plum forgotten ta scarcity o' coffee in this dam-able Territory."

Nellie cleared her throat with a laugh. "Beans remain scarce, with the United States mail restrictions. Not, of course, because merchants cannot import them, but because the *Saints* strictly forbid coffee, fearing the unnatural stimulation its ingestion excites in the humors."

"Moreover, nary a person can come in or out of this territory without permission of himself, the Laird Brigham," concurred Clayton.

The reappearance of that endearing Scottish vocabulary warms my heart. 'Lord' Brigham certainly fits!

"If we might return to the subject?" Nellie prodded.

"On the road from Cache Cave to Echo Canyon, Nauvoo Legion soldiers stood on both sides of the road in salute to the new governor."

Nellie felt her mouth hang open with surprise. She cast about for a brilliant riposte, but nothing jumped to mind.

Finally, she said, "Merciful heavens, 'tis a miracle."

"I knew we could reestablish détente," crowed Obadiah. "I shall depart at once for the Beehive House and join the planning of a welcome celebration."

Nellie raised her eyebrows. "I hardly think Young will *welcome* the new governor."

"He must," said Clayton, as he loaded more butter and honey on another piece of bread.

***

Several days later, new Governor Cumming, accompanied by his wife and a host of new judges and other federally appointed people, straggled into town.

The dark angel himself, Wild Bill Hickok, assembled a band, and it seemed that every Mormon remaining in the city gathered at the first note.

"They have literally *struck up the band* for the entrance of our new governor," Rosalinda shouted to Nellie over the heads of their children, as they gawked at the wagons full of ragged-clothed federal officials.

The two women, accompanied of course by all of the children, ran to join the crowd lining the streets. To their amazement, Young greeted the new governor in person.

Mrs. Lucy Ann Decker Young announced a welcome dinner reception for the following night.

Back at home, grateful to be invited, Nellie dug a gown she'd not worn since she left New York from her cedar chest. Shaking out the wrinkles, she tried to decide how to make it presentable.

Have I sufficient time to add new sleeves? Maybe a quick appliqué of trim around the bodice will heighten its appeal?

Rosalinda stopped by on her way to visit her husband at the dry goods store. "What shall I wear to the dinner tomorrow?" she asked. "Do I have enough time to make new sleeves, or should I just add some trim to my green crinoline?"

"Great minds think alike!" Nellie raised the dress she sat basting. "Praise the Lord you were invited."

At Rosalinda's quizzical look, Nellie added, "I worried that since your recent arrival precluded you from meeting the Missus Young in charge of social events, your presence might have been overlooked."

"All the Mormons have left," Rosalinda said with an airy laugh. "Who else could they invite?"

***

They left all the children at Nellie's house, with Rosalinda's oldest daughter in charge, to attend the 'state' dinner.

"You be good girls and help Adelaidia with the babies," said Nellie to her daughters.

"How I wished you lived next door," said Nellie to Rosalinda when they at last left the house.

"I live just three blocks away! 'Tis rather a greedy desire," joked Rosalinda. "Considering the miracle that I am here at all."

Nellie laughed. "Greater proximity would have ensured our punctuality for this event."

"True. At least your husband left in advance to attend to his important business. He entrusted our escorting to the good stewardship of Mister Wells."

They giggled and looked over their shoulders. Mr. Wells did not notice, engrossed in conversation with a neighbor. Like a dog with a bone, Wells grabbed the ear of the man and tenaciously held fast. The poor man failed to get a word in edgewise as Wells spun a long tale about the history of the waistcoat.

A gasp of horror escaped Nellie when she met Mrs. Cumming in the receiving line. Emaciated and barely able to stand, the poor woman seemed to operate on sheer willpower alone.

"How lovely to meet you," said the new governor's wife. "I do hope we have opportunity to get better acquainted."

Nellie smiled and said, "'Tis my desire too, to know the amazing woman who survived a winter without supplies. I know of your pedigree and education and, if there be any truth to the many rumors, you used these to embrace the challenges presented to you and devise many makeshift comforts to outwit the elements."

A light seemed to brighten Mrs. Cumming's eyes. She squeezed Nellie's hand in gratitude before dutifully turning to the next guest.

Delighted at their placement at the dinner table across from Mrs. Cumming, Nellie and Rosalinda soon established a rapport with the ravaged woman. When their husbands left to join the men in the library for cigars, the three women sat in the parlor together.

"This is our second welcome dinner, in fact," Mrs. Cumming confided. "Due to our deprivation, I dared not ingest more than a few bites at the first. I watched the other officials fill themselves to the brim and then pay the price for the overload of digestive system."

"Where in heaven's name was the first dinner?" Nellie asked. "I do not believe any towns have been settled between here and the former Fort Bridger."

"Cache Cave," Mrs. Cumming replied, taking a genteel sip of her wine.

Nellie and Rosalinda exchanged blank glances.

"The Cave of signatures functioned as the secret headquarters of General Daniel H. Wells. It was the General who dispatched his spy Orrin Porter Rockwell to escort us across Mormon lines, through the breastworks along the Emigration Trail."

"I was not aware the United States had a General Wells," Nellie replied with a frown.

"No, the Nauvoo Legion's general."

"A general in the army that we citizens loyal to the United States are assured does not exist?" asked Rosalinda.

"That very one," said Mrs. Cumming. "I cannot tell you how much it warms my heart to find like-minded intelligent women here in the barren desert of 'Deseret'."

"Behind enemy lines," agreed Rosalinda.

"Dinner in Cache Cave?" asked Nellie. "I remember that cave. My daughters were sure it was haunted."

"It may well be, with all the mystery and intrigue plotted there. Not to mention the murder of Egan's second wife's lover," said Mrs. Cumming.

"Egan! I do recall that name. He was the first person to be tried for murder in this territory."

Both ladies stared at her.

"My attorney husband oft speaks of landmark cases. We joked about Egan's defense. All the accused said in his own defense to the criminal charges was, 'A man who seduces another man's wife must die.' Imagine!" said Nellie. "However, the like-minded Mormons found this justification so reasonable, their territorial legislature passed the Justifiable Homicide Act in 1852. It can be nothing less than a direct outcome of the Egan case."

"Be that as it may," said Rosalinda, "I cannot imagine a dinner party at the Cave. I assume you had fresh game, spit roasted with nary a vegetable to grace your plate?"

"Yes. Quite. However, my ravenous, nutrient deprived organs could not process more than a few nibbles of delicious game. My Governor Cumming, however, remained the very picture of health throughout the ordeal, and dove right into the feast. We dined with General Wells, Orrin Porter Rockwell, and 150 of the armed men of the non-existent Nauvoo Legion."

My worst nightmares confirmed by the details of Missus Elizabeth Cumming's experiences.

Nellie shook her head and said, "I do recall Clayton mentioning a member of Young's First Presidency secretly re-arming the Legion our Congress once forced to disband. The entire United States Army presumed it was they who lined the ridges of Echo Canyon, waiting to gun down anyone not authorized by Young himself to pass into this territory. But my husband put no stock in this rumor."

"More's the pity," said Rosalinda.

"However," said Mrs. Cumming, "perhaps your husband's reassurances and optimism ensured the best results of this impasse, which in fairness to him did come about without bloodshed."

"Without *known* bloodshed," Nellie muttered.

Rosalinda squeezed her hand in agreement.

To Mrs. Cumming, Nellie said, "They did, however, almost cause death by starvation."

Mrs. Cumming looked chagrinned. "I confess agreement. However, I do believe we arrived here in one piece. Somewhat perversely, my husband rather enjoyed his winter holding court with the other officials and plotting his gubernatorial successes." She sighed. "Surely, the malnourishment and cold forever compromised my health, thus, we arrive safe if not sound. Now we must use all our wits and strength to make this uneasy alliance into a true partnership between federal authorities and Latter-day Saint authorities."

"Quite the challenge confronts us," said Nellie. "But as we prepare, may I offer some of my herbs and tinctures to help you regain your stamina?"

Mrs. Cumming looked pleased.

"Rosalinda and I shall call on you tomorrow with a basketful of remedies to aid your digestion, your humors, and rebuild your strength."

Mrs. Cumming sighed. "My prayers have been answered. I am not only reunited with the fairer sex, but have found two women who offer companionship, intelligence, and a skill set for which I hunger."

"Pun intended?" Nellie asked.

And at Elizabeth Cumming's affirmative nod of the head, Nellie added, "Then I truly have found a genuine kindred spirit in you. I shall delight in becoming better acquainted."

CHAPTER 20
Would You Like to Come Over for Tea?

Block 75 on South Temple Street, July 1858

As the days sped along, Nellie's hopes for added gravitas in Obadiah's position dissipated in spite of Brigham Young's bestowing an 'inheritance' of a new, larger house and acre of land on her husband. While she hoped it signified some elevation in Obadiah's status, she saw little change in any aspect of their situation besides the perk of the rent-free larger house. The new house seemed to her an attempt to buy Obadiah's allegiance.

The new, federally appointed governor had arrived without armed conflict and without the federal posse, but they all still feared the potential clash of the United States Army with the Nauvoo Legion.

Tarnation, the only saving grace of the Governor is his wife.

The addition of Elizabeth Wells Randall Cumming bolstered the ranks of non-Mormon, educated, sophisticated women to a new level.

Tarnation, Missus Cumming elevates the level of education of the Mormon women too.

But Alfred E. Cumming! To date, a timid milksop in the overpowering grasp of Young. He exhibits less spine than a marionette on strings, dancing to every tune that diabolical brigand plays.

Nellie shook her head, overwhelmed with negative thoughts as she filled the teakettle. Those thoughts took on monstrous proportions and hampered her assembly of the dirty laundry. She glanced out the back window and saw Emma and Elizabeth skipping around their new, larger garden while feeding the chickens. The sight gladdened her heart, mitigating her nagging worry of the precariousness of their life here.

The kettle steamed and water bubbled and whistled. Nellie hummed.

Elizabeth burst through the door, screaming, shattering the quiet and waking baby James. "Emma struck me. Emma struck me."

"I truly did not," Emma panted, as she ran in after her sister, and both girls, wailing, followed Nellie down the short hallway to the baby's cradle. "You pulled my doll so hard her head snapped off, and *it* struck you on the arm. Now you have ruined my best companion."

Nellie snatched her red-faced, squalling baby from the crib. Willing calm, she rubbed his tense back with an experienced, soothing hand, and at least one portion of the screaming stopped.

Her girls continued to bicker.

She cradled the baby upright against her shoulder gently patting him, and he gave a satisfying burp. Nellie smiled, inhaling his sweet scent.

My lavender infused water for his bath makes this sweet infant all the more huggable. She breathed in deeply. *Moreover, even in the midst of this racket, the lavender scent still soothes.*

Suddenly, her nose wrinkled at a sour smell, and she felt his liquid spit-up permeate her dress and dampen her shoulder. She retched and reprimanded herself.

I must remain calm. Just a small test of my patience and equanimity as a mother. Thank you, Lord, for my patterned calico, able to hide a myriad of sins.

"Sweet pumpkins, cease your caterwauling," she said, glaring at her daughters but keeping her temper.

They both stopped crying, but they pushed each other into the kitchen, each girl anxious to speak first to clear her name of the accusations leveled by the other.

"Emma would not share," said Elizabeth, at the same time that Emma asserted, "Betsy hogs all the toys."

Nellie shook her head.

The truth lies somewhere in between, in a competition begun at the birth of the younger girl.

"The responsibility of each of you does not depend upon whether your sister behaves well. In every situation, you both must behave only with love and kindness, no matter how the other responds."

Nellie gave up trying to knead the bread one-handed. She whirled around with James still on her shoulder and caught both girls with their tongues stuck out at each other.

She shook her head. "Sit down on the floor, and you each may have a turn holding your baby brother."

Both girls dropped to the floor and simultaneously said, "It's my turn first."

"Who straightened their coverlet this morning and brushed their teeth?" Nellie asked.

Emma raised her hand, and Elizabeth dropped her head.

"Emma, you may have the first turn. Betsy, you run up the stairs, and as soon as you have completed both tasks, your turn shall commence."

Elizabeth stamped her foot.

"Don't look so sad. Remember to perform your tasks before you play, and tomorrow you may have the first turn. Moreover, today's schedule promises reasons to rejoice. Missus Wells comes to tea, bringing Lemuel, Adelaidia, and baby Priscilla. Thus, babies will wait in line to be held, and you may romp to your hearts' content in our big garden with Lemuel."

"Shall we have cinnamon bread for tea?"

Nellie laughed. "If I ever get the last bit rolled, you shall soon smell your answer."

Elizabeth scampered up the stairs, and Emma took the baby.

Let's pray for a domestic tranquility at least long enough to get the bread in the oven.

***

Elizabeth Cumming took a genteel sip of her tea. "My travails surely encourage me to savor the finer things in life. I feared I would never again attend a lovely tea such as this."

"I am pleased you could join us. I'm am sure your presence is much in demand as the newly arrived Governor's wife," Nellie said, and beamed at her, a bit star struck at the list of the learned woman's accomplishments.

"We refrained from inquiring, but we remain anxious to learn the details of your trek across the country," said Rosalinda.

"If it is not too painful, we would feel honored if you give us a quick sketch of your arduous journey," concurred Nellie.

Mrs. Cumming hesitated.

"Even though *we* have not discussed it, perhaps that is the only question posed to you since your arrival here," guessed Nellie. "We can discuss it at another time. Or not at all." She looked anxiously at the thin pale face of her guest, as the woman stared at her teacup.

Mrs. Cumming answered in a quiet voice, with large pauses in her narrative. "Although the mountains surrounding us loomed bleak and windy, we encamped in a basin, so surrounded by hills that the winds reached us very gently.... A most rigid economy in... the distribution of provisions, we observed of necessity, to give us some assurance of being fed till spring."

Nellie and Rosalinda exchanged glances.

She begins quite in the middle of her odyssey. Mercy, the arduousness of the conditions has taken its toll on her finely strung and educated mind.

"We cut up the vandalized wagons for fuel. We found the mules dead by their sides, abandoned." She shuddered. "Destruction of newly crafted wagons, traveling their maiden voyage, felt like a sin we had not the luxury to avoid."

All the devastation and hardship I faced on my cross-country trek rush back to stare at me from the vivid picture painted by this frail woman of steel.

Tears threatened as Nellie realized, *I was one of the lucky ones, only brushing the specter of disaster, whilst others felt its true sting.*

She glanced at Rosalinda, who held her handkerchief up to her eyes. *My dear friend relives her own trauma too.*

"Mercy," Mrs. Cumming continued, "one cannot calculate the vastness of the damage done in this *non-war*. Truly, our accompanying armed forces caught many of the perpetrators and placed them under guard. With some of the *Destroying Angels* of the Mormons arrested *in media res* of destroying more of our wagons, the wheels of justice turned. Governor Cumming cheerfully went about the business of establishing an extemporaneous government—dashing off proclamations to Young and reports to Washington, all sent by scout. He got the judges established in a temporary court and commenced a trial of the Mormon perpetrators of this treason."

Nellie and Rosalinda exchanged glances.

I must sort this befuddled woman's 'in media res' story and try to reassemble it to glean some sense of the sequence of events.

The three women sat in silence for a moment.

"Sometimes, we had no food at night," said Mrs. Cumming.

Nellie took the woman's hand. After two months in civilization, the thin appendage felt almost claw-like, with no substance to it. "We pour our heartfelt sympathy upon you."

It was all she could think to say.

Silence reigned again, but for the ticking of the grandfather clock and the muted sounds of children's voices coming from the other room.

"'Tis almost astonishing, how men remain singularly focused on their profession," commented Rosalinda.

"True," Mrs. Cumming answered, and her lips turned up in a fleeting smile.

Nellie sniffed. "Surely, we afford them that luxury by attending to every other detail of survival, so they can *work* the choicest part."

Elizabeth Cumming laughed. "Amen! I applaud your candor, Missus Wright. I see we are of like mind, and I shall take it as a sign that we are of like heart as well."

After the brief lighthearted moment, a dire thought must have struck her, for Mrs. Cumming paled, sighed, and returned to her tale. "The morale of the troops caused me more hardship than even the grueling physical conditions we faced. In the very cold weather, the teamsters seemed more like madmen than human beings. Much sin abounded, as the cold and privations seemed to make them crazy."

Nellie again felt at a loss to respond.

Emma broke away from the playing children and skipped over to join the ladies for tea. She smiled at Mrs. Cumming and said, "It seems, though, despite your ordeal, *you* kept up your morale and thanked God for whatever you could search out that was good."

Mrs. Cumming beamed back at her. A soft pink blush warmed her cheeks, and her smile softened her entire face. "That's right, my little lady. I do believe our optimistic attitude and prayers were our salvation."

She took a healthy sip of tea and nibbled at a crumb at the edge of her cinnamon roll.

I must use my midwifery skills to further encourage this nascent sign of life returning to this skeleton of a woman. Perhaps I can further diagnose the ill effects of her deprivations.

Nellie said, "When you walked in, I noticed you favor your left leg. Does it pain you?"

"Frostbite took its toll upon my feet. My left foot, discolored and swollen, fared the worst. My worn boots, worse for the continual travel, did nothing to protect me from the unanticipated *October* winter weather. On our trek from Fort Laramie, we walked constantly, even through snow. I was unable to delay our journey to attend to my foot, thus it continued to swell."

"Hells bells, that must have been agony," sympathized Rosalinda.

Elizabeth Cumming shook her head no. "In truth, both my feet were so numb, I experienced no pain, only tingling, with occasional bursts of a sensation akin to what I imagine an electric shock might feel." The frail woman sighed. "I confess not feeling my feet made the trekking all the more difficult. 'Twas quite the sensation. I walked by rote and custom, astonished that my feet still functioned. I often looked down, as if to verify they remained attached to my limbs. By the second day, I developed red blisters, but only the ones on the bottom of my feet emanated pain. Mercifully, those eventually burst. When we made camp, the weather moderated slightly and I ceased walking. Thus, at last, it improved, and I was again able to wear a shoe."

Elizabeth Wright rushed over from the game of marbles she enjoyed with Lemuel. "You poor, dear lady! You walked in the snow without shoes?"

Mrs. Cumming nodded and hugged the little girl. "Thank you, my sweet," she whispered into the top of the child's head.

Thank heavens I bathed all the children last night, or else Betsy's hair might not smell as sweet.

Rosalinda made sympathetic noises as Nellie said, "As you tell your sad tale, I mentally compile a protocol for the reinvigoration and restoration of your health. When you leave this evening, I shall waste no time before compounding salves for post-frostbite treatment, as well as herbs for internal disorders."

"Mercy, you find me already vastly improved. I feared I would never walk again, not only because of the frostbite but the inflammation in my joints. Thus, I forced myself to keep moving about in the camp to combat these maladies."

"The exact medicine required," Nellie assured her.

"Betsy," Adelaidia called. "Come back to finish our game of marbles. And Emma, come join us children!"

"I prefer to sit with the ladies," said Emma, smiling up at Mrs. Cumming and pouring herself another cup of tea.

My sweet little lady! She always does prefer the company of adults. Perhaps she finds our company easier and less unpredictable than that of the other children.

Nellie leaned over and whispered to Emma, "Since Adelaidia is many years your senior, perhaps you can share your second cup of tea with her. As a good hostess," Nellie added, when she saw Emma readying an objection.

Emma put two cookies on her saucer, poured another cup of tea, and took the feast back to the game of marbles.

I know I don't have to warn her to be careful with my good China. Emma is less likely to spill than I am!

Nellie turned back to her own guests. "Dear Missus Cumming, you are well on your way to recovery, but I have some supplemental aide I can offer you to hasten it, and ensure your limbs return to their previous peak performance."

Rosalinda clucked. "It must have frustrated you beyond despair to be so close to your destination but forced to stop and suffer in the cold."

"Yes, my husband wished to forge on ahead, but we had no animals," confirmed Elizabeth.

"No animals?" asked Rosalinda. "How ever did you even get to Fort Bridger without them?"

Elizabeth Cumming shook her head. "Of course, we had them when we left Fort Laramie, but a raid upon our train at night left us *relieved* of half our livestock in the morning. The Mormons we later captured blamed it on the Paiute Tribe. The slow death of the rest of our poor beasts was yet another consequence of the dastardly behavior of the legions of *Saints* sent to plague us. They burned all grasses and destroyed all foodstuffs in our path, thus there was no corn to feed the animals. At the remains of Fort Bridger, there mercifully grew grass, but it was only enough to prevent the rest of the herd from dying, not enough to aid their regaining of vigor sufficient to complete our journey."

Elizabeth Cumming sighed. "Notwithstanding the Mormons' burning seventy-two of our provision wagons, with care and a rigid economy, we had enough to feed us through the winter. I am living proof that we survived!"

"It seems even more of a miracle," marveled Nellie, "in light of these further details, that you *did* maintain your morale."

"The saving grace, the manna from heaven, came in the form of mail from the States, and occasionally, even a package with emergency rations found us. Thus, I savor this tea and these delicious fresh baked luxuries," said Elizabeth, taking another nibble on the cinnamon bread.

The ladies watched a look of utter delight sweep over her fine features.

"My word! The joy of the kind words from my sister, and the newspapers reporting the state of affairs of our nation, sustained me for a week. Moreover, reading about the dastardly deeds of Brigham Young convinced us of the dire necessity for our mission."

Nellie looked at Rosalinda, who looked as vexed as she felt.

"'Tis more than we can say for ourselves," said Nellie. "The demonic prophet closed off all roads into this city, and we not only get little mail, we've had very little news of the world. Not even to mention we have no knowledge of the *activities* of the self-titled governor other than what he allows us to know."

"'Tis a grim state of affairs altogether," confirmed Rosalinda.

"But now you and our *true* Governor have arrived, and our malady shall heal," said Nellie.

"Yes." Elizabeth smiled. "We must count our blessings. Moreover, even in the worst of the time, another mercy was the capture of a few of the Mormons concerned with burning seventy-two of our wagons." She chuckled. "This kept Judge Eckles busy conducting a fair trial. Letters were found upon the accused, signed by Mormon authorities, *ordering* the destruction of our provisions and animals, telling where re-enforcements were to be placed, and who to call upon to assist in doing it. We also found a cipher, agreed upon by the Mormons for further communication, which enabled us to break their coded letters.

"My sleuthing provided another joy. Cracking the code meant we thwarted another attack on our remaining animals and wagons. When anticipating assault, our dragoons kept the wagons under guard, day and night."

"So," said Nellie, "you found conclusive proof that no tribes were responsible for the unprovoked attacks on your company?"

"Correct. A blessing that conferred certainty on our position, at least, and confirmation that our encampment at the burnt-out fort afforded our most likely chances for surviving the winter."

"Feelings of abandonment and loneliness must have exacerbated your suffering," said Rosalinda with a sympathetic pat on Elizabeth's thin hand.

"While I longed for female companionship, I did not suffer for lack of company. In fact, many crowded our little camp, which I suppose helped keep me warm! We erected tents and other protections less than half a mile from the main camp of the dragoons and enlisted men. All our traveling companions were likewise forced to halt their progress with us. Under pain of death, these *gentile* merchants were forbidden to enter the Great Salt Lake City. Unfortunately, only a very few of their goods aided our survival. But Governor Cumming dispatched a demand to Washington that all the merchants be well compensated by the States for their aide during warlike conditions."

Not pausing for comments, Elizabeth continued, "Chief Justice Eckles—"

"I was pleased to hear Justice Eckles numbered among your learned company when you mentioned the arrest of the Mormons keeping him busy!" interrupted Nellie.

Elizabeth nodded. "We were a troupe of distinguished, newly appointed Federal officers, including, District Attorney Hockaday, Superintendent of Utah Indians Les Tomay, and two or three other civil officers. The men were in high spirits indeed, despite the conditions, for they set about interrogating and trying the Mormon attackers.

"Mister Cumming's proudest moment occurred when a search of a Joseph Taylor, a so-called Major in the Nauvoo Legion—the army recruited in explicit violation of the United States Constitution, mind you—revealed a direct order confirming *the upper echelons of the Mormon Church* dictated and planned all their devilry. Mercy, I can recall the orders verbatim, I heard them so oft attested in court:

> "On ascertaining the locality or route of the troops, proceed at once to annoy them in every possible way. *Use every exertion to* stampede their animals and set fire to their trains. *Burn* the whole country before them and on their flanks. Keep them from sleeping, by night surprise attacks; blockade the road by felling trees or destroying the river fords where you can. Watch for opportunities to set fire to the grass on their windward, so as, if possible, to envelop their trains. Leave no grass before them that can be burned. Keep your men concealed as much as possible, and guard against surprise."

Elizabeth Cumming shook her head in dismay. "At least then we knew the reason for the delay and difficulty in our progress. It was not just misfortune. The Mormons blocked our Army's entrance into the Salt Lake Valley and prevented us from obtaining lifesaving provisions."

Nellie and Rosalinda, shocked at yet another confirmation of the malice of the Mormon people, clicked their tongues in sympathy for Elizabeth's plight.

Elizabeth smiled. "Thank the good and merciful Lord we left this treachery behind us. Yes, we were quite the party of survivors."

"You suffered at every turn," said Nellie, "whilst on my journey, I bemoaned the fact that my Mister Wright had no benefit of prestigious, learned, co-travelers...." She interrupted herself.

How must this sound to Rosalinda?

She amended, "...that were federally appointed."

My thoughtless words! Once again, I have failed to adequately consider the import and nuance my utterances convey.

Nellie strove to cover her mistake and winked at Rosalinda. "I certainly had benefit of at least one learned friend, and I rejoice in the company Mister Wright did find. Necessity often makes strange bedfellows, but I have made lifelong friends."

She turned to Elizabeth. "Moreover, our journey did end rather more successfully than yours."

Goodness, now I have demeaned Missus Cumming's suffering and privations. Honestly, sometimes I wonder at my own stupidity.

Elizabeth frowned, but she continued her conversation on a positive note. "Furthermore, all the different detachments of troops, dispatched from the States during the past summer, assembled near us so that we had peace of mind in our sufficient force to repel an assault. Upon arrival at the burnt-out fort, our climate was temperate, compared to the October winter storms we weathered whilst traveling. During that warmer interlude, my foot returned to boot size."

Elizabeth gave a little, repressed laugh, as if she was so unused to making the sound she dared not indulge in it. "Not *my* boot size, but rather dear Mister Cumming's. He made a great show of lacing his one old boot up for me every morning. Although I still loathed the anguish of taking it off every night."

With this declaration, little Elizabeth Wright bounded over to the ladies and looked at both of Mrs. Cumming's boots. "I guess you did get yourself better. Your boots are both the same size and they're both lady's boots."

The ladies all laughed.

Thank you, Betsy, for breaking the tension caused by my stupidity!

"Yes I have!" Elizabeth Cumming continued when the laughter died down. "At first, I slept in my odd combination of boots. In fact, we dressed and undressed only once in two or three weeks when we first made camp."

"Can I do that, Mama?" asked Betsy. "It sounds much easier than changing and bathing."

Mrs. Cumming laughed again. "Less time consuming, perhaps, but not very comfortable for our persons. There were no means of washing, of course, after the weather again turned so very cold, and so badly off for fuel too, as we were. I'm afraid it has caused some embarrassing, and lasting, conditions."

"Nothing my midwifery skills cannot undo," Nellie assured her. "You must just allow me to examine and diagnose your ills, then I shall find a cure."

Mrs. Cumming glanced at Rosalinda.

Rosalinda sprang from the settee announcing, "Come, Betsy, I do believe I hear my darling Priscilla calling for me." She tactfully hurried the little girl out of the room towards the sound of the other children.

"First, we shall address the issues you have already mentioned," said Nellie, taking Mrs. Cumming's hand and examining it. "As I mentioned, I shall distill tinctures for arthritis and mix salves for easing stiff joints and facilitating movement. As for new complaints, please be assured I hold my medical assessments in the strictest of confidences. I divulge patient information to no one, not Rosalinda or even my husband. So please, tell me your symptoms and concerns."

Elizabeth smiled. "I feel confident I rest in good hands. You shall see most of my complaints for yourself, but the one I must confide in you rather feels like a failure on my part. I am loath to disclose it."

"Please don't hesitate. We must not judge ourselves so harshly. Most times, disease and illness come through no fault of our own," reassured Nellie.

Elizabeth hung her head and whispered, "No monthly courses. My overland journey reduced me to an old hag. No monthly courses since frostbite set upon my foot in October."

Nellie gave Elizabeth a hug. "Fret not. 'Tis our person's natural response to extremely harsh conditions which only now, in this land of plenty, shall abate sufficiently to permit healing. You had no control over the weather, nor the compromising of your food supply."

Damn those Mormons. And yes, Lord, I do mean damn. Harming yet another innocent bystander, Brigham remains unchecked in his pursuit of dominion over his territory.

Nellie took a deep breath and continued, "Thus with good nutrition and proper temperature regulation, we shall soon have you fully recovered. Moreover, I have herbal remedies for that specific complaint. Do not fear, with this protocol and the good nutrition available here in the Great Salt Lake City year-round, you soon shall be living in high cotton."

Nellie gave Elizabeth's hand one more pat and then passed her a piece of cinnamon bread, still warm enough to emit an enticing aroma. "The first step is re-stimulating a hearty appetite. Please, savor a bit more bread than the crumbs you have thus far sampled."

Nellie caught Rosalinda's eye, and she came back, carrying Priscilla, and sat down again with the baby on her lap. The precious two-year-old sucked her thumb and stared with smiling blue eyes at the other ladies as she played with her mother's hair.

Elizabeth's eyes teared.

I dare not reassure her that motherhood could still be in her future, for there is no certainty, and I just swore I would keep her confidences.

Shaking her head as if to clear her tears, Elizabeth answered a question not posed. "At first, I would have been hard-pressed to describe the landscape surrounding our makeshift camp. My swollen and bedeviled foot held me captive and unable to assess my surroundings for almost a month. I found consolation in the picturesque view surrounding me. Majestic Rocky Mountains stood watch behind us, and Wasatch Mountains rose to the heavens in front. At last, when I healed enough for a shoe, I discovered the wonders of our spectacular surroundings, as well as life-preserving wood, and water, and grass under the ridges of our grand neighboring hills."

Subject changed. Duly noted.

"I admire your undaunted optimism and fortitude, despite your desperate conditions," said Nellie. "Our courage falters here with every rumor of Mormon *revenge* exacted upon unsuspecting gentiles. Revenge? Ha. I call it brutality and cruelty."

Rosalinda chimed in. "The all-seeing *prophet* continues to call on the faithful to pull up stakes and leave town. The doom and gloom may not pertain to us. In fact, our growing *gentile* numbers may be part of the cause, but with so many abandoned houses, the town resembles a ghost town."

Nellie said, "'Tis an unnerving environment, although the decrease in *Saints* has mostly accrued to our benefit. Some left veritable estates, large houses, and tracts of land, grander than even this house, which Mister Wright assumed for a mere fraction of its worth, complete with fertile gardens and healthy livestock."

Rosalinda sighed. "And my Mister Wells just walked into riches — a full inventory of high-quality dry goods to shepherd whilst the Mormon owner wanders in the desert, at command of their *prophet*, forced to find a new home and begin again with only the clothes upon their backs. Our only fly in the ointment? Mister Wells believes the owner will return the second this skirmish is resolved. Thus, even if he is not out of a job, his position will be much reduced."

She shuddered. "Please, God, not resolution through more of our blood sacrificed."

Nellie threw Rosalinda a warning glare.

Must she continue, heedless of the impact of her words on our frightened, perpetually listening children?

Nellie renewed her vow to avoid free discussion of the tensions while her children were within hearing distance. She and Rosalinda could gradually enlighten Missus Cumming as to the machinations of the diabolical dictator. In the meantime, she took some consolation in the fact that Elizabeth Cumming's husband, the new, duly appointed governor, would assume control and steer them into the protective fold of the States.

"Did nothing deter you or cause you to lose heart?" she asked.

Elizabeth sighed. "'Tis like reliving a nightmare to think of our journey, since we reached the summit of the Rocky Mountains and winter weather at one and the same time. Once at camp, with rest and healing for my foot and at least some modicum of shelter, I felt some hope. But sorrows still crowded into my heart. My good pony, my six-years-old friend, whom I rode so much in the previous part of the journey, was lost in the snows."

The corners of Elizabeth's mouth turned down, and she paused, closed her eyes, and patted her chest. With a gulp of air, she added, "He probably starved to death. I forced our entire entourage to remain near camp two hours searching for him, but eventually we could spare no more time. He had eaten from my hand so long.... When we had only three bushels of corn left for fifty-five mules, food for five days, he ate my bread with me, morning and night. He was my pet, and I still miss him very much."

Nellie tried to lighten her guest's mood. "Your presence restores our optimism that your husband shall advise Young this Territory no longer functions as a Theocracy. We embrace the command of a strong, forceful Governor."

Elizabeth extended her hand as if to slow Nellie's runaway train of strong thoughts. "I am afraid my dear Alfred might have a different strategy in mind. He prefers catching his flies with honey, not vinegar."

Nellie and Rosalinda exchanged glances.

This strategy will not suffice. Our only hope resides in a robust, compelling leader, willing to go toe-to-toe with this mad man.

Elizabeth was still shaking her head 'no' and extending her hand trying to still Nellie.

Every time hope springs in my heart, another obstacle rears its ugly head.

She smiled weakly at Elizabeth Cumming. "We shall pray Mister Cumming's strategy will be every bit as effective in curbing Brigham's." She took a deep breath and tried to find diplomatic words to voice her fears, yet mask her disappointment in Elizabeth's view of her husband's capabilities.

But as Nellie sat there, bolt upright, twisting her hair, she could not keep her bitter anger from her voice. "No, no, honey shall not aide us! We need drastic measures to curb this Territory's tyrant, and stop his abuse of power and fusion of church and state. Our dire situation can only be rectified with a strongman's policies as extreme as an Overland Trail trial by jury and immediate hanging."

Both ladies stared dumbfounded at Nellie's harsh words.

Nellie sighed.

Maybe in this untenable political climate, even the companionship of like-minded women offers no comfort.

***

That night, Nellie confessed to her husband, "I fear I was unable to curb my feelings about new Governor Cumming, or my tongue." She shook her head sadly as she continued scrubbing the pots.

Obadiah lounged at the table while they listened to their daughters' chatter as they changed into their nightgowns. He looked up from the letter he read and chuckled. "Who bore the brunt of your passionate words this time, my Cornelia Rose?"

She sighed. "A woman I had hoped to make my new confidante."

"Do not keep me in suspense. Out with it," commanded Obadiah, beginning to get impatient.

"Elizabeth Wells Randall Cumming," Nellie said, on a sigh.

Obadiah exploded. "Of all the people to alienate! I have spent the past few days currying Governor Alfred Cumming's favor, only to have it all undone by your runaway tongue?"

Nellie stiffened and tried to redeem herself. "I suppose I enhanced the problem by engaging in a bit of melodrama. In truth, we resumed cordial conversation, and the woman seemed no less friendly for my tirade."

Obadiah buried his head in his hands. "You unleashed a tirade of criticism of the lady's husband, and you believe all remained rosy in your newly budding friendship? Use your rational facilities, wife. Or is it true woman's heads are constructed differently, so they do not have the brainpower to think logically?"

Nellie drew in a sharp breath. "Thinking rational thoughts increases in difficulty when you are worried that at any moment, out of a clear blue sky, five thousand of our United States' finest soldiers shall come storming down South Temple Street."

"In light of your duress, I shall make you privy to confidential negotiations. Young made one more concession to achieve accord: Federal troops will not be resisted when they establish camp, and eventually a fort, just outside the city."

"Contrary to Young's bellicose mantra, which Hannah Tapfield King repeated just yesterday in my parlor: 'We shall prevent States troops from even crossing the Jordan River, much less than parade through the streets'?"

"I assure you, United States soldiers shall not march through our streets," said Obadiah. "Now compose a note, *tonight*, extending excuses for your outburst and plead for her forgiveness, and all will be well. *If* you learn to curb your tongue."

He leaned in for a kiss and Nellie made fists to prevent herself from slapping him.

***

The next morning dawned crystal clear and pristinely beautiful.

After breakfast, Nellie postponed her chores. "What say we take an early morning stroll to break up our routine?"

Her daughters dropped their dust cloths and ran to the door.

"Why do we gets to have fun instead of work, Mama?" asked Elizabeth.

"I have an important letter to post, and I want to make sure it is delivered today," said Nellie, pulling on her gloves.

They strolled down the street enjoying the morning's fresh air.

I 'spose it's silly I ever feared armed men storming past my front door.

"The cavalry is here!" a tall man on horseback shouted as he charged down West Temple Street.

"Tarnation," said Nellie, swerving the baby buggy back onto the boardwalk and pulling Elizabeth out of the wet gutter. She and her brood stood watching in amazement as a whole battalion of United States soldiers rode in after the imposing, shouting figure.

All civilian movement stopped.

Riding four abreast, platoons of U.S. Cavalry trotted down the street.

James started wailing as her daughters both asked questions at the same moment, but no one tore their eyes from the rows upon rows of men on horseback.

"It is the United States Cavalry!" Nellie explained to her children. "See our grand old flag? See the bars on that man's hat, indicating he is a general? We are protected at last!"

"From what Mama?" Emma worried, color draining from her face.

"Where is everyone?" demanded an imposing figure.

Should he not be riding to Brigham's house and demanding an audience? Nellie wondered, while hope—for an end to the constant fear of Mormon subterfuge—surged through her.

Nellie looked around the town, seeing it now through the United States Calvary's eyes. Only a handful of people stood on the normally busy thoroughfare into the heart of the commercial district of town. When the Wright family had first arrived, so many people walked the streets, so many wagons crowded the roads, often it took considerable time to progress down the street. Now the few residents remaining stood frozen in their tracks, their distress at seeing the Army, at not heeding Brigham's command to burn and flee, visible on their faces.

Relief emboldened her. She stepped forward and shouted, "General Johnson, Brigham Young awaits your arrival." As an afterthought, she added, "So does our new Governor Alfred Cumming."

The General wheeled his horse around to stop right in front of her. "I am indeed General Johnson, commander of the posse, dragoons, cavalry, and foot soldiers. We need no permission from that tyrant Brigham Young to travel through this Territory in the United States of

America. As decreed in the Accord, we shall march through town and commence construction of Camp Floyd, on the Jordan River, at the city limits."

Horses snorted and pranced while the civilians listened in amazement.

"Since we've been deprived of our mission of *posse comitatus*, someone up there givin' it to that spy Mormon, Orrin Porter Rockwell, we shall renew our efforts to complete the rest of our mission: establish two or three forts in the area."

This news thrilled Nellie.

I feel like the most important person in town. The General explains his strategy directly to me!

Thank you, most Merciful God! The United States Army moves right into town! I shan't have to daily fear for my husband's life, nor for the safety of my children. Halleluiah!

A true sense of relief settled over her with these words.

The General saluted her and all the men in rows behind him followed suit.

"Loyal citizens, we come to ensure your safety. We salute you as we ride right on through and set up camp a little ways south," said Johnston.

"Perhaps when you are settled, you can come back for tea?" asked Nellie. Then her face burned with shame.

I shall never be more than a dim-witted sap. Imagine asking a General to tea in front of his Cavalry?

The General took off his hat and swept her a bow. "You provide the true marker of our success. We have secured civilization in this Utah Territory."

A tiny bit of redemption for my stupid invitation.

CHAPTER 21
On the Road Again

Block 75 on South Temple Street, March 1859

Obadiah rushed in through the front door and the gust he brought with him contained more than the tail end of the March wind.

"Time to travel!" he announced. "Who wants to hitch up the old prairie schooner?"

The girls squealed. Nellie froze, her dinner preparation suspended in mid-stir. Even baby James's attention was arrested, mid-spoon bang.

"Can we truly travel again in our Conestoga?" asked Emma.

"Oh, Papa, where are we going?" shouted Elizabeth.

"Papa, you promised I could drive," said Emma, as James banged his cup in affirmation.

"Now hold those horses, children." Obadiah scooped the adorable eleven-month-old into his arms and sat at the table hugging him in his lap. Then he reached for both girls and hugged them on either side. "It is time to make the circuit rounds. Now ladies, and gentleman." Obadiah paused to smile at James as he waved the spoon he still clutched in approval. "Your Mama vowed: whither I go, she will follow. Since you ruffians are attached to her, I suppose that means you must accompany us as well."

He laughed as they shouted, "Huzzah!"

"Husband, when do we leave?" Nellie asked, drying her hands on her apron, all thoughts of stirring the stew gone from her mind.

"In the morning," he announced, and reached for his paper.

"Heaven help us!" Nellie exclaimed. "Have you no thought to the preparations necessary before we embark on such an outing?"

Obadiah frowned. "Wife, your cunning husbandry ensures we are as well provisioned on the trail as in our snug new house here." He smiled and reached over to pull her into his arms.

She melted in his embrace and hugged him back, smiling with love in return. After a minute, she jumped back up, panic at the enormity of the task rising and seizing her with anxiety.

Obadiah picked up his newspaper and shook it out calmly. "I have every confidence this trip will contain no deviation from the norm, and we shall be fully and appropriately provisioned."

"But, husband," Nellie said, the panic now surely visible in her eyes, sharing space with her fatigue. "I cannot adequately prepare us in just one night, especially since tomorrow is washday, and James's schedule remains erratic and somewhat capricious."

"Hmmm, well," said Obadiah, his eyes continuing to read.

"Obadiah, I beg your attention. We must not sabotage our journey with unnecessary aggravation and delays engendered through inadequate time for preparation. Why I am certain you first said these very words when I last proposed a spur of the moment venture."

"True, true," he mumbled.

"So then, it is acceptable for you to leave at the end of the week, in three days' time?" Her heart beat fast as she boldly contradicted his timetable.

"Three days' time?" Obadiah blinked, looked up from his paper, and leaned back on his chair, suspending the two front legs in the air.

Nellie winced in dread. She hated such slovenly behavior in front of the children, but more harrowing, the tilting back in the chair and the repeating of her words were usually a prelude to chastisement.

"Three days' time?" he said again, looking her full in the eye as her stomach clenched in anticipation of the criticism to follow. He hooked his thumbs inside his suspenders and pivoted the chair around so that it only stood on one leg.

Nellie and the children stood holding their breath, as suspended in time as the front legs of the chair were in space.

"Why," he said, "I suppose that three days' time might be the preferable arrangement, now that I reflect upon it. That would allow me the leisure to pursue a few matters that I am loath to leave pending. Furthermore, I suppose that it might behoove me to arrange another meeting with our fine President Young before our departure, perchance enabling us to head towards Saint Georges after my official business. We will be nearby, so we can explore that neck of the Territory." He leaned forward.

The chair's legs re-grounded as a soft whoosh of breath released from the rest of the group.

"How very prudent." Nellie smiled and turned back to her stew.

"Father, I will pack for the girls," promised Emma, and Obadiah recaptured her with a hug.

"I will pack my kit with emergency provisions," promised Elizabeth. "And I'll get my bow and arrow," she shouted, running from the room.

"It will be difficult to wait that long," complained Elizabeth to Emma, as they watched their brother crawl up the steep stairs to the children's room.

Nellie rolled her eyes at the innocent comment, thinking, *et tu, Brute?*

CHAPTER 22
Here Comes the Sun

Nellie's New Kitchen, Block 75, May 1859

"Daily, I thank our most Gracious Lord that you arrived here safe and sound," said Nellie, gripping the chair back in her kitchen and grimacing.

Rosalinda studied her. "You mentioned this quite frequently when I first arrived, but you have not alluded to gratitude for my presence recently. Yet you do so with a grimace on your face. What prompts this sudden vocalized thanksgiving?"

Despite the pain coursing through her body, Nellie smiled. "My labor pangs," she said, and waited for Rosalinda's reaction.

Rosalinda took her by the hand and led her around the table. "All right," she said, with an even tone to her voice. "Let us keep you moving until you no longer have the strength. I'll pack the children off to my house, via the dry goods store to alert Mister Wells he must assume supervision at closing time. Then you shall dictate the herbs and ointments I must assemble."

Gratified completely by this response, Nellie smiled. "Rest assured, I assembled all that we could possibly need in this basket, and we shall review my plan step by step before I lose coherency."

She doubled over in pain at the end of her sentence.

Contraction over, Nellie laughed. "Merciful heavens, 'tis a joy to contemplate this delivery with you. For James, I endured the foolish antics of Lucena as she fled the scene, and then the dire counsel of Mary Ann Angell Young. Hannah Tapfield King's assistance only slightly mitigated that trauma. Of course, James arrived and brought such immediate joy it wiped away all pain, suffering, and annoyance."

Rosalinda laughed. "That seems to be the case with childbirth. If we remembered the particulars accurately, we would never do it again!" A frown darkened Rosalinda's face. "Fiddlesticks! If I had realized you were so far along, I might also have fled town before you requested my assistance."

Nellie's face fell. "Do you fear you cannot aid me?"

"Mercy, no! I fear my own terrible ordeals shall refresh in my memory. Rest assured, we do not want to relive my trauma during the birth of Priscilla."

"I do agree midwifing a birth evokes all the pain involved in giving birth oneself, but I beseech you: help me! Priscilla's beauty, giggles, and sweetness surely eviscerate the pain caused by her entry into the world." Her voice rose, and then caught on a sob as a contraction wracked her body.

Rosalinda laid a soothing hand on her shoulder and smiled at her. "I stand by to assist, and shall remain with you until we welcome a new member of the Wright family. Indubitably, I would have gone to hell and back to bring joyful Priscilla into my life. But please, my dear friend, do not use words like 'eviscerate.'"

Surprise sprang to her countenance, mercifully obfuscating some of the pain from the ongoing contraction.

Surely this word is in my intimate companion's lexicon?

"'Evisceration' is too close a description of labor pain!" said Rosalinda.

They both laughed.

Thank you, Lord. Comedy might well provide unanticipated relief from the discomfort of childbirth, further enhancing its reputation as the best medicine.

CHAPTER 23
Hit the Road Jack

The Wright Residence, June 1859

"William has barely graced us with his presence on this Earth for a month. Surely, even you, Cornelia, my hardy pioneer woman, should see the benefit of not traveling so soon after you gave birth for the fourth time, especially since no necessity exists for your journeying."

"But 'wither thou goest, I will go.'" Nellie burst into tears. "You would leave me friendless amongst these godless people?"

"You might rightfully attach many epitaphs to the Mormons, but *godless* is the last thing applicable."

"The deplorable acts they commit in the name of God sicken me."

Obadiah twirled his mustache. "Stick to facts, dear wife. We do not *know* in hard and cold particulars that they committed any deplorable acts. Your Mormon neighbors treat you charitably and some engage in openly friendly behavior. Furthermore, your confidantes, Rosalinda and Missus Alfred Cumming, hobnob and commiserate with you daily. That suffices to meet all your necessities."

"I might quibble with your definition of *necessities*. Is it not imperative for husband and wife to remain united through thicket and thin woods?" she pleaded. "How can you abandon me to continue dreary domesticity alone for a fortnight?"

As if waiting for the cue, William started crying, and Nellie heard a crash followed by a slap and an older child's cry. She rushed from the room and returned minutes later, holding the baby in one arm and pulling a sobbing Emma with the other.

She saw the set of Obadiah's jaw, and his unsmiling eyes, and knew her protestations fell on deaf ears.

He shook his head. "I journey a mere fortnight. Surely, you can *hold the fort* for the limited duration of two weeks. I have faith in your husbandry. Moreover, this household seems to thrive of its own accord. Your management skills are hardly required to maintain it."

Nellie felt her eyebrows fly so high on her forehead, for one hysterical moment, she pictured them skyrocketing off her head.

The household runs itself? Does Mister Wright say this to deliberately wound my sensibilities or is he deliberately obtuse?

She tugged at her hair and decided not to get sidetracked. "If I were back in civilization in New York, I would have a bevy of women surrounding me, providing extra support, post-childbirth. Here I have only one true intimate, with her own cares, responsibilities, and charges. Yet, you cavalierly assure me I shall be fine."

She plopped down at the kitchen table, fumbled with her clothing to nurse William, and put a soothing arm around Emma's shoulders. "I shan't achieve *fine* without stupendous duress and effort on my part," she said.

In truth, the very thought of sitting on that unforgiving, hard bench in the Conestoga hurts my innards, not to mention my unmentionable areas. But Lord have Mercy, is this the harbinger of our lives to come? Must I remain here, marooned, tied to the anchor of domestic responsibilities, whilst my husband explores parts unknown and partakes grand adventures?

"I hired a Mormon girl to help with cooking and cleaning whilst I am gone," Obadiah said. He planted a kiss on the top of her head. "You must concede, in truth, this shall assist you more than I, since I must devote my time to *my* primary responsibility: breadwinner."

Meaning you confess ineptness in the running of the household, except to warm my bed?

Nellie bit back the vitriolic words and contented herself with only thinking them.

I must not sour my own milk with repressed anger, but instead think only loving thoughts.

***

"I, for one, rejoice in the Lord that your husband dissuaded you from travel," said Hannah King, her still strong British accent lending an authoritative ring to the proclamation.

Heat rose to Nellie's cheeks.

The unmitigated gall! Truly, this woman appointed herself my surrogate mother, but I require none. Furthermore, I certainly do not need a meddling old aunt, a high and mighty wag....

"Lord save my soul, I see my words struck a false note. I merely rejoice for my own personal reasons." Hannah put down her teacup and bent closer. "I have suffered such losses! My beautiful Georgie's tragic death grieves me hourly, and now my intimate companion, Mister Samuel Francis Niesen, returned to England on a mission trip." *Sob.* "My back buckles under the weight of this pain, but the Lord strengthens me with your love and kindness."

Nellie patted the older woman's hand in sympathy, tears in her eyes. "Yes, my dearest Hannah, I shoulder your sorrow too." She paused, sure there was something else on her friend's mind.

Hannah hesitated again. "You see, I have this matter, unresolved...." Faltering, she looked behind her as if to catch any eavesdroppers.

Nellie suppressed a smile. At her feet, James played quietly with his tin soldiers, while in the next room, his two older sisters read their lessons, and the baby slept.

"What troubles you, my dearest Hannah?" Nellie asked.

"A situation on a most compromising part of my person. Lord save me, I am loath to discuss this, much less expose this area to view. Howsoever, I trust you, and you alone, to assist me."

"I never betray my patient's confidences nor discuss their ailments with anyone," assured Nellie.

"Even your dear husband?" fretted Hannah.

The absent one, who no longer makes me privy to affairs of state, even ones that effect my well-being?

"Certainly not," said Nellie with such vehemence that Hannah raised her eyebrows.

Her own problem consuming her, Hannah fretted on. "'Tis most embarrassing. My Savior, save me from this pestilence! I seem to have some type of an eruption on my posterior. And whots worse—Lord! the trials I endure—I am unable to urinate without pain."

Nellie smiled her reassurance. "I can diagnose this without viewing the afflicted area, if it causes you too much embarrassment. I have found winter evergreen effective for strangury. I shall make a strong decoction from the leaves and stems. You may sweeten this with molasses and drink as often as you like, but at the minimum, three times a day."

Hannah looked visibly relieved. "I shall write these instructions in my diary and follow them faithfully. I offer you my heartfelt gratitude. Thanks be to God for your skill and knowledge."

Patting her hand again, Nellie said. "But, my dear friend, this diagnosis merely forms an educated guess—not the most efficacious way to ensure healing. Furthermore, you have seen me in the throws of labor, the ultimate compromising position, so there is no cause for awkwardness during this examination. Please let me examine the afflicted area and verify this concoction shall heal you most efficaciously."

Hannah nodded with a glum expression on her face. "Lord deliver me from the indignities my frail and ailing person must endure."

Nellie led her friend to the birthing room and, with the utmost professional and matter-of-fact manner, examined the sore spot. "'Tis merely a boil, not a fistula. The remedy is simple and painless. I shall make a poultice to draw out the infection, and then a salve to perfect the healing."

Hannah hurriedly righted her clothing saying, "Thank our Gracious Lord for this petty and easily malleable malady. Your loving ministrations ensure it shall no longer destroy my happiness. My dear, the Angels have sent you to me. Who could envision, that lovely day on the trail when I first made your, and your darling daughters', acquaintance, that God would bless us with such a lasting friendship?" She gave Nellie a hug.

Nellie smiled. "Your health remains in my good hands. Please never hesitate to approach me for any pains, large or small."

"I shall never forget how you turned the tide of the strange mountain fever which gripped my son Thom on the trail." Tears sprang to Hannah's eyes at the recollection. "I feared the Lord would take him from me, but your remedies defeated the terrible disease."

Nellie hugged her again. "I do find immense satisfaction in caring for others." After a slight pause, she said, "Now, back to the business at hand. For that nasty boil, I shall furnish you with a poultice of white pine tree gum and marsh rosemary. A cold infusion shall insure no virtue evaporates by heat. These astringents shall cleanse and heal the inflamed sore."

Almost to herself, Nellie added, "If this and the decoction fail to produce the desired diuretic result, I can always steep some wild carrot seed in a pint of boiling water and offer that."

CHAPTER 24
(K)Nights in White Satin

Pioneer Square, Great Salt Lake City, July 1859

Rosalinda hailed Nellie from across Fourth South Street.

Nellie paused the baby carriage on the threshold of the entrance to the cooper and waited for her friend to join her. She glanced at her daughters, but they still had their noses glued to the store window, watching an apprentice bend copper bands for new barrels.

"Have you seen the travelers just alighted from today's stagecoach?" Rosalinda asked.

"Whilst I continue to rejoice in the resumption of normal operations of the coach and mail since Governor Cumming declared the roads reopened on May 11th, no, I do not make a habit of meeting the stagecoach," Nellie answered with a smile.

"I marveled at the passenger attired entirely in dazzling white. How could one's clothing remain white after such a long and arduous journey?"

Nellie laughed. "Even an amateur sleuth like me, with *superior* — " She winked. " — inferential reasoning skills could not deduce anyone's identity from the two pieces of information you imparted: stagecoach and dazzling white."

"The man dressed head to toe in white," Rosalinda repeated. "White suit, a white overcoat, and a white hat. He even had white hair and carried a white umbrella. Did you not see him?"

"Another clue! A gentleman! I surely would have taken note if I had! Who is he?" asked Nellie.

"That piece of information I had hoped *you* would supply," said Rosalinda.

"I'll need just a few more clues."

"A big wig from your area of the woods, New York City. Curiously, he was in the company of that woman we met on the trail. I have two clues for her identity: she wears an Amelia Jenks Bloomer costume and totes a shotgun."

Nellie laughed. "With just those clues, this time I do know precisely whom you mean: Hannah Keziah Clapp. Mercy! I wonder what brings her here?"

"Speak of the devil," whispered Rosalinda, and gestured to a bloomer-clad woman striding down the street.

"Hannah Keziah Clapp," Nellie called. "How delightful to meet you again!"

The two women embraced, kindred spirits reuniting in hostile territory.

"You remember Rosalinda Wells?" she asked Ms. Clapp.

"Delighted to meet you, or see you again," said Clapp, thrusting her hand out to Rosalinda and shaking it vigorously. "Whichever applies."

Suppressing grins, Nellie and Rosalinda exchanged glances.

"Thousands of questions percolate in my thoughts that I believe only you can answer," exclaimed Nellie. "But the most important one: can you dine with us, or take some tea? We must devise some leisure to refresh our acquaintance."

Hannah looked up and down the street. "Well, I don't fancy myself a lady calling at teatime, but as the headmistress of a school eddycating young women in Michigan, I have cultivated some expertise in socializing. I mastered the art of fostering patrons and placating parents who only want young women conversant in the fine arts."

Hannah looked like she would spit on the ground, but then thought better of it. "You are acquainted with the type, them that object to their daughters reading the news and thinkin'. Thus, I believe I have transmuted that particular social skill into a general demeanor of sociable behavior. I shall call in two days' time. Does half two suit?"

Nellie grinned. "Why of course. Rosalinda and I shall await you at my house, Block 75 facing South Temple Street. I look forward to seeing you."

Hannah scowled, "Hells bells, I've committed now. Yet, I'll be pleased to spend some time with ye. I'm hoping ye keep company with other strong-minded women. Ye found some in this infernal place?"

"Interestingly, yes. Besides our present company, you will be pleased to meet a highly educated woman from the East accompanying her federally-appointed husband."

Hannah clapped Nellie on the back. "See you anon." She nodded at Rosalinda and strode off back toward the center of town.

Nellie and Rosalinda smiled at each other and Nellie rocked the baby carriage.

"Where are your children?" she asked Rosalinda.

"Adelaidia, bless her heart, minds them whilst I make a quick dash to the dry good store to bring Wilburforce his lunch and purchase some flour, needed for my supper preparations."

Nellie sighed. "I wish I had an Adelaidia."

"Your girls, although young, are good helpers," said Rosalinda.

The girls pulled their noses away from the window to smile at Mrs. Wells.

"Indubitably!" agreed Nellie. "Moreover, the Mormon girl Obadiah retained whilst he was away, Melissa Mellen, continues to assist with light housekeeping once a week. Before long, that blessing of a girl shall master the art of cooking. Or at least, cease to burn every dish she touches."

Nellie suddenly handed the pram to Rosalinda. "Merciful heavens, I either see a mirage or Mister Horace Greeley, editor of the *New York Tribune*, and resident of Chappaqua, New York, a veritable neighbor to my hometown of Sing Sing."

She dashed across the street.

"The man sporting dazzling white!" Rosalinda said as she grabbed the handle of the baby carriage.

Puffing wind, Nellie reached the man's side and said, "Mister Greeley, forgive my bold advance, but I must greet and welcome you to the Great Salt Lake City!" She stuck out her hand and pumped Mr. Greeley's. "I hail from Sing Sing, and had the good fortune to meet you on a steamboat traveling the Hudson River."

A thought darkened Nellie's cheer and clouded her face.

Merciful heavens: 'good fortune'?

She suddenly recalled that their meeting occurred on the first half of a trip to West Point that saw her return aboard the ill-fated ship the *Henry Clay.*

Mercy, the misery that transpired when the boiler blew and burst into flames. Hundreds died before we could rescue them.

She shook her head trying to stop her runaway thoughts. *Tarry a minute. Mister Greeley traveled on the first ship. He was not aboard the ill-fated Henry Clay. He will not take umbrage at my word choice.*

Greeley peered into her face. "You do look vaguely familiar, but I am afraid I can't quite recall any specifics...."

Nellie said, "I actually met you on two steamboat voyages, but the specifics do not matter. I delight in finding you in this remote Territory. Again, welcome to the Great Salt Lake City, and if I may be so bold, whatever in the world brings you here?"

"I travel by Wells Fargo Coach to heed my own advice: 'Go West, young man, and grow up with the country!'" He laughed. "Before the bloom completely leaves the rose, I thought I should see what I urge many Americans to discover."

She smiled. "I hope your stay affords sufficient time to dine at the home of my husband, Justice Obadiah Weber Wright, and myself."

"I would be delighted to accept your invitation to dinner." Greeley gave a courtly bow. "However, I am staying in the Beehive House itself, thus I am beholden to its schedule. Missus Young has made me quite comfortable, but I have yet to meet the *American Moses*. I shall advise you when I am free. Perhaps, in my reconnoitering, I shall be introduced to your husband, in which case I shall compare schedules with him."

She curtsied and ran back across the street to Rosalinda and her children.

"Our social engagements became quite pressing with the arrival of this stagecoach and the man all dressed in white," she said. "Rosalinda, not only are you coming to tea with Hannah Keziah Clapp, you are coming to dinner with *Old Honesty* himself, Mister Horace Greeley."

Rosalinda wagged her finger in mock admonition. "I presume this personage all dressed in white, this Mister Greeley, for whom you just dashed across the street like a fool to engage in conversation, merits this wanton risk?"

Nellie laughed, so happy at the sudden appearance of this revered person from the East that Rosalinda's criticism had no sting. "Your disapproval shall evaporate when you speak with this learned man. His credentials know no limits: famous editor of the *New York Tribune*, noted orator, political pundit, and sponsor and promoter of the first World Industrial Exhibition in New York City."

Rosalinda shook her head. "So I have read. Howsoever, you don't see me abandoning my babies and running all catawampus across the street." This time she gave an exaggerated waggle with her finger.

Nellie giggled. "New York City should bear *great* as part of its official title. It earned the moniker." She looked at her surroundings. "Not the likes of this... metropolis. Indeed. Quite pretentious."

Rosalinda linked her arm in Nellie's and dragged her, and the pram, past the coopers into the dry goods store.

Nellie glanced behind and saw that Emma and Elizabeth followed them. Her two boys still slept soundly in the pram.

"You invariably revert to the negative," said Rosalinda, "when reminded of your upbring in the East. We dwell here now and fashion this wild desert into habitable civilization." She turned Nellie around and looked her full in the eye. "Furthermore, your great hero Mister Greeley may be sporting a white ensemble with nary a wrinkle nor any dust, but his head looks like he hasn't washed it since he left Chappaqua!"

The two women giggled and parted ways to go about their business.

***

Horace Greeley shook his head. "The man's appearance, quite frankly, took me quite by surprise. Portly in build, plainly dressed, no air of sanctimony or fanaticism. His conduct seemed outright good-natured. Not what I was expecting from all reports."

"Yes," said Obadiah with a wink. "Prophet Brigham Young does not quite appear the villain that the State's press sketches."

"Ah yes, the *press*," said Horace with a wink of his own. "What would I know of the opinion of the press?"

"*Mister* Young's appearance cloaks a devil in sheep's clothing, none-the-less," blurted Nellie, earning a withering glance from Obadiah.

Wilburforce Wells cleared his throat.

Goodness no! Here comes an endless diatribe by Wilburforce, beginning with his impressions of Young and ending who-knows-where?

Nellie stared at him.

Wilburforce caught her eye, and when he jumped, Nellie suppressed a smile.

Rosalinda must have kicked him under the table!

"I do believe Young prides himself on his larger-than-life reputation," Wells began.

Nellie saw him jump again.

Wells paused. He shook his head. "I concur—we must maintain a vigilant watch and investigate every rumor of malfeasance." He took a gulp of his wine and looked down.

Mr. Greeley said, "I must compliment our hostess for the finest meal I have eaten since I left the great metropolis of New York."

Nellie murmured her thanks for the compliment and a silent, *Thanks be to God, and to Rosalinda, for restraining Wilburforce's tongue!*

As they lingered over coffee and dessert, Nellie sought to bring greater diplomacy to her words. "As editor of the prestigious *New York Tribune*, I am sure your sources for your opinion of the man prior to meeting him are well researched and confirmed."

"Yes, I am privy to all the news sources," confirmed Greeley. "Whether it is reported truthfully in other newspapers or not, my paper strives to deliver the facts, and then, in addition, our opinion on the state of the Union. That chubby man surrounds himself with every little luxury. I gleaned he amassed quite the estate. Gee willikers, he owns dozens of properties just to house all of his wives! Of course, he only admitted to fifteen, but my brief sleuthing reveals at least a score more."

Rosalinda giggled.

Nellie saw her jump as Wilburforce kicked *her* under the table, and suppressed another smile.

Turnabout is fair play.

Nellie congratulated herself for serving a tasty meal on an elegant table. She reveled in her achievement. Responsibilities fulfilled, she relaxed to enjoy stimulating conversation with her exceptionally distinguished guest.

Just like the company Mutter and Papa kept at their soirees in fashionable Sing Sing. Perhaps with Rosalinda's aide, and less giggling on her part, we might just craft a civilization out of this desert.

Nellie stole a glance at Rosalinda and her husband, both listening intently.

Moreover, thank you, Lord, for gracing the gregarious Wilburforce with the wit to remain silent in the presence of an erudite, learned man. Yea, his superior intellect stores a wealth of information, which I long to hear communicated before this evening ends.

Obadiah shifted uncomfortably. "I understand great speculation as to the existence and extent of Young's harem runs rampant in the States. But here, the general public rests comfortably in the knowledge that Young seals himself to old women simply to ensure them entrance to heaven, and of course elevate their legal status above *indigent widow* in this world. He only provides them comfort and comfortable surroundings."

Nellie raised her eyebrows.

My husband now defends Young's harem?

'Old women'? Hardly! Young married that poor Elizabeth Fairchild when she was a mere child of fifteen! Outrageous! Has Obadiah not met wife number fifty, Harriet Barney on several occasions? At age four and twenty, my exact age, she cut quite a dashing, risqué figure in her ball gown this Christmas Eve.

'Providing them comfort'? Indeed.

Horace Greeley leaned across the table and smiled at Nellie. "Yes, that thick set man of fifty-five enjoys life immensely. Most assuredly, despite his exhortations to the contrary, he is in no hurry to get to heaven."

The dinner guests laughed.

Amidst the laughter, Nellie rose to clear the table and serve the claret.

Rosalinda jumped up to help her.

"Most certainly stimulating conversation from quite the fascinating man," Rosalinda said, as they stacked the dirty dishes.

"Yes, thank you for your assistance in keeping the dialogue flowing."

The women smiled at each other.

"I have always been impressed at his words, but dazzled by his deeds," continued Nellie. "I read of a most dramatic illustration of Greeley's sense of fair play: after the conclusion of the New York World Exposition, some French exhibitors voiced dissatisfaction with the whole Exposition, allegedly because some of their exhibits arrived back in France damaged in shipping. United States political opinion thought their discontent more likely derived from the French's disappointment in the paltry financial boost the exhibition provided. In any case, these disgruntled exhibitors sued for indemnification. Greeley alone, of all the exhibition supporters, sought to placate them. He traveled to France to help give restitution.

"Then, for his troubles, they clamped him in jail." Nellie shook her head. "Guilty until proven innocent in France, that country does not afford the protections our fine nation provides. 'Twas a devil of a pickle to obtain his release."

"Still," Rosalinda whispered. "He would be a bit more impressive and effective if his head didn't look so dirty."

"I shall advise him," said Nellie. She took off her apron and picked up the tray with the glasses full of claret.

"You shan't!" exclaimed Rosalinda.

"I will," declared Nellie.

"This, I must witness," said Rosalinda, shedding her own apron and scurrying back to the dining room behind her hostess.

Balancing a tray with glasses filled with claret, Nellie placed one at each spot and said, "Sir, ever since I read you, and you alone, went to France to placate the disgruntled exhibitors at the World Exhibition and were tossed in a filthy French jail for your efforts, my admiration of you solidified in stone."

"Affirmative." Greeley rubbed his hands together and looked thoughtful. "The Exhibition of the Industries of All Nations championed a noble enterprise: the ingenuity and enterprise of the United States displayed for all the world to see." He sighed. "'Tis a pity it did not turn a profit for those men bold enough to recognize the opportunity it presented and invest in this exhibition."

Obadiah seconded the opinion. "My hopes rose when I read in your fine newspaper that in the second year, when the initial excitement and hubbub had somewhat abated, P.T. Barnum assumed promotion and running of the exhibition. I believed that ultimate showman had a chance at turning the tides. I understand though, even with Barnum's publicity, it hardly paid for itself, much less than made a profit."

"Correct," said Greeley. "But let us not forget that success is not measured by profit alone. True, I had to defend our integrity and attempt amends. 'He who postpones the hour of living rightly is like the rustic who waits for the river to run out before he crosses,' as I oft say."

He paused, and visibly brightened. "The magnificent exhibition still accomplished its purpose, however. All our inventions, all our grand ingenuity, appeared on the world stage, on display for the public to view. All over the world newspapers reported of the marvelous time-saving inventions: the sewing machine, the velocipede, the elevator safety brake. Why, now Mister Elisha Otis installs passenger elevators in so many new structures, the sky is the limit for the number of floors. I've seen edifices with fifteen floors in New York City scrape the sky!"

Nellie addressed Rosalinda. "Judge Wright and I saw these wonders!"

Obadiah nodded with a smile. "Cornelia Rose and I share fond memories of viewing revolutionary improvements in machinery, and the excellent display by Colt of its new revolvers."

Nellie made a silly face at her husband's penchant for guns but added, "Remember, distinguished gentlemen, the velocipede? My sister and I experienced a thrilling ride in that four wheeled contraption and propelled ourselves about the fair! I read that inventors continue to refine that machine. In France, two inventors took the original two-wheeled *Laufmaschine* and perfected it into the *dandyhorse*. Now a Scottish blacksmith added a treadle, making the two-wheeled velocipede workable by cranks connecting the wheels."

Nellie giggled. "And I mustn't forget *meine Mutter's* favorite inventor, the German, Herr Phillip Moritz Fischer, who invented the *Tretkurbel fahrrad*, a bi-cycle with pedals! I have even read someday we shall all not only *own* two-wheeled velocipedes but also horseless carriages!"

"Aye, magnificent discoveries, indeed." Greeley rubbed his hands together. "All triggered by our Exposition. Yessir, those who believe the illusion that times past were better than times that are now are sorely mistaken, yet have always been with us, since the dawn of mankind."

As the dinner guests pondered these words, Greeley took a sip of claret and continued. "The grand Crystal Palace, erected for the glorious Exhibition of the Industries of All Nations, graced our fair city for many years, as did the Latting Observatory. I exulted in the parade of impressive events at the Palace, and I welcomed the tourists seeking the splendid vistas the *tallest tower in the world* provided of the great New York City."

Nellie smiled and agreed. Warm memories of her visits to the fair and her own spectacular views from the tower flooded her. She smiled, until her eyes clouded with tears as she mourned the loss of those opportunities.

Blinking them back, a thought struck her, and she looked at Mr. Greeley with anxious eyes, "Mercy, you spoke in the past tense! I know my own visits to these cherished monuments shall never be repeated, but what prevents the rest of the world from viewing them?"

"Tourists from across our nation and around the world still flocked to both places, until of course the Latting Observatory burnt to the ground and the Crystal Palace followed into oblivion with its demise last October."

"Demise?" Nellie tried to bar her rising emotions from her voice. "I don't understand. Engineers constructed that building using only the finest materials and the latest technology."

Greeley nodded sadly. "Be that as it may, we have yet to develop the technology to prevent fire from ravaging our fine structures."

She mourned the loss of this treasured structure, full of memories.

"But no one from home mentioned the fire!" she practically shouted, now reminded of her dearth of unfiltered news.

Tarnation!

Since the day Clayton delivered her package, she'd only received seven letters from New York. Moreover, the one from her brother Patrick, the pithiest correspondent of all her relations, hardly deserved the nomenclature 'letter.' Deprived of most of her mail since the day they arrived, Nellie felt the sting of its grievous loss. Governor Cumming recently reopened the borders, but there had been no accounting for all the mail that should have arrived when the borders were closed and guarded by the Nauvoo Legion.

Her reverie caused her to miss some of the conversation around her.

"...but only just recently burnt to the ground," concluded Mr. Greeley.

Newspapers from the States barely trickle into this city. 'Tis little wonder an event such as this does not reach my ken.

"Fear not." Greeley assuaged. "The Latting Observatory continues to inspire. For example, a few weeks before my journey here, a Monsieur Eiffel called at my office requesting any mechanical specifications of the tower my newspaper office might still retain. He scrutinized these, as well as all our back issues reporting on the tower, for some project he contemplates. He visited the tower during the 1853 World Exhibition and showed me quite detailed drawings he had made at the time. I would not be surprised if he gifts the world with some grand and beautiful tower of his own design, sometime in the near future. In any case, someday, tall buildings shall grace other cities, providing the panorama of the Latting Observatory in London, Paris, or even towering over the Great Pyramids of Giza."

Greeley beamed at the assembled guests. "Yessir, architects, newly formed in a professional organization called the American Institute of

Architects, just hosted a lecture on the wonderous structure of the Latting Observatory and concluded it shall ever inspire them to obtain greater heights."

"I do so enjoy a well-crafted pun," interjected Nellie.

Everyone laughed.

Nellie watched Wilburforce's face suddenly brighten.

I must applaud him later. For one so unused to remaining silent and listening, he displayed excellent restraint tonight. I hardly remembered he sat at the table!

Horace Greeley continued, "Moreover, builders all over the world shall use the Latting inspiration and the Otis technology to construct these tall buildings. Thus, the influence of the Exhibition shall endure forever."

***

As Mister Greeley took his leave, Nellie found an opportunity for a private, hushed conversation with him. "If I may be so bold, as an old admirer, nay even a neighbor, as to catch your ear for a moment?"

Horace's bushy eyebrows raised in surprise. "Surely. But why the cloak and dagger mystery?"

"'Tis a rather delicate matter. I hesitate to broach it." All at once, Nellie did not want to ruin the success of her dinner by saying anything this personal to Horace Greeley, revered journalist and statesman.

"Out with it. You are a midwife. Give me my diagnosis." Greeley squeezed Nellie's hand and looked at her, full in the eyes.

"I believe you should avail yourself of the fresh mountain water we channel through this fine city," Nellie said. "I believe your credibility and clout with the tyrant who reigns here, and all his minions, would increase exponentially if you would wash your hair!"

Greeley scowled at her through his glasses.

Then he gave a loud guffaw. "And they call *me* Old Honesty!"

Nellie tugged at the recalcitrant strand of her own hair. "I do hope you will forgive my counsel, if inappropriate, but, put simply, I hold you, my childhood hero, dear to me. I have followed your writing and *your* counsel for so long, I cannot bear anyone, much less than the vile characters who populate this territory, to speak ill of you."

"My good woman, I agree." Greeley clasped her hands and peered into her eyes with an earnest expression. "I shall avail myself of the bright, sparkling water that flows into every garden. These same streams which impressed me so upon my entrance to town shall make a new man of me. I shall assume their air of freshness and coolness once these waters diffuse and wash away my travel woes. Thus, I shall be better able to impress the locals with my person, maintain my stellar reputation, and win my interview with *The Prophet* himself. All my loyal readers of the *Tribune* await my report, preferring my views and the formulations of my own impressions of *This Strange Creature* to those expressed by sources with fewer credentials.

"I shan't disappoint them."

With that he took his leave.

The next day, Elizabeth Cumming, Nellie, and Rosalinda sat with their children nestled around them, waiting for tea with their other visitor from the United States.

A dearth of friends with which to gather, yet now, thank you, Lord, good company surrounds me.

"It's either feast or famine," Rosalinda whispered into Nellie's ear, just at that moment.

"I cherish you, my friend," said Nellie. "I just considered that same thought."

Miss Hannah Keziah Clapp clattered into Nellie's parlor room. "Here I am all bucked up in my Bloomer costume and best hat, sporting the *pièce de résistance*, my pistol," she announced. "Of course, no attire would be complete around here without some type of firearm, now would it?"

Intrigued, Elizabeth Wright ran to Hannah Clapp and introduced herself with a curtsey. "I'm Betsy."

"I'll have none of that curtsying claptrap," said Ms. Clapp, extending her hand to shake Elizabeth's. "Although I am right glad to make yorn acquaintance."

"Clap-trap. I adore your wit, Missus Clapp!" Betsy smiled.

"My title is *Miss*. I brook no quarrel with my unmarried state. It gives me the luxury to answer to naught but my own good sense," said Ms. Clapp, grinning broadly and fiddling with her holster.

Merciful heavens, Betsy takes every word to heart. Who would think a ladies' tea could compromise a young girl's decent upbringing?

Nellie poured out four cups of tea and asked, "Miss Clapp, did you travel here with the esteemed journalist, Mister Horace Greeley?"

"Mercy no, he travels with swift luxury in the Wells Fargo Stagecoach. I arrived using far humbler transportation."

"Not another emigration wagon train?" asked Rosalinda.

"I am afraid so," said Hannah Clapp. "But I wear my Freedom Costume, ready for anything, and my mettle shall measure up to any test. Besides, I meet the nicest women on the trail."

Nellie grinned. "I remember well the circumstances of our meeting. We discussed the efficacy of crossing a rapid river at a particularly precarious point. I recall you vociferously advocated for fording. You shouted: 'Any lady afraid of getting her hoop skirts in a bunch go on back home to the States.'"

Hannah Clapp slapped Nellie on the back and hooted, "Excellent recall."

She certainly could not teach ladylike deportment at her school.

"I am most pleased to make your acquaintance." Elizabeth Cumming contributed to the conversation. "These learned ladies have spoken highly of you. We daily confer and commiserate over the plight in which we residents not complicit in the Mormon faith find ourselves. But I have confidence our new governor shall right the ship."

Hannah Keziah Clapp said, "Jumpin' Jehosaphat, Governor *Cumming* be of assistance? Hardly! Have you never met the chap? I'm only here on a stopover, but I have seen enough. A superannuated, brandy-soaked, Buchanan Democrat, Cumming shields his eyes from all evil doings here behind his belief that the Territories should control their own peculiar institutions in their own peculiar ways."

Stricken, Nellie looked at Elizabeth Cumming, who sat bolt upright, a smile pasted on her face.

Nellie took a deep breath. "Hannah Keziah Clapp, allow me to formally re-introduce Elizabeth Wells Randall Cumming."

Silence filled the room.

She rushed on. "I do apologize. My dereliction of hostess duties rendered this embarrassing moment. But we shall overcome! Missus Cumming, as you can tell from her response, projects quite a different impression from her husband. Educated, erudite, of Boston descent, she shrinks not from heated debate. Nor does she shirk an opportunity to guide political situations in a fair direction. We shall all enjoy each other's company."

Ms. Clapp had the grace to look embarrassed. "My aspersion to Governor Cumming was merely observational. I meant no disrespect."

"I must add, in fact, as Elizabeth knows, I rather share your opinion of his efficacy," said Nellie. "Apologies, Elizabeth, for my blunt expression of my opinion."

"No offense taken," said Elizabeth with a gracious wave of her hand. "Howsoever, I must say—"

Nellie and Rosalinda held their breath.

" —there are many ways to skin a cat. My husband employs a sophisticated strategy: cultivate Young's favor in order to guide him effectively."

Nellie and Rosalinda sighed with relief.

Just as I would expect, Missus Cumming expresses her rejoinder with diplomacy and grace.

"That said," said Hannah, "I shall continue voicing my opinion of your Territory's new governor. The man assured me that I, as a citizen of the United States, have nothing to fear of the Mormons while passing in their territory— *their territory* mind you— *if* I do not discuss their religion with them nor argue with them at all, or meddle in their religious views, but simply pass through quietly."

Wincing for the feelings of Elizabeth Cumming, Nellie bit her tongue.

I can't imagine Miss Clapp doing anything quietly.

Hannah clamped Nellie on the shoulder and Nellie winced again.

"Can you imagine me, quiet?"

All the ladies laughed.

Hannah pointed at Nellie and said, "I knew you were thinkin' it, so why not jest say it?"

Sidestepping the accusation, Nellie picked up a teacup and asked, "How do you take your tea?"

"Tea?" Hannah made a face. "Do ye have naught stronger? There are no Mormons among us, correct?"

Without pausing for an answer, Clapp leaned forward and confided, "I have heard tell that Young banned whiskey imported from the States. I guess he doesn't want the good stuff from the States to cut into the profits from his own distilleries."

"I would not imagine the Mormons own distilleries," ventured Nellie, "since all their faith permits them to consume is Valley Tan, a foul beverage with hardly any alcoholic content."

"Think again, sister. I have it on good authority that spy Orrin Porter Rockwell owns an inn and brewery at the stagecoach stop in Point of Mountain, not more than twenty-four miles south of here."

Rosalinda agreed. "My Mister Wells, too, has heard rumors of the depth and breadth of the Mormon participation in the profits of the forbidden alcohol industry."

"Am I the only one unaware of the spirit of the Prophet's profits?" asked Nellie, triggering the desired tension-breaking laughter.

The ladies sipped their tea.

"I see your Prophet hierarchy fears the loss of their heads." Hannah Clapp smirked.

The ladies looked questioningly at Ms. Clapp.

She continued, "I attended a service at the Tabernacle on Sunday, and I noticed heavily armed soldiers guarded Mister Young and the Quorum of Twelve."

The other women looked at each other.

Another alarming topic.

Nellie sighed. *I must not close my eyes to the dangers surrounding me. I must ferret information from every source.*

"What are your impressions of the Great Salt Lake City?" asked Elizabeth Cumming.

"Are all people indigent here?" asked Ms. Clapp.

"No," Rosalinda answered. "The Mormons as a people are quite prosperous. As you yourself observed, there are lush gardens that feed us all and livestock aplenty."

"Excepting Lord Pratt, Herber C. Kimball, and Lord Wells, I observed a barefoot congregation at the armed service." Hannah touched her pistol with an absentminded gesture while she sipped from her teacup held in the other hand. "No hoops for the ladies. Shirtsleeves, no waistcoat for the men. 'Twas a straggly bunch at best."

"It must have just been that particular service," said Nellie. "In my attendance of a Mormon meeting, just to cut through the cow slaver and hear the bottom facts straight from the prophet, the faithful seemed well-fed and well-turned out."

Rosalinda spoke. "The Mormon Church taints our news and the Utah war impedes our ability to receive letters or newspapers from the rest of the country. Inversely, I imagine little word of the true goings on here ever filters to the East. Lord knows, *we* don't know, and we wonder if our States' government has a true picture of the machinations of the maniac self-appointed king of this territory."

Nellie interjected, "Now that Horace Greeley has ventured into our town, a full, unbiased report of our condition shall appear in the

New York Tribune. As for our dearth of information, Missus Cumming's arrival gave us great insight to nefarious activity in our own backyard, of which we were completely unaware. Now the tide shall turn, with our Army's establishment of a camp just forty-seven miles from here." She frowned and twisted her hair as she spoke, belying her consoling words of greater safety.

"I have visited the camp," Hannah Clapp began, but Rosalinda interrupted her.

"But surely Young has now ceded power, or at least your husband, our duly appointed governor, forces Young to share his power?" Rosalinda turned to Elizabeth Cumming.

Elizabeth gave a sad smile. "Only a modicum of authority, I am afraid. Young has his followers trained to accept no authority other than the Mormon priesthood." She brightened. "If I ever get to the States again, I shall have a good deal to say."

"Hannah," said Nellie, then paused. "If I may call you Hannah?"

"No," said Clapp with startling bluntness.

First, she insults the woman's husband, then she refuses my offer to be on a first name basis?

Stuttering with surprise, Nellie managed, "Forgive me—"

"Call me H. K.," said Hannah Keziah Clapp, reaching out and slapping Nellie on the knee.

Obliging, Nellie asked, "H.K., did you go to see Mister Young?"

"Balderdash! I had no desire to meet the scoundrel. I consider him guilty of treason and not worth the respect of an American," said H.K. "Twelve-foot-high mortar walls surround his house, or should I say complex? Tall watchtowers stand guard at a rod's distance apart. Does this not cast a gloom upon the city?

"Furthermore, why are none of your houses painted, only the high muckety-mucks'?"

"Why, I suppose we have not lived here long enough," Nellie confessed. "In truth, Mister Wright and I only moved to this new, grand abode within the last six months, and I confess I am ignorant as to whether we own this house or just rent it."

Realizing how stupid she sounded, Nellie added, "There was some mention of an *inheritance share*. I have been meaning to educate myself on the state of my position here, but with my ever-increasing brood and my midwifery—"

H.K. gave a gruff guffaw. "With the plethora of babies borned daily, I would imagine that you have no time to even sleep! I met a young boy of about eight years of age, Brigham Young the third, I am told. I guess the prophet has so many children he has to number them!"

"However did you chance upon Brigham the third?" asked Rosalinda.

"I confess, in spite of my lack of interest, I entertained an audience with *the Lion of the Lord*. In all candor, I did not expect the sanguine temperament exhibited by that stout chap, and thus, I endeavored to do my part to make the meeting pleasant."

Strange, Nellie thought as the ladies finished the last of Nellie's delicious herb bread with the last pat of freshly churned butter. *Why the cloak and dagger feigned ignorance of Young if H.K., in fact, had a formal meeting?*

"Dear ladies, how do you survive in this foreign land?" lamented H.K. "I know we are not on American soil here. Yes, I saw the American flag waving over your and the Governor's house, Elizabeth, on Independence Day, but every other place hoisted the Mormon flag."

"We didn't," protested little Betsy, jumping up and knocking over her teacup.

I should be accustomed to her excitable nature by now, Nellie thought as she soundlessly wiped up the spill with her good napkin.

"Of course, you did not, good Betsy," said H.K., pulling Elizabeth toward her and beaming at her. "I appreciate you invitin' me to call you by your nickname. I delight in the beginnings of our intimate companionship, and I welcome the distinction it creates between you and our present company, the illustrious Elizabeth Cumming, woman of fine learning and intellect. For some day, you'll be a woman of fine learning and intellect, and but for your nickname, I won't be able to tell you apart."

H.K. sat Betsy on her lap and squeezed her affectionately.

"I've made it my business to eddy-cate women. Did your Mama tell you I hold the post of *principal* at the Lansing Michigan's Female Seminary? I taught many young ladies, some almost as precocious as you." H.K. lifted Betsy's chin to smile into her eyes, and Betsy beamed back.

Betsy glanced nervously at Nellie, who smiled and nodded.

"Anyway," H.K. continued, "this strange land certainly hosted an interesting celebration of Independence Day. I watched uniformed soldiers of the Independent State of Deseret, armed and on horseback, patrolling Brigham's harem. To my astonishment, Brigham came out on the steps, inside the wall, and gave a short speech."

H.K. turned to Elizabeth Cumming. "Where was your husband in all this?"

Elizabeth started, taken aback, so Nellie said quickly, "There was a separate celebration at the governor's house for—"

"The few loyal emigrants in whose bosom still burns the spirit of '76?" H.K. again interrupted.

"Yes," affirmed Rosalinda. "The spirit burned so fervently, some of them wanted to pull down the foreign flags and hoist up Old Glory herself in front of every household. Did you not hear the ruckus they made?"

"After Brigham's speech, I left town. I celebrated forty-seven miles away. I called on Colonel Albert Sydney Johnson at Camp Floyd. You ladies should pay him a visit as well. He can set you straight about the clandestine operations afoot. He comes from a long line of straight shooters—he'll keep you informed."

"We have met him," said Rosalinda.

"Did he come for tea?" said H.K., her raised teacup covering what Nellie was sure was a smirk.

"Upon occasion," replied Nellie, a trifle offended.

The unmitigated gall! This woman postures a bit too grandly for me. Too big for her Bloomer Britches.

She took a deep breath.

I mustn't take offense, or be petty, she counseled herself.

She sought to soften the angry tone of her voice. "He also joined us once for a lovely dinner. I must admit we were quite relieved when our gallant armed forces of the United States Utah Expedition rode into town, shortly after Elizabeth and the Governor finally arrived."

"Two hundred *thousand* dollars have been paid out of our government's funds to Brigham directly for lumber to build the new fort," advised H.K.

"Necessitated, of course, by the fact that the Mormon's seditious and treasonous army razed the other forts in the area," confirmed Elizabeth Cumming.

"And ninety-two supply chains, at last count, raided and razed," added Rosalinda. "Mister Wells, being temporarily in the dry goods business, keeps accurate running count of such things."

"Not one word of good about the lot of them can be said by any of the soldiers or officers of our Army," confirmed H.K.

"Dire circumstances indeed surround us," said Nellie, sinking into gloom despite her enjoyment of the intelligent female companions present.

"How do you find your lodgings in this city?" asked Rosalinda.

Nellie gave her a grateful smile for the subject change, but it faded when she heard H.K.'s reply.

"I am living at the *Utah House*, the home of a man with three wives. The first wife is talkative. I try teachn' them a better way, if only to revenge the man. He is one-and-seventy, and he preaches to me constantly. One day, he told me, it will be the business of the *Saints* in the next world to teach the gentiles the true way of the gospel, if they had not heard it in this life. But he warned, as he had already preached to me in *this* life, if I don't heed and believe *The Word* now and come follow this faith, I will burn in hell."

"They passionately believe their faith," said Elizabeth, in a diplomatic tone.

"It don't make no never-mind to me. I believe the whole lot no more than a bunch of wicked land pirates. Judges like your husband, Nellie, should bring them to justice or send them to their kingdom come, I care not which."

Nellie sat silent, unable to form a reply.

In truth, I do not disagree with her.

"The men cavort about, licentious knaves every one of them. The women, miserable slaves, not one in twenty can read. It grieves me, for it is true the world over. Yet these women think they have all the rights and privileges they want. Yes, they claim their system is beautiful if only I understood it. The children are half witted...."

H.K. paused and sighed sadly. "As an educator, their uncompromising, fanatical ignorance breaks my heart."

None of the women could disagree.

The gloom permeated the room, settling around Nellie's shoulders. It shrouded her in quiet despondency, like she donned a moth-eaten mantle in a musty cellar that provided no comfort or help in finding the stairs back to the warmth of the main floor's hearth.

CHAPTER 25
Back in the High Life Again

At Home in Block 75, August 1859

Obadiah's rough shake of her shoulder jolted Nellie awake.

"Have you not heard the incessant crying of our youngest offspring?" he demanded, a grumpiness to his sleepy tone.

She bolted out of bed and scooped William from the cradle. His screams immediately lessened to a disgruntled cry. She fumbled with her nightgown to allow him to latch and climbed up into their bed at the same time.

Happy gulping noises replaced William's wail.

"Can you not use the rocking chair in the parlor?" Obadiah grumbled. "I must appear in court this morning."

"How thoughtless of me," Nellie said, hoping her sarcasm did not penetrate his sleepy brain.

Still nursing, she climbed back down from the bed, wincing as her feet again hit the cold, rough floorboard. She crept into the parlor so she did not interrupt William's contented nursing.

Appear in court? Welcome and astounding news.

Just last week, Obadiah had confided that the Mormon stronghold on order and authority kept his docket in court virtually empty. The confraternity of bishops continued to adjudicate all matters both religious and civil. Perhaps he convinced the bishops to bring at least water rights adjudication back to the County Courts, or perhaps Governor Cumming began to assert his rightful authority. Nellie vowed to seek Obadiah's thoughts and opinion on this subject in the morning.

***

Nellie hurried past Obadiah's tidy study in the dawn's early light, with one arm already full of mending and the other aching under a basket of freshly picked vegetables.

The sound of Obadiah's cheerful voice followed her down the hall. "After tending to three matters here in court today, I shall review pending matters in other towns. 'Tis time to make the rounds, Nellie," he called. "There are one or two matters on the docket in the other courts in my district."

Nellie sighed. Obadiah had traveled back and forth to Fillmore City several times already this summer in an attempt to encourage the Mormons to use the federal judicial system.

His frequent journeys on the circuit since William's birth left Nellie alone juggling all the domestic chores. Milking the cow did not bother her, but she could not stomach mucking out its stall. It was small consolation that the grandeur of this house paled in comparison to their home in Sing Sing, but still, it was larger than their first house here, and the added domestic duties impacted her ability to raise her increasing brood.

She shook her head.

Not enough hours spin from a day to accomplish even the most pressing of tasks. My body aches from lack of sleep, and childbirth does exact its toll.

She had known a trip was imminent, as Obadiah had kept his messenger hopping this past week. Now she expected him to exert the same pressure over her activities. His expectation that she prepare his supplies and pack his clean clothes would upend her newly formulated routine, adding more work and more upheaval.

"Merciful Heavens, I miss the coffee beans of New York!" she complained.

She knew the official policy of the Latter-day Saints demanded total abstinence from alcohol and foreign stimulants, thus placing coffee and whiskey on the contraband list. But she knew many a Mormon with a secret line to spirits of all types. Why could she not find a consistent supply of coffee beans?

She shook her head and searched for a solution. "I shall ask Wilburforce Wells, in his new position as subtler for the Army, to locate a source. The United States Army surely receives a steady supply from the East via their provisions wagons."

Issue resolved sufficiently, Nellie turned her attention to her blessings.

She prayed, "I thank you, Lord, for the resiliency of my corporeal self, that you gifted me a back strong enough to shoulder these burdens. Thank you, Lord, for the daily renewing blessing of my children. I apologize that I must cram my prayers of gratitude into chicken feeding and laundry scrubbing time. My joy should never cease if my life included a husband who shouldered a bit more of the domestic burden."

She shook her head again.

I shan't pity myself any longer. I feel certain the Lord must tire of my endless stream of complaints.

Obadiah caught her arm as she scurried back to the porch to check the drying laundry, carrying a folded pile of his undergarments. "I devised no pleasure from waking you in the midst of your deep slumber this morning. Your angelic face in repose warmed my heart."

Nellie smiled, instantly sorry for her treasonous thoughts.

"Howsoever, I must sleep undisturbed so I can continue to provide for this burgeoning family," Obadiah observed.

Nellie shook off his hand. "Of course," she replied. "I understand full well the scope of each of our responsibilities in this joint endeavor of raising a family."

She turned to leave.

Obadiah again caught her arm. "Why rush away?" He smiled.

"To pack your things!" She tried to brush him off. "Before our colicky son again awakes to express his discomfort. I have yet to get to the garden for more catmint, and our poor son's colic disturbs the whole family's rest."

He counseled, "Let me teach you how to work smarter, not harder. Have the girls gather the catnip and submerse it in stream water while you—"

"No! The leaves must be infused in *warmed* water—not cold, straight from the stream—and then steeped for several hours. I shan't allow the girls near the hot stove! I have salved too many burns on other mothers' children."

She held up her hand to stop her husband from speaking. "Before you suggest it, I cannot simply pour boiling water over the leaves and have baby William drink it. Boiling water lessens the herb's efficacy. Moreover, it must be administered by the dropper-full, which increases the difficulty. 'Tis time well spent, however, as it relieves some of the spasmodic pain our poor little son suffers."

"What will *you* wear?"

She shook her head, uncertain how to respond to the non sequitur. "I beg your pardon?" she asked, and then flushed with anger.

I haven't leisure to play this mental subterfuge of a parlor game.

"Should you not simultaneously engage your daughters to pack *your* bag for your return to the intended capital city? I would imagine you ladies longed for an opportunity to don your finest gowns, and we cannot allow the boys to appear anything but well turned-out." He smiled.

Dumfounded, Nellie froze in place.

"Are you not pleased to again accompany me on rounds?" asked Obadiah.

"I am invited to come?" she asked.

"Invited?" he asked. "Nay! Welcome!"

"Oh goodness, gracious Lord!" she cried and turned on her heel to run out of the room.

"Can you spare not a moment for a grateful embrace of your husband?" he called to her retreating back.

"Not if we leave in a mere week's time. I must infuse much more catmint so I might drink some too." She tossed her words over her shoulder.

His responding laughter floated back.

She smiled.

Then panic struck her.

How shall I ever prepare us in time? So many supplies to list and gather! Pack sufficient provisions for four children and two adults? I can hardly expect to find a garden by the side of the road sprouting nourishment. The planning required overwhelms me. Should we bring a chicken? No, foolish. One egg a day shan't suffice for six people.

I must not forget my herbal remedies for maladies encountered on the trail!

How ever shall I assemble the necessaries in time and still attend to my domestic responsibilities?

She chided herself.

I mustn't allow melancholy to dominate my emotions.

She willed herself to be cheered by the news. They would travel together on an excursion again. The whole family would journey to Fillmore City.

My cup runneth over.

She rejoiced in the new opportunity to see the friends they had garnered in that home away from home. Moreover, the time there would provide relief from the endless tasks of running the household.

No menial preparation tasks shall daunt my determination to enjoy this endeavor.

"Who said 'a mere week's time'?" Obadiah's words broke her reverie.

Nellie ran back into his study, holey socks and dirty vegetables protruding from her arms.

"Huzzah, Obadiah! When shall we depart?" She waited, a look of expectation shimmering on her face.

"In two days' time," he said, and burst out laughing at her alarmed face.

"I must have time to make the preparations!" she wailed.

"Woman, calm thyself. You are yet again creating a mess," he scowled at her.

All joyous thoughts again fled from Nellie as she smarted from the criticism and returned his scowl.

"Do not pucker thy face so, it is unsightly." He gave a big laugh and grabbed her in his arms, sending turnips to the floor. "I jest! I prefer you rejoicing!"

"Then do not rob me of my joy, just cherish me for it rather than chastise me!" she said angrily, crushed in his hug, head tilted at an uncomfortable angle, trying to keep the rest of the vegetables and clothing in her arms.

"We leave on the thirteenth," he stated. "That should afford you abundant time to ready the wagon and establish the smooth running of our humble abode in our absence. Moreover, don't give too much care to your attire. Whatever you don, even if it be a gunnysack, you shall still outshine the rest as the prettiest and fairest maiden in the room."

Surprised at the sudden compliment, Nellie looked at her husband.

He grabbed her in a bear hug again, planted a kiss on her cheek, and hopped back into his chair. He turned back to his desk and buried his nose into work.

Nellie retrieved the scattered socks and pants, picked up the turnips, and scowled at the dirt tracked across the parlor floor. Still grimacing, she turned to leave, her mind leaping to the details of the journey preparation.

Did the baby outgrow his nightshirts? Where did I store the next size? I must harvest the green beans, wash the comforters for bedding, and find a handyman.

How could she possibly secure the prosperity of their sturdy little house, its productive garden, and robust livestock in ten days' time?

'Tis nigh impossible to generate smooth operation of our domestic enterprise whilst I attend to daily chores. How will I ever ensure...?

She spied a vagrant turnip as she exited and had to once again dump her armful of paraphernalia to repossess it.

"Such an unseemly view," Obadiah muttered.

Surprised, she turned to see him staring at her rear end, shaking his head, as she straightened herself.

"Displaying thy considerable 'caboose' without modesty."

"Considerable? It is not large! Moreover, thou art my husband! Surely, my bending in your presence is not unseemly." She blinked back tears, so overwhelmed by the tasks that lay ahead and so sleep deprived, she could only take his words at face value and feel affronted and mortified.

"Do not take offense, I merely tease." He burst out laughing. "Fear not, 'tis still a welcome sight, enhanced only when the view is repeated in our bed chamber when thee wears only thy night cap."

Merciful heavens, I find little humor in this. Teasing seems an unconvincing ruse, a mere excuse to insult me and take advantage of my beleaguered, besieged condition.

Nellie, blushing and furious, grabbed her bundles and charged out of the room so quickly that the fire flared in the fireplace with the swoosh emanating from her swirling skirts.

CHAPTER 26
Your Love Is King

On the Southern Trail, September 1859

"It's just like the old days of our great emigration," said Obadiah, laughing as he swung Nellie up on the wagon and handed their three-month-old baby to her. Still smiling, he helped the other three giggling, chattering children clamber up over the big wheel into the back.

She returned his smile. "'Tis even more superb, blessed with two additional children, both wonderful, rambunctious boys. Further contributing to our good fortune, a journey of only one month requires far fewer provisions, affording us the wagon space to fit our high-spirited brood."

She scooted over on the seat to snuggle closer to her husband, relishing his good clean scent and powerful arms.

With a laugh and a shout, he flicked the reins, and the horses sprang into action. The children clustered at the back of the wagon and watched the city fade behind them, but Nellie looked forward, toward the open road. Hugging the baby with both arms, she appreciated the luxury of sitting still, without feeling compelled to darn socks. Little William gurgled and cooed as they trotted along, and at the least sign of fussiness, she nursed him.

"Let's have a tune," chirped Elizabeth, and Emma stuck her head out of the wagon cover to agree.

Riding the full circuit with Obadiah felt like pure Heaven.

Their first stop, Provo, required just a short two-day ride.

Nellie sang, "Over the river and through the woods to Fillmore City we go!"

"I don't see no forest," said James. "I only seed little trees here and there."

Nellie got such a laugh from her son not seeing the proverbial forest for the trees she did not even bother to correct his grammar.

"The horse knows the way to carry the sleigh—"

"At any rate there's no snow, neither," interrupted James.

"Why must you take everything so literally?" asked Emma. "Just join Mama in singing!"

After many hours of satisfying progress, they found a cozy spot to stop for the night.

Nellie bustled about, setting up camp while Obadiah dug a quick trench and started a fire.

Elizabeth picked up Obadiah's rifle and pranced around, pointing the gun at any noise she heard coming from the scrub brush.

Nellie glanced at her daughter as she pulled her stew pot from the box of cooking equipment, and chided, "Elizabeth, remember your gun safety."

"I shall supervise this budding hunter," said Obadiah. "The horses are picketed, and it seems a good time to find dinner!"

Nellie filled her big stew pot with vegetable broth carefully packed in a glass jar with a cork stopper. "Emma, did you know that last year a Mister Mason patented a new way to seal jars with a threaded metal lid? The lid screws into grooves in the glass."

Emma shook her head no, not interrupting the song she sang to baby William.

Nellie smiled. "I suppose this revolutionary invention impresses no one but cooks. Your grandmother and all of your aunts each own some. Their letters made me rather jealous. These jars are but a small reminder of the important time-saving conveniences families in the civilized States enjoy."

She swallowed a lump of homesickness, longing for her former life replete with all the modern conveniences that she was forced to leave behind. Yet, she knew her yearning for innovative equipment masked her true feelings of bereavement for the loss of her family.

Nonsense. My true family surrounds me here.

She shook her head, and her voice resumed its happy cadence. "Once the invention finally comes to the Great Salt Lake City, I suppose sealed jars shall alleviate great waste in spoiled food, and help preserve jam forever in my kitchen too."

She acknowledged the invaluable assistance of her daughter. "Thank you for your loving care of your brother. I love you even though you do not care about jars."

Emma looked at her in surprise and they both laughed.

Nellie began chopping onions and carrots as she waited for the stock to boil.

Emma, bouncing William on her hip as she ran, scampered to her with some juniper and thyme to spice the stew.

Within fifteen minutes, she heard a single shot. In short order, Elizabeth ran out of the woods triumphantly holding a plump waterfowl. Obadiah charged out behind her, shotgun broken open over one arm, one-year-old James in his other, in hot pursuit.

"Elizabeth, you shot a pheasant?" Emma shouted.

Elizabeth giggled and nodded.

Merciful heavens, how could that scrawny little four-and-a-half-year-old even hold a rifle?

Nellie frowned. "All by yourself?"

Elizabeth nodded her head vigorously. "Yes, I did."

Nellie looked at Obadiah.

He grinned. "Little Betsy, 'twas not *all* by yourself. I did help hold the gun and squeeze the trigger."

Elizabeth's little face fell, but then she said, "But I looked through the scope and told you *when* all by myself, right, Papa?"

"Yes, you did!" He picked her up and tossed her in the air.

"I'm a skilled marksman!" Elizabeth giggled.

Skinning the waterfowl took no time and Nellie had it, and a few more spices, in the pot within ten minutes.

Just in the nick of time too!

Thank you, little William, for waiting to shriek your protestations of hunger until after I replaced the stewpot lid.

Soon the Wrights rubbed their bellies, full as the moon shining overhead, and relaxed around the dying embers of their dinner trench. Emma began singing *Yankee Doodle Went to London*, and they all joined in, filling the air with the cozy sound of beloved songs from their cross-country journey.

One by one, Nellie helped each child nestle into some warm bedding and get cozy for the night.

Lying under her own comforter, surrounded by her children, listening to the last crackles of the fire and looking at the stars, she felt a wave of happiness wash over her whole being.

Obadiah leaned over her and whispered, "The moonlight highlights all your beauty, my angel. Your exquisiteness grows every day of our lives together. I love you dearly."

Tenderly, he bent and kissed her. She slipped her arms around his neck and returned the kiss. His kisses got longer and deeper, and in seconds he was tugging at her clothes.

She broke away, laughing quietly in the starlight. "Mercy, husband, we are surrounded by the children."

"They sleep in *heavenly peace*," he joked. "An extremely deep, un-waking heavenly peace."

He tugged at her shirt. "What are you wearing?"

She laughed again. "I could hardly wear a nightgown in the middle of the high plateau."

"All the better to toy with me?" Obadiah's smile lit his eyes.

Nellie's smile widened. Anticipation flushed her cheeks and warmth bubbled through her body. She kissed his chin while he fumbled with her clothing.

"Mercy!" she said. "This harkens back to the first days of our wedded bliss."

He looked deep into her eyes, his face, suffused with sincerity, clearly visible in the moonlight. "My love and longing for you percolates just as intensely as during our first coupling."

"For me as well," she said, enjoying the delicious tingles emanating from her core and shooting through the rest of her body. "I hope we never lose this passion."

"We shall ensure it never slips away."

Nellie ran her fingers lightly along Obadiah's well-muscled forearms and treasured the feel of his hands on her body.

My cup runneth over with joy... and passion.

Suddenly, he rolled them over and she rose on top of him. She felt the cold night air whip her hair, tickling her shoulders and teasing her back. The moon and the starlight shone above her head until she raised her face to the sky and felt a star travel down her body and explode inside her.

She bit her lips to keep the erupting joy from bursting from her mouth.

Later, as Obadiah's snores joined the hoot of the American barn owl and the croak of the western chorus frog, Nellie reveled in the comfort of his arms still around her. She embraced the blissful feeling of knowing everyone she loved most fervently in this world slept around the embers of their campfire with her.

CHAPTER 27
What the World Needs Now is Love

Fillmore City to Mountain Meadows, California Trail, October 1859

"Finally in Fillmore!" shouted Elizabeth.

Nellie grinned. "Is that a battle cry, or a campaign slogan—like *Fifty-Four, Forty or Fight*?"

"Neither," said Elizabeth. "I am just happy to be in a genuine substantial city!"

"Don't know as I would call it a 'substantial' city." Obadiah laughed as he unpacked the wagon.

"The capitol building stands in grand majesty," said Emma. "The ostentatious design highlights the fact that the rest of the town looks ill-constructed."

"Yet the original blueprint designated the building we see as only the first wing of an imposing edifice," said Nellie. "The architects intended to create the largest government building in the whole United States."

Emma said, "Betsy's right. Such a monumental capitol would make it a grand city indeed."

"Plans oft go awry." Nellie smiled. "The Utah Territory Legislators changed their minds. After they invested in making the government seat here, they voted to move it back to Great Salt Lake City."

Elizabeth scowled. "Now I am angry that the capital left. I would think that the legislators would have better things to accomplish than to move the capital hither and yon, leaving impressive edifices standing out alone in the high plains."

"One would think." Obadiah laughed.

"Leaving the place looking half-baked," said Emma.

"Now it's just a one-horse town," agreed Obadiah, and tousled both girls' hair.

Nellie smiled again.

The building projected its visions of grandeur. However, the rest of the town left much to be desired. Fillmore City provided a picture-perfect one-horse town indeed.

***

Our week-long stop in the former capital of the territory passed in a heartbeat, Nellie thought as she watched Obadiah hitch the horses to the wagon. Just as she swung around to climb aboard, Emma came running out of the tiny house they had rented.

Waving Nellie's prized red-checkered tablecloth that doubled as a picnic blanket, and a pair of Betsy's bloomers, Emma shouted, "Look what I found!"

"Dear angel," Nellie said, grabbing her in a hug that almost smothered baby William, still clutched in her arms. "But for you, we Wrights would have scattered our belongings across the United States and almost all its Territories! Once we have commandeered a location for even several hours, all our belongings blend into those already there, such that I can never discern what we have overlooked. Thank you, my sweet."

"I thank you," said Elizabeth, giving a bow. "And my brand-new best Bloomers thank you. For without them I cannot be a modern woman like H.K. Clapp."

Betsy danced aboard the Conestoga with her bloomers as a partner.

That infernal H.K.! Full of claptrap herself! Such a poor model for my daughter. Such a bad influence.

Nellie scowled.

Emma caught her look. "Mama, have I done something wrong?"

"Merciful heavens, no!"

Horrified that her own petty jealousy caused Emma consternation, Nellie gave her oldest daughter another hug and confided, "I must take myself to task for my many foibles."

Emma hugged her in return. "We all have them, Mama," she said and followed her sister into the wagon.

Always wise beyond her years, Nellie mused with pride.

Obadiah swung James into the back of the wagon and then sprang to his own seat.

Nellie clutched William tighter and jumped in.

"Giddy-up!" called Obadiah, and the four horses tugged with all their might.

"Our mighty horses are the strongest in the land," shouted Elizabeth.

"My-tee horth!" echoed James, jumping up and down and waving his hat at the horses.

"They sure step mighty prettily," agreed Emma. "Especially considering the weight of this wagon."

"Just your ribbon collection alone requires a team of horses," joked Elizabeth.

"Pshaw," said Emma, giving her a good-natured shove.

"Our forward travel resumes in the direction of Cedar City. In a few days' time, after some well-chosen stops, we shall circle back home," called Obadiah.

He started singing *Camptown Races* and the children joined the chorus.

Nellie had enjoyed the merry days of visiting while Obadiah attended to business. Only the amazing nights filled with family dancing and guest-laden soirees surpassed them. The happy hours they spent in the former capital simply flew by. The large non-Mormon population had welcomed the Wrights, making Nellie feel more at home than in the Great Salt Lake City. Reluctant to leave, she took solace in the thought that more pioneers resettling from the States arrived daily in Utah Territory, and even the Mormons of Salt Lake indulged in dancing.

Emma intoned *Amazing Grace,* and Nellie joined in, singing with her whole heart.

***

The next night found them in Parowan, a small town newly populated by Mormons who had followed their leader's directive to flee the Great Salt Lake City and re-settle south.

Their journey unfolded, day after blissful day, soaking in the sunshine, even fending off some rain, as they traveled south through the high plains. They either camped in the woods or stopped in every village along the way to Mormon-settled Cedar City.

"Might we attend a court case opened to the public when we arrive in Cedar City?" asked Nellie one morning on the trail.

Obadiah glanced at her. "It's a court, not a three-ring circus."

"I am well skilled at keeping toddlers and babies quiet, and our daughters have an appropriate amount of decorum for the courtroom."

He laughed. "I'm sure."

But she persisted in petitioning him.

At last, he relented. "On the last day in Cedar City, you may attend an hour of the afternoon session."

She clapped her hands, startling baby William, but she laughed. "Good news! Not only because you have acquiesced but because you have such a full docket that your court will be in session all day."

He joined her laughter. "An astute observation, my clever wife." He smiled at her, beaming with pride.

"Of course," Nellie answered. "I recognize the havoc wreaked upon our judicial system by the Mormon's extensive use of their own ecclesiastical courts rather than the federal court system for civil matters, including the legitimacy of land titles, water rights, and various other civil issues. Thus, I proudly assume that your exceptional reputation for impartiality, and your impeccable judgment, has the lot of them flocking to your courtroom."

"I thank you for your faith in me. As you may well imagine, many disputes over the channeling and use of clean water arise in this arid land. I expend great effort to wrest at least this one civil matter from the control of the Mormon bishops." His grin deepened as he pulled her into his arms. "Moreover, I shall continue to strive to meet your standards."

Her heart filled with tenderness at his embrace.

***

On their last day in Cedar City, Nellie brought her little troupe of justice admirers to the courtroom as she promised.

Obadiah looked up and gave a fleeting smile but then got back to business.

We hardly made a peep — how did he hear us? No matter. Maybe at heart, he harbors a pride in sharing his profession with his family.

She sat them all down and they fixed their attention on their father. Nellie skillfully contained her children's squirming and whispering to a minimum as she kept her admiring eyes trained on her husband's command of the courtroom.

Mayhap people do not exactly 'flock,' she thought, from their hidden perch in the corner.

But she observed a steady trickle of adversaries appear before the court. She wondered if Obadiah's reputation truly did bring some petitioners from the Mormon courts back to Federal Court for a more just determination of their grievances.

Or are these merely the disenfranchised members of the Church seeking justice? Would any Mormons brave their fear of retribution from their town bishops to seek federal redress?

Nellie evaluated all supplicants and guessed their complaints from her carefully chosen roost. The Wright family perched in the shadows of the balcony, hiding behind a pillar. Her children remained unobserved, and not a single eyebrow rose at their lack of decorum. Nellie nursed William when the need arose, all the while observing the rank-and-file people of the Church of the Latter-day Saints.

The hour flew by.

***

The Wrights loaded their wagon and rode back on the trail that same night, trying to get a jump on the next day's travel. As she bounced along next to her husband, Nellie commented, "On an individual basis, I find the Mormons quite pleasant people. Those in court today seemed quite reasonable. Moreover, we've encountered friendly faces everywhere, even in Cedar City."

Through gritted teeth, Obadiah replied, "I have chosen my battles carefully and my allies with even more scrupulous care. You must always trust my judgment in that regard."

She looked at him in surprise. "Pray, what behavior have I exhibited that betrayed even the faintest distrust of your judgment?" She tugged at her hair and added, "I trust it implicitly."

He barked a bitter laugh and said, "One would be hard pressed to be assured of that conviction, in light of your unceasing indulgence in the art of cross-examination."

Nellie turned her face away, trying to hide her hurt.

"Do not, ever, underestimate the immense benefits of befriending President Young," he said.

She twisted back to reply but, at his glaring look, chose to keep her mouth shut.

Mercy, I wonder what bee alighted in his bonnet. Befriend? More likely you have been beguiled.

She shook her head.

Friendship with Young comprised a double-edged sword at best.

But she said nothing.

While Obadiah picketed the horses at their new campsite, Nellie sang her husband's praises as she assembled their dinner.

"Did you see how many petitioners sought your father's wise counseling and adjudication?" she asked her children.

"Yes," answered Elizabeth. "But every one of them paid tribute in turnips! I am mighty sick of the sight of them, and we didn't even start to eat them yet."

"Goodness, Betsy, my sweet pumpkin." Nellie laughed.

"Exactly, Mama. I would much prefer they were pumpkins," scowled Elizabeth. "At least then we would be assured of a pie now and then. Now all we'll eat is mushy turnip, and turnip soup, and turnip stew. No one ever made a turnip pie!"

Nellie kept smiling. "No matter. We can trade some with the Wells and other neighbors when we get home, in exchange for other vegetables."

"Honest? I won't have to eat a single one?"

"Do not misquote me." Nellie laughed again. "Some turnips shall find their way into my soups and stews. Perhaps even tonight! It is just their nature."

"Tonight?" cried Elizabeth.

Nellie smiled in sympathy. "Betsy, you would never have known if I hadn't told you. My sweet, our stew also contains partridge and fennel, and many other wild herbs. Just smell the delicious aroma."

Her daughter crossed her arms and pouted.

James ran up next to her and copied her stance.

"'Tis no good to protest, as the stew has warmed sufficiently to eat right now," said Nellie, gathering her skirt into her hand as a potholder and lifting the pot out of her cooking trench.

Just in the nick of time too, as William started crying. She nursed him right on the spot as she ladled the bubbling repast into bowls.

Emma and Elizabeth passed out the plates and the biscuits.

"How blessed we are that the Lord has provided this delicious supper for us," said Obadiah in conclusion to their dinnertime blessing.

"Didn't Mama help by cooking it?" asked James.

Everyone laughed.

Nellie caught her precocious little toddler in a bear hug and whispered into his hair, "Thank you for acknowledging my efforts on your behalf. I love you fiercely."

James pulled back and looked his mother in the eyes. "You're a tiger mother?"

Everyone laughed again.

"Who taught James about tigers?" Nellie asked.

Emma sniffed. "Just because he is a little boy does not mean he should be unschooled in the wonders of the world."

The family's laughter pervaded the dinner. The exhilarating night, with its clear fresh air complete with stars, elicited high spirits from all the Wrights as they feasted on leftover rabbit stew with freshly added turnips. Their playfulness did not diminish as dinner concluded and Obadiah picked up his fiddle. They sang while washing dishes—even James splashed water around trying to help.

As Obadiah played tune after tune, Nellie and her daughters gathered the leftover food, sealed it in tins, and covered it with their gutta percha tarp to prevent any remaining delicious scents from luring animals closer.

When finally they had completed their chores, the whole family danced to Obadiah's fiddle in the light of the campfire. Nellie felt she could never be happier, surrounded by her brood and dancing under the starry sky.

I continue to be so truly blessed. Although, 'tis a great responsibility: he to whom much is given, much is expected.

She shook her head. Tomorrow would provide sufficient time for sobering thoughts. Now was the time to revel in the present and give thanks.

"Goodnight, I love you." Nellie tucked each child into soft comforters assembled on another gutta percha tarp to keep the damp ground at bay.

"Goodnight, I love you," the children answered back, giggling and whispering it to each other over and over as they tried to settle down and sleep.

The happy whispering echoed the 'I love you' around the mountainside and through the canyons.

Later, lying under the comforter, surrounded by her children, listening to the last crackles of the fire and looking at the stars, she let the peace and contentment wash over her and lull her to sleep.

The next day dawned just as rosy.

"Next stop: Enterprise," shouted Obadiah gaily as they pulled out of their campsite on the far side of Cedar City.

Nellie turned to him in surprise. "Enterprise? I thought Cedar City was the farthest extent of our journey. Why have our plans changed?"

"The weary and work-worn never rest," he replied.

But a rush of horror surged through Nellie's heart. "But now our path must follow the trail of that infamous Arkansas wagon train, the murdered Fancher party!"

"I *know well* to which train you refer. You do not have to further elucidate for me, woman! Do not fret so, especially when we have an audience." He threw a glance over his shoulder into the wagon bed, but the children were all playing happily, ignoring them completely. "The path forms the well-traveled southern route to California."

He held up his hand, as if trying to stop the objections he assumed she would be making. "I know Brigham Young closed the immigration route shortly after we arrived, but do not forget: Governor Cumming reopened the route the following May. It surely has been well traveled by the multitudes since that unspeakable incident. There is no need to fear."

"Except that Young could revoke travel *privileges* through the entire Territory for *unapproved* travelers at any time again. Just like he did back in '57," mumbled Nellie.

"Look, Papa, Mama! Indian village!" shouted James. He started whooping and hollering.

"It is a village of the Ute," informed Obadiah.

"Quiet!" commanded Emma. "We don't want them to hear us!"

My thoughts exactly.

She tugged her husband's sleeve. "Were not the Utes responsible for the massacre?" she asked in a barely audible whisper, and shivered.

"I believe Young found the Paiute tribe responsible for this attack," he corrected.

Nellie rolled her eyes. "In any case, that tribe still inhabits this region." She paused, then said, "That theory still does not correlate with the Paiute's reputation as a peaceable tribe. They have never been known to attack people. An honorable group, the Paiute's only transgressions entail little more than an occasional pilfering of food from emigrants' livestock."

Obadiah leaned back on the driving bench, his voice assuming a lecturing tone. "On information and belief, the emigrants in the Fancher party deliberately poisoned the water supply in these parts when they passed through, to deter the Paiutes from stealing their valuable livestock. Thus, their attack was a one-time atrocity, a retribution for harm caused."

Nellie frowned, considering her husband's answer. "Who or what is the source of these allegations?"

Obadiah ignored her question, giving her a *don't-say-anything-else-in-front-of-the-children* look.

"Now, now, we have nothing to fear," Obadiah said again, this time loudly. "Relations between the Latter-day Saints of Utah Territory and the Ute and the Paiutes are presently most harmonious."

"Fiddlesticks. Of course, the Yew-tah Indians!" shouted Elizabeth. "Now I know why the land received the name 'Utah Territory'."

"Obviously," said Emma a trifle haughtily.

"I am quite certain you only recently discerned this yourself," chided Elizabeth. "Do not act so smug!"

"We know it is difficult to fathom," said Nellie. "The larger Ute tribe has divisions called the Paiute and the Goshute."

Aside to Obadiah, she said, "I hardly need to remind you: *we* are not *Saints*. This good relationship shall not protect *us*."

Despite her fears, smiling people in the village waved or shouted friendly greetings as the Wrights' wagon rolled past. With relief, she smiled and waved back.

The day's journey continued without any impediments until they disagreed over which trail in a fork in the road led to Enterprise.

Studying the map details, Nellie finally pointed left. "I believe our path heads that way."

"We merely follow the California Emigration Trail. The clearly delineated main route! What impedes your cognitive abilities?" asked Obadiah.

"I'm having difficulty making heads or tails out of this *Irish huddle*. What is this jumble?" She showed the paper to him.

"It is merely trail notes I sketched from my last journey," he replied.

The horses ambled on for a while.

"I do not believe we should now head in a southerly direction." Obadiah tugged his mustache. "We must aim west. At times, dear wife, you do not have the best sense of direction, or at very least your orientation twists."

"Would *you* like to decode your map?" asked Nellie.

He just stayed the course of the horses in reply.

Another round of joyful sound broke out in the back.

Nearly an hour has lapsed, and yet we seem no closer to recognizable landmarks. She fretted. *Have I chosen the wrong direction?*

She turned the map this way and that. "Were we not at this juncture when we chose our direction?" she fussed. "Now it appears we could have been here." She pointed.

Obadiah glanced over, shook his head, and shrugged his shoulders.

"If 'twere the latter scenario, then we travel in the wrong direction," muttered Nellie, pulling at her stray lock of hair and twisting it around her finger.

They followed a fresh mountain stream.

How far wrong can we travel when we have fresh water at our ready? She tried to cheer herself.

Rounding a sharp bend, with the stream still in view, they entered a bleak and desolate place.

The wind picked up suddenly and juddered through a man-made pyramid of stones piled near the stream.

Abruptly, mid-song, the children stopped singing.

Obadiah pulled the horses to a stop.

An eerie silence descended upon them.

Even the horses stopped snorting.

Obadiah gave a long low whistle. The whistle joined the wind reverberating off the cairn, pinging around the meadow, and bouncing along the mountainside.

"So, this is what Judge Cradlebaugh found!" Obadiah twirled his mustache as his gaze swept the dismal scene before them. "Little wonder the man is mad to investigate! This very scene screams of foul play. It must have confirmed every rumor, every suspicion the good judge held. I wondered why he strode in, gunning for bear, demanding access to documents and witnesses."

Nellie stared at her husband. "The judge seeks to hold the Paiute accountable for these deeds?"

Obadiah stared straight ahead and mumbled, "Culprits must be found."

She frowned at his strange response.

But the eerie echoes and the dismal sight that confronted them obliterated her thoughts, arresting her attention.

She shivered.

Their path through the mountains had been lush with vegetation and bright with sunshine. The place that stretched before them now loomed arid and devoid of even grass.

Stones gathered hastily and stacked pyramid style, several crudely constructed crosses, and a bedraggled American flag, stared grimly down at the Wrights.

But what protrudes around the stones? Why would someone place sticks there? Where would one even obtain sticks? We left the trees far behind.

"Merciful heavens," Nellie blurted.

Thinking better of her utterance, she immediately clamped her hands over her mouth.

Her children were too mesmerized by the monument to hear her.

Bones! Not sticks! Bones surround the stones.

Human bones piled one on top of the other formed a crude burial mound.

Hundreds of human bones!

Nellie shivered again, but the chill created by the visible remains of poor innocent souls, and heightened by Obadiah's grim words, could not be shivered away.

"It's a memorial," whispered Elizabeth.

Something about the sad, desultory scene made them all speak in hushed tones.

"We must pray," said Emma.

James burst into tears, which woke up baby William, who let out a wail. Soon the big girls joined them.

Nellie could no longer stop her own silent tears. She looked at Obadiah. He pinched the bridge of his nose, and Nellie knew he tried to prevent himself from crying.

"Hail Mary, full of Grace," Nellie began, and, beginning with Emma, the sobbing, childish voices of her offspring chimed in. By the time they got to "Blessed art thou..." Obadiah's strong baritone rose above them all.

Nellie next prayed. "Hail, Holy Queen, mother of mercy, our life, our sweetness and our hope. To thee do we send up our sighs, mourning and weeping in this valley of tears...."

Obadiah looked at her. "Remarkably appropriate. Which prayer is that?"

Hysterical laughter threatened to break Nellie's reverent praying. She did not answer but finished the prayer, and motioned to him to 'gee up' the horses.

She gathered her shawl tighter around her, but the chill permeated her bones.

Tarnation! The damage I have inflicted upon the tender sensibilities of my poor innocent children by my erroneous navigation! Joining our voices in prayer constitutes the only way to mitigate the harm to the family.

"I'm glad this is not our stop," whispered Elizabeth.

Nellie heard Emma whisper back, "I think we took a wrong turn."

As they lurched past the horrific pile of bones and hustled away, remorse overwhelmed Nellie.

We indeed have traveled exactly the wrong way, at my direction. Worst of all, I exposed my offspring to the most hopeless place on earth, the scene of the so-called 'darkest deed of the nineteenth century' — the Mountain Meadows Massacre.

"*Mea culpa.* My contrition knows no bounds. I have led us astray," Nellie said, leaning her head on Obadiah's arm and trying to pat his hand.

"I well ken," he said through tightened lips.

He moved his hand away, grabbed the horses' reins and said nothing more.

"Merciful heavens, the perpetrators of this most atrocious crime wander at large, anonymous and lawless, free to terrorize and steal at will?" Nellie tried to keep her voice from rising with her terror.

She shivered again, at first in anger at the horrendous carnage perpetrated here, and then at the grim realization that the fading daylight left them few options for distancing themselves from this spot.

Please, God, no! Do not forsake us whilst stranded at this horrible place! Nellie screamed inside her head.

A look at Obadiah revealed he just reached the same realization.

She whispered, "I have isolated us almost a days' ride away from either our destination of Enterprise or a return to Cedar City. Where can we go from here?"

Obadiah grabbed the map and scrutinized it. Then he threw it on the wagon floor in disgust. "I see little choice but to travel three miles around the rim of the meadow toward the north."

"Does that not leave us dead square in front of the Hamblin's house, with its bird-eye-view of this massacre site?"

The home of the Hamblin settlers remained the closest habitation to this site. The superstitious Mormons claimed the deceased from the Arkansas emigration train haunted the area and cavorted and moaned in the wind every night.

Now I can see why.

This ominous ambiance prevented any new claimants from settling on any of the surrounding land.

Obadiah seized the reins. "We shall stop well before those vile, unhelpful Hamblins, and make a campsite, as usual, all our own."

The wilderness contains wilds and terrors that shall surely prevent the lot of us from sleeping, worried Nell.

She did not communicate her fear to anyone.

Mercifully, they traveled far enough away to find a ridge that hid the view of the grizzly monument site.

Within an hour of eating cold remains from yesterday's supper, the children's spirits revived. No boisterous laughter marked their preparations for dinner and bed, but love and appreciation for each other permeated their speech.

When they were all tucked into their comforters around the fire, "Goodnight", and "I love you" once again echoed and rolled around the mountainside.

A nascent hope took shape in the mire of Nellie's gloomy thoughts.

Perhaps our love creates a balm strong enough to assuage this brutal wound.

"May the blessing of our love and the succor of our Holy Lord help rectify this atrocity," she prayed.

In the end, with the aid of God, all we can do is proclaim and perform acts of brotherly love for all. We must pray and hope that this example influences others to act only in kindness as well.

Despite the warmth of the dying fire, Obadiah's body heat, and the warm comforter, Nellie shivered.

Can we truly ignore the enemy and his dastardly deeds that surround and threaten us?

CHAPTER 28
Everybody's Talkin' at Me

Great Salt Lake City, April 1860

Nellie breathed in the clear crisp air and lifted her eyes to the snowcapped mountains, praying. "Thank you, Lord, for the uneventful winter—full of fears, yet no disease plagued us, and we had fuel and food aplenty. We laughed and prayed with our neighbors. Through Your mercy, we enjoy Your continued blessings."

"Truly," agreed Emma. "The snowy mountains reflect God's majesty, Mama."

Sunshine poured through the windows and they scrambled to prepare the morning's breakfast.

"Yea, verily they sing God's glory," Nellie responded.

"I like watching it snow up in the mountains whilst we enjoy sunshine and mild temperatures down here," said Elizabeth, skipping into the room with a full dustpan, dangerously close to spilling all her laboriously gathered dirt back onto the floor.

"One more blessing for which to thank God each night," Nellie confirmed. "When we want our fill of snow and cold weather, we simply drive our carriage up the winding road into the mountains. In the meantime, we are free to live comfortably, without expending much effort on chopping firewood."

James ran in with an armful of sticks. "Then why do I gots to gather all this kindling?"

My brilliant little two-year-old, inquisitive and useful beyond his years.

"The weather still chills us," chided Emma. "Especially at night. Do you want to lie in your bed without Mama first passing the bed warmer?"

"No!" he shouted.

"Then do your job without grumbling, right, Mama?" asked Emma.

"Ideally, yes. Although, 'tis natural to grumble a bit. I confess *my* guilt in sometimes complaining about the enormity of my daily tasks." Nellie straightened from her position at the stove and looked lovingly at all her children, now scattered around the kitchen completing their tasks. "I hope to eradicate my petty complaints and supplant them with more gratitude for our many blessings."

Elizabeth laid forks on the table.

"Bacon," screeched James.

"Our sumptuous meals offer reward for all our hard work," said Nellie, placing a platter of bacon and eggs in the center of the table.

Elizabeth threw down the dustpan and helped herself.

Mercifully, Betsy managed to dump the dirt into the bin first!

***

"Marketing is such fun, Mama!" shouted Elizabeth.

"I had plum forgotten," agreed Emma, smoothing her hair under her bonnet and adjusting her shawl. "What with all the infant tending I must do of baby Will whilst you scurry out to market alone."

Nellie grimaced.

I loathe that I must make this lovely little girl more responsible than her age demands.

"Your complaint is duly noted. However, nature may have relieved you of this chore already. Grown hale and hearty and the ripe old age of eleven months, Will has proven himself ready to accompany us all on a family outing."

Feeling validated, Emma grinned. "What must be readied before our departure?"

"Naught!" Nellie laughed. "Even the boys remember the fun. They practically dressed themselves, with no coaxing today. They have been chomping at the bit to begin our excursion to the marketplace."

Elizabeth shouted, "I'll get the pram from the shed."

"My goodness," exclaimed Nellie, "you wonderful children truly expedite our exodus for our excursion."

The group started out in high spirits. They chattered and played, meeting several old acquaintances on the State Street's boardwalk as they paraded to the market.

After fifteen minutes of pleasant encounters and exchanges, even Emma could not prevent herself from expressing her anxiety to get to the dry goods store.

"Mama, please! If you *visit* with yet another person, we shall never arrive!" exclaimed Elizabeth.

Emma nodded her head vehemently, and James pulled her by the hands.

"Oh no!" exclaimed Emma. "It's Mary Ann!"

"Emma, it is not polite to call an elder by her first name," reproved Nellie.

"But Mama," protested Emma. "If I call her Missus Young, you will have no idea to whom I am referring!"

Elizabeth and James chortled. Even baby William giggled, just to join the merriment.

Nellie smiled. *I must admit my children speak the truth.*

She remained optimistic for a brief encounter, since Mary Ann Angell's vitriol had decreased since Brigham granted this second wife her wish of her own residence. Although evicting her from the Beehive House and sending her to live in the dilapidated White House seemed a mixed blessing to Nellie, she might now even call Mary Ann friendly.

Mary Ann's sharp voice called, "Hallu, Missus Wright. Stop walking. I must speak with you."

The children groaned and Nellie rolled her eyes.

I suppose Missus Young's change of domicile does not stop her wagging tongue.

While it might have slowed Mary Ann's access to information, she still earned the nomenclature 'church bell' daily.

"Missus Wright, when *did* you arrive back in civilization?" asked Mary Ann, almost before she was even within conversation distance.

James groaned again, but Nellie stopped the baby carriage and turned around to face Mary Ann.

Nellie listened without complaint or comment to an unadulterated stream of propaganda, straight from the Discourses of Brigham Young, with a peppering of complaints thrown in for good measure.

If all I do is agree, the conversation shall cease, she tried to telepathically communicate to her children as they danced with impatience around her.

But, merciful heavens, what a trial to refrain from interrupting Mary Ann! I find this infuriating subterfuge of the truth most unpalatable.

From the corner of her eye, Nellie saw James whisper something to Elizabeth, who in turn whispered to Emma.

In her most respectful voice, Emma said, "Excuse us, Missus Young, but I am afraid our brother needs the outhouse, urgently, so we must scurry away."

Obligingly, James hopped from foot to foot.

When Mary Ann said, "One last item...."

James pinched the front of his pants and hopped a little faster.

Did his pants just darken with moisture?

Nellie grabbed his hand and interrupted Mary Ann. "My apologies, we must leave. Never fear, we shall resume our conversation at just this point, just as soon as possible."

They rushed toward the dry goods store, Nellie sure that Mr. Wells's former employers would accommodate the urgent need.

"Did you not just use the necessary right before we left, as instructed?"

"Of course, Mama," said James, allowing himself to be dragged along.

Suddenly suspicious, Nellie looked past the arm of her son that she tugged and saw his face, not only placid instead of panicked, but laughing.

"I'm sorry, Mama," Emma finally confessed. "'Twas the only polite thing we could think of."

"Completely plausible, too. Right, Mama?"

The impish grin of Betsy evaporated Nellie's ire. She burst out laughing, and so did all the children. Even Will hooted from the baby carriage.

Finally entering the dry goods store, Nellie was surprised to see Wilburforce Wells behind the counter. "Mercy, Mister Wells, I thought you had been relieved of your position here and were now installed as the sutler for our welcome United States Army."

"Relieved of my position?" sputtered Wilburforce. "*Au contraire!*" He took a deep breath.

Here comes a diatribe. Good thing James does not truly have to urinate.

"Spreading rumors that I have been replaced ices the cake of atrocity baked by the *facinorous, notable-cowardly, hourly promise-breaking* Elders' collusion to proliferate only Latter-day Saint commerce and exclude competing *gentiles'* businesses! As if a mere merchant could best me at trade, with my superior sutler's experience...."

Nellie frowned, puzzled. "But...."

Wilburforce held up his arms and looked around. "As you can see, I stand before you in all my glory."

"Yes, of course, but—"

"I'm just funning you," Wilburforce interrupted again. "Yes, when the Mormon owner of the store came back after Young recalled his 'burn and resettle' command, I received a demotion. But the flap-mouthed fustilarian never relieved me of my responsibilities. As I just mentioned, the business needs a valuable man like me."

"But," Nellie began again.

Once again Wilburforce Wells cut her off by raising his hand for silence. "Yes, I hold the position of sutler for the Army, but I do continue to oversee some operations here on a part time basis, as well as barter for favorable rates of exchange for provisions."

Nellie shook her head, annoyed at the excessive amount of 'cat and mouse' played for such a simple explanation.

A crash in a corner of the store saved her from engaging in further conversation.

Elizabeth started crying. "Mama, I did not mean to!"

Nellie rushed over, leaving the pram at the front counter. "Tarnation! What transpires here?"

Elizabeth cried, "It wasn't my fault. James forced me!"

"Besty, James is a *two-year-old*. He cannot *force* you to do anything!"

The clatter came from a box of buttons, overturned and scattered on the floor. Nellie surmised that Elizabeth, attracted by the pretty buttons, had reached in to touch them and then knocked them over.

"It wasn't my fault," repeated Elizabeth.

"Gee willi-wiskers, not mine!" shouted James.

"We can sort this out later. For now, you will both pick up every button, make sure they are not dusty and return them to their proper place," Nellie said, with quiet reproach in her voice.

Nellie turned back to find Wilburforce, but he was right behind her.

"Mercy!" Nellie jumped back, narrowly escaping a head-on collision.

He shoved the pram he dragged over at her. "Madam, you cannot leave your baby unattended at the counter."

Nellie's face registered her hurt and shock.

Wilburforce let out a long laugh. "Pribbling pignuts! I'm only funning ye."

Perturbed, Nellie asked, "Since when have you become such a jolly jokester?"

"Well now, that's an interesting question. My Rosalinda, of course, always loved my sense of humor. Howsoever, I trace my most recent dalliance into situational comedy and prankster-ism to certain life-changing incidents. The origins of...."

Now I have queried myself into a fine kettle of fish! I shan't be able to concentrate on my list of purchases as this silly windbag blows on.

She edged back to the shelves where the last of the buttons rejoined their companions, the spools of thread, and began looking for the sewing items she needed.

"I heard a bit of gossip you may be interested in," said Wilburforce, when he concluded his tale about his sense of humor.

Mercy no! I've had my fill from Mary Ann.

Elizabeth piped up. "No thank you, Mister Wells, we just had a long conversation with Missus Mary Ann Angell Young."

Luckily, Mr. Wells laughed as loudly as the Wrights.

Nellie looked at her friend Wilburforce Wells with renewed gratitude.

His continual drawing of the longbow may constantly irritate me, howsoever, I do appreciate his good humor, whatever its origins!

Seeing that he had her attention, Mr. Wells jumped into his tidbit of information. "Yessir, back in March, Congress ordered an official investigation of the Massacre to determine jist what went on, what how."

This must be the investigation Obadiah mentioned at the Monument in Mountain Meadows. Has Judge Cradlebaugh already begun?

Surely, as an officer of the court, my husband would be privy to this enquiry?

Nellie smiled at a new thought. *Mayhap Judge Cradlebaugh has enlisted my husband's aid in the examination of evidence, thus obligating him to maintain strict secrecy.*

Wary of discussing such an important topic with Mr. Wells, especially in front of her children, Nellie whispered, "It seems prior investigations concluded with the determination that the massacre was, in fact, an Indian uprising."

She raised her voice to conversation level, thinking she could conclude the topic. "In fact, I believe Brigham Young, as Territorial Superintendent of Indians, advised Congress last year that the tragic incident's origins lie in a dispute which has since been resolved."

Wilburforce looked right and then left, and put his hand up to whisper to Nellie. "That new Governor Cumming attempted a lame investigation of that there atrocity, but he collapsed into Mister Young's snare! That flap-mouthed, fool-born, foot licker just turned the whole matter over to Mister Young and let him continue to spin yarns about the matter, rather than delve into the truth of the events."

Nellie gasped. "Why, Mister Wells, your comments rather take me aback! Surely you have spent many a leisure hour with me, sometimes in the company of that good Governor, yet said nary a harsh word to or about the man."

Wells had the grace to look sheepish. "I do always like to think the best of a man. Certainly, when imbibing a shared *supine* supper and a *scintillating* glass of sherry."

Nellie suppressed a giggle, sure Wells meant 'sublime' rather than 'supine,' but Wilburforce sped on, oblivious.

"Sure, clay-brained Cumming re-opened that emigration trail through Cedar City, but those-in-the-know have cottoned to the fact that it warn't Injuns attacking them poor emigrants."

He leaned closer and dropped his voice even lower, and despite her best intentions, Nellie bent closer to hear.

"The Mormon Militia leader of Fort *Harmony*, ironically, and Brigham Young's adopted son, a Major John D. Lee, created that fictionalized account of massacre to remove any suspicion from Young and the hasty-witted hierarchy of the Mormon Church. Since Young ordered the creation of the fiction, he had no qualms about relaying it to our esteemed senators and representatives, to throw them off the scent."

Nellie shook her head. "I do believe our good Governor Cumming would press for a truer answer if what you say were true."

"With all due respect for our Governor," began Wells. "And yes, truly, I have enjoyed his company many a night at your fine dinner table, granting me insight into his methodology and reasoning. Thus, I do believe over time our Governor became convinced that the threats to the territory's peace of an aggressive inquiry into the Mountain Meadows Massacre, in his mind, outweighed the benefits."

Somehow Wells's attempt at diplomacy caused Nellie to cave. "I appreciate your delicacy, Mister Wells, but unfortunately, we both know the gentle man lacks the will to challenge Young."

Angry at herself for her own candor — *to the second biggest gossip in town, no less* — she searched for words to erase her admission of doubt in the governor's ability.

"Yessir," continued Wells, "our folly-fallen, still newly minted Governor Cumming should have tackled that there atrocity first thing. Head on! But you agree: he lies dormant, just like putty in Mister Young's hands. Cumming relinquished power, delegated the whole matter to Mister Young, and let that almighty devil continue to spin yarns about the matter, rather than dissect the incident himself."

Poor Elizabeth Randal Cumming! Her husband may never assume the true might and mantle of governor. He dances to Young's tune. Mercy, she is more 'man' than he! Cumming's feeble attempt at investigating the Mountain Meadows Massacre pacified no one.

Nellie sighed, the responsibility of rectifying the governing of the whole territory burdening her as if she were culpable for its dysfunction.

Truly, Missus Cumming rightly appraises the situation, realizing her husband shall not advance his agenda without enlisting and winning influence with Brigham, but what profits our government in winning little skirmishes when we surrender big battles like this without a fight?

Feeling disloyal to Elizabeth, the Governor, and Obadiah, who towed Brigham's party line as well, Nellie attempted to retract her statement of criticism by repeating her first response. "I have it on good authority that Mister Young reassured Governor Cumming that aggrieved Indians were responsible for the unfortunate fate of the Fancher wagon party. I shan't second guess Governor Cumming's reasoning putting faith in Young's conclusion, since Young holds the position of Superintendent for Indian Affairs. Cumming believes as Agent, Young stands in the best position to determine what had riled the tribe and report that summation back to Washington."

"All well and good," said Wells. "Yes, we would all like to believe that. In fact, we have swallowed that tale for nigh two years. But folks with more distance from the situation, by *moldwarp*, it doesn't sit right with them in Washington. That's why they deputized this Judge Cradlebaugh. Washington can see what we perhaps turn a deliberate eye from. Cradlebaugh's investigation will confirm: the tale just doesn't ring true."

Nellie shook her head and bent over a shelf, looking through skeins of wool.

***

Later that night, darning socks in the candlelight as they sat enjoying the fresh spring breeze drifting through their parlor, Nellie broached the controversial subject with Obadiah.

"Speculation on the perpetrators of the Mountain Meadows Massacre again runs rampant through town from the new Congressional Inquiry. Do you recall hearing any results from Judge Cradlebaugh's fact-finding examination of the whole horrendous tragedy?"

"I keep well apprised of the new scrutiny of the incident. I offer my complete cooperation to a fellow federal appointee and colleague on the bench." Obadiah shuddered. "I cannot recollect this matter without aching for the hapless train involved. You recall our depth of mourning for the poor souls when we stumbled upon the monument during our circuit rounds."

"Of course. A more lonely, dismal place I have never encountered." A tear rolled down Nellie's face. She took a long shuddering breath, tugging at her stray hair. "Howsoever, the gossip now concerns accountability for the culprits."

Obadiah stroked his mustache. "The cry for a pound of flesh, and some good-old-fashioned hangings, once again resounds throughout the Territory. However, Young spoke of this incident to me himself, as well as to Governor Cumming, thus I am privy to precise details of the whole matter."

Side-stepping the implicit challenge of his claim of superior knowledge, Nellie asked. "What were his precise words?"

"Young first broached the subject shortly after we arrived. We discussed whether our wagon trail had any encounters with hostile tribes. Young candidly relayed the entire incident of the savage Paiutes viciously attacking those emigrants." Obadiah shuddered again. "The gruesome details he confided haunt me still today."

"Omitting, of course," said Nellie, "any mention of the reports that Brigham's counsel met and decided to encourage that attack? Perhaps no mention either of the rumors that Latter-day Saints were, in actuality, the attacking party?"

"How often have I counseled you to spurn rumor and conjecture?" countered Obadiah. "Governor Cumming has seen fit to place the whole thing in Brigham's hands and follow his lead. Who am I to counter his decision?"

Nellie blinked in confusion and tugged her hair. "I thought you were a man with uncompromised integrity. One who aligns with truth and justice, no matter who opposes it."

Obadiah looked as if he would say something, but Nellie rolled on.

"That vile, reprehensible man." Nellie snorted. "Equally reprehensible are the apparatchik men who fail to stop him."

"You know not of what you speak! Hysterical woman, we must learn the facts *before* we form our conclusions."

Nellie's ire flashed. "Thus, we grant the man who vows blood revenge on *gentiles* free reign to bury the whole matter under the carpet. Brigham excels at fulfilling his own prophecy: 'I am the Lion of the Lord. I live above the law.'"

"Bury under the carpet? How many times must I implore you to restrain from mixing your metaphors?"

"My metaphor? *That* is the part of my statement that perturbs you?" She abruptly changed the subject. "Has Cumming truly assumed the gubernatorial reins of the Territory?"

Obadiah laughed and looked sheepish. "I concede that point. No, not yet. I hope to convince Mister Young to allow some responsibility to Cumming, or at least officially acknowledge his tenure at the helm by the beginning of next year."

"But Cumming's governorship began nigh two years ago." Nellie shook her head. "Must you placate and pander to Young for the poor dupe Cumming to be granted permission to exercise the authority his title demands?"

"The man possesses the savvy to recognize, just as I do, he can do nothing without the help of President Brigham Young."

"Must you call him *president*? It seems just another acknowledgement of the man's sway. Rumor has it Young used the same dirty tricks he now employs against the States to obtain *approval* for his supreme command of the Mormon Church."

She took a jagged breath and tried to quell the despair rising in her. "It could take another year for Cumming to confront Young. By then, it may be too late."

"Better late than never," replied Obadiah with a twist of his mustache.

Nellie's heart sank even further. In deep despair she grabbed another holey sock.

Now I know the true hopelessness of our situation. A threat even worse than the alarming prospect of war with the States. Obadiah used a cliché to express a complicated thought.

CHAPTER 29
Already Gone

Back to Great Salt Lake City, May 1861

Nellie adored riding the circuit with Obadiah, surrounded by her dear little pumpkins.

Their hardy group of pioneers exceled at employing their skills in the wild. Contemplating the beautiful landscape around her, she wished the joyful two-month journey rolling through prairie would last forever.

A good night's sleep, however, continued to evade her. Every night, when they camped on the road, she crafted six beds from gutta percha tarps, buffalo skins, and large cloth sacks or ticks filled with feathers and strips of cloth from old clothes. Warm comforters, in colorful patterns, made the coziest top layer. But in spite of her skillful bed making, she still felt the hard ground under all those layers.

No matter, as I have reasoned, in this condition it is difficult to sleep anywhere, so I might as well enjoy the freedom of the road and the scent of pine as I slumber.

Nellie blushed with her next thought.

Obadiah's passion simply runneth over in the wild. Dear man. Dear handsome, desirable, hot-blooded man! What continuous joy. The pleasure the Lord grants us in our union has not diminished with the years.

Thank you, Lord, for the gift of this passion.

She blushed again.

Thank you, Lord, for the gift of this corporial pleasure!

Nellie tried to devise reasons to extend their trip. While rumbling through the red cliffs, surrounded by canyon walls, she proposed a side trip to explore the Saint George area. She asked Obadiah if there were any other towns waiting for his services they could visit now. She worried that this blissful honeymoon feeling would dissipate upon resuming the cares of daily life back in Salt Lake.

A message for Obadiah dashed those hopes.

Governor Cumming, anticipating that new President Abraham Lincoln would not renew his governorship, resigned.

Obadiah hitched their horses.

The Wrights raced back to Great Salt Lake City to ensure Obadiah played a role in determining how to fill the newly created leadership void.

Thus ends our cocoon of passion and contentment, in a mad dash to stem the bleeding.

***

Wagon still rolling, Obadiah jumped down at the Beehive House, threw the reins to Nellie, and dashed through the arch.

She trotted their children and possessions back to their house. But in the time it took to learn the news, and the ensuing journey, their rush had gained them no advantage.

The Cummings had already left, and Brigham had already resumed all gubernatorial duties.

Yet again a victim of this Territory's politics, Elizabeth Cumming departed last week without opportunity to say a proper goodbye.

I shall sorely miss the wisdom and intimate companionship of Missus Elizabeth Wells Randall Cumming.

Shaking her head and wiping her tears, Nellie resigned herself to yet another loss. One more deprivation and hardship to suffer, courtesy of his Lordship Brigham Young.

Moreover, the Cummings left town so abruptly, not a whisper of them remained, even though barely a fortnight had passed since Alfred Cumming's cessation of titled office.

My sense of bereavement deepens at their disappearance. Vanished, as if they were never here! I do so hope dear Elizabeth continues in the regime I prescribed for her, so she can one day birth the heir she so desires.

She retrieved some dried lavender from her pantry to stem the headache from her excessive tears. She inhaled its fragrance deeply, allowing its soothing properties to reduce the pounding in her ears and the pain across her right eye.

She patted the large baby she carried within her, soothing them both.

I must solider on. After all, my presence here would not have prevented her departure.

I must focus on blessings.

She acknowledged that her absence spared her the awkwardness and anguish of exchanging goodbyes. She determined to pour all her feelings for Elizabeth into a letter and maintain a brisk, steady correspondence. Like the ties she cultivated and sustained with her mother, and Anastasia, and Augusta back East, as well as Agnes in Chicago....

I shall spend the entirety of my days writing! How wearisome.

She sighed again.

Buck up! She told herself. *Don a pretty frock, or at least a clean apron, and adopt a cheerier disposition. After all, letter writing has its rewards – a return response with news from home and a wonderful respite from changing diapers.*

Thinking of the plethora of letters from New York that had greeted her on her doorstep when she returned home, she smiled.

I shall savor reading each one. Those missives shall warm my heart each night as surely as our crackling fire warms my toes.

I shall see you on paper, my cherished friend Elizabeth Wells Randall Cumming. Fare thee well.

Nellie whispered, "You'll have a little one soon, my sweet Elizabeth. You have regained the strength lost from your winter of '57-'58, and your courses have recommenced. Keep up the regime and the Lord shall do the rest."

Praise the Lord, I still have Rosalinda. Although she does come burdened with her loquacious appendage, Mister Wilberforce Wainright Wells! Mercy, I mustn't be so judgmental of my dear friend and wonderful ally in this foreign world.

While tying on a clean apron, she chuckled to herself. One needn't be a soothsayer to have foreseen that Young would not let the dust of Cumming's retreating footsteps subside before usurping gubernatorial authority again.

As Nellie poured a fresh coffee into Obadiah's proffered cup, she said, "Without a skipping beat, Governor Cumming vanishes and business as usual resumes. I had hoped, somehow, our situation would become more transparent now that the mere figurehead resigned."

"Do not dismiss this change summarily," Obadiah counseled. "This upheaval may provide opportunity for me to win the confidence and respect of Mister Young. Have you no vision? Without Cumming's interference, and by posing no threat to Young's acting-governor's authority, I shall support—and guide—his actions."

Have you still not secured the confidence of that abominable man?

She answered, "Do you not believe Governor Cumming thought he accomplished the same thing?" She shook her head. "Now, emasculated and enfeebled, Cumming retreats home. Depriving the man of all powers, Brigham obliged Mister Alfred Cumming to sit quietly by and achieve nothing."

"*Au contraire!* Governor Cumming employed cunning," Obadiah countered. Then he conceded, "In spite of his attention-seeking vanity. He knew full well the Mormons' displeasure that he had come to replace their omnipotent leader, but Cumming eased their concerns and established a good relationship with the entire Mormon counsel. His gubernatorial accomplishments include resolving various and sundry Indian issues, constructing new roads and bridges, overseeing the sale of public lands, ensuring the security of our United States Mail Service, and managing lawlessness, including cattle rustling and murder."

He grinned at her. "You are a beneficiary of that secure postal delivery, as I see from the fat stack of letters on our *étagère*."

She dismissed her bounty with a wave of her hand, determined not to allow him to sidetrack her thoughts. "We know full well the lack of apparent lawlessness results from the Mormons' control of the judicial process. Superfluous federal appointees gnash their teeth with vexation."

Obadiah frowned. "Must you always focus on the dark side of the picture? You yourself reap the benefits of Cumming's and my skillful negotiations. We secured the reopening of the borders, thus reviving and reinvigorating normal trade routes. Not only do a flood of emigrants flow through our town again, but you, my Cornelia Rose, may enjoy your morning coffee, and other imports, courtesy of Alfred Cumming and yours truly."

He planted a kiss on her cheek.

Surprised, Nellie smiled at him. "I suppose I shall reconsider my dismay."

She picked up the newspaper from the kitchen table when a headline caught her eye. "Merciful heavens, new, larger problems rear their ugly heads. Officially, war has erupted between the North and the South! The skirmish occasioned by the firing on Confederate troops at Fort Sumter and the surrender of Union forces now marks the start of a Civil War."

"Yes, my dear, I was loathe to tell you." Obadiah squeezed her shoulder.

She did not look up from the newspaper. "A Union man, a certain Colonel Elmer Ellsworth, friend and former law clerk of our new President Lincoln, was killed capturing the Confederate flag in a Virginia hotel. His friend, Private Brownell, who accompanied Ellsworth into the hotel and avenged his death, said that Ellsworth could not bear to witness the newly seceded state of Virginia's flag flying so close to our capital.

"Mercy, visible from his window in the White House, it taunted President Lincoln daily!"

"Yes, I am familiar with these events," confirmed Obadiah. "This sensational event shall trigger more conflict than the Confederate troops firing on Fort Sumter in South Carolina's Charleston Harbor. At least no one was killed there. In fact, the Fort battle merely embarrassed our United States Army. They surrendered less than thirty-four hours into the siege."

"But it sealed our fate, tearing our nation asunder, pitting brother against brother!" exclaimed Nellie. "Lord, have mercy upon our souls. We are at war."

Another thought struck her as she paced the length of the kitchen. "Tarnation! You must not attempt to shield me from incidents, however terrifying, that directly impact our lives!" She shook her head in anger. "I never agreed to this change in our relationship. I never wished sheltering from the truth, and I'll not abide it now. Hiding information from me! In New York, I had many trusted sources of information, including the daily press. Moreover, there you shared every intrigue to which you were privy. Now here, with only Mormon propaganda to distill for word of world events, you no longer confide in me the earth-shattering events of our country?"

Obadiah caught Nellie in his arms and with a patronizing air replied, "With your still nascent role of mother to this burgeoning brood, I did not want to unnecessarily burden you with my man's world of dangerous politics."

"I must wait to read the news in my letters from home?" Squirming, she shook her head in disbelief. "Please, swear to me you will no longer keep secret or withhold any bit of information that concerns the welfare of the country, *and* our position in it. I rely on you to supply me with information I can obtain nowhere else here in this God-forsaken place."

Obadiah removed his hands from her arms with an angry jerk. "I have warned you repeatedly: I shall not tolerate such unseemly language in our home."

He turned on his heel and stalked out of the room.

Why must I sabotage my own agenda with my rough language? Nellie cried. *I shan't ever even think a foul word.*

She snatched the newspaper from the table and gave it an angry shake, then scoured it for further information.

"Tarnation!" Nellie's newly sworn resolve crumbled with the viewing of the *Deseret News's* next story.

That dastardly Young's arrogance only increases!

Her eyes raced over the detailed print. Brigham Young traveled to the desolate site of the Mountain Meadows Massacre and viewed the monument hastily erected to honor the departed souls. Nellie shivered as she read, recalling the eerie feeling surrounding them when they stood in that meadow of horrific butchery.

Brigham Young had the gall, the temerity, to destroy this homage. *And now he brags about his deeds to this propaganda reporter?*

She lifted a kitchen chair and slammed it, hard, back down on the floor. *Mercy!*

No. God our Father, show no *mercy. None should be given this cocky, audacious man who holds himself above the law and arrogantly believes in his right to control others' lives and deaths.*

Like a horror scene from which she could not look away, she picked up the *Deseret News* again and read one more excerpt. A quote from Young's opinionated preaching on the unfolding of skirmishes back in the States made Nellie's blood boil. "The Civil War will destroy the United States. God will help us smite our enemies without more bloodshed from us."

She crumpled the paper and threw it into the cook stove.

That smug Brigham takes our country's troubles as a verification of his path and a sign from God!

Suddenly Emma burst into the kitchen, with James following closely behind her shouting, "To market to market to buy a fat pig."

'Tis little wonder I never finish reading the newspaper.

But Nellie smiled at the interrupting children. "Did I forget today is once again marketing day?"

"You couldn't, Mama," said Emma. "Could you?"

I shan't let these dark thoughts rule my days.

Elizabeth came in with William toddling behind her.

"...Right here to Mama," said Elizabeth.

William collapsed onto Nellie's skirt and tugged it.

Nellie laughed.

With my children, my most cherished blessings, literally surrounding me, how can I let these worldly troubles consume me? I must employ any method in my means to influence the world toward the good, and permit myself, simultaneously, to feel the glory and joy of our Lord.

But as they strolled down the street to the grocer for produce Nellie had not grown in her own garden, the weight of the world descended upon her again.

A most unusual sight interrupted her thoughts.

Two lovers walked down Main Street, arm in arm, alternating between gazing into each other's eyes and stopping for an embrace. They seemed an unlikely pair. The man was clearly much older than the woman who prettily, daintily, and youthfully danced at his side. That they were both smitten was clear to see. They seemed oblivious to all the noises, commotion, and people on the street.

Lord, have mercy! Could that man be....

"It's Mister Young," Elizabeth said in a stage whisper.

James pointed and whooped.

Emma and Nellie quickly shushed him.

Nellie and her brood were within earshot of the couple, but the pair continued their walk, and passed the Wright family, unaware of their surroundings. Nellie felt sure that her feet were rooted to the ground while she followed the couple with her eyes, mouth agape.

Snapping it shut, Nellie pointed them all in the opposite direction and managed to steer them forward as the questions and comments came.

"It *is* Mister Young!" confirmed Emma.

"Who is that girl?" asked Elizabeth.

"Why are they all lovey-dovey?" sneered James.

"Did Mister Young get married *again*?" asked Elizabeth.

"Isn't that his fifty-hundred wife?" asked James.

He and Elizabeth giggled.

"You may well giggle," said Emma, "but I do believe the number you spoke as a gross exaggeration is not far from the truth!"

Nellie's head swam, trying to invent a plausible yet proper explanation for a behavior she abhorred. But the questions kept coming.

"I thought your friend Mary Ann was Misseth Young," said James.

"Where did that lady come from anyway?" asked Elizabeth.

"She just comed here last year," informed James. "Remember, we used to run into town to meet the travelers' wagons?"

"I marvel at your memory, James. Three-year-olds are not renowned for their recall of facts," said Nellie with her own giggle.

"My chum said Mister Young met her on Emigration Pass," said Emma, "when he was welcoming a wagon train of new converts. It was 'love at first sight.'"

Nellie only had a second to wonder *who could have told her that?*

"Mister Young is going to build her a new house," informed Emma, "across the street so she won't have to share with Lucy Ann Decker, now that Mary Ann Angell had to leave and move to the White House."

"Is Mary Ann Angell in charge of our government now?" asked James.

Nellie tried to prevent laughter from choking her. "No! Not for a millisecond. Whyever would you ask that?"

"Because if Mister Young made her move to the White House with President Lincoln, I figure it's on account of he wants someone he knows to run the States. 'Cause in the sermon, Young always talks about the government's in-ter-mini-al meanness and slipper shod management."

Nellie could no longer restrain her laugh.

"Using the same name for two entirely different houses can be confusing," she said, tousling her son's hair. "Brigham Young's white-painted dwelling that now houses Mary Ann Angell stands next-door to The Beehive House, right here in the Great Salt Lake City. *The White House* that President Lincoln occupies is the nickname for the dwelling our United States President resides in, back East in Washington, District of Columbia."

She hesitated. *Should I tackle the whole 'in-ter-mini-al' and 'slipper shod' statement or just let it ride?*

"That makes more senthe," lisped James.

"Why would a lady who looks *my* age have any desire to cavort with an old geezer like that?" asked Emma.

"I am sure she is older than eight, Emma," was the only response Nellie could muster.

Tarnation! Mayhap by less than a decade.

CHAPTER 30
Waiting for the World to Change

The Birthing Room, June 1861

Hannah Tapfield King helped re-categorize and seal the herbs remaining while Rosalinda scrubbed all the surfaces and gathered the soiled linens.

"The Lord fortifies me," said Hannah, "and makes me immortal until our work is done. I'll just boil another kettle and get this laundry soaking."

"I can't have my dear friend doing my washing!" Nellie said laughing. "Besides, very cold water from the spring is needed to wash out all the blood. You can have Emma fetch the cold water and then leave it all in the tub. I have a girl who comes to help with the never-ceasing chores on Mondays."

Hannah dumped the soiled linens in the tub as instructed, and circled back with kisses for Nellie and the newborn baby.

"The Lord has blessed you with a strong constitution and a suffusion of bravery, Cornelia Rose," said Hannah. "Birthing that big boy would have taken the stuffing out of a weaker woman than you."

Tears in her eyes, Nellie confided, "I could not have fared so well without the help and hard work of each of you, my dearest friends."

Hannah sat down beside Nellie on her bed, gently caressing the head of the newborn. "The excess of joy from this little angel shall provide redemption from the pain."

Rosalinda leaned over and whispered, "You and this little prince had to do a little hard work yourselves."

The three friends burst out laughing.

Hannah kissed Nellie and said, "Obadiah seemed a trifle surprised at the sight of this robust boy. Does he not expect this after the evidence your other children provide?"

More laughter responded to her question.

"With this cheerful spirit to sustain us, I shall take my leave." Hannah sailed out of the room, grabbing a slice of Nellie's jellyroll. "For my tea."

"'Twas an interesting combination, little Jeremiah," Nellie confided to her new son. "A duet of women, as unlike in both temperament and political views as any could be, eased your entry into this world. I wager Admiral Bird had these exact ladies in mind when he coined the term 'polar opposites.'"

Giddy from this ordeal, I prattle nonsense, but my utter relief at the safe birth of my new son, and my complete happiness, releases into words any thought that crosses my mind.

"Rosalinda," she said, "I thank you especially for your help. After all, you shall be in my position any day now." She watched her friend tidy the rest of her room.

"I jest know in my bones he's a boy," gushed Rosalinda, patting her bump. "He's just felt different from the other two right from the get-go."

"Mercy," said Nellie. "All this child-birthing befuddles my brain. I almost said, 'but you already birthed a boy.' I plumb forgot you adopted Lemuel."

Rosalinda laughed merrily. "Oft times I plumb forget too. And you *know* Wilburforce just dotes on the boy so much, it is quite clear he embraces Lemuel as his true son."

Suddenly Nellie burst into tears. "All the poor boy has left of his family is his last name," she said, sobbing. "Losing his entire family in the river crossing changed the course of his entire life."

Stricken, Rosalinda stood speechless.

Nellie turned her tear-filled eyes toward Rosalinda and cried harder. "Merciful heavens! I can only apologize for my thoughtless utterances. Labor and delivery addle my brain and cause me to babble gibberish. Of course, the tragic accident changed Lemuel's life, but your love and care resurrected him. His new life with you makes him the happiest person I know. Maybe his optimism expands *because of* the severe loss of his original family, and the tragedy engenders additional love and appreciation for his *new* family. All I know is you provide an ideal home for him, including the bonus of doting sisters."

Rosalinda gave a tentative smile. "I do wonder what I have done to the lad sometimes. What possessed me and gave me the gumption to take him unto my own and not send him back East to his kinfolk, the way that awful Missus Clayton insisted we should."

"How could he have fared better, sent back like an unclaimed letter to some kinfolk that did not want the burden?" demanded Nellie.

"Jiminy Cricket, I don't know. But blood is blood. Moreover, here he lives smack dab in midst of turmoil plaguing us daily. One ominous situation partially resolves but remnants spill over into another controversy. Every day we hear tell of fresh Mormon atrocities from our fellow States citizens. Mind you, though I am a citizen of the United States, I refuse to call myself a *gentile*. That Brigham propagates evil. He proclaims himself an angel, yet evidence of his devilry lurks all around us. We live in constant fear that Brigham will suddenly take umbrage at our presence and evict us. Or worse, we will get caught in the crossfire when our good States Army tries to clip back the old tyrant's ears."

"Now who speaks nonsense?" Nellie responded. "Lemuel would have fared little better in the States. Torn asunder by Civil War! I still cannot grasp the enormity and despair of this division. Why, it renders our great democratic experiment of 1776 a failure!"

Nellie shook her head, tears overwhelming her again. "The deplorable state of the world quite overwhelms me. From the moment we arrived here, rumors flew that Brigham conscripted an army rather than cede power to our Federal Government's newly appointed governor. We landed right in the middle of a precarious situation that seemed to spread a threat to democracy like a plague throughout our whole nation.

"Moreover, there is no rest for the weary. I hear snippets of Young's Armageddon language still." Nellie paused for a moment and said, "Although, in truth, Young's self-absorption and aggrandizement may help us at this exact moment. In a twisted way, his arrogant sermon this past Sunday may diffuse the tension here."

Rosalinda drew a chair to Nellie's bed and said, "Do tell. You know Mister Wells and I do not attend services at the Tabernacle."

Neither do we.

Nellie did not bother to correct her friend. Only fully baptized Latter-day Saints can enter The Tabernacle. The rest of the inhabitants of the city heard Young's 'holy words of wisdom' at the Bowery.

Instead, she dove into her story. "This past Sunday, old Brigham leaned his corpulent body over the pulpit and shouted, 'Let the North obliterate the South. What care we? It is to our advantage. Lincoln will be too busy now to harass and persecute us. We can continue our industrious way of life without the constant fear that at any moment the United States will employ whatever means they choose to relieve us of our autonomy.'"

Nellie squirmed in her bed. "'Tis simply torture to hear his bombastic, narcissistic words. Shouted, no less, under color of the Lord's authority in a space of worship consecrated to God. Sure, the wrong version of God, but our Lord and Savior none-the-less. Yea, these words ooze blasphemy along with treason."

Rosalinda shook her head. "Then whyever do you subject yourself to such torture? I myself refuse to step foot in any dwelling in which Young might pontificate."

"But how else to learn of the true state of this Territory than from the mouth of the devil himself? How else to obtain confirmation of the rumors—we may not live in the States or feel the brunt of that civil discord, but we are still at war. We still reside behind enemy lines."

"I'm confused," said Rosalinda. "What is the good news?"

"A mixed blessing. Since Brigham feels President Lincoln, preoccupied with the War Between the States, has no time to scrutinize Young's antics, Young might cease his belligerence and allow life to settle into pleasant commerce and industry."

"Or," warned Rosalinda, "he might use the opportunity to cause all sorts of devilment, believing it shall remain undetected, and thus fear no consequences."

"True." Nellie sobbed again. "Moreover, it is uncertain whether we should fear the Tribes our existence here displaces, or whether the treachery of the Mormons exceeds even our worst fears, what with their constant cry for revenge and their *Destroying Angels*."

Rosalinda wrung her hands. "They still cry for blood revenge?"

"Perhaps you *should* attend Young's weekly service. It is in his preaching that I find the true state of affairs here. Mister Wright does not keep me informed. In spite of my protestations, he continues to attempt to shelter me." Nellie's frown deepened and she shook her head. "I guess I am forced to agree, my anxiety knows no restraint. Evils and malfeasances abound here."

"'Tis no surprise to me. I knew this fear was in yourn heart too. Just neither of us choose to discuss it," said Rosalinda, wiping away a tear.

"Mercy, I gave birth mere hours ago. Perhaps 'tis not the best time to attempt resolution of all the problems of this Territory."

Nellie struggled to lift herself into a less painful position, and tightened her grip around her new baby while she searched for a happier topic of conversation. "Rosalinda, I apologize for my careless speech concerning your extraordinary gesture of love, adopting Lemuel. From the bottom of my heart I sorrow, seeking your forgiveness.

"One bright thought: you shall shortly have your chance for revenge. I would wager your new little one shall make its appearance in the next fortnight."

Rosalinda's smile now reached her eyes, and she gave a loving gentle stroke to her abdomen. "Shucks, I already have a name picked out," she said, almost shyly.

"You do?" asked Nellie, a new worry instantly striking her heart, having been through enough midwifing of childbirth to know the precarious nature of labor.

"Sure. I know in my heart and soul he's a boy, so of course there is a name all dusted and ready."

"Mercy! Will you keep me in suspense, or will you reveal the name?" Nellie asked, glad they were talking about happy things now.

Rosalinda looked at her. "I woulda thought you, of all the perceptive people I know, would have already guessed."

Nellie searched her mind, finding a dearth of ideas. "I guess I must blame my lack of perception on my selfish preoccupation with Jeremiah's birth."

Rosalinda's smile brightened. "Little Jeremiah, we shall note the day, not just for your entry into this world, but that your mother's extraordinary brain slowed to match the pace of ordinary humans."

Nellie smiled and hugged her baby tighter.

I guess she chooses not to confide in me after all. I shall not capitulate to superstition, but it's probably for the best.

"Wilburforce Wells, junior of course," Rosalinda said with pride in her eyes.

Nellie shook her head. "But of course. How silly of me to not think of the name immediately. I know our sons shall be the truest of friends." Shifting again in the bed, she added, "Jeremiah and I stand ready to help you." She kissed the top of her new baby's head, careful to avoid the soft spot. "Won't we, my sweet boy?"

Rosalinda gave Nellie a hug.

Nellie enjoyed the embrace for as long as she could endure the rest of her body's discomfort. "I truly do mean 'stand.' You recall how painful sitting is right now. Ouch!" She complained and winced from the pain caused in her abdomen from her nursing baby.

Rosalinda's smile froze on her face. "I should never have assisted you in this birth."

Nellie burst into tears again. "I did apologize for my thoughtless words."

"Silly goose, it's not *that*." Rosalinda sighed. "For a moment, I plumb forgot the ordeal awaiting me. After all, Priscilla celebrated her second birthday this past June." She shuddered. "My baby's kicking reminded me what's comin' down the pike. And you just brought all the details back for me in vivid color. Now what did I do, getting myself in trouble like this?"

Both women burst out laughing.

Nellie stroked her newborn son as he nursed and said another silent prayer. *Thank you, dear Lord, for the safe delivery of this precious bundle of joy. In a world fraught with death and tragedy, thank you for this gift of new life.*

***

The first two weeks of little Jeremiah's life passed by in a blur for Nellie. In between the baby's constant nursing, burping, and only short naps, she focused her attention on her other children, happy to rely upon Hannah and Rosalinda and some kindly neighbors for gifts of meals.

She vowed to clean more thoroughly when the baby got older, as she stepped over a pile of Emma's and Elizabeth's dirty stockings.

Sweet Melissa Mormon... mercy, that can't be her last name! I know it is something that begins with an 'm'... can triage the kitchen spills and clean where necessary until I regain some vigor.

"Your hardy welcome of your new little brother warms my heart," Nellie said to James as she tried to prevent the baby from choking in his big brother's enthusiastic hug.

"I do like babies, sure," said James. "But when will he talk, better than William?"

Nellie smiled. "William learns very quickly. As the biggest brother, perhaps you can practice some patience, for little Will has only been your brother for two years. He still needs you to teach him many more things. But take heart, his language skills improve daily."

"So, you mean this new boy can't do anything better than Will?" James looked crestfallen. "Aw shucks. Do we need to keep him?"

Nellie hugged him, ignoring the tears that sprang unwelcome to her eyes.

Emma rushed into the room. "When can it be my turn to hold Jeremiah? Betsy's hogging him."

This dispute I welcome.

At least the girls' acceptance of their brother, even though it fostered more competition between them, confirmed their bond with the newest member of their clan.

CHAPTER 31
How Far Is Heaven?

Block 61, Great Salt Lake City, July 1861

Nellie padded around the kitchen. She ground enough beans to brew the coffee strong enough to stand her spoon upright, trying to compensate for her complete lack of sleep... again.

She shook her head.

I mustn't exaggerate my troubles. If I commence an optimistic dialogue with myself, my outlook shall glow rosier. Restated: I enjoyed almost three hours of sleep.

She hummed and waltzed around the room, hugging Jeremiah who snuggled right under her chin.

"Lord, thank you for my blessings. I count five — all my little ones. What a charmed life I lead — five times of confinement, five beautiful children. Dear Lord, keep me pleasant and loving through the day. I know that lack of sleep brooks no excuse for unkindness and ingratitude."

Turning in her waltz, Nellie knocked over the sack of coffee beans, which she had left open on the table while she ground the few for the morning. Tears sprang to her eyes.

'Tis of no consequence, she counseled herself. *Betsy and Jimmy will be only too happy to pick them up and grind me a week's worth of coffee.*

Rosalinda burst into the room. "Something don't feel right."

It's five o'clock in the morning! Nellie thought, but she sprang into action.

Carefully, she put Jeremiah down. "Hush, hush, little one. You've just been fed, and all is well with the world."

Rosalinda panted next to her, winded from her journey to Nellie's kitchen.

"Did you sprint here to induce labor?" Nellie smiled. "Have you forgotten the nature and sensation of labor pangs?"

"No, no, you don't understand," Rosalinda cried. "Something ain't right."

Nellie snapped into midwife mode. "Water gushed down your limbs? Cramping in your abdomen?"

"No," Rosalinda wailed. "I haven't felt the little feller move all night."

Nellie frowned. "Do you remember exactly when you last felt him move?"

Rosalinda continued sobbing. "I haven't felt him since yesterday."

"In the morning? In the afternoon? Last night after dinner?" Nellie asked.

Rosalinda put her hand to her head and her shoulders shook. "I can't remember!"

Nellie took a deep breath, put her arm on her friend's back, and asked in a calm soothing voice, "Did you feel him when you laid down for sleep last night?"

"No, *no*," wailed Rosalinda.

"When you cooked supper?" Nellie slipped her arm down to hug Rosalinda. "Think, my dearest friend. Any details you remember may help me diagnose our situation."

Hiccupping now, Rosalinda said, "I remember he kicked something fierce yesterday morning. And when I didn't feel him all the rest of the day, I thought he was just taking a long nap. But I ain't felt him since."

Nellie's heart sank.

But she adopted a brisk tone. "I shall awake Obadiah. He will fetch Hannah and Mary Ann Angell Young, and Adelaidia shall attend to all the children and help them with their lessons."

"Not Mary Ann," wailed Rosalinda.

"We must enlist all skills," said Nellie, taking her by the hand and bringing her to the cot she used for her midwifery business.

"Can we at least go back to my house?" asked Rosalinda.

***

Rosalinda writhed in agony, tears streaming from her eyes, her stillborn baby clutched in her arms. "No, no!"

Crying herself, Nellie applied fresh compresses and tried to staunch Rosalinda's bleeding.

A new thought pulled Rosalinda to a sitting position. "You must baptize him, or our Lord will turn him away from them pearly gates.

Hells Bells! You have to baptize him." She reached her hand out as if to grab onto Nellie and pull her onto the cot with her.

Nellie blinked. *I'm a midwife, not a priest, have mercy!*

Rosalinda flopped back down. Her sobbing turned hysterical and fresh blood darkened Nellie's newly applied compress.

How can I tell her that her baby cannot receive baptism since he is already dead? Our faith requires conscious acceptance, or at least consciousness.

"Nellie, please. You know any good Catholic can validly baptize." Rosalinda's voice now came out in a whisper, as if she didn't have the strength to make it any louder.

Nellie tied a new bandage into place and moved to the side of the bed.

Still crying, Nellie made the sign of the cross on the baby's forehead, as Rosalinda clutched him tighter in her arms. "I baptize you, Wilberforce Wainright Wells, junior, in the name of the Father and of the Son and of the Holy Ghost. Amen."

"Amen," said Rosalinda, sobbing.

Nellie reached for the baby, but Rosalinda just clutched it tighter. "No, no. I cannot part with this little angel. No, no. This cannot be his fate." Rosalinda turned her tear-streaked face to Nellie and demanded, "What did I do wrong?"

"Nothing! Nothing at all. We know not why this sometimes happens. Perhaps—"

"Don't you dare say 'the will of God.' How could God be so cruel as to will this?" Rosalinda demanded, face fierce with distress.

Nellie shook her head, searching for an answer to help her friend in this horrible time of grief.

Perhaps I should stick to a subject I have studied thoroughly, and leave the will of God to the learned priests.

"Medical study has not advanced sufficiently to allow me to know for certain. I would guess that for some reason your baby—"

"Junior," inserted Rosalinda.

Nellie raised her eyebrows but continued. "For some reason, Junior could not sustain his own life." She stood and gently took the baby from Rosalinda. "I know this hurts. I know this is an unbearable burden to shoulder, but I am here to carry it with you. We know your little angel looks down upon us from heaven. His saintly soul is in good hands. The best. He is with our Lord now."

Tears streaming down her face, Nellie turned and cleaned the baby and wrapped him in the blanket that should have held him as a squirming bundle of joy.

"I must hold him again," demanded Rosalinda.

Nellie placed the bundle in her arms, tried to swallow her own grief, and went into the kitchen.

Emma stood at the stove watching the kettle boiling. "Oh, Mama," she said, and burst into tears too. "I went to the room to help you and I heard you baptize the baby. Lord in heaven, Mama, why?"

Nellie sighed. "I suppose only God knows."

She had noticed the chest of the baby seemed malformed, concave rather than convex. She tried massage to stimulate the heart, open the lungs, but the baby did not respond.

Perhaps this malady prevented a lifetime of hardship.... But I have yet to discuss this with Rosalinda. I must wait until she is stronger, or until she asks.

Emma reached for her mother and they cried silently. "I... I boiled some more water for you, thinkin'...."

Nellie gave her a final, grateful hug. "Yes, I know. We would have used it to.... I'll use it now for a healing tea for Aunt Rosalinda."

Minutes later, Nellie returned to the birthing room and offered a cup to Rosalinda. "Here, drink this."

"What is it," Rosalinda said in a small voice, tears still sliding down her cheeks.

"Just a bit of chamomile tea with a special sprinkling of cardamom."

Rosalinda took a gulp, and then some more sips. "What is card-a-man?"

A good sign – a question expressing interest.

"A spice I brought from New York. I studied at an apothecary that imported the spice from England, but it is grown in British Ceylon."

"How do you still have a supply?" Rosalinda said, the distraction temporarily checking the flow of tears.

"I preserve some seeds from each crop and continue to successfully grow it here," said Nellie. "The obliging Missus Hannah King allows me space in her greenhouse for cultivating some of my herbs."

"Herself is it," said Rosalinda, and made a face.

Nellie smiled. "I know you hold no love for Hannah, but I also know you bear her no ill will. Her ministrations here in this time of tragedy aided us both. In any case, the cardamom carries nutrients, healing benefits, and special properties that function as a natural tranquilizer."

"I don't need a tranquilizer," Rosalinda protested, halfheartedly.

Nellie sat down on the bed beside her friend and gathered Rosalinda in her arms. "After this ordeal, my friend, let us employ all the remedies I possess to ease your burden." She kissed Rosalinda on the head and stroked her friend's hair until Rosalinda fell into an exhausted sleep.

Gently, Nellie extricated herself and ran to find her children.

"All is well here," reported Emma, looking up from her sampler. "Adelaidia took Lemuel and Priscilla over to the dry goods store to convey the sad news to their father. Jeremiah is asleep—Betsy rocked him—and James and Will play amicably."

Relieved, Nellie flopped into her rocking chair. Then she saw her two boys, heads bent together, squashing beetles with their fists, encircled by every toy the family owned, sporting telltale milk mustaches, and honey visibly stuck to their hair.

The Wrights' new grandfather clock struck nine.

Merciful heavens, I thought days had passed since Rosalinda's torment began. No wonder Jeremiah sleeps. The whole ordeal only lasted four hours!

"Our little angel Jeremiah certainly picked the right time to enjoy a prolonged slumber," said Nellie, and burst into tears.

Emma rushed over and gathered Nellie into her arms. "Don't fuss, Mama. I know you did everything you could."

Surprised, Nellie lifted tearing eyes to her daughter. "Emma, my sweet, you have always displayed wisdom beyond your years. Thank you for these comforting words."

"We never understand the ways of the Lord. He does not promise us a pain-free life. He only promises the strength and the resources to endure it," Emma said.

Nellie stared at her eight-year-old daughter. "Your comfort and wisdom astound me."

Emma offered a sad smile of thanks and got up to sit in the rocking chair. "Mama, should you not nap whilst Jeremiah sleeps? I do recall oft hearing you counsel every mother whom you midwifed, 'sleep whenever the baby sleeps,' even though you never do as you instruct!"

Nellie laughed. "'Tis nigh impossible, with other children to feed! Moreover, I must brief Mister Wells when he arrives."

"Adelaidia can attend to her father. He shall hurry here immediately upon receipt of the news to comfort Aunt Rosalinda. I shall wake you at the slightest disturbance," said Emma, and pointed to Nellie's bedroom.

Mercy, the rigors of the Overland Trail most assuredly caused this child to assume adult responsibilities prematurely, Nellie fretted.

But she hauled herself wearily from her chair and dragged herself to her bedroom, where, fully clothed, she collapsed on the bed and fell asleep instantly.

Forty minutes later, Nellie jumped awake at the sound of her newborn's cry. Fresh tears streamed down her face.

Nightmares plague me. Thank you, Lord, for sending my angel to awaken me. Jeremiah lives! He did not die in childbirth.

But then she remembered her dearest friend still in the birthing room, clutching her stillborn baby. Heartbreak and guilt assailed her.

She prayed, "Lord, my gratitude for the gift of five children knows no bounds. Lord, make me worthy of these blessings and guide me to assist my intimate friend. Dear God, help me console my dearest friend who suffers my worst nightmare."

She splashed some water on her face and scooped Jeremiah from his crib. He calmed as soon as she began to nurse him.

Upon hearing a shout, Nellie scurried out to examine the state of her household. Jeremiah, oblivious to the movement, continued his contented feeding.

Emma and Elizabeth stood in the middle of the parlor arguing.

"What discord puts you sweet daughters at odds?" asked Nellie.

"Thank heavens you are awake!" said Elizabeth.

"Whatever is the matter, Betsy?" asked Nellie.

"Missus Wells just keeps crying," said Betsy.

"So does everyone else in the Wells family," added James, spying into the birthing room.

Emma said, "I know you said to wake you, but I feared for your own health."

"Me too, Mama!" said Betsy. "But you are the most important person here. We can't do anything without you!"

"My sweet pumpkins, thank you. You have held the fort for my much-needed rest."

She hugged both her daughters, and James ran over to hug them all too. She kissed the top of each of their heads, as they all listened to the sobs and voices of the Wells family. "'Tis right and proper that the family gather and grieve together."

"But it's so sad, Mama," said Betsy.

"It's *terrible*. They are *all* crying," said James, now crying too.

"I know, because death *is* sad. Some difficulties in life quite overwhelm us and fill us with grief. When sadness and hardship predominate, our circumstances look bleak and unendurable. While knowledge and science have made great strides in understanding the human body, we still only partially grasp the mystery of life. Moreover, there are some things beyond our mortal ability to rectify. So be extra loving and kind to all our friends in the Wells family and support them through this tragedy. Pray daily. That is all we can do."

Toddler William scooted to them and joined their hug. They clung together for a long moment, until baby Jeremiah began to cry.

"Now, you brave helpers, you may go back to being children and leave the rest to me."

***

At the end of the long day, Nellie once again fell dead asleep as soon as she lay Jeremiah in his crib after his last feeding.

She felt she barely closed her eyes when she heard crying. Upon opening one eye and seeing Jeremiah still slept, she closed both eyes and thought she just imagined the sound.

But in her semiconscious state she heard it again.

The cry comes from the boys' bedchamber!

Nellie drew on her robe and bumped into the bassinet. Jeremiah's wail of protest broke the silence of the room. "Tarnation!"

Obadiah mumbled, "Hopping horsefeathers," and turned over on his other side, pulling the pillow over his ears.

Another wail arose from the boy's bedroom.

Nellie scooped Jeremiah into her arms and patted him while she stumbled across the hallway.

James lay moaning in his bed.

"Jimmy, my little pumpkin. What ails thee?" Nellie whispered into his ear.

In response, her son moaned louder and tugged at his ear.

Nellie bounced Jeremiah onto her shoulder and tried to prompt a burp as she scrutinized James's ear.

Jeremiah squirmed and started fussing again as James ratcheted the moaning up a notch.

Saints in heaven, this tells me nothing. I need more light so I can determine the source of his irritation.

In spite of the circumstances, Nellie smiled at her own pun. *Ear-itation! Ha.*

Jeremiah calmed.

Does he sense I relaxed into a smile?

One-handed, she helped James into a sitting position.

His eyes flew open, and he looked at her with a dopey expression, but he stopped moaning and whispered, "Mama, is it time to get up?"

"No, my little pumpkin. You were crying, so I came to comfort you and determine the cause of your ailment."

"It hurts."

"What does?"

"My whole of head."

I hope not his hole head.

She bit her lip.

No time for jokes. But I must keep my spirits up. Lord knows my lack of sleep alone can sour my temperament and my milk for the baby.

This is no time for philosophical discussions with myself either.

Nellie fluffed James's pillow. "Sit up here just a minute whilst Jeremiah and I fetch a candle."

Nellie scurried into her bedroom and located the candelabra by her bed.

Will there be a day I again read in bed before sleeping?

She lit the four candles with the taper she had in her hand. She hesitated to pick it up with Jeremiah still perched on her shoulder.

She felt his calm rhythmic breathing, though, and cautiously peered at the baby's face.

By what bona fide miracle does this good little baby slumber? No matter, I shall take full advantage of reclaiming my other hand.

Gently, she tucked Jeremiah back into his cradle. She knew she could not rush, even though any second now James would resume his moaning. She left her hand on the baby's back, a warm, reassuringly firm touch.

Slowly, slowly, she lessened the pressure her hand exerted, and then slowly, slowly, withdrew her hand. Almost afraid to stand fully upright, she backed away from the crib and only stood when she got to the nightstand to pick up her fully lit candelabra.

She snatched it off the table so fast the candles flickered wildly and threatened to extinguish. Sighing, she cupped her hand around the flame and crept back to the boys' room.

James sat, eyes closed, sucking his thumb.

Good heavens, he must suffer terrible pain.

James had not sucked his thumb for over a year, but this development lent credence to her theory that her son had an infection of the ear. Sucking on his thumb relieved some of the infection's pressure.

Nellie tried to look into James's ear without disturbing him. She held the candelabra close but could not see inside. She shook her head. What little she saw looked red and inflamed, sufficient evidence to act upon her suspicions and determine a course of treatment for an ear infection.

She prescribed first a dose of decoction of mustard seeds and mullein leaves wilted in warm milk to stop the underlying infection. She followed that with a dropper full of heated vegetable oil to alleviate the pressure and pain.

Hours later, medicines administered, and his small hand held until her poor sick son fell back asleep, Nellie, chilled to the bone, crept under her comforter and closed her eyes.

Just as she drifted off to sleep, Jeremiah began to fuss.

No, no, no! Nellie screamed in her head.

Please God, no. I am exhausted and frozen. Please let my baby sleep so I can sleep.

But the baby's movements increased in sound and frequency, and he began to cry.

Obadiah tapped her shoulder and said in a sleepy voice, "Cornelia, my love, our baby cries for his mama."

Nellie made a face in the dark. "Yes, sweetheart, I can hear him, but I am still hoping he can settle himself. I fed him a mere two hours ago."

"I do not desire to hear the full report, nor the cries of the baby. I must be in court tomorrow and I need adequate rest to function. Please ensure he cries no more," he ordered. "At least not within my hearing distance."

He flopped over with an angry movement and again put the pillow over his head.

***

In the morning, Obadiah strode into the kitchen impeccably dressed.

Nellie sighed with relief, grateful she could not see the small scorch mark she made when she applied the hot iron to his shirt. The starch she had concocted supported his collar smartly, she observed.

I had a devil of a time pressing that shirt!

He unfolded his morning newspaper and sat down at the table, reaching for the fresh pot of coffee. "Good morning, my dear Cornelia."

Nellie brought over a biscuit and a fried egg and gave him a smile.

"I must say you are looking wan and tired, my love. Perhaps you should nap this afternoon to ensure your preparation for potentially another sleepless night tonight."

Nellie shook her head. "Whenever would I have leisure to nap?"

"No need for surliness. I merely seek to aid you during these first few months of our new baby's residence." He shook out his paper and started reading, not bothering to wait for her reply.

CHAPTER 32
The Heat Is On

Nellie's Dining Room, August 1861

"Tarnation, whatever possessed me to offer to host the latest round of visiting firemen? How can I prepare a four-course dinner on a day hotter than Hades?" Nellie grumbled as she pulled a cherry pie from her potbellied stove.

My face already flushes with perspiration and the sun has barely risen.

Obadiah stood from his leisurely breakfast and arrested her in mid-flight, hot pie threatening to burn her hands. He wrapped his arms around his wife and nuzzled her neck.

Tarnation, assistance would be welcome. Why must he restrain me?

Obadiah, oblivious to her plight, kissed her neck and whispered, "Because you are the sweet, loving handmaiden who furthers our common purpose."

Nellie pulled away and almost tossed the pie onto the table. She stuck her burning thumb in her mouth and looked ruefully at her scorched dishtowel.

"But I will thank you not to curse in front of our impressionable children."

Nellie looked around in surprise, thinking one had escaped from the tidying they were supposed to be doing in the parlor. "What impressionable children? I see nary a one."

Obadiah sighed. "I seek to comfort and aid you in your feeble attempt to remain calm in the face of minor adversity and I am rebuffed for my efforts? Incorrigible woman. You deal not in political unrest, seditious uprisings, disaster or crime. You have not the daily tasks and woes I face in my work. You simply prepare a formal dinner for ten persons."

"Ten persons and our own five children," Nellie muttered. "Dear God, why did I volunteer to host this party on such a hellish hot day?"

She snatched the pie before it marred the table and turned to place it on a cooling rack.

Elizabeth stood right at her elbow.

Merciful heavens, I have been overheard!

Chastened, she added, "'Tis a privilege to have such honored guests as Orion Clemens, new Secretary of Nevada Territory, his brother, and two other dignitaries from the States gather at our table for dinner."

Nellie stole a glance at six-year-old Elizabeth.

Her daughter took that as a cue to speak. "Can I try the cake now?"

Nellie frowned.

"Just a little bite?"

Her sweet face gazed at Nellie imploringly and Nellie's resolve wavered.

Elizabeth pressed her advantage. "You know I favor vanilla flavor! Can I make sure it tastes good and isn't burnt?"

"I shall make a deal with you. Yes, you can try the cake." Nellie winked. "Just so you can confirm its deliciousness! I would not want to serve inferior cake to our esteemed guests. Luckily, I chose a rectangular pan, or we could not hide the sampling."

As Nellie cut a thin slice from the cake and then centered the remains on the plate to keep the trimming unnoticeable, she said, "Of course, you will be on your best behavior tonight, and impress our company with your grownup manners."

Elizabeth smiled, taking small bites and savoring the sweetness.

Nellie returned the smile. "Please do your best to help your little brothers with *their* manners too. Furthermore, you must say our Grace before meals tonight at the table. Do not forget to bow your head with reverence and speak slowly and distinctly."

Elizabeth lingered over each bite.

Nellie resumed sprinkling herbs over the roasting goose, giving it another quarter turn on the spit.

Obadiah frowned at Nellie.

She didn't bother to respond. She fanned her hot face and tried not to notice the sweat trickling down her back.

She picked up her conversation as if there had been no interruption. "Moreover, 'tis a pleasure to gather our friends to meet such men, passing through our Territory with news from the States and stimulating conversation.

"My dearest husband, can you retrieve a stick of precious cinnamon from the pantry, please? I am up to my elbows in this herb paste for the goose." She put her hands in the air and showed the paste smeared all over them. She scratched her nose with one hand, spreading the smear.

"I cannot be at your beck and call. Do you think I have naught to occupy my time than to fetch things? I just conveyed the important matters on my desk demanding my immediate attention." Obadiah gulped his last bit of coffee and stalked out of the room.

With tears stinging her eyes, Nellie tugged a stray strand of hair into place before remembering her dirty hands.

Elizabeth stared at her, in the middle of chewing her last bite, and pointed.

Nellie laughed. "I know, Betsy! I have just greased my hair. At least now that pesky strand will stay in place!"

Elizabeth laughed, ran to the pantry, and came back with the cinnamon stick. Then she picked up her doll and ran out the backdoor.

Nellie smiled. She appreciated her daughter's help, and knew Betsy did not want to linger for fear she would be enlisted for further kitchen duty. She decided to let the big girls play a while, for she knew she must employ them later.

In the afternoon, Nellie managed to wrangle all of her babies into a nap at the same time.

James made a valiant protest. "I am practically *four* years old, Mama. I don't need a nap."

Nellie found a cherished picture book and convinced him to put his feet up on the divan while he 'read' it, and soon he was snoring too. She smiled at the sight of her three-year-old curled next to the open pages.

***

The Wright women scurried around, ironing a tablecloth and napkins, cleaning silverware and setting out the nice dishes.

"Mama," said Emma, "these plates are not nearly as beautiful as the good china you gave to Aunt Anastasia when we left on our Overland Journey."

"I am surprised you remember them," said Nellie.

"The butterflies and flowers were such pretty colors," Emma replied.

"No matter," said Nellie. "Aunt Anastasia can enjoy them now. These are as pretty as I could find in this neck of the woods, and shall have to suffice."

Anxious to finish the last of the preparations in time to freshen up and put on her best dress, she turned to her youngest daughter and said, "Betsy, at six o'clock, just as our company arrives, please pump a pitcher full of fresh water."

"Do I have to?" asked Elizabeth.

"Yes," Nellie said. "The men will still be parched from their stagecoach travel."

"Why can't Emma do it?" Elizabeth scowled.

"She will be diapering William or holding Jeremiah."

"Why can't I—"

"Would you really prefer to change a dirty diaper?" Nellie inquired.

Elizabeth looked down at the floor.

"I thought not. Everyone must do their part to ensure our dinner party is successful."

"Not father," said Elizabeth.

Nellie flinched. "Your father bears many burdens and shoulders much responsibility to ensure our family is well fed. He works hard, which earns us the money to afford the seeds for our food, and the purchase of livestock and fowl."

"But we still have to plant the seeds, and weed the garden," said Elizabeth, full of rebellion. She pinched her nose. "And muck out the stalls."

"You shall aid this family by completing your assigned chores. End of discussion," said Nellie.

***

By some miracle, everything stood ready when the front doorbell chimed announcing their guests.

Jeremiah let out a holler.

No matter, I am free to hold him whilst we imbibe a whetting of our whistles.

Emma had already placed the hot buttered rolls on the table, so Nellie planned to pass the baby off to Emma when she brought out the main course.

Nellie turned at a sloshing sound.

Elizabeth, pretty as a picture, walked into the room with a pitcher of cold water, straight from the pump.

"You darling girl," Nellie whispered approvingly as her daughter placed it on the table. Elizabeth turned around and Nellie saw the front of Elizabeth's dress was darkened and drenched with water.

"Betsy," Nellie began.

But Elizabeth grinned and whispered, "It feels nice and cool. I don't want to be dried and hot."

Nellie shook her head with a grin.

The evening progressed nicely. She managed to get all the food to the table, hot, and serve it family-style with tremendous help from her daughters and a little help from Obadiah.

As the serving plates were passed around the table, Nellie said to Elizabeth, "Time for our special Grace before meals."

Elizabeth stared at her blankly, and finally whispered, "What should I say?"

Nellie frowned and whispered back, "What we always say, plus what I told you this morning in the kitchen."

All of the guests had finished serving themselves and they sat, waiting for the signal to begin.

Nellie kicked Elizabeth under the table.

Elizabeth bowed her head in an angelic pose. Everyone else at the table followed suit.

Elizabeth cleared her throat and prayed, "Dear God, thank you for our bounty and the good company we keep. Dear Lord, why did I volunteer to host this party on such a hellish hot day?"

Mortification assaulted Nellie's entire body.

"Merciful heavens," she whispered into the dead silence.

Every person in the room roared with laughter, including the children.

When will I learn, it is not the lessons I mean to teach which find purchase, it is the conduct I demonstrate without any thought that my children absorb! Dear God, let me be a better example for my children.

She wiped away a tear.

Rosalinda whispered across the still laughing gentleman between them. "Make that a tear of mirth. You have *nothing* to be ashamed of." She raised her voice and lifted her glass. "A toast to our hostess. Cornelia Rose Wright, you have many fine attributes, but your sense of humor caps the climax."

Rosalinda winked at her and looked around at the assembled guests. "I never imagined my friend, in spite of knowing her vast capacity for humor and punning, would plan such an elaborate joke as this. Engaging the services of a youngster. Well-done, Betsy! Three cheers for the Wright family."

Elizabeth looked abashed but pleased as the company answered Rosalinda's three 'Hip, hips' with three resounding 'Hurrahs!' and the men chugged the entire contents of their glasses.

Mercy, I hope we do not run out of wine!

Tarnation, that Betsy! What in all the heavens and the Earth possesses her? Is she purposefully trying to simultaneously embarrass me and raise her father's ire, dunking me in further hot water?

She shook her head, shooting Elizabeth a look-that-could-kill, and drew her lips into a grim line.

Just you wait until we are in the kitchen, Elizabeth Violet Wright. I intend to give you a stern talking-to.

"Comedy sets the table more elegantly than a host of beautiful dishes," said the youngest man of the traveling dignitaries. He gave a boyish grin, which, combined with his tousled hair, created a rakish charm.

Nellie moved her lips from their grim line to a forced smile.

"Of course, I've been told I am gifted with a 'joke mind'." The younger Mr. Clemens leaned toward Nellie with his earnest but jovial eyes staring straight into her own. "As the accompanying brother, not important in my own right except by relationship, along for the joy of the adventure, and maybe to gain untold riches on a cache of gold, I reflect a touch of humor adds more than levity to a dull day. Indeed, it adds a spark of light that ignites our creativity, our hope, and our joy."

Nellie smiled, grateful for the gallant attempts to relieve her acute embarrassment.

That devil Elizabeth. Did she say that deliberately?

She looked at her daughter who sat with excellent posture and perfect table manners innocently nibbling her green beans.

Indubitably deliberate!

As the guests began to eat, the younger Clemens turned to her. "Orion and I traveled past all nature's wonders, including wild specimens of rugged scenery, banks of snow in summertime, a natural icehouse underneath prairie sod, and a dry lake of saleratus, to name but a few."

"The Rocky Mountain South Pass, The Ice Slough, and Soda Lake!" Nellie exclaimed.

Samuel Clemens nodded, and sensing he had found a likeminded conversationalist, continued, "Mountain peaks with long claws of snow grasping them, tower so high, they would have to stoop to see Mount Washington, that little hill we call a mountain back East."

Nellie closed her eyes and sighed. "I remember the grand vistas as if I traveled yesterday."

Clemens chuckled. "In bottom fact, I did travel yesterday. It took a mere ten days to travel here by stagecoach from New York City."

"Jumpin' Jehoshaphat. A modern wonder. It took us almost four months."

"Yea, I saw a sad, bedraggled lot of Mormons tramping wearily their way west, coarse-clad and driving their bony cattle along. Many a disgusted sheep." He shook his head. "A sorrier looking bunch I never did encounter."

I hope our wagon company did not appear that disheveled when we entered town.

Nellie shook her head, no. In spite of their many hardships, she had managed to keep her kith and kin well fed and in good spirits.

Mister Orion Clemens, the freshly appointed Secretary of the newly incorporated Nevada Territory stood and addressed the table at large. "May I raise a glass to toast our host and hostess on this fine occasion of delicious food and convivial conversation."

All the guests cheered after Obadiah hastily refilled some of the men's glasses.

"We are pleased to visit this stronghold of the capital in Utah Territory as we travel through," Orion continued.

Young Sam Clemens said *sotto voce*, "The residence of the only Absolute Monarch in North America," eliciting titters from the guests within earshot.

Secretary Clemens frowned. "We certainly appreciate acting Governor Brigham Young's introduction to you, esteemed hosts and new friends. I thank our hostess for preparing this fine supper of the freshest meat and fowl and vegetables—a great variety and as great abundance. Let us continue our conversation and feast." With a glare at his brother, he resumed his seat.

Unperturbed, Samuel resumed conversation. "I'll say one good thing about that ruling plutocrat: his protocol compelled him to introduce us to you *gentiles*. I would imagine 'tis a strange thing, to be transplanted into this fairytale. To me, the Great Salt Lake City unspools as a land of enchantment, goblins, and awful mystery."

This clever young man speaks in riddles.

Has a new governor not already been appointed by President Abraham Lincoln? Why is Brigham still acting governor?

Goblins? Merciful heavens, all my nightmares rear their ugly heads, their reality confirmed into worries for the day.

But Nellie had no time to dwell upon this menace.

Samuel already broached an even more controversial subject. "I had a curiosity to ask every child how many mothers it had and if it could tell them apart. I gawked in doors opened suddenly in the street to see a Mormon family in all its comprehensive ampleness."

"But no one here admits to marriage to more than one woman," said Rosalinda with an exaggerated wink.

The conversation whirled and swirled around Nellie as the guests finished the main course, and she fretted about the food still cooking in the oven, lurking imminent dangers, and her recent social humiliation.

Which disgrace (ha! an excellent pun) shall be underscored and worsened by my husband's lecture on the topic later this evening.

Obadiah refilled the wine glasses.

She and her daughters jumped up to clear the plates and to bring out dessert.

Rosalinda came out to the kitchen to help.

"Rosalinda, thank you so much for having Adelaidia put the boys to bed tonight. I could not manage one more thing."

"What a lovely dinner party you confected," said Rosalinda, clearing food scraps into a bucket and stacking dirty plates at Nellie's big sink as fast as Emma and Elizabeth could bring them in. "It's purring along like a kitten playing with a ball of yarn."

"Other than the enormous social gaff of the Grace." Nellie glared at Elizabeth, who just shrugged.

"The levity created by your daughter's Grace set the perfect, happy tone for a delicious dinner," said Rosalinda, dismissing Nellie's complaint with a wave of her hand.

When Nellie still frowned, Rosalinda whispered, "Besides, you and I know the children could overhear much more damming words coming from our mouths. Consider yourself lucky. Or a very good mother."

Nellie felt some relief at her friend's comforting words. "Thank you so much for your rescue," she said. "You salvaged an untenable situation."

With the main course dishes cleared from the table, Nellie dispatched vanilla cake, pie, and new plates back to the table with Rosalinda and Emma.

Elizabeth came forward holding her hands out for forks.

Nellie said, "Just a minute. *What* were you thinking when you prayed that Grace?"

Elizabeth opened her mouth to reply but Nellie steamrollered ahead. "How could you, a smart young lady, utter a sentiment like that to our esteemed company? Surely you knew full well the import of your words!"

Elizabeth hung her head, but then she lifted stormy, defiant eyes, "Well, you said it. You said to say what you said, and that is what you said."

Nellie's mouth returned to a grim line. "You feel no remorse for the inappropriateness of your smart-alecky response?"

"You said I should always tell the truth." Elizabeth stared at her, still stormy-faced.

"*Now* you decide to tell the truth? Never when your sister objects to your behavior?" Nellie threw up her hands. "There is a difference between telling the truth and blurting information not for public consumption that will hurt people."

"I told a joke. I was trying to be funny."

Suddenly tears streamed down Elizabeth's cheeks, and Nellie noticed how unusually red her lips were.

We did not eat any foods that would stain her lips that color.

Nellie softened immediately and gathered her daughter in her arms, forks and all. She kissed her damp cheek just as Elizabeth breathed a long, sobbing, "I'm sorry."

Nellie noticed the foulness of Elizabeth's breath, and felt the girl's forehead with her eyelid. She diagnosed a fever.

"Elizabeth," she said gently. "Do not fret. I am sorry your words upset me. Yes, they were funny, but they also placed me in a precarious position. But you apologized, and I'm sure you meant no harm. Tell me," she said, pulling her daughter down into her lap as she eased onto the floor.

Mercy, all *my kitchen chairs were pressed into service for the dinner party?*

"Does your throat hurt?"

"Yes, Mama. Something awful," said Elizabeth, and she swallowed with obvious difficulty.

"My love, you should have told me."

"It only just happened at dinner," said Elizabeth. "Before Grace."

And I, like a mean ogre, chastised you, my precious daughter, whilst you feel ill! Merciful heavens, will I ever learn to curb my temper? Or my tongue? Will I ever gain greater compassion and motherly skill without first making these terrible mistakes?

Stroking her daughter's hair, she whispered, "I love you, my petite pumpkin, and always will, even if you provoke me to temper. I shall brew you a tea just as soon as the kettle boils, and you can either sit back down for dessert or go to your room for a nap."

Elizabeth started crying harder as Nellie stood back up.

"I want dessert. Vanilla cake and cherry pie are my favorites, but I can't eat them. I just want to save them."

A bad sign.

Nellie said, "Was that your dinner plate, returned with the food barely touched?"

Elizabeth hung her head. "I know. I am 'sposed to eat everything I put on my plate."

Nellie gave her another hug. "Not when your throat is sore. Fret not, my sweet. It already found a home in the slop bucket. The pigs shall enjoy my fine cooking too. You shall take the tea and tuck yourself into your cozy little bed. Ask Adelaidia to read you a story, but do not hug her or get too close to her. Explain to her you feel unwell. I shall come with herbs to nurse you to better health as soon as our guests leave."

Elizabeth straggled out of the room forlornly carrying her tea, and Nellie ran back to the dining room and her waiting guests, carrying the forks.

"I do enjoy hearing your impressions of the city," said Nellie, immediately restarting a conversation with Samuel Clemens, seated next to her.

"A grand general air of neatness, thrift, and comfort permeates this place; perhaps it is not so odious a place for a *gentile* to dwell," opined Mr. Clemens. "'Tis little wonder the streets are so broad and level, given the city lies in a broad flat plain as large as the state of Connecticut."

Nellie smiled her agreement. "That was my very first impression upon viewing the city, straight out of Emigration Canyon. Currents sweep down from the mountain ranges on two sides of the city with fresh cleansing air, around the clock."

"I take it that here, to date, you've skirted the Yellow Fever and Cholera that periodically plague the cities in the East?" asked Mister Clemens.

"Yes, quite handily. I do attribute the dearth of disease to the ingenious irrigation system of the Mormons," she answered.

"Quite so. I observed a limpid stream rippling and dancing through every street, in place of a filthy gutter, and great thriving orchards and gardens behind every trim sunburned brick house— apparently branches from the street stream wind and sparkle among the garden beds and fruit trees," agreed Sam Clemens.

"It does rather confirm my theorem that contaminated water initiates cholera," she said.

Mr. Clemens raised a quizzical eyebrow. "You have a theorem?"

She replied, "I am a trained, skilled midwife. In addition, my father was one of the main engineers of New York City's Croton Aqueduct construction, completed in 1842. Privy to my father's work, I have familiarized myself with learned men of medicine's hypothesis that contaminated water caused many a disease in New York City. I incorporated this thesis into my midwifery practice and counseled many an emigrant to test the water supply before imbibing."

"Excellent execution of this thesis! And the Mormons have perfected the system here. Moreover, your city here is so healthy, I am quite sure your one resident physician is weekly arrested and held under the public vagrant act for having *no visible means of support*," quipped Samuel.

Nellie laughed.

This man's humor quite delights me. I can't think when I have had a more interesting, funny dinner guest.

She frowned.

If Elizabeth's joke released this humor, I should heap commendations, not chastisements upon her.

He continued, "I do believe I witnessed all the wives in the Lion's House draw in their breath at once, as I saw the walls of the house suck in. And when they all exhaled at once, I could see the walls swell out and strain and hear the rafters crack and the shingles grind together."

Nellie laughed harder. *I mustn't speak, lest he stops!*

"After this experience, I certainly imagine ten or twelve wives is all I will ever want. My dear, keep me aligned with this principle and never let me go over it."

Wiping tears from her eyes from laughing so hard, she said, "I do so adore your droll sense of humor."

"Sometimes humor is my only defense," he said. "I must admit I rather lost my sense of it during the interview with the Holy Man himself. While the Saint appeared a kindly, dignified-mannered old gentleman and his conversation flowed sweetly, peacefully, and easily, like a summer brook, I saw the craft in his eye. I chafed in indignant silence as he completely ignored me, despite my efforts to draw him out on his highhanded political views and disdain of Congress. Nonetheless, I was unprepared for his humiliating slight at the end of our interview."

"His slight?" she asked, her voice now devoid of amusement.

"As we retired from his presence, he put his hand on my head and asked my brother: 'Ah, your child, I presume? A boy or a girl?'"

"Tarnation, the gall of that humbug," Nellie sputtered.

Samuel Langhorne Clemens shrugged. "We ne'r-do-wells sometimes do make something of ourselves. And when I do, I shall surely exact my revenge — if not by the sword, then perhaps, one day, by the pen."

Nellie shook her head, angry for her newfound friend.

He does have a youthful look about him, but I wager he is more or less my own age.

In answer to her unspoken question, he said, "'Twas a diabolic insult, I shall grant him that. Although I am but a lad of six-and-twenty, I have already enjoyed several diverse careers: printer apprentice, newspaper journalist, and most recently, until our new domestic Civil War put a stop to all river traffic, Missouri riverboat pilot."

And what have I accomplished in my same number of years?

She shook off her self-deprecating thoughts, focused on the inquisitiveness this man inspired in her, and marshaled her questions. But just then the men rose from the table and retired to Obadiah's library for cigars and brandy. She and the women folk enjoyed their own after-dinner party in the kitchen, up to their elbows in suds.

As the ladies finished their last sips of tea, the men came into the foyer to retrieve hats and coats. The brothers Clemens began their goodbyes.

Samuel Clemens reached for Nellie's hand and, smiling, looked into her eyes. "We shall continue our travels West. However, I doubt this superb, hearty meal and fine company will be excelled should we travel all the way to Hawai'i. In any case, we cannot continue our conversation, for I shan't have time to further my probe into the curious animal of Mormonism. Our stage departs at dawn. Thus, I abandon the idea that I can settle the *Mormon question* in two days."

"The pleasure of your witty conversation ensures that I am the beneficiary of this wonderful evening, not you." Nellie grinned.

His smile deepened. "I do thank you for leaving me well fed and happy. The men provided the icing on the cake of your delicious dinner in the thrilling evening stories about the assassinations of intractable *gentiles*. I cannot easily conceive of anything cozier than your husband's den, smoking pipes, and listening to macabre tales of Wild Bill Hickok, the Destroying Angel, shooting down men and women *gentiles* like so many dogs. Or the tales of old men who, enjoying so thoroughly their marriage to a maid, then marrying her sister. And her sister's sister. And then the maid's mother, aunt, and grandmother. And because the second sister is the favorite, the grandmother waits on her hand and foot!"

Shaking her head, she could not think of an adequate reply.

Now laughing, he continued, "Because of this impartial warning, I shall not take more than four wives, nor shall I be one of the heedless people who often come to Utah and make remarks about Brigham or polygamy and tomorrow morning find myself lying up some back alley contentedly waiting for the hearse."

She drew her breath in sharply.

Why am I never privy to the tales of terrible deeds and awful intrigue happening right in my own backyard? If my husband wishes to 'protect' me by not advising me of dastardly deeds, I shall redouble my sleuthing skills to have a more realistic assessment of our position here.

With only her eyes showing her anger and determination, Nellie said, "I wish you a pleasant, safe journey. And I do so hope to read your report of your travels one day. Your clever observations of the circumstances which surround me shall sustain my sense of humor over my current precarious predicament."

Mr. Samuel Langhorne Clemens took both of Nellie's hands into his own and stared deep into her eyes. "I shall leave the Great Salt Lake City a good deal confused as to what state of things exist here, after the gentlemen's conversations tonight. In fact, I question in my own mind whether a state of things exists here at all! Never-the-less, may the goddesses of fortune and democracy sustain you, my precious hostess, for in you, I see true human decency, which one glimpses only occasionally in this world where force is the only recognized authority."

Nellie hesitated and looked to see where Obadiah stood in the room. *Out of hearing distance.*

In a rush, she said, "I do so hope, for all of us *gentiles'* sake, you find and seize the right opportunity to exact your revenge."

CHAPTER 33
New Light

Great Salt Lake City, February 1862

"I did so wonder," Nellie confided, "about the abrupt departure of Governor John Dawson, but my new increase in domestic duties left me quite unable to do more than speculate."

Clayton's eyes twinkled. "A hearty congratulations for the strappin' lad. I see he coos and wriggles about in a manner to bring joy to th' heart." He caught little Jeremiah up in a bear hug.

The boy stared at him wide-eyed.

For an anxious moment, she thought her son would burst into tears at a stranger's abrupt embrace. Although Jeremiah still gazed uncertainly at the big man, the baby giggled and pulled Clayton's hair. Hard!

He winced but laughed. "I 'spose 'tis fairly played, wee bairn, after a stranger takes liberty to hug ye. There's a good lad now." He plopped down into a kitchen chair with eight-month-old Jeremiah still in his arms.

Surely, Jeremiah shall wriggle from this embrace to explore greener pastures, as he does any time someone other than me manages to capture him.

But the baby settled into Beauregard Cornelius Clayton's lap, picked up a lock of Clayton's hair again, and began to suck his thumb.

"Aye, the couthy lad 'll bide awee." Clayton smiled, his twinkling eyes capturing Nellie's gaze. "Now, back to ta business at hand. The fleeting Governor Dawson."

"Nicely punned." Nellie smiled.

But a frown replaced his genial demeanor. "Nellie Entwhistle, that short-lived Governor openly opposed Brigham. T'is as foolhardy as a chicken kissing a fox."

She gasped. "You don't mean they killed him, do you?"

"Mebbe not, but not for lack of trying. Dawson lasted a mere three weeks before ta Danites, those damn Destroying Angels, ran him out of town. Did your husband not advise, ta Danites brutally beat ta poor man near to death, at Pawley station?"

Nellie clutched her hands to her racing heart.

He shook his head. "But for our good Lord sending ta Wells Fargo wagon at that precise moment, and ta conductor snatching Dawson from that scalawag Wild Bill Hickok's hands, we woulda had a funeral to plan. Ta coach driver whipped up the mules and just kept riding. Ta fresh team awaiting them had to chase that coach almost to ta shores of the Great Salt Lake before ta driver felt they could safely stop to replace ta horses."

She exploded. "That scurrilous jack-a-nape! That odious, evil Young! How can he call himself a man of God?"

As Nellie paused for a breath, she frowned.

But how is it I never heard this information?

"Men continue to commit dark deeds in ta name o' religion. When will they learn? Look at ta history of me father's poor country, Scotland."

Clayton shifted in his seat and tickled Jeremiah with his finger. The baby erupted in laughter.

'Tis quite the infectious sound. Jeremiah's joy lessens the direness of our state of affairs.

"Truly," said Nellie. "Evildoers have plagued mankind since the dawn of time, but here we have a single individual who somehow commands the power to dominate and direct thousands of followers. The outrageous self-aggrandizement! The manipulation of truth to suit his own designs! The hubris, the pretension, the posturing," she sputtered in indignation. "I pity the poor puddin' heads ensnared in his web. God have mercy on their souls."

"I do agree ta man thinks ta sun came up jest to hear him crow," he said. "Simmer down, bonnie lass. I dinna want to aggravate you so."

Clayton got Jeremiah to giggle again.

Nellie smiled.

He changed the subject. "Speaking of the Wells Fargo coach, I encountered a man at ta stagecoach stop in the mining camp, Gold Hills, in the Colorado mountains, who, but for his conversation, I would never have noticed. Perhaps you might recall him, a lad named Samuel Clemens?"

"I did so enjoy his droll humor," she said with a smile.

"He entertained a group of travelers at lunch with an anecdote of a certain young hostess residing in ta Great Salt Lake City, not a *Saint*, who asked her child to say Grace before a meal."

"Merciful heavens, he did not!" Nellie gasped and tears sprang to her eyes.

Clayton's laugh burst forth so loudly, it frightened Jeremiah, who wailed to be released.

She gathered her baby in her arms trying to hide her crimson face. "Surely, this anecdote confirms I am hardly a saint."

"Eureka! I knew t'was you." The sound of Clayton's hearty laugh filled the room. "Don't get poked up. Once again, your humor guides ye through a difficult temper. Ta man did not mention a young hostess, rather he recounted, 'Gentiles fed us and feted us. And provided entertainment. A rogue of a boy at the feast, when asked to say the grace he was taught intoned, 'Why the hell did I ever invite this lot to dinner on a night as hot as Hades'.'"

"*Betsy did not say that!*" Nellie emphasized each word.

Clayton bellowed his laugh so loudly all four children ran in to see what was happening.

"I just knew it were you, Nellie Entwhistle," Clayton said as Emma and Elizabeth ran to hug him, shouting, "Mister Clayton!"

"Did you come to fix my shoes?" asked Elizabeth.

"Why, wee Betsy, ye remember me?"

Nellie muttered, "Will my mortification never cease?"

But everyone ignored her as the girls laughed and joked with Clayton. Emma cut him a large slice of the cake Nellie had just finished making for dinner. Elizabeth got him a fork. Clayton dug right in as James and William asked for a piece for each of the children.

Nellie began to deny that it was a cake-eating occasion when Emma asked, "Please, Mama, we could finally have that picnic on the porch with our tea set. The winter sun does shine so perfectly this afternoon, erasing many days of gloom."

Relenting, Nellie prepared them a tray and sent the whole lot outside with tea and cake, allowing her daughters to play hostess to their brothers.

Still red-faced with shame, she protested, "I've become the laughingstock of the West."

"I'm surprised at ye, carrying on so. Ta man obviously sang yer praises, thrilled ta pieces to tell ta titillating anecdote. Nay, he dinna stop complimenting ta feast he had enjoyed. Moreover, he never mentioned yer name. No one in the world knows it was you. Jest me.

I'd know your *modus operandi* anywhere, little braw Nel. Afterall, I've known ye since ye were a wee lass of seven, and I've loved ye from the day I met ye."

Did Clayton just proclaim his love for me? In my condition?

Unfazed, or maybe just not realizing the full import of his words, Clayton merrily continued. "And I knew it were your little scoot Betsy. Not some plucky boy. She brings a spark of joy ta me heart, jest like her mother. 'Ta apple never falls far from ta tree. I remember her on ta trail, her antics cheering us all along. And ta shoes I repaired for her, you would 'ave thought I'd given her me pot o' gold."

"My poor Betsy took sick at that dinner." Nellie felt her chagrin at her own anger toward her child all over again. "A flaming sore throat with a headache and fever. God's grace alone prevented it from blossoming into ague or croup."

"God's grace, with a wee help from your herbal medicines, I'd wager," he said, the twinkle back in his eyes. "But I'm sorry ta bairn felt all peely wally in her thrapple."

She chuckled. She could not resist those eyes, or the Scottish words that still crept into this mysterious man's vocabulary. Moreover, the delight of all his compliments!

I have not felt so appreciated in a month of Sundays.

"That's me bonnie lass. Ye must always look on ta bright side. Things could always be worse. Besides, as I jest saw again, ye bairn's a Macintosh, jest like ye."

She sighed. "Aye. But for the undercurrent of strange rumors and evil deeds, I enjoy a life abundant with God's blessings."

She paused and remembered her newly received letters from home.

"Mercy, the terrible war waging in the States confirms evil abounds everywhere. *Mutter* advises that only Anastasia's West Point-graduated husband, Mister Zetus Searle, who long ago declared himself a pacifist and resigned his commission, remains at home. My brothers Patrick and Jerome, both keen to fight to end the abomination of slavery, enlisted a year ago. Agnes sent me a long, fretting missive from Chicago advising me her husband, Armistead L. Long, honoring his West Point training, joined my brothers, fighting under that crazy General Hooper. Beside herself with worry, poor Agnes's letter contains naught but anguish.

"Perhaps this dire situation causes an increase in Agnes's appreciation for her husband," she finished with a wry smile.

He smiled in return. "We must always look for ta silver lining in ta cloud. Now, I don't rightly feel as if I can joke about a thing like this, but if I recall, was not your brother-in-law Long a fellow who lacked decisiveness?"

"'Tis true," she confirmed. "I am sure Patrick regaled you with the tales from the West Point Cotillions where poor Armistead could not decide which of my sisters he fancied."

"Aye, ye'r brother spun quite ta tale from that little sit-i-ation. In fact, ifn' ye hadn't said that Agnes wrote ye, I wouldna remembered if it was Anastasia or Agnes he fancied."

"He chose Agnes, but let us pray he doesn't fancy Anastasia." She grinned.

Mercy, my warm reminiscences of those happy times make me quite giddy, and perhaps almost inappropriately cavalier in my speech.

Clayton's eyes twinkled again.

Nellie hugged her baby with one hand and poured more tea with the other.

She allowed herself to enjoy the happy conversation with this old friend who constantly surprised her with the depth of his knowledge of her childhood and her family in New York. She recalled his longstanding friendship with her brother Patrick, and his employment by her father on the Croton Aqueduct engineering crew.

She frowned.

But I thought his family moved back to South Carolina. Or was it North Carolina? Merciful heavens! Right now, both those states are rebel members of a different country!

A sudden burst of fear and gloom clouded her eyes. "The current state of the world rips apart the very fabric of our lives and threatens our democracy. Since the day we arrived, I've lived with terror. First the terror of war exploding right in this town overshadowed my life. I've lived in dread so long, it now feels the natural state! To add the terror of my brothers, and countless other friends from New York, engaged in the fight to save the Union... my worries oft overwhelm me. Would that at least my brothers were deployed to the branch of the United States Army camped forty-seven miles away from here! Then that terror might somewhat subside, if I ignore the new vacuum in the governor position vacated by Dawson."

Nellie shook her head and tugged at her recalcitrant hair. "That vacuum hardly matters, in any case. 'Tis clear Young runs the territory with or without a figurehead appointed by the States."

He agreed. "Yes, and a-course, Dawson was run out of town because he dared to assert his authority rather than grovel before Young."

Not exactly the words I want to hear.

She made a face. "Furthermore, we grapple with the sinister mystery of the Mountain Meadows Massacre. Who attacked that innocent, California-bound wagon train? Who is the enemy? Brother fights brother in Mississippi and Maryland. Yet do I dwell amongst the enemy here?"

Normally an undemonstrative man, Clayton reached out his hand and squeezed her shoulder. "'Twas no coincidence that suddenly, prominent Mormons hold possession of the well-known riches of this wagon train in cattle, horses, mules, and other property."

She blanched. "Surely, you malign these misunderstood people with your broad suppositions. Surely, this statement merely fosters hostility between warring interests and bears no grounding in the truth."

Clayton's mouth set in its grim straight line and looked as if he would debate her.

But shaking his head, he looked at her with anxious eyes and only said, "My darling Nel, my deep concern for yer wellbeing in this God-forsaken place knows no comfort."

The concern and compassion of her friend arrested Nellie's heart.

'Tis quite unexpected to have this brawny, stalwart, enigma of a man express such empathy.

She lowered her own eyes before they revealed her innermost, tumultuous thoughts.

Clayton remained silent, so Nellie looked at him.

Unexpectedly, the twinkle returned to his warm eyes. "Hannah Keziah Clapp spoke the truth."

"I do admire that Bloomer-clad woman," she said. "But whatever does H.K. Clapp have to do with this terrible clandestine affair?"

"Naught other than identifying ta Mormon conspiracy. Ta evidence abounds: emigrants from Arkansas suddenly attacked. Arkansas, the very state where the *Saint*, Parley Pratt, was killed by ta jealous husband of ta woman he took for his twelfth wife. Rumor has it that Mormons believed ta murdering husband was among the people on that wagon train. Thus, ta slaughter served only justifiable revenge."

She stayed silent, weighing this 'rumor.'

Clayton took a large bite of his remaining cake, and then pressed his finger into the crumbs, eating them one at a time.

Nellie blanched at the sight, but then took it as a compliment to her cooking.

Through his mouthful, he said, "That brings to light another matter. I attended Mormon services last week, just to hear the warmongering straight from ta horse's mouth. He preaches the mercy of killing infidels. He assures his faithful, slaying *gentiles* purifies their souls. He dirties not his own hands but incites others, in addition to the Danites, to perform heinous deeds in the name of God."

Clayton leaned back in his chair and drained his cup of tea. He eyed the rest of Nellie's fresh bread and the wedge of cheese.

"Please, help yourself to more," she urged, remembering his nomadic ways caused him food insecurity.

Mouth full again, he mumbled. "Bide awee, I do suddenly recall I witnessed a rare instance of Brigham dirtying his own hands. From a secure position I saw Brigham Young, himself, yank some stones from the monument to ta massacred and heave them into ta scrub brush."

"Mercy me," she gasped. "You personally verify information I long to receive yet somehow am not privy to."

He ducked his head, resuming his unassuming quiet pose. "I *did* train to scout. Many an Army officer seek my services. But I do surely appreciate your implied confidence in me.

"In my official capacity, I saw an open display of imperiousness — in fact, arrogant disrespect of the most audacious nature. Last May, my assigned scouting route had me patrolling near ta community settled in Enterprise. I detoured to pay my respects to the poor victims of ta Mountain Meadows Massacre. I offered a prayer at ta monument I had ta honor to help Van Vliet and his dragoons erect. Young, surrounded by a posse of the Quorum of Twelve, ha! More aptly ta Quorum of *criminals*, had ta audacity to order them to destroy ta monument. Using stealth, I stayed hidden and witnessed ta defilement."

Clayton passed his hands over his eyes. "Infuriating."

"You witnessed that sacrilege with your own eyes!" Nellie shivered. "A new high of hubris superior to any the 'Lion of the Lord' previously attained. The one time our circuit journeys took us past that sinister place, my emotions quite overcame me at the sight of the monument."

She felt a chill shimmy through her, in spite of her pregnancy-elevated body temperature, and rubbed her arms for warmth. "The sheer number of bones! We prayed for mercy for the restless spirits of all the unfortunate victims that truly haunt the purlieu. The wind made eerie noises attending to its daily business, and even the sun shrouded its light in a cloak of shadow."

Nellie could not stop venting her contempt and fear of Brigham Young. "Merciful heavens, is there no end to the evil to which this man will stoop? Some of this vigilantism seems alcohol-induced! How else would sane, God-fearing men carry out these commands? Yet, Young preaches total abstinence from all alcohol and unnatural stimulants.... Unless rumors are true that he also distills the rotgut and profits from abuse of the written church directive."

"That's another kettle of fish altogether," said Clayton, and he winked! "But, a' course, it's true. Orrin Porter Rockwell, Brigham Young's infamous bodyguard, earned his fortune brewing spirits ta Mormons are forbidden to drink. Since Young knows all his officers' exploits, you can bet your bottom dollar he gets a cut from Rockwell, and many other breweries as well."

"Confirmation of their continued devilry from two trusted sources," she said, throwing up her hands. "Hannah Keziah Clapp spoke of seeing Rockwell's brewery at his Inn in the south."

"A Mormon alone finishes every wee dram before the rest of us can touch it. Ta only way to get him to stop drinking is to invite one of his brethren to ta party." He shook his head. "Ta exclusively Mormon refresher, Valley Tan, made of imported *fire and brimstone* is somehow permitted. Rotgut! A fouler tasting dram I ne'r threw down me thrapple."

Clayton made such a funny face in response to the remembered foul taste that Nellie laughed.

"The prohibition against public drinking establishments casts a salutatory effect on the demeanor of the town." She reflected. "'Tis truly in appearance a most orderly and pleasant place to live."

"What a kingdom this self-proclaimed king has built for himself. No public saloons and no private drinking except for Valley Tan. If I got a cut of every drop of Valley Tan consumed in these parts, I'd be in no hurry to get to heaven either," he said.

Beauregard Cornelius Clayton must finally enjoy his circumstances. I've never heard him speak at such length, and with so much cheer. True, his meliorism always shows through his infrequent speech, but I never suspected he had an optimistic and loquacious side to his personality.

"A bonnie blessing on ye, Nel, and ta wee lass ye carry," he said, preparing to leave.

Surprised, Nellie blurted, "How do you know it's a girl?"

"I told ye, wee braw lass. I know ye, Nellie," he answered.

And the Scottish terms of endearment and the twinkling eye gaze sent tingles down her spine.

Shaken with tender feelings, Nellie turned her head away and whispered, "Mercy, Mister Clayton, it saddens me to see you depart. You brought me sunshine and a little bit of home."

Clayton gave her one more twinkling look and bounded out the door.

CHAPTER 34
Adalida

Great Salt Lake City, August 1862

It's hard to fathom the galloping of time!

The Wright family had dwelled in their well-constructed, sizeable house for three years already. Nellie grudgingly acknowledged the effective strategy of the autocratic Brigham Young. Deeding them the impressive home right in the hub of town had reeled her husband in close, both figuratively and literally.

"I retrieved the perambulator from Missus King," announced Elizabeth. "But mercy, her little grandson exacted some vengeance upon this conveyance! No matter, Mama. I scrubbed it and then trimmed it with fresh blue ribbons for little Jeremiah."

A nicety I'm sure will be lost on the little chap.

Nellie took a closer look, and a renewed appreciation for her daughter's hard work dawned. "A surprise, thoughtful detail enhances your fine work: jingle bells festoon the ribbons. You dearest daughter, Betsy! Jeremiah shall adore that!"

With all her Mormon sister-wives, Nellie was unsure why Louisa had to borrow *her* perambulator.

She suddenly grinned.

I suppose dear Louisa alighted in town to visit her mother for just a fortnight. Moreover, I cannot pretend that I would not prefer a gently used stroller to one that sees more use than a cook's chow wagon in the army.

She shrugged. Hannah Tapfield King and her daughters remained her dearest friends. She would gladly continue to do them good turns.

"Prince Jeremiah, your carriage awaits," she announced with a happy laugh. "We are off to the market."

"I hope we meet lots of people today," said Elizabeth. "I want everyone to see my new dress."

"It did turn out well," agreed Nellie. "If I may say so myself."

Elizabeth protested, "You did not sew it! *I* sewed on *all* the buttons."

Nellie glanced at the buttons, a crooked line of soldiers marching up the entire length of the otherwise-perfect dress she meticulously stitched for her daughter. Suppressing a grin, she said, "How could I forget what a fine job you did."

With everything at last assembled, they strolled closer to the city center.

"Look, there's the Wells family." William pointed.

Rosalinda and her three children stood on the boardwalk at the corner of State Street. Rosalinda and her oldest daughter, Adelaidia, appeared to be having a heated exchange.

"Perhaps we should give them wide berth. It appears they could use some privacy," Nellie observed.

"If they need privacy, why would they be shouting on the street, Mama?" asked James.

"Well, I *gots* to marry him, Mama," shouted Adelaidia.

Merciful heavens, they do not discuss the dinner menu!

Nellie tried to steer her children clear of the group as she watched Rosalinda gape and clutch her swollen baby bump.

"Hells bells, Adelaidia! As I live and breathe, I never thought a daughter of mine would *ever*...."

It was no use.

Elizabeth and James planted themselves right between Lemuel and Priscilla, looking expectantly from Rosalinda to Adelaidia.

Adelaidia turned beet red and gasped. "Gosh, golly, Mama, no! Not that. No! Not *that kind* of gots to. Why *that* would be most indecent!"

Rosalinda's breath suddenly left her, and she gasped for air.

"How could you ever even suggest that, Mama? My Captain Nicholas Bartlett Pearce is too honorable a man. Mercy, I knowd he comes from Arkansas, but that ain't a lawless state. And a' course we don't know of his upbringing, but he comports himself as a gentleman in his own way."

Rosalinda just stood there, gasping and clutching her belly.

Adelaidia's oblivious tirade rolled on. "Heck. And yes! I do mean to cuss. I'll cuss up a storm to save my reputation. *How* could you think that of me? Why, you know me, you know my upbringing. You up-bringed me—"

"Adelaidia," Nellie finally interrupted her, "I believe your mother's utterance came from shock at your statement. As you can see, there has been a new development."

"Yes, my Captain Pearce and I intend to marry this week, as he has just been transferred back to Arkansas to command its troops in the War Between the States."

"Fight for Arkansas?" cried Emma.

"In the States' war?" asked Elizabeth.

Lemuel and James made their fingers into guns and fired at each other.

Have mercy upon me for my anger at this young girl's self-absorption of youth!

Nellie grabbed Rosalinda by the arm but addressed Adelaidia.

"Dearest, your mother has suddenly gone into labor, and we must all abandon our marketing plans and get her right to my confinement room."

"But we need to get me a weddin' dress," said Adelaidia.

The contraction finally passed, and Rosalinda panted and said, "My sweet little girl, I'm so sorry that your news surprised me so."

Lemuel said, "I wish I was a captain."

"Me too," said James. "But not for Arkansas."

Rosalinda ignored the boys. "I know you, sweetkins, and I have witnessed you fall in love, in between your dutiful fulfillment of your chores at home, your mastering of your schoolwork, and your sewing enterprises—"

"Don't forget all my child watchin'. I've been doing that since I was a wee tyke," said Adelaidia, anxious all her work be recognized.

"We do quite rely upon you, dear Adelaidia," said Nellie, hoping to help diffuse the situation.

"Yes," said Rosalinda. "I have noticed your cheerfulness has taken a whole new dimension and I am overcome with joy for you. However...."

Adelaidia rolled her eyes. "Why does there always gots to be an objection?"

"Heck!" Rosalinda put her hands on her hips. "We don't know the young man's family. We only know his fellow soldiers."

"But he is abandoning his fellow soldiers if he is going to fight for Arkansas," whispered Emma to Nellie.

"I don't see how that makes any never mind," said Adelaidia. "I love him and would follow him to the ends of the Earth."

Mercy, Arkansas feels like it could be the end of the Earth. So far away from here, right next to Mississippi in the middle of the War... I pity my poor friend Rosalinda.

"We shall discuss this with your father.... *Ugh!* Oh." Rosalinda took a step forward and fell onto her daughter.

Nellie knew she needed to get Rosalinda to the birthing room.

Third babies come on fast, at least for some lucky women.

"But Arkansas's a rebel state," said Lemuel.

"He's gonna fight for the wrong side," said William.

"Don't marry him," said Elizabeth. "You don't want to be a rebel."

"You support the abomination of slavery?" whispered Emma.

"No, not at all," said Adelaidia. "I love Captain Bartlett and he loves his home state. He's just fighting for his state."

Nellie's conscience prickled. "In truth, we should not ostracize the man for following his sense of duty. We have the same problem in our own family. Your grandmother's most recent correspondence advised that your Uncle Armistead now fights for Virginia."

Nellie's children stared at her.

I should not have told them here! Look at their stricken faces!

"Perhaps we should move this discussion from the center of the city to the privacy of our parlor." She tried to forestall further public display of discord.

"Brother against brother!" exclaimed Rosalinda. "This terrible war, which all predicted would be short, drags on and on, solving none of our nation's problems but creating new problems in our families. It hurts to think—" The rest of her sentence could not find passage in her groan-choked throat.

"Let us haste to my home. We can continue this discussion later," said Nellie, tugging Rosalinda's hand and guiding her toward her home.

"Good afternoon, ladies," a tall, good-looking man interrupted. He made a sweeping bow, bending low, and on the way back up he met the boys' eyes and saw their look of outrage. He hastily added, "And gentlemen."

James eyed him suspiciously but said, "Good day, Captain Bartlett Pearce."

"That's General Pearce to you, boy," boomed the man.

Startled, Nellie opened her mouth to rebuke him, but then the man gave a boyish giggle and said, "Don't that sound *grand*!"

Adelaidia rushed to his arm and swooned, "My dearest."

Rosalinda groaned.

Nellie looked to see if another contraction overwhelmed her friend, but it looked like Rosalinda merely reacted to the Captain-General's bombastic Southern drawl.

"Mama," said James, "how could you not tell us Uncle Armistead switched sides?"

"I can see not telling the little ones," said Emma. "But how can you not confide in me?"

"The tumultuous state of the world reaps problems for adults, not for children," said Nellie.

"Mother, I am hardly a child." Emma drew herself up to her full five-foot height with dignity.

Nellie sighed. "It's true, Emma, at birth you were already imbued with the wisdom of the ages."

"My dearest Ada. You cannot marry this man, however charming," said Rosalinda.

"I declare!" said General Pearce and stomped his foot.

Rosalinda shook her head. "Sir, I shall ask you to come to our home and present your case directly to my husband and me, as any proper gentleman would do."

"I shall arrive at your doorstep promptly at four o'clock," said the General with a crisp salute.

Nellie interjected, "Rosalinda, you might still be a bit... busy at four."

Rosalinda gasped as another contraction swept through her body. "Flapdoodle, that was a dandy."

The contractions seem less than two minutes apart. I had better keep Rosalinda moving or this baby might come right here on the street. Another thing we do not want happening in public!

"My sweet child, you've lost all reason," Rosalinda said, gasping as she walked slowly forward.

"But, Mama, I'm in love, as I hope my intended knows full well."

Nellie looked over her shoulder to see Adelaidia gazing up at her beau with stars in her eyes.

What is he still doing here?

"I think you have been dismissed," Elizabeth said pointedly to the general.

Nellie could have kissed her, but she was too busy supporting Rosalinda.

The Captain-General blushed a sickly crimson, abruptly dropped his fiancée's arm, and raced away.

One problem solved, temporarily.

Rosalinda kept up her arguments. "What might feel like love could just be a passing phase, made all the more romantic since he charges off into battle."

Adelaidia looked doubtful. "I truly adore him. Did my Captain... er... General Pearce mention how much he hated patrolling the West an' was itchin' to see the real action in the South?"

Rosalinda groaned and clutched her belly.

"I do declare," Nellie drawled in a southern accent. "My home seems to have migrated, I say my-grate-ted, farther away during our brief for-ay toward the market."

She winked at Rosalinda. "Adelaidia, you must learn how to speak properly now."

"Quite devoid of humor," said Rosalinda through gritted teeth and pinched Nellie's arm. "Completely." She shook her head. "The foolish lad seems ill-prepared for the true hardships of war. He shall be shot within days of his arrival at the front line."

"Mama, that pain of yours got your brain addled!" said Adelaidia. "He won't get hurt on accounta — you heard him — they just made him a General. All generals do is stay at headquarters and have coffee served to them. He 'splained it to me. And sometimes they strategize over maps with his aides, but that will still be far away from the actual fighting. He can't pass up this opportunity to advance."

Rosalinda threw up her hands.

"Oh, Captain-er-General, I love you," teased Lemuel.

James made kissing noises and Adelaidia swatted him with her fan.

They turned the corner and Nellie's house appeared a few yards away.

"We shall discuss this with your father," Rosalinda said, by way of conclusion.

Nellie looked at the posse of children that walked behind her on their way back to her house.

Emma ran to her and whispered, "Perhaps we *children* can accompany Adelaidia to the dry goods store. We big girls can mind the little ones whilst perusing material suitable for Adelaidia's trousseau, in case Aunt Rosalinda and Uncle Wilburforce grant her permission to marry the captain."

Nellie winced at Emma's emphasis on the word 'children.' She gave her daughter a quick, sideways hug. "Once again you save the day, my dearest daughter. 'Tis a grand plan. No harm can come from looking at cloth. When you ladies have had your fill, return to the Wells's home and feed the children some lunch. Perhaps you might also supervise their lessons."

Emma's face fell. "But we planned a backyard picnic at our house for lunch today. Furthermore, what if you need my help? And everyone will be anxious about Auntie Rosalinda."

Nellie considered. "True. All right, bring the troops to our house when you have finished ogling goods at the store. If you find Mister Wells at the store, tell him of the turn of events."

"He could well be at the store," said Emma. "If not, I'm sure Adelaidia would not mind if we took a detour to the fort to find him."

"The fort is far too far away!" protested Nellie.

"That new commander, Colonel Connor, started moving the fort closer to the city," said Emma. "Troops are clearing a large parcel of land on the east bench above the city. We can walk to it from here."

This child observes everything!

"Mercy," Nellie replied. "I only learned of the plans for the new Camp Douglas last week. Mayhap I should ask you for the news instead of your father."

Rosalinda stumbled and Nellie turned back to the business at hand.

Rosalinda needs my help more than Emma needs further instruction.

Squealing, the girls turned Jeremiah's baby carriage around and ran back toward the dry goods store. The three boys followed close behind, using sticks as rifles to shoot at each other.

***

Hours later, Rosalinda still labored.

Nellie massaged her friend between contractions with soothing liniments, helped her change positions frequently, and encouraged her to push.

At last, Rosalinda delivered a baby boy.

Wilburforce rushed in as Nellie handed the cleaned and squawking baby to Rosalinda.

"I just knew he was a boy," both happy parents said at the same time.

"Wilburforce Wainright Wells junior, welcome to the family," shouted Wilburforce.

When the children heard the news booming through the house, they all rushed in to meet the new kid.

Nellie said, "Make your introductions quickly for I must still attend to your mother."

But as the Wells children greeted their new sibling, Nellie's children and Obadiah crowded into the room. The happy celebrations resounded throughout the house.

The noise was so overwhelming, Nellie hardly heard Rosalinda whisper, "Something is happening. Oh, Lordy."

As Nellie pushed her way through the crowd back to her friend's side, Adelaidia said, "I cannot wait until my Bartlett meets his new brother-in-law."

"Speak of the devil," shouted Elizabeth.

"Here he is," said Lemuel.

All heads turned to the back of the room.

"I say, I am most apologetic about my interruption," drawled the Arkansas General. He swaggered a bit, enjoying all eyes upon him, obviously used to being the center of attention in any room. "But as I understood it, we had a meetin' scheduled for four o'clock sharp, and I found no one at the home. I told myself while it would have been more precise to affix our appointment at sixteen hundred, which is four in the afternoon in Army jargon, there is no chance I misconstrued the time or that I should have assumed we would meet at 4 o'clock in the morning."

The room filled with laughter so loud it obscured Rosalinda's sharp cry of pain.

Nellie looked at Obadiah, hoping to communicate that he should usher this silly man out. She was about to tactfully escort him out herself when she heard Rosalinda panting. Nellie turned back to her friend just in time to realize another baby was on its way.

"Everyone clear the room," Nellie shouted. "Now! It seems another sibling is on its way."

Nellie held her friend's hand and helped her bear down again. Then she lifted the blanket and saw the baby's head emerge.

The general said, "I say, I say, I—"

"Get out!" Rosalinda screamed.

Nellie looked over her shoulder to see the Captain-General standing there gaping, paralyzed in his place while watching the baby emerge from Rosalinda's womb.

"Adelaidia," Nellie shouted. "Retrieve your fiancé."

The young woman appeared at the door. "There you are, my sweet. I lost you in the crowd exiting the room! I hope you.... Merciful Heaven Above!" she screamed when she looked at her mother, and she pulled her beau into the hallway.

Nellie eased the baby's shoulders into the world and chuckled as she heard the Captain-General say, "Now we *must* get married. It is my sacred duty. I don't think I can ever unsee a gory sight like that."

Merciful heavens, what will this scalawag think when he gets to the front line of the war?

With skilled hands, Nellie guided the baby out and lifted him to Rosalinda. "It's another boy!"

Nellie wiped the baby's face, anxiously checking for breathing.

That was an awfully long time between births!

The baby moved and gave a small cry.

Halleluiah.

Nellie placed him on his mother's chest.

Rosalinda cried happy tears and embraced her second baby. She caressed him gently, marveling anew at the miracle of delivering a second healthy baby.

"Where is Junior?" asked Nellie.

"I've got him in my arms," said Wilburforce from the doorway. "Is it safe to come back in or do you have another one in there?"

Rosalinda smiled. "I think I'm done," she said wearily.

"I'll come, but I shall avert my eyes to err on the safe side," said Wilburforce. He walked to the head of the bed and put his hand on his wife's arm.

Nellie delivered the placenta, and she said, "That's it for the babies, but give us a minute to finish the processes. Rosalinda, you nurse this one while I complete our task down here."

Rosalinda smiled wearily and tried to get the newest born to latch.

"Wilburforce?" she asked.

"Yes, my dearest, bravest pioneer woman," he replied, eyes still fixed in the opposite direction.

Through her smile and tears of exhaustion, Rosalinda whispered. "I think we must change your baby's name. We can't be having one of them being 'Junior' and one not."

Then she beamed at Nellie. "Thank you, Lord, for the blessing of this grand dilemma."

Nellie smiled and patted her hand. "Yes, what a wonderful problem!"

"Indubitably," responded Wilburforce, still averting his eyes toward the doorway. His happy laugh infected the entire family again trying to crowd back into the birthing room. "We are in quite the pickle."

CHAPTER 35
Isn't She Lovely

Great Salt Lake City, January 1863

"I refuse to name the child Lucena, after that dolt of a woman." Obadiah shook out his morning paper and began to read.

"But I hold Lucena in my heart, and the girls simply adore her."

A sob caught in Nellie's throat at the thought of never seeing her blithe friend again. "Without her friendship during those early months in this Territory fraught with strangers and intrigue, I doubt I would have survived."

Frowning, Obadiah shook his head. "Cornelia, whilst you are not often prone to excessive drama, when you do stoop to this obvious feminine frailty, you pull out all the stops."

She just sobbed harder. "We already have an Elizabeth!"

"Blast these histrionics."

"My confinement nears its end," she sobbed. "I know I carry a girl."

"A pox on your riddles, wife. I cannot fathom your meaning."

Obadiah slammed his porcelain cup into the saucer, shattering it. Hot coffee spewed all over the table. He sprang to his feet, overturning his chair, before the boiling liquid reached his trousers. He stood looking at the mess, newspaper dangling from one hand, face twisted in disgust.

She ran to get a dishrag, and a contraction slammed her so hard she fell toward the table. Between clenched teeth she grunted, "*Lucinda* now makes her way into this world."

If she had not still been riding the wave of the contraction, she would have giggled at the expression on Obadiah's face.

I see the penny dropped!

"I accept your compromise as to the child's name," he said, gently taking her into his arms. He kissed her on the top of the head and then kissed her on the cheek.

His expression changed to gleeful, and he whispered into her ear, "But I do believe you bestow a tremendous handicap upon our new *son* when you name him *Lucinda Iris*."

Contraction over, Nellie smiled at him and allowed the warmth of his embrace to soothe her. "I rejoice, for we shan't let quibbling over a trifling matter blight our joyful union."

She relaxed in his arms a moment, ignoring the puddle growing on the floor.

She clamped her mouth down as much to brace for this next wave of pain as to prevent herself from voicing, *I have always known I carried a girl. Mister Clayton just confirmed my belief.*

Obadiah read her gasp of pain, clutch of her belly and clench of her jaw correctly. "I shall fetch Rosalinda immediately," he said, grabbing his hat and almost running out the door.

Nellie looked at the coffee staining her tablecloth and running down the side of the table to join her water that broke on the floor. She sat down on the chair with a loud "oof" and watched the coffee drip.

Emma appeared at her side and took the cloth from her hand. "Mama, I shall attend to tidying the kitchen. You must rest for the enormous chore ahead of you."

Nellie looked up at her in surprise.

Emma laughed. "Goodness, Mama, I have assisted you in your midwifery ministrations so often, I too can now detect the progression of events. Just as you taught me." She straightened her shoulders and looked proud. "I declare myself ready for you to recognize me as a qualified assistant, ready to follow in your footsteps."

Nellie burst into a fresh onslaught of tears.

Alarmed, Emma ran to embrace her. "Mama, I did not mean to overstep—"

"Tears of joy, my little pumpkin. Emmeline Rose Wright, you always bring me tears of joy."

They enjoyed a tender embrace before Emma whispered, "Perhaps I should dispense James to fetch Mary Ann Angell Young to assist as well."

Nellie looked up in surprise. "Tarnation! I would prefer you did not. Certainly, that cantankerous woman provided adequate assistance in a pinch for James's birth when we knew no other qualified women."

"Yes, but now Missus King traveled to visit her daughter Louisa in Fillmore City, and I do not think any other—"

"Whyever would we seek Mary Ann Angell Young's company," Nellie interrupted with a smile for her considerate daughter, "when we have you and Rosalinda to give expert care? Furthermore, I can supervise!"

Emma laughed. "First of all, my dearest mother, even *you* can see it is unwise to plan on being both the supervising midwife *and* the patient. And secondly, for all her curmudgeonly behavior, Mary Ann possesses the competence of a skilled midwife."

Emma looked down. "Moreover, ever since that nasty old Brigham Young dismissed her from the Beehive House last year, and Lucy Ann and Clarissa Decker Young assumed command, I do feel sorry for her. She seems ostracized in the land of her own people."

Nellie smiled.

My dear, sweet, kind Emma.

"Emma, you thoughtful, charitable girl. Actually, no. I must acknowledge, you thoughtful, charitable *young lady*. I am honored to have you assume the position of my apprentice and assistant."

"Thank you, Mama, for recognizing, since I just turned ten, I *am* practically a grownup," said Emma.

Nellie grinned despite the sharp pain knifing across her abdomen. "Do not hurry the process, my sweet. But at any age, you cause my cup to runneth over with joy."

The contraction peaked in an extreme jolt of pain and Nellie bent double. "Merciful Heavens!"

"Should be any time now," said Emma, rubbing her shoulders. "Aunt Rosalinda should be here in a jiffy. That seemed a good strong contraction. You must be well on your way."

Nellie reached for her daughter's hand and Emma led her to the bedroom.

CHAPTER 36
Groovin' on a Sunday Afternoon

Camp Douglas, May 1863

As the two boys noisily licked the bottom of their pudding bowls, Obadiah announced that his duty the next day involved a field trip to the new Camp Douglas, completed last October on the east bank of the city. "I must reconnoiter the fort and verify some facts regarding the circumstances of a new case I prosecute."

Alleluia. Perhaps the Mormons' vise grip on justice in this Territory has finally loosened, at last allowing Federal judges to perform their duties and enforce the laws of the United States. Of course, my husband guards his tongue with his usual caution in his role as an officer of the court, ensuring all details of federal litigation remain confidential. It suffices that Obadiah lets slip he has a case!

This hopeful sign came in the same month that Obadiah's colleague, Justice Waite, resigned his commission in frustration over his empty court docket. Waite's circuit encompassed territory consisting of the hard-core faithful, Mormons who followed every commandment of Young. They had scorched their first homesteads, burning their houses and crops, and re-settled farther south in Waite's judicial territory.

Beaming at her husband, Nellie said, "'Tis unfathomable the 'Lion Above the Law' and his Quorum of Twelve obstructed justice by adjudicating civil matters in church courts for so long. Perhaps now we shall not lose more good men."

"Must you always jump to such extreme conclusions in response to my simple statements?" Obadiah shook his head.

She frowned. "I simply deduce educated inferences from what little information you divulge."

His face darkened into a thundercloud.

She switched to a different tone. "Surely, dear husband, you take rightful pride in gaining enough of Mister Young's trust to ease the tyrant's tight-fisted control over the matters in your district."

He gave a tight-lipped smile, his face clearing as he picked up the newspaper and began reading.

"Might I please accompany you?" Nellie asked, beginning to clear the supper dishes.

"Cornelia, isn't it enough that you keep me here in Great Salt Lake City instead of on the trail, whilst you recuperate from your latest confinement? Must you smother me with your constant attendance of me, even as I employ my skills at my profession?"

Stung, Nellie paused, dirty dishes stacked in her arms, and stared at her husband.

"Missus Wright, this is not a church picnic!" Obadiah said, frowning.

"What joy, a church picnic!" Emma clapped her hands as she strode into the room. "I can hardly even recall ever attending one. Why, the last one occurred so long ago, the details do evade me."

Nellie chuckled. "'Twas last summer," she said. "We went on a *church* picnic with the Wells and several other Christian families with whom we worship."

The news spread like wildfire and one after another, each of the Wright children ran into the kitchen.

Elizabeth looked doubtful at the truth of this statement. "I may not recall the specifics, but I certainly do remember the fun!" She shook her head so vigorously her ribbon fell off her braid.

"Could we please go on a picnic, Father?" asked Emma.

"Picnic?" shouted James. "Complete with hoops and running races and Mama's fried chicken?"

"Fried chicken?" echoed William.

"Now you've gone and stirred the hornet's nest!" growled Obadiah, his eyebrows still knit in consternation.

Yet I can detect a glimmer of acceptance of this idea.

"We have so few opportunities to enjoy these niceties of civilization with your all-consuming responsibilities and demanding superiors," observed Nellie.

"Hopping horse feathers, I most certainly did not envision a whole parade of Wrights traipsing up to the embankment when I informed you of the commitment my duties demand. I will, of course, conduct my tour and my business on my own," Obadiah said, still frowning.

"Oh, Father," said all the children in one disappointed breath.

Elizabeth shook her head. "We are so disappointed in you."

All the children gasped.

Nellie stifled a grin.

I guess she has heard that admonition once too often to not use it herself! I hope she did not trip his anger.

She frowned with anxiety.

Obadiah paused, his head down.

The Wright family waited, scarcely breathing, for his thunderous reaction.

"Elizabeth Violet Wright," he whispered in an ominous voice.

He shook his head and tilted it to the side.

Then he raised his voice.

"Now that the cat is out of the bag about my trip to the new, conveniently located Camp Douglas, perhaps we could think about a picnic this Sunday after worship."

Nellie could see a small smile forming.

The children jumped up in one accord with a loud, "Huzzah!"

Obadiah burst out laughing and gathered William into his arms in a hug.

Nellie let out a silent 'Huzzah' herself.

A picnic! What joy. A treasured event, so infrequently indulged. Moreover, the cherry on top of the 'sundae.'

Nellie laughed aloud at her own pun.

Now I am sure to see the encampment of United States troops at Camp Douglas for myself. Thank God for Elizabeth and her wayward tongue.

***

Sunday dawned sunny and clear, ensuring the entire Wright family appeared freshly pressed and ready for church in record time. Nellie felt proud every time they stepped into the 'gentiles' church.

Not only do I nearly burst my buttons with pride at my beautiful family, I am proud of myself for gathering a committee and appropriating the proper building for our small non-denominational chapel.

Nellie's committee also devised a liturgy for a Sunday Worship, concentrating on singing shared Christian hymns, combined with the high points of a Catholic Mass and the preaching of the Baptists.

Nellie doubted any of her children heard a word of that day's service, even the always attentive and proper Emma. Between juggling baby Lucinda so she did not disrupt anyone else's worship, and her own anticipation of picnic fun, even Nellie would be hard pressed to give a comprehensive synopsis of the priest's sermon. They all hurried away to their wagon without even stopping for Rosalinda Wells's crullers at hospitality—a recent unanimous family favorite.

The trip up the embankment to the South Bench took a little less than an hour. The children spent the entire journey singing, the boys punctuating the ending of each song by jumping in and out of the wagon. The aroma of the fried chicken, prepared last night and kept in the cellar on this week's block of ice, tickled their noses. James declared it was already making his mouth water.

"Wonderful!" shouted Obadiah, reaching his long arm into the back of the wagon and pulling James forward for a hug. "Because we brought *watermelon* for dessert!"

"Huzzah!" they shouted with laughter.

"Wherever did you procure a watermelon in May?" asked Nellie.

Obadiah glanced at his wife with a warm smile. "I work in mysterious ways!" he intoned.

Nellie smiled but pressed his arm.

"All right, our Prophet experiments with glass houses for growing vegetables in the winter."

"*Our* Prophet?"

"Bottom fact, his gardener dabbles in experimental horticulture. But the gift originated with President Young. He shares his bounty with us."

Nellie raised her eyebrows in disbelief.

That's debatable. That man amasses much wealth merely by conflating the church's treasure with his personal finances. Who finances the greenhouses and the gardener? Without a doubt, the tithing faithful. Share his bounty? Hardly.

Unaware of Nellie's stormy thoughts, Obadiah continued his agricultural observations. "Truly the temperate climate of this valley, nestled between mountain ranges, lends itself to prodigious crops, year-round."

Nellie swallowed her vitriol, determined to enjoy the fun outing on a beautiful day.

She took the high road. "Not to mention the excellent aqueducts and aquifers engineered by the enterprising Mormons to take full advantage of the water streaming off the mountain ranges."

The clear blue sky embraced them from overhead and the sun warmed their faces. Nellie drank in the beauty of the surrounding countryside.

"We are here," announced Nellie, eliciting another 'Huzzah' from the back of the wagon.

In no time at all, she spread the picnic blanket and presented the feast.

In short order, the only sound heard was happy munching.

The children dispersed to start games while Nellie and Obadiah finished their last bites of the chicken.

"I'll save the watermelon and cookies for after our games," said Nellie.

"Don't forget about the tour of the fort," said Obadiah over his shoulder as he sprinted like a kid to join the children at play.

As she focused on gathering the remains of the feast, crawling around the blanket retrieving anything salvageable, a shadow fell upon her.

Startled, she looked up into the air to see a tall man bending over her.

"Sure an begora, 'tis a mighty fine day for a picnic," announced the shadow.

Squinting, Nellie could not make out any features as she stared right into the sun.

Panicked, she scrambled to her feet, realizing for the first time Obadiah's and the children's running games carried them far off in the distance.

She and the sleeping Lucinda were alone at the blanket with an enormous stranger!

She whirled in front of the baby to protect her, but her movement turned her back to the sun and she saw his face.

Mercy! He is the spitting image of my own father! It's his Irish blood.

She drew a long shaky breath, with her hand over her heart.

The man smiled, and she felt as if she had always known him.

"Madam, allow me to introduce meself." The man bowed.

Thank goodness my father's doppelgänger did not arrive whilst I nursed the baby!

"I am Colonel Patrick Connor, ma'am, at your service!" The officer bent over Nellie's proffered hand.

She curtsied and replied, "Missus Obadiah Wright, I thank you kindly."

"Why, Attorney Wright never mentioned he had such a charming and beautiful wife," said the colonel.

She blushed at the unexpected compliment.

"For you, I'll reveal me real nomenclature: Patrick Edward O'Connor, a lad straight from the quays of Donegal. I dropped the "O" along with me brogue when landing as a lad of twelve on the streets of New York, and made assimilation into America my main goal in life. But I'm proud to be a Hibernian."

Still flustered, she grasped at straws for a reply. She mimicked a brogue saying, "Me own father hailed from County Cork, just a hop, skip and a jump from your childhood home."

"And you were born in the old country?" he asked, incredulous.

She blushed even redder. "Mercy, no. I meant no disrespect."

The colonel looked a little confused.

She stammered, "When I hear someone speak in the brogue and cadence of my father, I can't help but lapse into the tongue meself."

"An' by the blessings o' Saint Bridget, a right fine employment you've made of it." The colonel laughed.

Goodness, Lord, will I never cease to embarrass myself?

She tried to right the ship. "We Wrights enjoy a fine Sunday picnic atop this hillside, near your campsite. I hope that is not somehow against regulations?"

At this new apprehension, she looked anxiously at him.

"Sure n' begorra, I do believe the only ting 'twould go against Army command would be to deny the highest-ranking officer a taste o' that lip smacking chicken!" he said with a smile, rubbing his hands together.

"Mercy, by all means, do have a seat and enjoy a bit o' repast. I am afraid it is rather slim pickings once the Wright clan has tucked in!" She laughed.

She unpacked the food she had just re-deposited in the picnic baskets.

Why does Obadiah not sprint back here to help me entertain the commander of the States Army in the Territory of Utah?

But Obadiah had not even glanced her way since he joined the children's games.

The Colonel dined on some pieces of chicken with a swift dispatch that even her son William could not match. He sampled the cold caraway and vinegar cabbage and dug into the potato salad with relish.

"The best grub since Donegal!" he muttered, wiping his lips with satisfaction. "Can you allow me ta escort you around the grounds here, my dear, as a repayment of the kindness of sharing your fine sup?" He jumped to his feet in a limber movement and extended his hand to Nellie.

She took one more nervous look at Obadiah, still engrossed in play, and then gave her hand to the Colonel.

Leaving the sleeping baby on the blanket, she walked with him to the edge of the embankment to look at the camp and the city below as he regaled her with an outline of his mission in Utah.

"In addition to keeping the civilized world safe from savages, I spearhead a crusade to encourage more *gentiles* to settle in the area. Fortuitously, my men and I discovered the very thing to entice new settlers." He leaned closer to her and whispered, "Missus Wright, I have discovered a vein of silver runs right underneath your picnic blanket!"

Nellie turned, eyes widening with surprise and was even more surprised to find her nose inches from the Colonel's.

"My purpose," he explained. "I vow to further delineate the differences between the United States Federal Government's objectives and that of the Latter-day Saints. Moreover, our loyal citizens residing in this Mormon-controlled place lack a voice. Hell, they even lack any news or information of the rest of the world not tainted by the propaganda of Brigham Young and the Moronic Church."

Connor wiped his brow and looked angry. "I vow to thwart the treacherous and treasonous Brigham Young. I shall not rest until that scalawag is dethroned and de-clawed."

Hope rose so high in Nellie's heart, for a fleeting moment, she thought it would burst out of the top of her head. *At last, an unadulterated champion of American rights. In fact, one in a position to stem the tidal wave named Brigham Young!*

His facial expression intensifying, Connor asserted, "We must keep the loyal States' citizens in the area safe. We must keep this Mormon Church separate from our States' government! The atrocities these insurgents commit in the name of righteousness and revenge must cease. Yet they escape Washington's notice since quelling another rebellion preoccupies the Union at the moment. That crafty devil Young! He takes full advantage of Lincoln's and the States' current battle by expanding his interests whilst they look elsewhere. It makes a man's blood boil."

The tall man stared across the valley into the city of Salt Lake, with his fist clenched.

Further heartened by the ferocity and conviction of his words, she agreed with her whole heart. "Troubled times prevail! Our situation in this land has not improved one iota since our arrival. The subversion and subterfuge has simply taken a different shape."

"Tyrannical Young flagrantly disregards our United States and its federal authority," Connor declared. "Since they won't send me to the real fighting in the South, I've made it me mission to stop the rebellion here. The Indians do not pose the real problem. I took care of certain skirmishes, but when the dust settled, I saw that Young stood squarely behind all the trouble. No, *warring* won't be effective. Yea, ye heard that admission coming from one of the fightin' Irish! I must make our mines safe from sabotage and Mormon extortion. I must encourage non-Mormon citizens to live here and increase our numbers."

Nellie voiced her agreement, even though she was sure her husband would disapprove. "Your zealous rhetoric breeds hope within me, Colonel O'Connor, for you answer not to Despot Young and truly hold a position that could overturn the Theocrat's grip on the Territory."

They strolled back to the blanket, and at the sight of her beautiful baby sleeping so peacefully, Nellie renewed her vow to protect her children.

"You'll see," Connor promised. "I'm not a one-trick pony. I shall fight the Mormon propaganda on multiple fronts."

Nellie's eyes widened with surprise as he swore an oath under his breath.

"And with the help o' blessed Saint Bridget," he concluded, "I must disseminate true information to all loyal States citizens. I shall wage a war of words with that dictator Young. Why, I heard tell some folks here don't even know of Judge Cradlebaugh's presentation of the bottom facts of the Mountain Meadows Massacre to the House of Representatives this past February."

She stared at the man, mouth agape. Overcome with dismay at yet more information denied her, she dropped down on the picnic blanket. More to soothe herself than her sleeping baby, she caressed Lucinda's soft cheek.

"Even you," he said with a sad shake of his head at her reaction, "a learned woman with a prominent husband, has no access to this news. I feel duty bound to provide a supplement to the daily stream of propaganda, to inform all here of the true happenings both locally and in the world at large."

This news elated Nellie. "Would that you had the resources to bring this to fruition! Untainted news is a rare commodity here."

Connor warmed to his subject with her wholehearted endorsement. "I am quite sure you haven't heard that in the short time I've been deployed here, we not only moved the fort to literally on top of the city, but in addition to the silver that slumbers right below us, my men and I have discovered a vast resource of minerals in nearby hills. We can encourage miners to settle and make their fortunes.

"Our new governor Doty and myself have joined forces to keep Young's congressional lackey Kemp at bay. The turncoat Kemp attempts all measures to get our federal troops removed from this area."

Connor paused when he saw Nellie's blank expression. "Do I overwhelm you with all new information, my dear?"

Nellie blushed with embarrassment and chagrin. *I must seem a vapid fool, not availing myself of any of the information my husband must hold. Or worse, so poorly educated I fail to comprehend the intelligence my husband confides in me.*

"Buck up," he said with a warm smile. "We are down and out, but the only way is *up!* One of the many reasons 'tis for the best the *true States* citizens living in this community of boot-licking ruffians saw the back of that scalawag Cumming's head back in '61."

Out of respect for her friend Elizabeth Wells Randall Cumming, Nellie felt she must at least partially defend the honor of Alfred Cumming. "I do believe Governor Cumming became convinced the threats to the territory's peace incited by an aggressive inquiry into the Mountain Meadows Massacre outweighed the benefits of bringing the true culprits to justice."

"Don't succumb to that Blarney! When the villainous Young spun his yarn, he caught Cumming in his web, stripping the man of any gumption he mighta had, neutralizing his will, ensuring Cumming never challenged Young's edicts. He allowed Young, as Indian Agent for the territory, to attribute the massacre to an *Indian uprising* in his report to Congress, thus effectively sidestepping any inquiry into the culpability of the *Saints*."

Nellie shook her head and said, "We'd best leave sleeping dogs lie. That incident happened six years ago."

But Connor raised his hand and corrected himself. "No, not entirely preventing inquiry. Young's malarkey report did *not* prevent trustworthy Judge Cradlebaugh's thorough investigation and distillation of the facts, as he attested in Congress, where the probe continues still."

Nellie gasped in surprise. "But if there is evidence and a report revealing the true culprits, why have federal marshals arrested no one?"

Connor looked grim again. "Warrants have been sworn for the arrests of clergy and even bishops. Young and his agents, and the Danites, effectively prevented any of their own from being taken into custody. They refused to serve the court-ordered appearances, but Congress now knows the truth. Cradlebaugh persisted, and just this past February, he himself presented his findings. Now the facts are clear. Firstly, the order for the Indians to steal all the livestock of that hapless wagon came directly from Young himself."

Nellie felt the blood drain from her face. "And the massacre?" she whispered. "Who gave the command for that?"

"You well know," said Conner, the grim expression on his face deepening. "I can save my full itemization of the evidence for a full report to the loyal States citizens living in Salt Lake City."

Nellie smiled to herself. "Is it a philosophy that prevents you from granting the full nomenclature to this City?" she asked, with an assumed innocence.

He snorted. "Aye, a course. No self-respecting citizen could call this place *great* without choking upon the words! A damnable title, egotistical and overreaching, just like the tyrant running the place. A-rr-gg, the dastardly deeds that no one here knows! Except for my camp, information concerning the happenings here remains inaccessible to those who need it the most. It could save lives!"

Connor barely paused for a breath and Nellie did not interrupt.

I feel as if I attend Miss Sarah's Lady's Finishing School again, and learning nothing, am forced to steal my brothers' schoolbooks to discover what they were taught. Colonel O'Connor's speech pours forth such a plethora of information, I feel delinquent not taking notes.

"Yea, the atrocities committed daily shall make your head spin! At least now we have concrete evidence that Bishops and the Mormon hierarchy were actual members of the party that committed the murders at the Mountain Meadows Massacre."

"But how is that possible that no one—"

"The bastards dressed as Indians."

Baby Lucinda screamed, as if suddenly in pain.

Nellie snatched her into her arms. "All those women and children, slaughtered." A tear ran down her cheek and, not thinking, she wiped it with the baby's blanket.

"*After* they surrendered," said Connor. "The true details of the horror are unspeakable. If you want to know more, I cannot bear to tell you. You must read the report."

Nellie gave a hopeless laugh that caught in her throat and sounded more like a sob. "Where would I obtain access to that? I can't even get unfiltered news of the world."

Connor attempted levity. "Even this little darling is outraged by this turn of events. At least the lack of information is a matter in which I can be of assistance. I shall undertake to apprise you, and every other true citizen of the States, of the workings of our government and news of the rest of the world."

Speechless, she cradled her baby, grieving again for the souls of the victims of the massacre. The fact that she now knew the Mormons purposefully killed them made this sorrow fresh and unbearable again.

"Those innocent souls were truly killed *after* they surrendered?" she whispered.

"Truly," he confirmed.

He turned away.

"I am loath to tell you this. The elders of the Church, re-garbed in their usual apparel, convinced the hearty group to surrender, and then shot them one-by-one as they were marched away."

Nellie covered her face with her hands and sobbed. "Impossibly, this horrendous tragedy is worse than I imagined."

She sobbed into Lucinda's bunting.

Connor awkwardly patted her on the back and said, "You must read the official report. The details are too disturbing for me to continue."

Nellie nodded into her baby bundle.

Connor's attempt to distract Nellie with a change of conversation plunged them into another subject she truly abhorred: the lecherous evils of polygamy.

"How can our Federal judges, like your husband, enforce the new Morill Act, extending the prohibition of polygamy to all territories of the United States, if the *de facto* leader of this United States Territory remains the biggest known polygamist in the world? 'Tis yet another reason to hang this abomination of a man," Colonel Connor moaned.

Out of the frying pan, into the fire!

As his speech reached a crescendo, she glanced at her family and caught a glimpse of Obadiah suddenly spotting her talking to the colonel.

Her husband stopped; mid-run, and stood up straight with his hands on his hips. He raised his hand communicating outrage and astonishment. His cessation of movement was so abrupt, James, concentrating on rolling a hoop, smashed right into him.

Nellie could feel the anger of his glare from across the field.

Adding insult to injury, I now shall have criticism of my deportment compounding my sorrows.

CHAPTER 37
Bang, Bang Maxwell's Silver Hammer

South Temple Street, Block 75, June 1863

Boom, boom, boom!

Nellie jumped, cold water from the washing pitcher splashing everywhere. The water-soaked spots on her dressing gown spread and cold wetness permeated her skin. She shivered with cold and fear.

Boom, boom, boom!

She snatched Lucinda from the bassinet almost the instant the baby wailed.

The children all woke up screaming and ran to her. She caught them in her other arm. Reassuring her brood that she was there and they would cope together, she turned to pick up the crying Jeremiah with one arm as she bounced Lucinda in the other.

"Do you think we are under attack?" Nellie shouted, running to their bedroom dragging along the children attached to her nightgown.

Obadiah, awakened by the sound, jumped out of bed and crept cautiously to the window.

On her knees, Nellie crept on the floor toward the window too, slowly and awkwardly, still carrying Lucinda and Jeremiah. All the other children beat her there.

An astounding scene unfolded before them. The quiet and orderly downtown street erupted with chaos. From their vantage point behind their second floor, solid pine frame of the window casing, they could see Brigham across the street, out on his high front stoop, in his nightshirt, brandishing his sword.

Boom, boom, boom!

My, he has chicken legs! How do they support his round form?

A bizarre question at a time like this.

Nellie stood straight and laughed. Her two babies in her arms stopped crying. "No! Silly me. 'Tis not a time for panic, 'tis a time of gaiety. The guns do not attack us, rather *turnabout is fair play*. Husband, where is thy usual calm under fire?" asked Nellie, laughing and leaning on his back as Obadiah struggled to load his gun.

"How can you employ such an inane platitude when we are under attack?" Obadiah said through clenched teeth.

Boom, boom, boom!

The rest of the Wright family all ducked below the protective pine sill.

Nellie stood firm and announced, "All is well! That is the sound of our United States Army cannons."

Her family turned and stared at her, hope and relief stamped on all their faces.

Boom, boom, boom, boom!

"It's a twenty-one-gun salute!" said Nellie.

"I only counted 19 bangs," said James, looking at his raised fingers.

Boom, boom!

"That just made 21," James shouted.

The girls looked a little less frightened.

The Wright family straightened up and stood looking out the window.

Brigham Young ran down his front stoop. Looking down from their second story window, the Wrights could only see the top of his head now, as the enormous wall still surrounded his land. His balding head ran back and forth.

But they could still hear him frantically shouting, "Summon the captains of the Nauvoo Legion. 'Tis a call to battle with the Army encampment!"

Nellie laughingly said to Obadiah, "What has Brother Brigham been up to that he could think that the United States Army would aim their fire at him?"

"Call out the guards," shouted Brigham. He ran to the Eagle gate and found a neighbor, who strapped on his guns as he ran to protect his Prophet.

"Find Herber Kimball. Find the commander of the Nauvoo Legion!" Mr. Young commanded.

"We are under attack?"

The question became a cry throughout the streets as people ran every which way, panicked and frenzied.

"Is it the Federals or the Confederates?" someone shouted from below.

Obadiah stared at Nellie. "Explain your reasoning," he commanded.

"Mister Wright, did you not listen to our supper guest last night, the United States Lieutenant who advised us that the troops planned a surprise for our country's Camp Douglas Commander?"

Obadiah paused in his attempt to load his gun.

"Did you not hear him confide in us that in honor of Colonel Connor's new promotion, his troops organized a twenty-one-gun salute for this morning?"

She stifled a grin at the sheepish look on Obadiah's face.

"Hopping horsefeathers! I saw you panic too," he raged, then dropped his gun and twirled his mustache. "Verily, now I recall his words to that effect." He removed the shot from his gun and remounted it on the wall.

"If our Army had a way to communicate with the people loyal to the States living here, perhaps we could have avoided this panic," said Nellie.

She saw Obadiah's reaction, ratifying her remark hit home, and smiled with satisfaction.

The children still looked warily up at Nellie.

"My little pumpkins, do not fret! Our United States Army devised a bit of devilment to honor their Commander whilst simultaneously goading Brigham Young," she said.

"A fine success they've made of it too," said Elizabeth, pointing out the window to Young, vehemently ordering people about, still brandishing his sword, his nightshirt flapping ridiculously in the morning sun.

The boys in the Wright family, all lovers of practical jokes, chortled with glee at the panicked and frantic movements in the street.

"Let's go downstairs so we can see the action better!" shouted James, and they all ran down the stairs behind him.

The chaos on the street was visible from all the windows on this floor.

"The cannons are pointed toward us," shouted an elder of the Church.

A man with a spyglass looked up at the embankment. "I can't see through the fire! I cannot ascertain the exact nature of the enemy!"

"But there are no more shots!" exclaimed a voice.

Even Obadiah chuckled at this.

"Is it the Rebels?"

The shout ran down the street.

Suddenly their back door burst open.

The Wrights gasped, terrified.

A sobbing Rosalinda, holding two wailing toddlers, fell into Nellie's arms. Big-eyed Lemuel and petite Priscilla scooted quickly in behind and slammed the door shut.

"The Utah War returns! We are under attack," shouted Rosalinda.

"No, no!" Nellie took her friend into her arms.

"The Rebels arrived in Utah Territory?" Rosalinda panted.

The wailing twins squirmed out of the group hug and screamed louder.

"No. All is well," Nellie said, and scooped Dudley from the floor to sooth him.

Or is this Dwight?

She checked the other twin to see which one's face was longer.

"You are quite certain?" Rosalinda demanded. Still shaking, she picked up the other squalling boy.

"Mostly," said Nellie absentmindedly, still focused on which boy she held.

And the twin in Rosalinda's arms—*I am fairly certain now* that *one is Dudley*—stopped crying.

Nellie shook her head. "Yes, yes! I am certain. 'Tis a bit of a practical joke."

She looked down at the little boy in her arms, who stared back at her wide-eyed. "Dwight?" Nellie whispered.

The baby opened his mouth and howled.

"I am so sorry, Dudley," Nellie said, and the baby stopped crying.

"Flummadiddle! What with Wilburforce already unloading merchandise at the store, Adelaidia up and married, I am left alone to defend home and hearth and four terrified children!" cried Rosalinda. "Bereft of a shotgun! Thank Goodness we managed to run through the back alleys the three blocks to your house. I don't know what I would have done if you were not here to help defend me. I panicked the whole way over, running in my nightgown, clutching the twins. What if you were on one of your excursions, thousands of miles out in the wilderness?"

Nellie could not resist a smile.

Yes, thank goodness when you are being attacked, I am here to join the merriment too.

"Do not fear, Rosalinda!" she said.

Dudley wriggled out of her arms and toddled over to his sister Priscilla. Nellie grabbed onto Rosalinda, still holding Dwight, and held her tight.

Nellie hugged her hard, and in a gentle, reassuring tone said, "We have it on good authority we are not under attack. That was merely a twenty-one-gun salute to Colonel Connor of the United States Army, upon the occasion of his promotion." She whispered into the top of Rosalinda's head, "Thanks be to God for our friendship and close proximity."

Nellie's sons welcomed Lemuel with a joint "Whoop!" and swarmed all over him. William gave Lemuel's legs a big bear hug while James leapt into his arms. Lemuel gave a tentative smile in return.

"Then why were the cannons pointed at us?" sobbed Rosalinda with relief. She tightened her grip on Nellie.

Nellie's sons, not big fans of the twin boys, especially not of their names, nevertheless stepped to the plate and tried to distract Dudley and Dwight with toy popguns.

"To provoke Brother Young," said Obadiah.

"I do hate practical jokes," said Nellie. "Often there is little humor in them."

Rosalinda straightened herself out and tried to comfort Dudley, back in her arms and crying so hard, now his nose was dripping and his face was all slobbery. "A great many more people were *provoked* besides that rapscallion Young," she said, and sniffled.

"After the terror of the never-officially-acknowledged," said Nellie, "nor never-officially-ended Utah War, I confess I first thought the war caught us in the crossfire, on the front lines." She put her hand on her chest and forced herself to calm her still racing heart. "But then I remembered the secret confided by our dinner guest last night."

Rosalinda shook her head. "Yet another reason I am sorry to have missed your dinner last night. I could have kept my calm had I known the secret."

Nellie walked back to look out the window, and her jaw dropped at the sight of Brigham, still running in circles in his nightshirt. A big snort of laughter erupted from deep within her.

Everyone just looked at her, and she snorted with laughter again.

Suddenly, she was laughing so hard tears streamed down her cheeks.

Surprised, the twins stopped crying.

Rosalinda and all the Wrights could not help but laugh with her.

"It is rather funny to see him get his come-uppance!" Rosalinda said, laughing and trying to wipe the laughter tears from her eyes while still clutching Dudley.

Or was that Dwight? Did they switch places?

Nellie laughed even harder.

If I ever mind them again, I shall mark one of them for identification.

Rosalinda picked the other twin back up and jiggled the heavy boys in her arms, still laughing.

Speechless with laughter herself, Nellie plucked Dwight from Rosalinda's arm, and her friend wiped her eyes with the hem of Dudley's nightshirt.

"Amen!" said Emma.

CHAPTER 38
Further to Fly

Home on Block 75, August 1863

Nellie hurried into the large front room where Obadiah conducted his official business, deposited a sheaf of paper, and refilled the inkwell while contemplating her growing family.

Her three boys grew like the weeds she couldn't keep away from her vegetables. She thanked the Lord for that large, fenced garden that provided ample space for the boys' excessive energy that found no outlet indoors.

Letting her gratitude flow, she reflected that their grander house provided sufficient room, even on the few days of inclement weather, to run and play. All the while, undisturbed, her husband could toil diligently and peacefully at his desk in the front room, with a bird's eye view of Young's headquarters.

She credited her husband's brilliant reasoning and persuasive speaking as the negotiation skills that wrested concessions from Young to the States. She admired his perseverance as he slowly and patiently wrangled Young's compliance with United States laws. Certain that Obadiah daily increased his influence, she smiled with satisfaction.

Moreover, at night, I am the beneficiary of his charms.

Nellie, lost in her thoughts, continued scooping up shoes, toys, and articles of her children's clothing scattered around the house, and delivering them to their proper place. She could hear the happy chatter of her children in the garden as they played. She smiled out window, watching them as she stood at the sink scrubbing a pan.

Obadiah rushed into the kitchen bringing a rush of excited energy. "Young just deeded us a ranch!"

Soap splashed in Nellie's face from the pan she dropped in surprise.

"If my calculations are correct, it is but a week's journey from here. Some of Young's scouts reconnoitered the area and returned with reports of ranch-able land in the southern quadrant, in fact due south from here. Perhaps the soil would lend itself to farming! A profitable herd of cattle and some other livestock already populate the ranch. We have been invited to set up a homestead there."

He paused as his excitement grew. "Imagine, my Rose, elevated to landed gentry!"

Nellie tried to match his enthusiasm. "What unanticipated bounty!" But her mind spun with dread and doubts overwhelmed her. "How far away did you say? What strings come attached?"

Obadiah deflated a bit. "Must you always perceive potential detriments?"

Nellie tried to smile and change her focus but her thoughts raced. "A ranch? At almost any distance, overseeing its operations from here shall surely challenge us."

"True, but we won't have to. We shall move all our kit and caboodle and reside in its splendor." Obadiah grinned like he just handed her the crown jewels.

"Relocate? But I've just expanded my garden this spring and it finally produces enough for us to sell the bounty of our crop beyond what we need to sustain us," Nellie said in confusion. "What need is there for an additional farm or a ranch?"

"We have been just handed, on a silver platter, an opportunity to be owners of acres of land, and you focus on your tiny garden?" Obadiah picked Nellie up and swung her around. "Expand your horizons. We shall have acres of gardens! We now own a ranch."

"Leave here? Move into the middle of the wilderness? Leave the schools and the community behind and relocate by ourselves? Miles away from neighbors?"

Blessed Saint Bridget, help me, what new tomfoolery is this?

"Leave the non-Mormon Church community I helped found?"

"You may stop asking the same question over and over, employing different words." Obadiah smiled. "I understand this announcement catches you by surprise."

She tugged at her stray lock of hair. "Why have the owners abandoned this ranch if it has proven itself a profitable enterprise?"

"You know I yearn to live in the wilderness. We often talked about our pioneering aptitudes. Our love of exploration and discovery spurred our journey here. Remember, we agreed only to a temporary residence in Great Salt Lake City. I continuously remained focused on determining a suitable location for our next home."

Shaking her head, she contradicted him. "Your promotion to Utah Territory Circuit Judge spurred our journey here. I agreed to temporary arrangements here but only with an eye toward moving *back East* when the time came."

She sighed. "*Back home.*"

She continued, "True, we have adapted ourselves so handily, I lost sight of the fleeting nature of our residence. But I have no desire to delve farther into the wilderness! Our home flourishes here!"

Obadiah just stood there, looking disappointed in her.

She knew he would unleash his fury into his persuasive words in short measure, so she hurried on. "Against the odds of being a minority in the Latter-day Saint community, we have established a cozy little home and firmly ensconced ourselves in this village. The children excel at their lessons and are quite fond of the schoolteacher. They have other children for companionship when they have completed their chores. We have musical diversions in concerts, there are speeches from famous traveling orators occasionally, and I am sustained by the companionship of Rosalinda, Hannah King, and several other ladies here. What can we gain by pulling up stakes now?"

Obadiah's mounting anger permeated every word of his reply.

"We must adhere to our strategy: to use this as a stopping point to ascertain other opportunities. We set a goal of staying two years. You knew that was the plan. You have changed the plan."

"I did not change the plan, it just evolved! We have flourished here for over five years now and I have fashioned us a home. Despite formidable obstacles! Just like our forefathers *and foremothers* before us, we conform to God's plan and have children in His image and likeness and provide for them. We settle into a community and help it, and our family, grow and prospers."

Nellie searched for persuasive words to explain her position, although part of her brain remained in shock at the sudden news that Obadiah wanted them to just pick up and leave.

"How would you even continue your work? Isn't every case you now hear tried *in Great Salt Lake City* in the new courtroom you fought so hard to establish?" She asked.

"You know I travel the jurisdiction's circuit to resolve disputes in other areas of the Territory. I can make our new ranch the seat of this circuit, maybe even establish a courtroom for the southern part of the Territory right there!"

If that doesn't cap the climax. Uproot the whole family and then have criminals loiter in my new parlor as they await adjudication. "I cannot even begin to consider the prospect of uprooting our home again."

"Brother Young blesses me with this ranch. We benefit from his largess. Moreover, I have earned this. I have labored with great industry and plied my diplomatic skills to our advantage, earning our Prophet's respect."

Our Prophet?

"I have long wished for more open spaces. Just think, cattle of my own and *one hundred and fifty* acres to raise them. It is my heart's desire. The prosperity of the ranch clinches the deal. We do not begin all over again, we simply take over the reins and stay the course."

"But look out the window at the growth in my garden! Lush vegetables ripen before our eyes, but they won't be ready to harvest for several months. You would deprive your daughters of the literal fruits of their diligent labor? Daily they weeded after their lessons, delaying play. Shall we just leave our produce to rot?"

"Brigham assures me that vegetables have been planted at the ranch. He has chosen to bestow favor upon me. He knows I crave more than a little patch of garden around an unassuming house. He knows I desire a ranch of my own!

"Brother Brigham insists that I take it as a token of his appreciation for my hard work. Brigham insists—"

"Brigham insists? Brigham! What care I of his opinion? Why do *you* heed his voice? Now you consult with Brigham to make *our* decisions? What of my desires, my plans for our family? Are you thinking of what is best for our family?"

"Our family shall prosper and flourish wherever I say we should abide. I have decided. *You* must bend to my decisions. I am the man. I am the breadwinner and head of this family. You do as I say."

Stunned, Nellie could not believe her dear, sweet Obadiah could be so insensitive to her needs.

Insensitive? No. Callous, unperceptive. He does not care enough about my needs to even discern them. How can we have enjoyed years of marital union and have my husband clueless as to what I cherish? How can he just assume whatever he wants shall suffice for me?

"What of the community of friends we have garnered here? I do not wish the children to leave their society. Who will school them? Who will help me with the chores? I am sure our one domestic shall not move with us to the wilderness."

"That is of no concern. We are self-sufficient. We will not need more help than the ranch hands who already reside there."

"Any womenfolk?"

Obadiah paused.

He has not even inquired.

He shrugged his shoulders and said, "Perhaps. You need not worry, the men there can help you with anything you need. I will see that they provide for you when I am on the road."

"You would leave me there alone?" Terror seized Nellie.

"Alone? Do you not have many children for companionship? Do you expect me to neglect all my other duties and responsibilities? You would not wish to cause negligence in my scrupulous attention to the legal needs on the circuit."

"But you now travel every month! Sometimes you are absent for a fortnight at a time! I know we try to accompany you regularly but as we now have school-age children, the difficulty increases."

Obadiah waived his hand dismissively. "It is far too burdensome for me to have the whole clan travel with me now."

Startled, Nellie stammered, "B-b-b-but I thought we agreed to travel together as a family. I have spared no effort or resource to accompany you, endowing you with the comforts of home as you journeyed. We have kept our spirit of adventure vibrant, and instilled in our children the joy of travel and exploration. Why, think of all the time together we shall forfeit. We will have no natural opportunities for telling the children our stories from our journey on the Overland Trail. First you decree we will pull up stakes and move, and then you advise you no longer wish my company on your Circuit?"

"Wife, many times it makes it more arduous for me to perform my duties when you and the children accompany me. Their antics distract me. Their crying and needs awaken me at night, when I need sleep to keep my wits keen for court. This makes it difficult for me to concentrate," Obadiah explained.

"But these are minor inconveniences! Is it not better that we are all together, thanking God for each other, sharing our burdens and joys together? I thought we were of one mind on this matter."

"Certainly we are of accord. It is laughable that you think there will be no other opportunities to tell stories to the children."

He shook his head with a wry grin at her foolishness, making Nellie even more upset.

"Now, Cornelia Rose, you must understand that you and the family in constant attendance makes the trial of travel oft times insufferable for me."

She felt sick to her stomach. The pain seared worse than morning sickness, this anguishing news like a physical blow.

As she thought about it, though, instead of hurt, she felt anger.

More arduous for him? The pampered man with all his meals prepared, and his bed made, under every imaginable kind of traveling condition? He who has had all his physical needs attended to as we traipse from one location to another? Insufferable *for him?*

She opened her mouth to rebut his statements but as soon as she began to speak, he interrupted her.

"I concede you have a fair point. I shall examine the viability of your continued company on the circuit. Howsoever, your presence at the ranch will be indispensable to ensure its successful operation," Obadiah decreed.

Nellie's outrage churned her stomach and tumbled from her mouth.

"I am sentenced to wither on a ranch, without a voice in our future together? Brigham has filled your head with such rubbish! I trusted that we labored in harmony and strove to choose a path for our journey through life *together.*"

"Do not include Brother Brigham in your invective. I know the correct way to perform my duties, and thus I know the correct path for my family. I don't need Brigham, *or you*, to make up my mind for me."

The outrage twisting in Nellie's stomach leapt into her heart. She stood there, dumbfounded, twisting her recalcitrant hair.

My loving husband metamorphosed into this unrecognizable monster?

"We leave in one month's time. You must get our domestic affairs here in order and pack the necessities for our move to *my* new ranch."

He took a deep breath. "Moreover, you are to trust my judgment. I have pondered extensively and earnestly about this. I have even prayed upon it. Shame on you for even contemplating I would undertake something harmful for my family. Your statements are merely emotional and are derived, I am sure, simply from the surprise of my decision. When you have had leisure to ponder this clearly, you shall see reason. Perdition is the sure penalty of further hesitation. You *will* cogitate the unmitigated benefit of this opportunity."

He threw his hands in the air. "Hopping horsefeathers! A gift is bestowed upon us to craft my existence in accordance with my dreams! You shall come to appreciate, as I do now, the meritless-ness of the arguments you espouse."

Obadiah stormed out of the room.

CHAPTER 39
Against the Wind

Great Salt Lake City, October 1863

"Marketing day!" shouted Elizabeth. "How I love this outing!"

"I do as well." Nellie smiled sadly, thinking of the many times she had felt burdened by the need to go to market.

What will I do on the God-forsaken ranch? How shall I purchase necessities I lack?

Pack lightly, indeed.

"I cherish the fun," agreed Emma, smoothing her hair under her bonnet and adjusting her shawl. "I shall miss this sorely when we move. However, Papa promises that traders and merchants shall travel to us! A different kind of adventure surely awaits us. Now, what must be readied yet before our departure?"

"Naught!" said Nellie. "We all awake in good spirits on our marketing day, ready to stroll through town. Your brothers chomp at the bit to begin our excursion."

"High-spirited ponies," laughed Emma.

Betsy wheeled the pram around to the front door, baby Lucinda already cooing within it.

"My goodness," exclaimed Nellie. "You wonderful children truly are prepared for our jaunt."

"Papa says we must always be ready for adventure," said James.

"Papa made me an explorer!" agreed William. "Just think, in a short while we shall have all new territory to explore, and shan't have to invent adventures on our trips into market."

The heavy-handed campaign of propaganda administered by Obadiah seemed to sway the attitude of the children toward abandoning this city life.

Do they truly embrace it?

No matter, for what are our alternatives?

Divorce?

I swore an oath before God to obey my husband. I know I have no rights of my own. My only rights come from my status as a wife. Maybe the villain Brigham does do the widow a service elevating her status to 'married' under the law to receive at least the rights of a married woman.

Stuff and nonsense!

Since Young refused to honor United States law, it seemed unlikely he would care about women's status under it.

'Wither thou goest, so goest I.'

Mercy, more blarney. But blarney I pledged to honor. I must accept that this is my fate and make the best of it.

Perhaps I can persuade Rosalinda to move with us!

She found some consolation in the fact that at least they would no longer reside across the street from the enemy, right under his scrutiny.

Now I truly have loosened my grasp on my reasoning abilities.

She pulled on her gloves and grabbed the baby carriage. "Here we go!"

The children displayed their high spirits, greeting many friends and acquaintances on the boardwalk as they paraded to the market.

With each encounter, Nellie felt like crying.

I shall miss each and every person, even those I find most irritating.

After fifteen minutes of pleasant encounters and exchanges, the group turned to enjoy the shops.

"Mercy, no!" shouted James, pointing down the street.

"It is as if, when we say we have had enough visiting, those words summon her!" exclaimed Elizabeth.

William hummed an ominous snippet of music.

At the ripe old age of four, his sense of humor fully matures! Nellie thought with a laugh.

Mary Ann Angell Young swooped down upon them.

"Cornelia Rose, when did you arrive back in civilization?" asked Mary Ann, almost before she was even within conversation distance.

Is this the only greeting Mary Ann has for me? Does she realize I am now sentenced to a life in the wilderness with no foreseeable reprieve?

Nellie tried to remember if she saw Mary Ann after their most recent, bittersweet trip accompanying Obadiah. Since his earth-shattering news, life had compacted into a small space filled with panic.

Oblivious to Nellie's dilemmas, Mary Ann rushed on without waiting for an answer. "We have had ever so many goings on since you've been gone." She pointed her finger at Nellie. "I am sure you heard tell of the aggression of the United States upon our poor kingdom in the news, so I shall not bore you with my version. However...." She paused to take a deep breath.

Tarnation, no! This big drawn breath usually presages a long tirade.

"...there may be a fact or two that the newspapers might not have reported with complete veracity."

Mary Ann Angell Young droned on and the children fidgeted.

"As if it were not insufferable enough, now several federal agents prowl around, *investigating*. Ha! More likely lying in wait to further malign and insult us."

Even Nellie had no interest in Mary Ann's version of the official Latter-day Saints' justification for destroying the United States' monument to the brave and wronged souls who were the victims in the Mountain Meadows Massacre.

I heard that oppressor Young's cocky preaching, one too many times. His snide declarations that the States' Civil War shall implode my valiant country, leaving Deseret free to govern itself, make my blood boil.

"Yes, we fought our Utah War to save souls and preserve our right to our Kingdom of God here on Earth. Missus Wright, I ask you, what business does the man-made government of those United States have in interfering with our Godly right to salvation?"

Mary Ann paused as if she expected an answer from Nellie.

Nellie was at a loss.

She asked herself again: *Did the Mormon sabotage of the United States Army truly constitute a war?*

In the end, it seemed more like vile and vindictive vandalism by the disgruntled Mormons. She found no points of agreement with Mary Ann's twisting of the events to make the United States look as if it were in the wrong.

But the thought of the Mormon's deceptive use of the Paiute's men to massacre an innocent band of waggoneers on their way to a better life still made her sick to her stomach.

Mary Ann must be deaf to the allegations that the elders of the church actually attacked the train disguised as Paiute, or how could she believe the propaganda that somehow their act of brutality was an act of aggression on the part of the United States?

Nellie shook her head and tugged at the strand of hair perpetually loose. Her anger and frustration left her speechless.

The United States dispatched more federal agents who identified some disgusted, former Latter-day Saint church members willing to testify to the complicity of some of the Mormon bishops.

The truth will out.

She regained her optimistic outlook.

Maybe Obadiah's efforts to help the investigation and establish the Federal jurisdictional systems here shall facilitate true justice prevailing, especially for ex-Mormons who have seen the light.

But at this point, it seemed unlikely that even the truth about the real culprits for the Mountains Meadow Massacre would deflate the loathsome lies that had circulated for years.

How much longer would it take to ferret out the truth and bring the culprits to justice?

Nellie tuned back into Mary Ann's voice, despite the tugs on her skirt and both her hands, and Emma's unladylike shifting from side to side.

"...a bunch of lies and written down and disseminated as if it were the truth!" Mary Ann said vehemently.

Nellie frowned.

She could not possibly be of a like mind with my *thoughts.*

What lies worry Mary Ann?

"Written when?" she asked tentatively, wondering if Mary Ann had already said.

"Why, daily... the paper comes out daily. It is a direct dictation from that Colonel Conner at Camp Douglas. Even named it the *Union Vedette*, if that is not a fine 'How d' ya do'! The very title of the new newspaper affronts us, an insult to every good Saint."

Nellie interrupted, suddenly interested. "You don't say? The commander of the United States Army stationed right here at Camp Douglas dictates the news and prints it in his own newspaper?"

She chuckled to herself. *Vedette: the lookout inside enemy lines. How clever!*

"As if there is a need for another voice to quarrel with our fine *Deseret News*. Why, our paper contains all the truth. There is not a lick more fit to be printed. *The Vedette* is just the mouthpiece for your States' Army's propaganda.

"Our Prophet Young said just the other day that Civil War will make short order of the United States. There shall be no States to unite once the North and the South have finished their fighting. Then we here in Deseret will resume our sovereignty as a nation. Our Brother Brigham shall no longer answer to men but will answer to the Almighty alone."

Emma coughed politely. Elizabeth and the boys began making vigorous hand gestures behind Mary Ann's back. Even Nellie felt that she had listened politely long enough.

"My dear companion, Missus Young," she interrupted. "I do extend my sincere appreciation for your earnest efforts in apprising me of the newsworthy events transpiring in my absence.

"Yes," Nellie raised her voice a tad to continue even though Mary Ann started to reply. "One of the many pieces of civilization—" She took Mary Ann by the arm and started walking her in the direction of the market. "—I hold dearest, and sorely miss in my many journeys into the wilderness, is the opportunity to converse with those I hold in high esteem."

Flattered, Mary Ann did not seem to notice she had been arrested in mid-sentence and steered in the opposite direction from her previous course of travel.

Finally in front of the shops, Nellie promised to come calling in the next several days. At this point, most of her children were already inside the tinsmith's.

She rapidly took her leave, but not soon enough to prevent Emma, the usually polite and extremely decorous young lady, from blurting under her breadth, "I, for one, shall certainly not accompany you!"

After purchasing a new grater at the tinker, Nellie made sure her next stop was a visit to one of the few shops not owned by a member of the Mormon Church so she could pick up a copy of General Conner's 'dictation.' In fact, she asked for a copy of every paper they had printed.

Only five issues? At least I am not that far behind the times.

With the papers secured in her marketing basket, and eager to read confirmation of all the reports of the investigation, she wondered if the children would be too disappointed if she cut short their errands.

***

When Obadiah came home to his supper that night, he found Nellie finishing the last page of the *Union Vedette*.

"By what manner did that vile rag come into my abode?" he shouted. "Why are you not preparing our evening repast?" He sat down at the table, still in his boots, with his overcoat still buttoned to the top of his chin from his walk back to the house in the chill of the early fall night.

Choosing to respond to the question for which she had an answer, she replied, "Observe the table beautifully laid by your daughters for our evening meal."

She pointed to the table under his elbow, where everything lay in the ready — plates and freshly pressed linen napkins, tin mugs already filled with milk for the children and mead for herself, Obadiah, and the young woman, Melissa Mellen, now assisting Nellie daily.

"Where is supper?" he asked, looking askance at her still.

"Breath in deeply! Does not the aroma tease your senses to good humor?" She smiled at him.

"My employment taxed me sorely today. The delicate negations I must daily conduct between diverse personalities with opposing loyalties require every ounce of education and skill I possess. I expect my meal to be ready when I come to the table, and my children waiting in attendance for me."

This was too much, even for Nellie.

"But Mister Wright, in fairness, your daily time of arrival is hardly better than erratic, and a fine stew simmers on the stove right behind you, almost at the peak moment of readiness. Moreover, it shall take but a single gong of the dinner bell to assemble all the children. Surely, you do not expect such a healthy, rambunctious bunch with such a fine aptitude for hard work and frugality with time to assemble at the table, waiting with idle hands? Furthermore, I know well your penchant for a hot meal, not one that has already cooled. How am I to —"

Obadiah held up his hand, "Enough, woman. This excessive verbiage further delays my supper." He looked down at her hand, still clutching the offensive paper. "While I ring the dinner bell, answer my initial inquiry as to the origin of this missive?"

"Surely, you are in daily contact with General Connor? You remember the camp he and our troops established at the south bench overlooking downtown Great Salt Lake City? We visited him there a few months ago."

"Do you think me a dolt? I have not taken leave of my senses! Verily, I could tell thee intimate details of the Army and its affairs far beyond thy ken," he said. "Ye know well, I merely wish to ascertain the means of entry of these lies into our home."

He waved the paper in front of her face.

"'*Lies*'?" Flabbergasted, she spit out the word. "A member of our United States government, a General in *our* Army, sworn to protect our interests, publishes this paper. At last, we have a reliable source of news not censored or altered by the *Lion of the Lord*! It is a far cry from the *Deseret News*, which serves only as a mouthpiece for the *propaganda of the faith*, as Elizabeth likes to say. The Mormon newspaper furthers the sovereignty of Brigham the tyrant. It facilitates group disobedience of Federal Authority."

"I have apprised myself fully of the information available from all camps," said Obidiah. "General Connor does not shrink from voicing his opinion. In fact, he shouts it, often in a particularly bellicose manner. I know full well the loyalties of Mister Young and the Saints' church, yet the *Deseret News* advises us of everything we need to know. We do not need to support this new avenue for General Connor's voice."

Nellie could not believe her ears.

When did my reasonable husband deviate from his philosophy to read all information available with an eye to obtaining the truth?

"But what of the other *gentiles* dwelling in this city in the wilderness? One must oft wait long intervals to receive intelligence of world events. I, for one, did not read Judge Cradlebaugh's address to the House of Representatives elucidating the Mormon elder's true roles in the Mountain Meadows Massacre until just now, printed in *The Vedette*. Yet published reports of the massacre appeared in the San Francisco press *four years ago*.

"Do our fellow citizens not deserve to hear an accurate depiction of the news? Moreover, a non-biased account of politics and States' policies should be welcomed by one in your position."

Obadiah opened his mouth, but hesitated.

Nellie was spared his reply.

The whoop and holler of the boys as they rushed upon their father in joyful welcome home curtailed further discussion.

"Hush now. You shall wake the baby and your Mama will not be able to dine with us," Obadiah admonished.

The boys' faces fell.

Obadiah shook his head but caught both boys up in his arms and tossed them into the air, while his daughters clamored for their turn.

***

Later that night, Obadiah returned to the subject. While cleaning dishes after supper and preparing the children for bed, Nellie marshaled more arguments, but Obadiah would not listen.

"Read the paper of lies, for all I care. In one short month, when we move to the ranch, I shan't be troubled with that rag finding you there."

The final nail in my coffin.

CHAPTER 40
Fly Me to the Moon

Great Salt Lake City to the South of Utah Territory, November 1863

Ordinarily, Nellie's spirits would soar at the sight of their trusty, modified Conestoga wagon piled high with possessions and supplies, oxen already hitched. Today, she looked back at their cozy house in the neatly sectioned neighborhood with the civilized boardwalks, and her heart sank low.

How can I tear myself asunder from the birth house of four of my children?

Does it not still wrench me daily to live thousands of miles from Mutter and Papa, and my siblings and their kith and kin? Yet now we finally have the full-time presence and protection of the United States Army, with a newspaper to advise us of the true happenings in our country, and I must forsake this new home.

Begin again? Bereft of Hannah? And Rosalinda?

"Mama, it seems a pity to abandon the rest of our ripened squash and eggplant to the chipmunks and birds," lamented Emma.

Her words almost burst the dam of tears welling in Nellie's eyes.

James ran out of the house, arms full of his treasures. He dumped slingshots, a toy boat, six books, a slate, chalk, and a pocketknife into the back of the wagon. "I need these at the ready while we travel. Now I'll rescue the last of our vegetable harvest," he shouted. "We will need sustenance for our great adventure."

"Take your knife," shouted Elizabeth from the garden. "It makes freeing the vegetables easier."

A tear rolled down Nellie's cheek, despite her resolve to contain her emotions.

Emma put her arm around her mother and sobbed. "At least all our possessions, all the way down to our vegetables, accompany us."

James called, "Yes, our treasures fill the second wagon to the brim!"

Nellie gratefully returned the hug and the sympathy.

"Do not fret, Mama," Emma said. "We shall all band together and enjoy this new challenge."

"You will be back to visit soon, and you always have a home in our humble abode," said a familiar voice.

Nellie turned to see Rosalinda just as her friend smothered her in a hug.

"We agreed that our tear-filled dinner last night would suffice for our goodbyes," Nellie said into her friend's shoulder.

Rosalinda pulled away. "I just followed my children here."

Nellie saw all the Wells hugging her children.

"Furthermore, I made this for you this morning." Rosalinda thrust a basket at Nellie.

Nellie lifted the corner of a pretty cloth, enticed by the aroma. "Your ginger cookies! How thoughtful."

Rosalinda smiled through her tears. "I tucked some of my apparently famous crullers at the bottom."

"You know those shall be devoured before we even leave the city limits!" said Nellie, and hugged her friend harder.

"Do not lose faith, or hope," Rosalinda whispered fiercely into her ear. "We parted once before and somehow wound up neighbors. Trust in the Lord, my dear friend, as I do."

Nellie pulled back, surprised.

I had little inkling Rosalinda possessed such faith.

Rosalinda choked on a sob as she said, "You, my friend, renewed my faith with your kind ministrations when I lost Wilburforce Junior. Moreover, you gave me new life, and hope, and helped me endure until I was rewarded with Dwight and Dudley. I owe you a debt of gratitude I can never repay."

"Merciful heavens, untrue! It is I who have undying gratitude for you. But for your daily love and support, I would just be a shadow of my true self. Tarnation! I do not believe I would have survived all the trials and tribulations of this city without you. You, and my love for you, shall always live in my heart."

"All aboard," shouted Obadiah.

"Just think," Rosalinda said. "Soon our whole continent shall be connected by rail and your ranch reachable with a short, easy voyage."

Nellie blinked back the tears, and pulled Lucinda a little closer to her chest as she felt the animals' strain with Obadiah's flick of the reins.

That pull usually triggered a surge of excitement, or at least a lift of spirits with the creak of the wheels laboring to roll, but not today.

The two older boys started running down the path, getting a head start on the journey.

"Goodbye, goodbye, farewell," the shouts echoed back and forth.

Nellie looked back at her waving friends for as long as she could. When they were no longer visible, she squeezed her eyes shut, trying to keep the vision of the smiling and crying Rosalinda fixed before her eyes.

Practical matters soon grabbed her attention.

She had squeezed all the cherished possessions they owned into their Conestoga, after filling up the pack mule wagon with more mundane supplies. She glanced into the back of the wagon, warily appraising the potential hazards of her packing. Using every square inch of space up to the wagon cover, the contents of her life snuggled together. She grinned in spite of herself when she saw yellow squash, eggplant, and zucchini peeking out from the folds of her expensive carpet, already wagon-carried from New York.

The children's coats tucked around valises left barely enough room for Nellie and the two babies to squeeze onto the spring seat. But from there, she watched Emma, Elizabeth, James, William, and Obadiah walk happily alongside the wagon.

The trail ambled through the flat Great Plains, a topography of vast nothingness stretching on forever before the eye. Space swept down from the distant mountains, blew everywhere, and materialized in wide plateaus punctuated only by cacti. Only the change of gently rolling scruffs of grass and prairie bush for cacti marked their progress. Nellie screened her eyes and looked forward, and then backwards.

We stay stationery in the middle of nowhere.

An additional rocking of the wagon brought Nellie out of her gloomy reverie. "James, do sit down on that of bit carpet right behind me for a minute, there's a good boy."

She turned around to catch James by the seat of the pants as he wormed his way into the wagon between a barrel of provisions and her antique chest of drawers, topped by her treasured book collection. But he jumped back out of the wagon, clutching his trousers.

"I can't sit down, Mama, we have to stop at the next outhouse!"

Nellie shook her head. "Then why were you trying to get into the wagon?"

The girls giggled.

Obadiah grinned, and even Nellie smiled at the thought of an outhouse perched on the side of this dusty trail. She pointed to the side of the road. Obadiah pulled the oxen to a halt.

"Another roadside stop for *The Necessary*, brought to you by James," Elizabeth quipped as she flew past her father and began turning cartwheels.

Even Emma seemed boisterous at the unscheduled stop and skipped by, heading toward a patch of violets peeking out from a buffalo hollow.

At least no chamber pot requires emptying whilst we travel the trail, Nellie thought, and jumped down with baby Lucinda. She pulled Jeremiah down beside her with her other hand. The three scampered across the prairie after her two daughters.

She caught a glimpse of Obadiah's broad smile as he called softly after her, "Now that's my Cornelia Rose."

The Lord has truly blessed me.

I embrace this life with my cherished children. What other course could even exist? My husband knows my best interests. He provides me with this wonderful family and he keeps us in his good care.

Together, they would embark upon a new adventure bolstered by their expanding band of hearty travelers.

Accepting her fate, she smiled in anticipation of the freedom of the journey and the fun of five nights of camping on the way to their destination.

Soon we shall view new vistas whilst remembering the highlights of our trip across this amazing land.

"Who can spot the first prairie dog?" she called after her children, tucking Lucinda firmly into her elbow and running down the trail after them.

Obadiah clucked to the oxen to start the wagons moving again behind them.

Their old reliable Conestoga schooner quickly caught up to Nellie, with the much-relieved James and the wide-eyed William perched on the wagon chair, fighting over who could hold the reins.

Obadiah relinquished control to the two boys and pulled Nellie toward him in an exuberant embrace.

She caught her breath at the crush and juggled the baby, but smiled up at him.

He plunked the still exploring Jeremiah up on the bench with his brothers and fell into step with his wife.

The three boys in the schooner, cooperating in driving the oxen, followed obediently behind. They all soon caught up to the giggling big girls, whose arms overflowed with wildflowers.

"My supplications to the Lord have been answered. I rejoice that you bend your energies again to our common purpose," Obadiah whispered in her ear.

Nellie laughed and leaned her head against his shoulder. "My dear sweet Obadiah! My cherished provider for our family!"

She looked out over the beautiful landscape.

Why should he not enjoy the fulfillment of his dreams? Why should I not renew my efforts to make his life just as he desires?

"All stands right with the world, my dearest."

Obadiah echoed her thoughts. "All is right with the world when we Wrights stand firmly together. Your eventual compliance with my wishes vindicates my holding steadfast to the pernicious belief in your obedience. Mayhap you can retain this lesson in your mind and trust that I know what is best for our family."

The thrust of his last words almost burst the bubble of her newly retrieved happiness.

But I shan't let Mister Wright's confidence in his own reasoning diminish my joy. My little brood surrounds me. What more company can I need? The Lord protects us and guides us as we embark upon a happy excursion through unchartered territory, carrying our home within our hearts.

This love is all I need to establish a physical new home anywhere Obadiah desires. In fact, anywhere the wind blows us, I can find my bit of heaven.

THE END

Book Club Guide

1. Many different personalities populate *The Path of Saints and Sinners*. Many of the characters are true historic figures. What insight did you gain into the actions of the real people in the novel? What surprised you most?

2. Which character did you connect with? Do you have an "Obadiah" in your life?

3. J.F. Collen's research and understanding of history is thorough and vast—what did you learn about this period in the United States from reading the book (and series)?

4. Have you ever been a part of an historical event, like hearing a famous person speak, or witnessed history in the making? Did that event cause any changes in your life?

5. Have you ever faced unfair treatment due to prejudice against you, or "your type"? How well do you think Nellie navigated the open hostility of some of the residents of Salt Lake City?

6. How would you adapt this book into a movie? Who would you cast in the leading roles?

7. Do you think Nellie did enough to assert herself under the steady stream of criticism from her husband?

8. How did the book make you feel? What made you laugh? What made you cringe? Did anything make you cry?

9. Can you empathize with the plight of any of the women in the story, including the true historical persons? Did you think Elizabeth Randall Cumming did a good job supporting her husband while staying true to her own beliefs?

10. If you could ask the author any question, what would it be?

About the Author

Jane Frances Collen has spent the last umpteen years practicing as a lawyer—but don't hold that against her! She has made a career of protecting Intellectual Property, but at heart always wanted to be writing novels instead of legal briefs. She has written award-winning children's books, "The Enjella® Adventure Series," using fantasy as a vehicle for discussing the real-world problems of children. She has tried to use her talent for storytelling for good instead of evil.

But her real love is history. One of her many hobbies is traveling to historical sites around the world and reading the biographies of the people who affected these places. Her books depict modern dilemmas in historical settings, with a touch of humor. Since only one of her parents had a sense of humor, however, Jane feels she is only half as funny as she should be.

She and her husband, to her husband's great relief, departed New York and now reside in Connecticut.

For more, please visit J.F. Collen online at:
Website: www.JFCollen.com
Facebook: Jane.F.Collen

More from J.F. Collen

Be sure to read the previous installments of the "Journey of Cornelia Rose" series, if you haven't already. As of this Book 4 publication, Books 1-3 are available, and Book 5 is pending.

Flirtation on the Hudson (Book 1):
Cornelia Rose, determined to make her own way, shuns the limited vocations available to proper women in New York in the 1850s.

Walk Away West (Book 2):
Cornelia Rose eschews the glories of New York City and the wonders of the 1850s modern technology, and heads out to unknown territory in the Wild West.

Pioneer Passage (Book 3):
Life on the Oregon Trail is full of more deprivations and difficulties than Cornelia Rose ever imagined, in spite of her research and preparations for the rough road ahead.

The Path of Saints and Sinners (Book 4):
Leaving the misery and difficulties of the Overland Trail behind, Cornelia Rose expected a happy welcome to her new life in the Great Salt Lake City. Instead, she steps into a bees' nest of new challenges.

Bit o' Heaven Ranch (Book 5):
Stranded in the middle of the high desert at a ranch hugging Hoodoo rock formations, Cornelia Rose tries to make the best of her new circumstances. But most days, her new ranch feels more like 'this godforsaken place' than a Bit o' Heaven.

More from Evolved Publishing

We offer great books across multiple genres, featuring high-quality editing (which we believe is second-to-none) and fantastic covers.

As a hybrid small press, your support as loyal readers is so important to us, and we have strived, with tireless dedication and sheer determination, to deliver on the promise of our motto:
QUALITY IS PRIORITY #1!

Please check out all of our great books,
which you can find at this link:
www.EvolvedPub.com/Catalog/

Thank you!